GW01464486

To my dear cousin Andrew

who left us too early

Literal Fireworks

Chapter 1

The first thing I notice when I wake up is how wrong my room looks. For a second, I forget my plans to move at the end of the summer. My bookcase holds about three-fourths of the books I own, my winter clothes are no longer in the closet, but put away in my uncle Eli's garage for the time being. My CDs and vinyl are stacked in the corner, waiting to be placed in a box and taped up until I arrive in Seattle, Washington, a.k.a., one of the furthest places from my current location. It looks almost as empty and scattered as I feel.

I officially decided to move two weeks ago and have been eager to get a head start on packing. With working for my uncle Eli, Ms. Elsie, and going to therapy twice a week, I know I won't have a lot of time. My tendency to procrastinate will most likely cause me to quickly fall behind with my packing, too.

There are a lot of memories I want to leave behind about this town, hence wanting to move three thousand miles away. Being a college drop-out, my mother who abandoned me, losing my grandmother and my dad, the accident. And her.

I'm anxious to leave.

I sit up in my bed, my feet touching the spot on the floor warmed by the sunlight shining through the curtains. I like to sleep with my window open, so the curtains dance as the wind blows through the ajar casement.

As I rub my hands down my cheeks, I reflect on the nightmare I had last night and the reality that it isn't just a nightmare. It happened, and I've had this dream a lot since the accident.

I can't tell if it's an oneiric moment from my recurring nightmare or a specific memory from the night of the accident. Either way, some version of what happened in my nightmare last night happened in real life. Every time I blink, I see those two lights. Two lights that changed my life forever.

That was seven months ago. I'd like to think that I'm impervious to these moments, but I know I'm not. I'm more self-aware than that.

I smell pancakes, so that must mean Jey is up.

Jey and I met in middle school, sixth grade to be exact. We were the only guys in our home economics class that semester. Both of us were quiet loners who had nobody else to pair up with, so we ended up as partners. We looked around, locked eyes, shrugged, and got to work. We were too scared to pair up with the girls in the class, an embarrassment to which neither of us would admit. At that age, when there was a strong possibility that girls had cooties, no self-respecting guy would admit to liking a girl.

We spent most of the semester goofing off. Our assignments mostly consisted of cooking baked goods, which neither of us had the skills or experience for, but I guess that was the point of the class. Our cookies came out too salty, our pineapple upside cake wasn't fully cooked, and when we made homemade ice cream, it somehow came out like cottage cheese. But we had fun. We would sometimes pilfer the delicious treats from the pair of girls that shared a kitchen area with us. So no matter what, we ended up leaving home ec with an upset stomach, either from eating recipes that had been made wrong or from stealing too many yummy desserts from our classmates.

That first day in home ec was also the first time I saw Laurel.

Jey and his family moved to Massachusetts the summer before sixth grade started. Our area of town is pretty small, and I had seen him hanging around with his younger brother a couple of times at the beach. I found out that they moved from Honolulu,

Hawaii because his dad got a job offer over here. Why anyone would move from Hawaii to Hull, Massachusetts is beyond me.

Since then, Jey and I have been best friends. He was my ride or die all throughout middle and high school. I spent a lot of time at his house because it was easier being there than jumping back and forth between my grandmother and my uncle. The Bishop family is well off, so there was a spare bedroom that was offered to me. But Jey had his own room, complete with a queen size bunk bed so I slept in his room the majority of the time. Sometimes, he would let his younger brother Dallas sleep on the floor, and we would stay up all night talking about whatever it was we talked about, eating too much popcorn and pop tarts and playing video games we probably shouldn't have been playing at such a young age.

His parents, Reggy and Elora Bishop treated me like I was one of their own kids. They made me lunches when I slept over on school nights, paid for my movie tickets when we went out, and they always got me a birthday present. Jey and I share the same birthday, so most of the time we did combined birthday parties. When we turned fourteen, I overheard Jey telling his parents that he wanted his own birthday party. But Mrs. Elora told him he should be happy to share a birthday with his best friend. And I never heard Jey complain about having a combined birthday party again. That made me love Mrs. Elora more.

Jey is the oldest of three. He has a younger brother, Dallas, and a younger sister, Naomi. I get along great with both of them, which makes me feel even more a part of their family. I don't have any siblings, so it's nice to think of Dallas and Naomi as my brother and sister.

I went on vacation with them once when I was fifteen to Surfside Beach, South Carolina. Dallas spent the whole time trying to impress me while Naomi kept pretending to be shy around me. I'm six years older and think of her as a little sister, so nothing was ever going to happen between the two of us. Thankfully, she now understands. She's also more into girls now, so there's that.

That trip was what really made me feel like I was a Bishop. Jey, Dallas, Naomi, and I spent countless hours at the beach, looking for starfish, making cities out of sandcastles, and eating way too much ice cream. Mr. Reggy rented a golf cart that week and Jey and I rode all around the neighborhood. Probably looking for cute girls to impress, riding with our shirts off and hats on backward, sand covering our bodies from head-to-toe, sunburn under our eyes and across our noses.

Our last night there, Jey and I thought it would be a good idea to sleep on the beach. His parents bought us a small tent and we brought all the extra pillows and blankets we could find from the beach house. We stayed up nearly all-night telling ghost stories, eating dry cereal, and playing stupid games like *Truth or Dare*.

"Truth or dare," Jey asks me. After playing never have I ever for ten minutes we got bored because we basically already know everything about each other.

"Dare," I ecstatically answer. I love a good dare.

"I dare you to set off the fireworks I bought yesterday," he says with a sly grin on his face. I had a feeling that was coming at some point.

I run back to the house, which sits right behind us, just over the giant sand dune. I book it up to the bedroom we called home this past week and check under the bed, the best hiding place Jey could think of. I grab the boxes of whatever it is he bought and run back outside. I'm pretty sure his parents don't know he bought these. Come to think of it, I don't even know how Jey got ahold of them. Honestly, I'd rather not know.

I find Jey digging a shallow hole in the sand, making sure the fireworks have a place to be set off. Ripping open the box, I set the first one up. I look up at Jey, realizing I should've grabbed a lighter or something, only to find he's holding a box of matches in his hand, a smirk plastered on his face.

He lights a match and touches it to the end of the firework. There's a hissing noise, causing us to run into the tent for cover and watch the firework shoot about fifty feet into the air. I was somewhat worried we'd get in trouble, but I'm having too much fun to care. We set off another one and I run around the beach in circles while hollering and laughing, jumping in the shallow water. The smell of fire roams all around us. We finish off with a box of sparklers and draw in the sky with them. I draw a wave and write my name while Jey draws a penis and laughs so hard he nearly face plants into the sand.

We go back to the tent and play a couple more rounds before Jey confesses one of his biggest secrets to me.

"I can't believe you never told me you kissed Audrey Tillie!" I shout, while throwing a pillow at him.

"Yeah, well it wasn't a big deal. And it was so awkward," he says groaning, his hands dragging down his face. "I didn't know what to do with my mouth, so I just left it there for five seconds before pulling away," he says, his face now growing red. That makes me laugh.

"Well…you have no right to judge because at least I've kissed somebody!" he mocks, sticking his tongue out. Now I'm the one blushing.

"Fine, whatever. It's my turn now and I pick truth," I say confidently.

"Do you like Laurel Owens?" It comes out of his mouth so fast. I feel like he's been waiting to ask me this for a long time.

"What? No, I- I-..." I stutter. "No, I do not," I respond with fake confidence. He already knows I'm lying.

We spent the rest of the night talking about soccer, burying Jey in the sand, and sleeping under the stars. Leaving that next morning was difficult for me; it meant going back to reality. One where I didn't have a family with two loving parents and three siblings. One where I didn't get to eat ice cream every night or go to fancy seafood restaurants or rent golf carts. Instead, my reality was jumping back and forth between my uncle and grandmother because my dad died and my mom bounced when I was younger. It was back to used shoes from the thrift store, peanut butter and jelly sandwiches every day, and worrying about whether or not my uncle Eli had enough money for groceries that week.

Being with Jey meant I got to escape my reality, even if only for a little while. Looking back, I think that was one of the reasons I spent so much time with him. Don't get me wrong, I love the Bishop family, but it was more than just spending time with friends. It was relief. That, and Miss Elora's homemade bread was the best thing on this earth I have ever tasted.

At home, Jey and I would spend most of our time out in the water. Since the Bishop's lived in Hawaii before they moved here, he'd learned a lot about surfing, skimboarding, and pretty much everything water related, which is why we would spend countless hours in the water every summer. Swimming, burying each other in sand, boogie boarding, floating, and sometimes late at night, we would go just to sit and talk while we picked up sand and let it mindlessly fall through our fingers.

Before Laurel, I spent almost every single day with the Bishops.

I decide to get up and take a shower after noticing how sweaty I am from my dream, hoping the quiet will help clear my mind. Removing my perspiration-drenched sheets, I combine them with the pile of dirty clothes at the end of the bed, throw it all into the washing machine, and numbly head toward the bathroom.

In the mornings, I often enjoy showering with the lights off. I find it to be more calming. I turn the water on, shut the door, get undressed, and don't turn on the lights. Because of the small window, I can see enough with the sunlight streaming in.

As I step into the shower, I let the hot streams of water fall down my body. The scars on my ribs are still sensitive and even though it hurts to have such hot water on them, I don't turn it down. I wash my hair and start on my body, lathering body wash over my skin as I run my fingers along the scar on my left side. I can feel the bumps from where the stitches sewed me back together. The cicatrix runs from the middle of my torso to my left side, a permanent reminder of the worst night of my life. Flashes of that night flick through my mind, as if I'm watching snippets of it through a View Master.

I stand directly under the faucet, letting the water rush down my body and hear the *plop plop plop* of the water hitting the shower floor, forming a small puddle by the drain. I wonder what it feels like to slide down a drain. Would it be calming, like cruising down a river in an inner tube? Or would it be like crashing down a waterfall full of rapids?

I stand there for what feels like hours, until the water starts to turn cold, and think about absolutely nothing. Except for what it would be like to slide down a drain.

I finish my shower, taking a little longer than I normally would. I grab a towel to dry off and head back to my room, just barely sneaking by Jey in the kitchen, and throw on a hoodie and some sweatpants. I don't have to go to work until this afternoon, so I decide not to get dressed yet. Looking in the mirror hanging on the back of my door, I see my unkempt reflection staring back at me. My dark brown eyes look like pools of ink, barely being held up by the bags underneath them. My face has a eight-day-old scruff. It's a deep brown like my thick, shaggy hair. Laurel once told me I looked good with facial hair. It didn't take me long to quit shaving after that. My hands find my cheeks, my fingers running along my more prominent cheekbones. My face has thinned out.

I haven't slept well since the accident and I can see the effects that sleep deprivation is causing to my face. I notice the freckles along the bridge of my nose, something else that Laurel has mentioned she likes about my face.

Because the weather has been so nice, I've been trying to spend more time outside. My therapist, Dr. Therin, suggested that I spend as much time as I can outside. He says it'll brighten my mood. So far, all it's done is give me more freckles.

I walk out of my room and into the kitchen to find Jey and his girlfriend, Paisley Aberforth, making pancakes just like I thought. Despite taking home economics in middle school, pancakes are about the only thing that Jey can make. His chocolate chip banana pancakes are my favorite, but I'll never tell him that. He's arrogant enough already.

"Good morning, Lane," Paisley says, throwing a handful of chocolate chips in her mouth. Jey gives her a look that says, "stop eating my chocolate chips" and Paisley responds by sticking her tongue out then throwing more in her mouth. He swats her leg with a hand towel.

Jey and Paisley have been dating for a year and a half and I don't ever see them apart. She hasn't officially moved into the house, but she basically lives here. They met at an event at the university Jey attended before he graduated early this past December. Apparently, it was love at first sight.

13

He lived on campus his freshman year and then decided he wanted to be more "independent." Probably meaning that he wanted privacy so he and Paisley could...you know.

At first, I thought that Paisley was only interested in Jey because his family has money, he was the star on the university's soccer team, and is a cocky, self-assured guy. For some reason, girls seem to love overly confident guys. But being that they've been together for so long, maybe it really was love at first sight.

Paisley's one of those girls that cares about turtles and knows everything there is to know about astrology. She wears boho clothing, is a very skilled artist, and genuinely cares about others. She's currently the manager of a soup kitchen where Jey and I used to volunteer when we were younger. Her family lives on a farm in Montana, but she moved out east for school. She has six younger siblings, all of which have names that start with the letter "P." Their family flew out for Jey and Paisley's graduation this past December and I got to meet all six of her younger brothers and sisters. I can't remember all their names, but I remember the smallest one. Her name is Pepper. She's two years old and definitely my favorite. She waddled around our backyard, her pigtails bouncing to the beat of her jerky steps. She kept handing me carrot sticks.

Don't get me wrong, Paisley's a great girl, but sometimes she treats me like I may break at any second. I don't blame her because sometimes I could break at any second, but I hate being looked at like that. Jey, Paisley, Laurel, and I used to hang out a lot before the accident, but now that I just seem to cause Paisley stress, I try to keep a distance. I admire that she cares so much, but I don't want her pity.

I nod over at her as I grab the top two pancakes on the stack and head to the pantry to grab the peanut butter and syrup. Jey only eats his pancakes with butter, which I find to be a sin.

"Take as many as you want," Jey tells me. "Some of the team is coming over soon, so you might want to grab more now if you think you'll want them."

"Thanks, but this is good," I tell him.

I finally feel like eating today. Two pancakes may not seem like a lot, but after the terrible appetite I've had lately, these two pancakes look like a feast. I head towards the backdoor to eat on the patio, taking my pancakes and grabbing a glass of orange juice before I go outside. It's a nice morning and I feel like being alone.

I eat my pancakes while listening to the birds sing and I watch the ocean roll in and out. Looking at the waves from a distance, the water seems calm, controlled. I can't help but think of the little critters and shells that get pushed around and pummeled when the wave finally crashes. Only up close can you see the destruction that waves can cause.

My life is a constant wave; hitting the ocean floor, being tossed around, only for the tide to pull it back out and do it all over again, nearly drowning those it takes as its prisoners. From a distance, my life could look calm and controlled. But up close, you can see the bruises and bumps I've taken from crashing and crashing and crashing.

I take a sip of orange juice and hear Paisley quietly say my name. My chewing pauses. I quickly shuffle over to the door and open it slightly so I can hear what they're saying. Luckily for me you can't see the back door from the kitchen.

"...you sure he's okay? I just really worry about him." I can tell by her voice that her face wears a stressed expression. She wears her emotions right on her face.

"No, I'm not sure. But he's been going to therapy twice a week. He told me he enjoys Dr. Therin and has worked on opening up, but he's been so damn private since his dad died. At least Eli's always said he's been more closed off since he lost his dad."

"Understandably. Well, why don't you just ask…" Paisley starts, but gets interrupted by Jey.

"I don't want to pester him, so I don't ask him too much. I don't want to push him away. I care about him, too, Paisley." Jey sounds like he may start crying.

I shut the door and walk back over to the patio table, suddenly losing my appetite. I don't want to hear the rest of the conversation.

Wasted Pancakes

Chapter 2

After I finish eating, I take my empty dishes inside, having thrown the rest of my pancakes into the bushes. I don't want Jey to worry about me not eating again, especially after he saw me take more than what I have been eating.

The second I step through the backdoor, Jey's head shoots up and he looks like he wants to talk to me. He quickly looks down at my plate and notices all my pancakes are gone. I see a flash of satisfaction cross his face.

I'm nervous he's going to ask how I slept last night. He knows about the nightmares. He is actually the reason I started going to therapy. He convinced me I needed to talk about my feelings with a professional, someone who knows what questions to ask, and what to say that'll help make me feel better … blah blah blah. I wasn't too excited about it at first, but after the accident, I needed help.

I know he cares a lot about my well-being, but I hate it when he asks about anything accident related in front of Paisley. It just makes her look at me like I'm a sick puppy.

"So, how'd you sleep last night? Sleeping any better?" Just as I thought. He tries so hard to be casual about it every time.

I take a quick glance over at Paisley while she's washing the dishes, trying to look oblivious to our conversation. I respond with a simple "Good," seeing as I don't want to talk about it. Even though it wasn't good. I hate talking about anything that reminds me of that night. On top of that, they're pretending like they weren't just talking about me. I hate that, too.

It's quiet for a second, besides the running water, when I ask, "How'd you guys sleep?" I don't know what else to say. I feel stupid for asking that.

Jey looks over at Paisley with a beguiling grin on his face while Paisley starts to chuckle. Now I wish I didn't ask.

"You know what, don't answer that," I say as I walk over to the couch, hitting Jey on the back of the head.

"You don't want to know about our intimate night together?" Jey asks, placing a hand on his chest, sounding genuinely hurt. Once he's finished being dramatic, he sets a stack of plates on the counter and grabs a fistful of forks from the drawer, placing them down next to the plates.

"No, I really don't," I say through a small laugh.

I grab the remote and start flipping through the channels. I have a couple of hours before I have to head over to the pottery shop, so I figure I'll watch something to pass the time in an effort to occupy my mind. As I click on *The Crocodile Hunter*, my phone vibrates in my pocket. Ms. Elsie is calling me. She calls me pretty frequently, so I answer without any hesitation.

"Hi, Ms. Elsie. How's your morning going?"

Ms. Elsie Lorray owns the pottery shop I work for. I spend most of my time there, not only working, but also making a lot of my own pottery. Sometimes I just sit in the back and sketch new ideas. I spend a lot of my alone time there, especially since it's just the two of us that work at Elise's Pottery Shop. We had an intern, but she graduated and moved away earlier this year.

Ms. Elsie was best friends with my grandmother. That was how I got this job four years ago. Most of the time, I make the pottery and she paints it, but occasionally we switch roles. She taught me everything I know about pottery. She taught me pretty much everything I know about art. I remember when I was younger, she would bring me to the shop after school and she would let me paint or create whatever I wanted. That was what really got me into art. She talked about art in such a deep way and I didn't know it could be so meaningful.

Ms. Elsie is one of the reasons I feel bad about leaving Hull. She relies on me a lot, especially since she's getting older and can't carry large slabs of clay or big boxes of heavy pottery or reach the highest shelves of the cabinets. The arthritis in her hands makes it difficult for her to do much.

Before I moved in with my uncle Eli when I was fourteen, I bounced back and forth between him and my grandmother. My grandmother, Hazel, who has been called Honey since she was in her twenties - and which she insists I call her - was kind of ditzy. She let me do whatever I wanted so long as I wasn't causing trouble. I was never a reckless or irresponsible kid, so she must've trusted me enough. Don't get me wrong, I liked to have fun. I just knew how to have responsible fun. Honey made me eat my vegetables and the crust on my sandwiches. She always had an inspirational quote to throw at someone. "Life is too short to worry about grass stains on new jeans" or "Eat cake and ice cream while you can 'cause soon enough, you won't have the teeth for it."

She made me go to church even though she would immediately go home and drink until Ms. Elsie came over to catch up on their soaps. A free spirit, she'd never really cared what people thought about her. She loved to dance and when I was younger, she would run around with me in the sprinklers in her front yard. Ms. Elsie would watch us as she sipped her iced tea from the front porch, laughing at us while we got soaking wet.

I didn't mind staying with her, but her house never felt like home to me. She took good enough care of me; buying me new things because my uncle Eli couldn't afford them, or a new outfit for the upcoming school year. But I think she had a hard time being around me. She was my mom's mother, and she seems to hold a lot of resentment towards my mom for running out on her family. I don't think it was ever Honey's intention, but sometimes I felt as if she took those feelings out on me.

Ms. Elsie used to come over to Honey's on Sundays after church and the three of us would play Skip-Bo together, after they caught up on their soaps of course. Honey always won, which is probably why it was her favorite game. Three months before I turned fifteen, Honey was diagnosed with Alzheimer's and was put in an assisted living home. After she was diagnosed, Ms. Elsie would take me to see her as often as she could. We would play lots of Skip-Bo. The doctors used to say it was good to try and remind Honey of who she was. Of who we were to her. When Honey started getting worse, she would forget a lot, sometimes even in the middle of a game. She would get a look on her face like her memory had just been swiped, then she would look at the cards in her hand and then look at me and Ms. Elsie. We usually left after that happened.

Honey passed away in her sleep five years ago. I was sad to lose her because she was one of the people I knew I could rely on. She was one of the few family members I had left. I don't know what I would've done if I didn't have Ms. Elsie. They both raised me during those couple of years of bouncing around like a pink-ball. It was always easier when Ms. Elsie was there. After I lost Honey, Ms. Elsie was the closest thing I had to a motherly figure.

"It's going well, darling." Ms. Elsie came over to the U.S. from England when she was in her thirties and still has a strong English accent.

"I was wondering if you could come in early for me today. I have to run to a doctor's appointment over in Hingham. I seemed to have forgotten about it. My old age is making me quite forgetful these days." She starts laughing and mumbling about her "old woman memory," as she likes to call it.

"Yeah, I sure can. I'm not in the mechanic shop today. What time would you like me to come in?" I ask.

"As soon as you are able to, love. I would really appreciate it." She's so sweet, I can't ever say no to her.

"Alright," I say. "I'll grab my keys and head out."

"Thank you, Lane. See you soon."

Just then, two cars pull into the driveway, and Jey's teammates pile out like a clown car. As it turns out they aren't a bunch of egomaniacs like I thought they would be. They're actually pretty cool guys. Well... some of them anyway.

"Dudes are here," Paisley says while standing over my shoulder, looking out the front door window. "Who was that?"

"Oh, just Ms. Elsie. She asked me to come in early today."

"Oh, sad. Jey was looking forward to having you around this morning."

I hang up the phone, wishing I could have these next couple hours off, but also glad to get away from Jey and Paisley, especially after learning that

Jey wanted me around this morning. I run to my room to quickly change into some black pants and a plain white t-shirt. I grab my jean jacket; it's still too cool in the mornings to wear short sleeves. I find my keys and as I head out the door, trying my best to avoid any small talk with Jey's teammates, I tell Jey I won't be back until later tonight.

I get in my truck and drive the three miles it takes to get to Elsie's Pottery Shop. I park it and walk to the door, expecting Ms. Elsie to hand me a list of things I need to get done. When I step inside, my stomach drops, and I feel like I'm going to be sick.

I slowly walk up to the counter where Ms. Elsie is talking to Mrs. Malani.

Oh shit.

The Apology

Chapter 3

"Oh, hello, darling. Thank you so much for coming in to cover for me. Would you mind checking out Mrs. Owens? I have got to get running!" She grabs her purse and shuffles toward the door, saying something to Mrs. Malani as she finally egresses.

I nod my head because words just won't form. I'm about to live one of the moments I've been dreading for so long. One I've been *avoiding* for so long.

As I walk behind the counter, I can feel Mrs. Malani looking at me, like she's staring into my soul. "Hello, Lane," she says with a shaky voice. Good, she's nervous, too. But she won't look at me.

"Hi, Mrs. Malani. How are you doing today?" I gulp, my throat suddenly becoming dry. My hands shake as I pick through her items.

"I'm well, thank you for asking." For the next thirty seconds, there's complete silence between us while I finish bagging her items, my shaky hands making the pottery clank against each other. I wince, but not because of the sound. I tell her the total and shakily hand her the bag. I notice she didn't ask me how I was doing.

"Thank you, Lane," she says with a flat affect. I hate this. I hate this so much.

She turns to walk out the door but suddenly, I'm yelling at her to stop.

"Wait, Mrs. Malani! I – I…" I start to stutter because I can't make my words come out. My heart begins to pound and I start to feel a little light-headed.

"I can't do this anymore." I almost shout while looking everywhere but Mrs. Malani. "I'm so sorry," I say with a quivering chin. I bite on the inside of my cheek, trying to stop myself from crying.

I force myself to make eye contact with her and make my feet move so I'm standing closer to her. Apologizing to Mrs. Malani makes everything feel so much more real. Like I actually have something to be sorry for. Trust me, I know I do. But speaking it into existence makes the ache in my chest hurt like hell.

I feel like I can't breathe. I've been holding that apology in for months. Tears start to form in my eyes. My palms are getting sweaty, and my heart is beating so fast, I worry it'll burst out of my chest.

I have been avoiding the Owens family for as long as possible since the accident happened. I ruined their lives that night.

She looks at me with tears in her eyes. Pure hurt masks her face. At first, she says nothing, and then turns to exit the shop. She pauses and turns her head ever so slightly and says, "Have you seen her yet?" she sniffles. I drop my head in shame. "No, I haven't." I look down at the ground, wondering what I can say to make this any better. I don't think there is anything I can say to make it any better. After a couple seconds, I speak up again as she starts to walk away.

"But I will," I say, taking a step forward, reaching out to her. "I just haven't been able to get myself to." I cross my arms, not in a defiant way, but in a way that makes me feel like I'm being held. "I know it's been months since the accident, but I just need to do it on my own time."

Mrs. Malani nods her head in understanding, but I know she holds me accountable for what happened. As she should.

I don't even see her leave; I just hear the clanking of her shoes on the tile and the door close behind her. My eyes have glossed over with tears, making my vision somewhat blurry. I've thought about what our first interaction would be like since the accident, but that wasn't really what I was expecting. I was hoping she would hug me and tell me everything's okay. Deep down I knew it wasn't going to be like that. I got exactly the reaction I deserved. But that doesn't make me feel any better.

I feel so guilty all the time and I just want someone to tell me it wasn't my fault. That I couldn't have done anything to prevent it from happening.

That night was the worst night of my life.

The Treehouse

Chapter 4

Laurel and I met when we were in eighth grade. She was new to our neighborhood; her family had moved in the summer before we started school that year. I remember watching them arrive the morning they moved in, but I don't remember seeing Laurel. I never saw her until that first day of school. I got up too late and ended up missing the bus, so my uncle Eli had to drive me to school.

She lived four houses down from my uncle Eli's house, so we got off at the same bus stop. We were the last stop on the route, so by the time we got home every day, we were the last two on the bus. She sat in the front seat and I sat all the way in the back like a loner, minding my own business, but watching her watch the world around her.

She would stare out the windows of the bus. It didn't matter if the windows were in her seat or not, she would look out of them. The bus driver was constantly telling her to turn around and sit down. I hated the bus driver for that. It made me sad that she was limited to seeing the world through only one window, when she so clearly wanted to see it through all of them.

Sometimes I would watch her walk home. She lived in a light blue, two story home with a huge treehouse in the backyard, complete with a tire swing hanging from the thickest branch. Back then I would've told you I watched her walk home because I was jealous of her treehouse. Looking back, I know that isn't why.

One Friday after school, we both got off of the bus like always. Her house is closer to the bus stop than mine, so I would walk behind her in order to watch her run straight to the treehouse the second she stepped off the bus. I always wondered what she did in there.

She was a good thirty feet in front of me when she suddenly turned around, making me freeze. We'd never talked before this random Friday, but that wasn't what made me freeze. It was the look in her eyes that sent ice through my veins. I felt like I was seeing into her when I made eye contact with her. I could see absolute happiness and pure joy, laughter that made you wheeze and smiles that could turn any frown upside down. But I also saw intense loneliness and a severe longing for a friend.

I knew those feelings all too well.

She looks at me for a second before saying, "You're Lane, right?"

I nod.

"I'm Laurel. You wanna come over? I have a cool treehouse we can hang in." She points over her shoulder toward the one thing I've been so curious about.

I stand there for a second, confused about what she just asked me. *Did she just ask me to hang out?*

I slowly nod again because I don't know what to say. I've thought about hanging out in that treehouse for almost a year now.

"C'mon, let's go. My mom always makes me a snack and puts it in the treehouse for me. There's a small bathroom in the treehouse in case you need to go." She says it so matter-of-factly, as if she knows I need to go, and as if it's normal for a treehouse to have a bathroom of any size.

I follow her to the treehouse, not really knowing what to expect. *How do I talk to her?* The only girl I talk to is Naomi and she's basically my sister.

I'm concerned my long, lanky legs are making me look really awkward. She's talking to me, but I don't really know what she's saying. I trip over a pinecone. I think I hear her say something about popcorn, but I could be wrong.

We go up the stairs and into the treehouse. I've never seen anything like this before. It has a small couch, nice hardwood flooring, a ceiling fan, a tiny mini fridge on a small desk, a giant beanbag, and a tiny little bathroom. There's a boombox and a digital DVD player with a large stack of movies next to the tiny mini fridge. She plops down on the couch and starts shoving popcorn in her mouth. I guess she did say something about popcorn.

She interrupts my thoughts and my glancing around and asks, "What's something on your bucket list?"

"My bucket list?" It's the first thing I've said since I got off the bus. Why is she asking me about what's on my bucket list? *What's a bucket list?*

"Yeah, like something you desperately want to do someday." Then answering my unspoken question, she says, "A bucket list is a list of things you want to do before you die."

"Um, I don't know. I never really thought about it before," I say feeling somewhat awkward. I stand there while she eats popcorn, not knowing if I should sit down. I'm suddenly more aware of myself than I ever have been. *Does my breath stink? Why am I so awkward?*

"Well, you should. Everyone should have a bucket list. Otherwise, how do you know what you want to experience in life?" I guess she has a point.

I stay silent for a second, trying to think of something to say, but also not wanting her to smell my breath if it stinks. I settle for, "I guess you have a point."

She hands me the bowl of popcorn and motions for me to sit on the beanbag, while she pulls a notebook out of her backpack. I sit on the beanbag and eat a few pieces of popcorn. It's kettle corn. She grabs a jar full of colored pencils and pens from the desk and jumps back on the couch. "How do you spell your name?" she asks me, picking out a marker.

"L-a-n-e."

I watch her write "Lane and Laurel's Bucket List" at the top in an awkward, jerky cursive.

"Now," she starts. "We have to come up with things to put on our bucket list. Things we have to do together."

I guess that means we're friends now. I'm not complaining; I've wanted to be her friend since that first day in home economics.

She's drawing stars all around the top of the page, switching colors every few stars, and accidentally gets some popcorn grease on it. The fact that she doesn't notice is kind of cute, focused as she was.

"Laurel!"

Laurel sighs and yells "Yeah, mom? You're interrupting something important," she states, continuing to doodle. Her eyes never leave the paper. That was something I noticed about her in home economics. She was always so focused on what she was doing. Her eyebrows would crease and she would stick her tongue out of the side of her mouth.

"Honey, we have to go pick up your dad from the airport. We won't be back until later tonight, so you can't stay here by yourself. You have ten minutes until we need to leave." That would be Mrs. Owens, I guess. I see her out in the front yard a lot, usually picking at the flowerbed.

"Ugh." Laurel sighs again. She looks up from her doodles and says to me, "We'll have to finish this later. I have to help my mom in the garden tomorrow, but you can come over after that."

I pick up my backpack off the floor and follow her out of the treehouse and down the steps. She's telling me all about the vegetables and spices they grow in their garden, her favorite being carrots. Mrs. Owens stands in the grass at the bottom of the stairs, her hand wrapped around the tire swing rope. I watch the swing move back and forth as Mrs. Owens lightly sways it.

When my feet touch the ground, she sticks her hand that was holding onto the rope out to me and says "Hi, Lane. I'm Laurel's mom. You can call me Mrs. Malani. It's so nice to finally meet you. I've heard so much about you." She wraps both of her hands around mine and they feel like the softest hands a mother could have. There's a sweet smile that forms on her face and it makes her eyes sparkle a little. She looks like she doesn't regret saying that last part, despite the flash of embarrassment on Laurel's face. Now I feel embarrassed. I notice Mrs. Malani and Laurel have the same smile. That same sparkle in their eyes.

I look over at Laurel as I shake Mrs. Malani's hand, finally realizing what she just said. *Laurel talks about me?* That makes me feel good.

"It's nice to finally meet you too, Mrs. Malani. Thank you for letting me come over."

"No problem at all! I'm glad Laurel has a friend to bring over," she says, but Laurel whines "Mom," under her breath while folding her arms across her chest. "I have lots of friends," Laurel tells no one in particular. But I know she doesn't. Sure, she has some friends at school, but I've never seen her bring anyone over before.

"Well, I better get going. My uncle's probably waiting for me. It was nice meeting you Mrs. Malani."

"You as well, Lane."

I start to walk to the front yard when Laurel starts talking as she follows Mrs. Malani into the house. "Come prepared tomorrow with all of your best ideas!" she shouts as she skips inside.

I run off for home with a wide grin on my face and an extra hop in my step. Ivy's car is in the driveway, and I feel like I couldn't get any happier today. *She'll probably have good advice about writing a bucket list!*

Ivy Riddenhouse is my uncle Eli's girlfriend. They haven't been dating very long, but I can tell that he really likes her. She's really nice to me and sometimes she brings me candy from the bowl she keeps stocked in her office. Whenever I have to hang out with Ivy until my uncle Eli can pick me up, she always lets me eat as much as I want.

I walk inside and see my uncle Eli reading today's newspaper, but no sign of Ivy. I guess he dropped her off at the hospital for her shift today.

"Hey, Laney-boy! How was school?" He always asks me how my day was. I usually tell him it was fine, which my days usually are. But today was actually a good day.

"It was good," I say honestly, grabbing some orange juice from the fridge and sitting down at the table across from him. He wears his reading glasses low on his face when he reads the newspaper which always makes me laugh. He looks over the top of his glasses when I speak again.

"Do you know anything about writing a bucket list?" I ask.

"A bucket list, huh?"

"Yeah, like what goes on one. Have you ever written one?"

I try to think of the last time my uncle Eli ever did anything fun. He has barbeques with his buddies from the shop sometimes and enjoys going on walks along the beach with Ivy, but most of his time is spent taking care of me or working at the shop.

"Despite what you may think of me, I used to be adventurous. I've never written a bucket list, but I've done a lot of things that are probably on people's bucket lists. I've been skydiving, swimming with sharks, and have traveled all over the United…." He stops talking and laughs when he sees the amount of surprise plastered on my face.

"I know, it may be hard to believe," he says, putting his hand up, "but I used to be such a thrill seeker." He chuckles.

He has a look on his face that makes me think he's remembering something good. A life where he did whatever he wanted because he had no responsibilities. I wish he could have that life again. Instead, he comes home from working long, hard hours all day. His permanently stained, calloused hands are proof of that.

I've been told I look a lot like my uncle Eli. He's my dad's twin brother, and even though they're fraternal and don't really look alike as much as twins should, I somehow ended up looking like my uncle Eli. We have the same big, black eyes, full heads of hair, and freckles that trail across the bridges of our noses.

For the next hour he tells me all about his favorite memories from traveling across the United States. He's been swimming with sharks, helicoptered into the Grand Canyon, hiked parts of the Appalachian Trail, has been parasailing, skydiving, and skiing. I never knew my uncle was such an adrenaline junkie.

"Are you making a bucket list?" he asks me when he's finished reminiscing about the past.

"Kind of. A friend from school said something about a bucket list today and I was wondering what types of things I should put on my list." That wasn't the whole truth, but it was enough of the truth.

"Oh, I see. Well I suggest that you should start with some smaller things, like run a 10k or…" he drags out the "or" while thinking of something else to add. "...eat nothing but ice cream all day," he says excitedly, like it's the best idea he's ever had. "And then work your way up to the bigger things, like sky diving or swimming with dolphins." This is good. I love ice cream.

"That makes sense. Thanks uncle Eli," I say, taking the last sip of my orange juice. I start to head toward my bedroom after putting my glass in the sink when I decide to tell him I have plans for tomorrow. I turn around and walk the five steps back into the kitchen.

"Hey, Uncle Eli, I was invited over to a friend's house tomorrow. Is it alright if I go?" I ask somewhat impatiently. I don't want him to know I'm hanging out with a girl I like. Let alone, a girl.

"Yeah sure, you going over to Jey's house?"

"No, it's a different friend," I say backing up.

Probably judging by my awkwardness and my unwillingness to give more information, he must know it's a girl. He moves his eyebrows up and down, with a mischievous look on his face, and that's my cue to run to my room. I hear him laughing from the table.

"Make sure you get your homework done for Monday," he shouts over his shoulder, still laughing. He knows school ends next week and I don't have any homework. He's making fun of me. *How rude.*

"Actually, Lane, can you come here for a second?" *Oh no, does he know I just lied to him?*

"What's up?" I ask, trying to mask my anxiety.

"I have a question for you and I want you to be completely honest with me." He looks really serious. He scoots out the chair next to me and motions for me to sit down. I take a seat in the chair, my leg bouncing with anticipation.

"Okay…" *This cannot be good.*

"I've been thinking….I know it hasn't been very long, but I was wondering how you felt…I want to ask Ivy to marry me and I just wanted to talk to you about it first. I love her and I want her in my life, but I want to make sure that you love her, too."

Oh, this is *good.* "Oh, yeah, I'm good with it. I like Ivy a lot."

"Are you sure, bug? Things will probably change after I've asked her. I just want to make sure you know that."

"Yeah, I'm sure. I think it's great!" I say, my happiness growing.

"I also want you to be a part of it when I do ask her."

"Thanks, Uncle Eli. I'd love that."

"Fantastic! Now, how should I ask her?"

The Bucket List

Chapter 5

I stay up all night trying to think of some ideas for our bucket list. So far, all I have is 'eat nothing but ice cream all day,' which I took from my uncle Eli.

After doing some research, meaning talking to my uncle, and thinking about things I want to experience, this is the list I have come up with:

Eat nothing but ice cream all day

Visit Boston Aquarium

Rock climb the Quincy Quarries

Go to a carnival

Skip a day of school ??

Try sushi

Read Harry Potter

Visit an abandoned amusement park

Watch the sunset overlooking the city

Try pottery

Eat food from a food truck

Go camping

Geo-cashing

Hike the Appalachian trail

Laurel told me to bring some of my best ideas, and these are all things I would really love to do. I'm a little hesitant about skipping school because I'm not really a rule-breaker, but I've thought about it before. Jey does it all the time and he's tried to convince me to do it before, but I haven't given in yet.

Some of these things I've already done, like go to a carnival. But these are things that Laurel and I are supposed to do together. Just from the interaction that we had yesterday, I know her list is going to be full of adventurous things, so I tried to add some of those to mine, too. Still, I have a feeling that our lists are going to be very different.

***

I stayed up after midnight coming up with my list and woke up dead tired at 10:45 the next morning. I take a really fast shower, so fast I didn't even realize I forgot to turn the lights on. It was actually kind of peaceful despite the rushing.

I get dressed and head to the kitchen to make breakfast for my uncle Eli and me. We always make breakfast together on Saturday mornings. Our go-to is waffles and bacon, but I see that he's pulled out stuff for breakfast burritos.

"Good morning, Uncle Eli," I say stretching.

I turn the corner and see Ivy making strawberry, banana, and spinach smoothies. She tries to sneak the spinach in there, thinking we won't notice. But it makes the smoothie a diarrhea green color.

"Oh, hi, Ivy," I say, waving at her, still stretching. I remember my uncle Eli's plans to propose to Ivy and I suddenly feel really grateful for my misshapen family.

"Good morning, bug," he says, greeting me with a smile before returning his attention to the stove. The sounds and smells of frying vegetables, onions and sausage for the burritos fill the air. I grab a bowl and start cracking some eggs, a smile plastered on my face.

He has quiet rock music playing in the background, which we listen to every Saturday while making breakfast. I start to hum along when he asks me about my bucket list.

"I heard you up late last night, were you working on your bucket list?" he asks.

"Are you making a bucket list, Lane? That's so exciting! Maybe I'll have to show you mine someday," Ivy says, dropping some spinach on the ground. She picks it up and plops it in the blender.

"I'd like that, Ivy. Yeah, I was. I think I thought of some pretty cool things. Sorry if I kept you guys up," I say. I kind of want to change the subject, so I ask what his plans are for the rest of the day.

"I have to run to the store to get some groceries and I have to pick up a couple of parts from Big Joe's that I'll need this week. Anything you want me to get from the store?"

"Just some more orange juice," I say, stirring the eggs.

"And some kettle corn popcorn."

***

Forty-five minutes later, we've eaten and finished all the dishes. I go back to my room to look over my bucket list one more time before heading over to the Owens' house.

It looks pretty good to me. I could maybe add one or two more things, but my mind seems to be drawing a blank. I pack up my backpack with the notebook that has my list in it and head to the bathroom. I check myself out in the mirror to make sure I didn't get anything on my clothes and I don't have any strawberry seeds in my teeth. That would be embarrassing.

I inch closer to the mirror when I realize I have a small pimple growing by my bottom lip. *Ugh. I hope she doesn't notice that.*

Approximately six minutes later, I head to the garage to get my bike. I thought about walking to her house, but biking will be faster. I hop on and bike the four houses down to Laurel's. With each inch I get closer to her house, the more nervous I am.

Parking my bike in her driveway, I follow the sidewalk to the front door. There are flowers all along the edges of the sidewalk, making a pretty spring pattern. I think of Mrs. Malani tending to her flower bed and I make a mental note to tell her it looks nice. There's a wooden O hanging on the door, probably for Owens, I assume. It looks like it was decorated by Laurel, completed with the names Matthew, Malani and Laurel following the curve of the circle.

I ring the doorbell and my stomach feels like it's going to be sick. I can feel my breakfast stirring around. It doesn't even ring twice before Laurel answers the door. She never told me a time to come, but I figured around noon was probably fine.

She swings the door open so fast it startles me. She has on a pair of overalls with a plain white t-shirt underneath that has a picture of a porcupine eating a popsicle on it.

"Lane! You got here at just the perfect time. Let's go!" She turns and runs, leaving the door open. I step inside and shut the door, quickly following Laurel through the house.

The inside of her house is nice. The living room, which you stand in when you enter the front door, is an open space with a large navy couch pointed at a TV. There are pictures of the Owens family perfectly hanging all over the room. Some of just her parents, some of just Laurel, some of the three of them, and some of Laurel with each of her parents. They look like a happy family. For a split second, a pang of jealousy and sadness hits me. But it's gone as fast as it came.

We make it to the back door when her father stops us.

"Laurel, don't you think you should give Lane a tour of the house?" He looks over at me and introduces himself from behind the large island in the middle of the kitchen. "Hi, Lane. I'm Laurel's dad, but you can call me Mr. Matthew. It's nice to meet you!" He's dressed in sweatpants and a t-shirt with his hair all tousled and looks completely different from the man I see getting into his car every morning.

Laurel slowly turns around, darting her eyes toward her dad.

"Hi, Mr. Matthew. It's nice to meet you, too. Thanks for letting me come over," I say, feeling a little embarrassed.

"I'll make some chocolate chip gingerbread muffins while you give him a tour, Laurel," he says rather enthusiastically.

Laurel huffs and lightly stomps her foot, and I start to tell her I don't need a tour when she starts talking super-fast.

"This is the kitchen," she says pointing to where Mr. Matthew stands. "That's the family room over there, and the dining room over there," she tells me, pointing to both rooms. "Around the corner is the sitting room and up the stairs is where all the bedrooms are. There's a bathroom around the corner, right there and there's a basement downstairs with a Wii and Guitar Hero. We can play later."

Oh, it's a three-story house.

She turns on her heel and gives her dad a look that says, "Are you satisfied now?"

He chuckles and gives her a look that says, "Not quite," but she turns on her heel and opens the door anyway. She runs out of the house, straight to the treehouse. I don't know how I didn't notice it yesterday, but there's a small above-ground pool in the backyard.

Next to the back, right side of the house is the garden. Mrs. Malani, who is still working in the garden, looks over at us, waves, and says "Hello, Lane! It's nice to see you again!" I wave over at her, saying hello and adding "Your flower bed looks really nice."

We walk up the stairs to the treehouse, once again feeling awkward about my long, lanky legs. Laurel climbs up before me and I can see the bottom of her feet are dirty. She must've helped her mom in the garden after all.

The second we get inside I can tell she's been working on her list for a while. There are papers and markers and colored pencils strewn all over the floor. Plopping down in the only open space, she clasps her hands together. She looks up at me where I am still standing in the doorway, and exclaims, "We have no time to waste, let's get started!" she exclaims, sifting through her pile of papers.

"You made a list of ideas and brought it right?" she continues, pointing at me, shaking her finger sternly in my direction.

I nod, slinging my backpack off and unzipping the first pocket. I pull out my notebook and hand it to her, while sitting on the beanbag. She flips through until she finds the last page written on. She skims the page, looking pleased.

"These are some great ideas, especially eating nothing but ice cream all day." Then she adds, "Good thing I'm not lactose intolerant." She laughs and a small snort escapes from the back of her throat.

Just then, there's a knock on the door and Mr. Matthew comes in with a plate of freshly baked muffins and two glasses of chocolate milk. He doesn't say anything but leaves them on the desk. He seems to know not to interrupt.

I smile to myself, then ask her, "What's on your list?" She looks up at me and says through a cheeky smile, "I thought you'd never ask."

I don't even know how she's able to tell which one is her final list because there are at least fifteen papers surrounding her on the floor. She must have started over many times. She grabs one written in purple marker and starts to read.

"Spend the night in the treehouse

Sneak into a movie

Ride in a hot air balloon

Walk on hot coals

Learn how to fly a plane

Read the largest book in the world

Visit the Statue of Liberty

Go to a Red Sox game

Walk the length of the beach

Visit Disney World

Paddleboarding, and finally

Go to Victoria Falls"

My first thought is that her list is a lot more
adventurous and daring than mine, just like I
thought it would be. She seems to read the
expression on my face and responds "I know, our
lists are pretty different. But I think we can take the
best things from each of our lists and combine them
to put on our official bucket list. Come sit next to
me."

I stand up from the beanbag, grab two muffins and a
glass of chocolate milk, and sit next to her. I hand
her a muffin, which she eats in one bite. She
watches me as I sit down and says, "You have a
pimple by your lip," her mouth full of half-chewed
muffin. *Oh gosh, I was hoping she wouldn't notice.*
But she goes right back to skimming through our
lists. It meant nothing to her, as if she told me I had
dark brown hair.

Despite my embarrassment, I look over at her. I
realize how perfect Laurel's skin is. Just the right
amount of red in her cheeks, cute freckles placed
sporadically on her face, as if God dipped a
paintbrush in freckles and just flicked it all over.

"What's Victoria Falls?" I ask, thinking about her list.

"You've never heard of Victoria Falls?" she practically gasps. I shake my head no.

"It's one of the largest waterfalls in the world!" Her eyes light up and she's speaking so animated, like visiting Victoria Falls is the only thing in the world that could ever make her happy. "It stretches between two countries: Zambia and Zimbabwe. But I want to visit the Zimbabwe side because it's much better. At least that's what Google says. It's my ultimate dream to go there."

She stands up and closes the bathroom door. Behind it is a small mural of a bunch of different pictures of what I assume is Victoria Falls. "I collect pictures of it, hoping one day that when I actually see it, it'll feel like I've already been there."

Even though the mural is made up of only about ten pictures, I'm impressed by it. There's some stickers and other random papers and drawings of Victoria Falls, which I'm assuming she made herself, that surround the mural. It's cute that she cares about it so much.

Okay, that's definitely going on our bucket list, I think. Not because I want to go, but because she wants to.

"How do you know about Victoria Falls?"

She stares at her mural, tracing one of the pictures with her finger. "My grandmother's been there. She actually used to live in Zimbabwe. Before she died, she told me stories about when she lived there. About what Victoria Falls was like. She said it was the most beautiful thing she had ever experienced. And it made me want to go someday. She said you can feel the water splash on you. It soaks your clothes and hair and there are rainbows everywhere."

"Wow, that's -"

"Yeah, I know," she cuts me off.

She sits back on the ground and gets my notebook, which she set beside her, and rips my list out of it. She moves the pile of papers and places our lists side-by-side on the floor. She stands up to grab our official bucket list she made yesterday off the desk and sits back down.

"So," she starts, "which ones from your list do you definitely want? I think we should definitely do eat nothing but ice cream all day, go to a drive-in movie, watch the sunset overlooking the city, and eat food from a food truck."

We spend the next thirty to forty-five minutes coming up with our official list. We scratch out a bunch of ideas, like walking on hot coals. She was adamant about how cool that would be, but I told her we would probably end up in the hospital with mangled toes and torn skin. She eventually agreed with me. We even add some new ideas. Eventually, we've compiled our list.

Lane and Laurel's Bucket List:

Eat nothing but ice cream all day

Ride the train from one end to the other

Go to a Red Sox game

Visit Kings Dominion amusement park

Watch the sunset overlooking the city

Spend the night in the treehouse

Try sushi

Visit all forty-seven lighthouses in Massachusetts

Go Geo-cashing

Try Paddleboarding

Ride in a hot air balloon

Sneak into a movie

Eat food from a food truck

Buy someone in need a meal

Visit the Statue of Liberty

Ride a motorcycle

Go to a drive-in movie

Go to a carnival

Visit Boston aquarium

Try pottery

Read Harry Potter and watch all the movies

Visit an abandoned theme park

Go to Victoria Falls

After we have our list completed, we spend most of
the afternoon hanging out in the basement. There's
a shelf along the wall that is full of all different
kinds of games. There's Candy Land, Apples to

Apples, Dutch Blitz, Monopoly, Ticket to Ride and so many others.

She turns on the TV and the Wii and puts in Mario Kart. I haven't played Mario Kart in a while. Dallas and I used to play all the time after school while we waited for Jey to finish soccer.

The next two hours fly by as we play Mario Kart, Wii bowling, Rayman Rabbids, and some Pictionary game. We eventually switch over to playing some board game I've never heard of and that's when I tell her about my uncle Eli proposing to Ivy.

"WHAT?" she yells. She doesn't even know them and she's excited. "That is so exciting! I love weddings. They're so magical and there's so much happiness."

"Well, he asked me if I had any ideas for proposing, but everything we thought of sucked. Do you have any ideas?"

She grabs my hand and runs us inside to tell her parents we're going to the beach and we'll be back later.

Our street is only a fifteen-minute bike ride to the beach, and since I rode my bike here this morning, we decide to bike. We bike most of the way side-by-side on the sidewalks in different neighborhoods, but I let her go in front of me when the sidewalks narrow. We cut through the neighborhoods to get to the beach faster. I notice summer flags swaying in the wind in front yards and beach towels drying on driveways as we zoom past houses, a tell-tale sign that summer is right around the corner.

I watch her in front of me and I notice her long caramel colored hair flying in the wind. It looks really soft, despite how tangly it must be from all the wind. I think I can faintly smell something fruity. *Must be her shampoo.*

She talks most of the way there, saying what she's most excited to do from our bucket list (which is to visit Victoria Falls), talking about school (which she hates), and even talking about how her hamsters, Marvin and Ted, somehow ended up having babies together. "I guess one of them is a girl," she shrugs. They're weird names for hamsters, but I don't think there's anything normal about Laurel.

After fifteen minutes, we make it to the beach. We attach our bikes to a bike rack and head down to the water. We take our shoes off and run to the sand. It's the first time I've been on the beach this summer and it feels good to have the sand in between my toes. The beach has always been one of those special places to me. After my dad died, I would sneak out late at night and come down to the beach and just sit and watch the stars. Looking back I realize how dangerous that was as a ten-year-old, but I was grieving and I didn't really care.

The water is still too cold to swim in, despite the warmer weather we've been having. But Laurel runs in any way. She must have forgotten that I asked her if she had any ideas for my uncle Eli's proposal because we haven't talked about it yet.

I've only known Laurel for a day, but she already makes me want to be a better version of myself. She makes me want to enjoy life more. It's possible that was just the bucket list idea, but I don't think it is.

I watch Laurel skip around the water, getting the bottoms of her overalls wet. She doesn't seem to care. She bends over and picks up some seashells and holds onto them like she's scared she's going to lose them. She tries to skip a rock, but it just hits a small wave and makes a plop sound. She runs over to me after a minute or so and starts placing the shells she collected onto the sand.

"I think he should do it here. At the beach. I've never had a bad memory at the beach before. Have you?"

I try to quickly think of a bad memory I've had at the beach, but being here with Laurel right now, I can't seem to think of the beach as a place where bad things could happen. "No, I haven't."

"Then it's settled!" she says, throwing her arms in the air.

I'm not quite sure what she's referring to, but before I can ask what she's talking about, she's already telling me.

"I have a plan. Just tell me the date he wants to propose and I'll get it all set up and ready."

"Okay," is all I say. I guess she won't be telling me the plan right now. It makes me wonder if she actually does have a plan.

She leaves whatever she was just making and runs back to the water. When I stand up to follow her, I see she's made a heart out of the shells she collected. I smile down at it and run after her toward the salty ocean.

Who is *this girl?*

Hesitantly, I step into the freezing cold water. The bottom of my feet get shocked from the freezing water and I jump back, tripping over my long legs. I let out a shout as I fall to the ground. Laurel turns around and laughs, even though she didn't watch me fall.

She walks over to me and I think she's going to help me up, but she actually pushes me closer to the ground. She jumps on top of me, looks me dead in the eyes, and says "I bet I can beat you to the ice cream truck!"

I realize then how green her eyes are.

She immediately jumps off of me and books it toward the ice cream truck parked by our bikes, throwing all the shells she just meticulously collected in the sand. Stunned and feeling a surge of competition, I get up and run after her.

I catch up to her in no time and she tries to push me over. In her attempt, I grab her arm and yank her backward. She lets out a mixture of a grunt and a yelp as she falls to the ground, making sand fly at my legs. Somehow, she manages to trip me before I can take another step. Both of us lay in the sand, laughing. I laugh so hard my cheeks start to ache and she clutches her stomach, saying that it hurts from laughing too much. She accidentally snorts and we start laughing all over again.

We lay in the sand, our heads right next to each other. I turn my head and look at her and through her laughing, I realize how absolutely perfect her smile is.

Once we get ourselves under control, Laurel starts making sand angels, which don't really look like angels because of the sand's rocky texture. She breaks the comfortable silence and says "We're gonna be best friends."

I Only Have Myself to Blame

Chapter 6

The second the door closes, I stumble to the front door, flip the open sign to closed, and lock the door. I numbly run to the back room, knocking over a display on the way there. I hear a crash, indicating I just broke something. I'm blacking out as I throw myself on the bathroom floor. After kicking the door shut behind me I try to calm myself down. Gripping my chest, I try to breathe deep, but I can't seem to get my breathing to even out. I try to think of anything but that night; basketball, furniture, brussel sprouts, hand-me-down clothes...but it keeps playing on repeat in my mind. If I never asked Laurel to come home with me that night, this never would've happened. She would still be in my life.

I try to remind myself I couldn't have done anything to stop the accident and it wasn't my fault. I was the one driving, but I wasn't the one driving drunk. Dr. Therin told me when I start to spiral, I should remind myself I couldn't have prevented the accident. The accident wasn't my fault and I need to stop blaming myself.

Dr. Therin also taught me that breathing deeply and finding something to focus on will help me calm down when my emotions start to spiral. I sit on the floor and start rubbing my hands on my legs. I think about the feeling of the back-and-forth movements. I try to feel the jean material on my palms and my fingertips. I move my hands up and down and up and down. *It wasn't your fault,* I remind myself. *Up and down, up and down.*

My breathing starts to slow down, but I keep repeating the back-and-forth movements.

I begin to whistle, like how my dad used to when he would try to calm me down. He would hold me in his arms and softly whistle in my ear, telling me everything was going to be okay. He was always there to comfort me.

Except now, there's no one here to tell me everything is going to be okay.

I start to calm down after a few minutes and the tears that were streaming down my face have slowed. I breathe deeply, in and out, trying to get control of my rapid, short breaths.

It wasn't your fault. I remind myself over and over again, willing myself to finally accept it.

With trembling hands, I grab some toilet paper and blow my nose. I rinse my face off with cold water to get rid of the puffiness and redness under my eyes.

I look at myself in the mirror and see a broken version of the person I used to be.

I turn around and leave the bathroom, wishing I could be whole again; wishing I could remove the black hole that's been slowly growing inside of me these past seven months.

It was your fault.

***

Ms. Elsie comes back from the doctor's three hours after she left with lunch for us. There's a sandwich shop in town we both really like and we like to treat each other every once in a while.

She brings the bag of food over to the counter and starts going on about the traffic on the way back from the doctor's office. I'm not really listening so I just nod and pretend I am. I unwrap my sandwich that I don't have an appetite for and take a bite. It's my favorite sandwich: turkey, muenster cheese, lettuce, avocado, banana peppers, BBQ potato chips, and a thin layer of garden vegetable cream cheese on a plain bagel. Ms. Elsie always gets a Mediterranean wrap and we split a large fry.

We eat and make small talk while sipping our lemonades. After a couple minutes, she looks at me like she wants to ask me something but is scared to invade my privacy. She asks anyway. She isn't really one for boundaries.

"How was Mrs. Malani?" she tries to say casually. She picks at her fries, not making eye contact with me. I stare at the watch on her wrist and say, "She was fine. She bought two bowls and two matching plates."

"Oh, is that right?" The silence is awkward and deafening. I count as seven seconds tick by on her watch. I know she wants to say more, but I don't want to talk about it. I cut her off just as she opens her mouth to speak again.

"Ms. Elsie, I know what you're going to ask me, and I would really rather not talk about it right now." I pick at my sandwich.

I slowly look up at her bright blue eyes and wait for a response. She hints at a frown but catches herself before she makes me feel bad. I really don't want to have another panic attack. It took me thirty minutes to calm down from the one I had earlier.

"Darling," she pushes my hair out of my face. "That's alright. I never meant to push you to talk

about it. I just wanted to know if you were okay."
She pauses before adding "Why don't you take the
rest of the day off? Go take a walk or do something
fun with Jey."

I'm worried I hurt her feelings. "Ms. Elsie, I didn't
mean to be rude. I was thrown off guard earlier, and
I didn't mean to take it out on you. I can stay the
rest of the day."

I don't mention that I don't want to spend the day
doing something fun with Jey.

She steps closer to me and takes my face in her
hands.

"Lane, I care about you a lot. I think of you as a
grandson, and I just want you to be okay. If you
ever want to talk about anything, including the
accident, I'm here for you." A pause, then "Have
you been going to your therapy sessions?"

I grab her elbows to steady myself, even though I'm
sitting down. "Yes, I have. And I know you care
about me, but I need to work on things on my own
time. It's going to take me a while to get there. But
I'm okay," I lie.

I can see her eyes forming tears and I look away
from her. Seeing her cry makes the ache in my chest
crush me harder. She drops her hands from my face

and takes my right hand in hers. Her bony, wrinkly hands feel soft in mine. They make me feel safe.

"Okay, I won't say anything about it again," and I know she won't. She lets go of my hand and starts to clean up lunch. She turns to me as she fills the to-go bag with our trash and says "I still want you to take the rest of the day off. I will see you tomorrow morning. Thank you for covering for me earlier." I appreciate her pushing me to take care of myself and my mental health. I know I don't do enough of that.

She shuffles off to the front door to throw the trash in the dumpster. Her short strawberry blonde hair has started showing some spots of gray and I think she's gotten shorter over the years. I grab my phone and keys from the counter and walk out to my car. Ms. Elsie meets me halfway and motions for a hug. Kissing me on the cheek, she reminds me she loves me.

I pull out of the parking lot and drive along the beach before going home. I find a parking spot and people-watch from my car, the ache in my chest ever present like I've been holding in a breath I haven't let out yet. I watch kids riding their bikes, parents yelling at them from behind to slow down and watch out for cars. I watch a seagull steal a

French fry from someone's plate. They swat at the bird, dropping half of their fries on the ground.

I watch three little girls play in the shallow water while their moms sip on something colorful. I watch an old couple slowly walk the boardwalk, hand-in-hand. I watch a group of teenagers listen to music and throw a football back and forth. All of them have no idea of the pain I feel right now. They're all probably carrying around their own pain.

It looks like it's going to storm, despite being so sunny this morning. Sitting at this beach reminds me of Laurel. I'm reminded of the first time we hung out at the beach together. She challenged me to a race and we both fell to the ground and never ended up getting the ice cream we were racing to. I miss her a lot and I start to feel the black hole expand.

I need to go see her.

Finding Hidden Treasure

Chapter 7

After an hour of sitting at the beach, I drive home. Paisley's car is gone, which must mean she's at the soup kitchen. But Jey's is still in the driveway. His soccer game must've been canceled because of the impending storm.

Inside, I find Jey asleep on the couch. I quietly tiptoe past him and head to my room, as if any noise I could make would possibly be louder than the cacophonous snores bellowing from his pie hole.

While sitting at the beach, I decided I may as well get a head start on packing if I'm free today. I picked up some banana boxes from Stop & Shop last week, so I get them out of the shed in the backyard and start packing.

I don't have a ton of stuff, which makes the process of packing and moving across the United States a lot easier. I took everything I owned from my uncle Eli's house when I moved here nearly five years ago. But now that I've started packing, I've been taking some finished boxes over to his garage. I have to go through all my tools in the shed, my random stuff strewn all over our house, my clothes and shoes, and all the junk left in my room. I own almost everything in the kitchen, so I'll have to wait until it's closer to the end of the summer to pack it all up.

I have decided today is the day to go through my closet. Mine is the bigger room in the house and with the bigger room comes the bigger closet. Jey and I decided the only fair way to choose who got the room was to leave it up to fate. One game of rock, paper, scissors. Whoever won, got it. I won, so I got the bigger room.

I grab my phone and go to my Spotify app to play a Pearl Jam radio station, but I decide to use my record player. I haven't used it in a while. Sifting through my records I choose Pink Floyd's *The Dark Side of the Moon* album and get to work going through boxes of old pictures, projects from middle school, and things my dad saved for me before he died. There are 6 boxes of junk on the shelves above my clothes. I pull the first one down, open it up and find old birthday cards, lanyards from the summer camp I used to go to, pictures from birthday parties, and a map one of my cousins and I made of our town to find buried treasure. That was when we thought we were going to grow up to be pirates. Looking through all these things makes me smile. It helps me remember that not all days are hard days. It reminds me of the time when my life wasn't filled with guilt and regret. When life was simpler. I pull out some of the birthday cards and read through them. I even found a twenty-dollar bill in one of them. I find my wallet on my bed and stick it inside.

One of the cards was from my uncle Eli for my tenth birthday. I smile back at the memory. He took me and my dad out on a boat that year and taught me how to fish. Inside the card was a picture from that day. My dad is in the background, driving the boat. His head is turned toward the camera and I notice he has a wide grin on his face, giving me a thumbs up with his other hand on the wheel. My dad was always smiling. I'm the focus of the picture. I had just caught my first fish of the day. It was a little one, but I was so proud of myself. I remember asking my uncle Eli if he could take a picture of me. We celebrated my birthday that night with cupcakes as the sun was setting over the water. The colors all morphed together and bounced off the water, making it seem like we were inside the sunset. My dad whistled happy birthday to me, which was one of our traditions because he couldn't sing to save his life. I enjoyed his whistling. Sometimes when I got hurt or was sad, he would whistle for me. It always seemed to calm me down. He would whistle random songs, sometimes he would even make up his own. I set the picture aside, making a mental note to put it in my desk drawer. That was the last birthday I got to celebrate with my dad. I want to keep that.

It's been thirteen years since my dad died, but I think about him everyday. I can't help but wonder what he would think of the man I am right now. If he would be ashamed of my mistakes. If he wasn't proud of me, I don't know what I would do. My dad was the one person I looked up to the most. I wanted to be just like him when I was younger. I remember I used to put on his shoes and follow him around the house, copying every move he made. I remember a picture of the two of us in my dad's bathroom. I'm in nothing but my diaper and a pair of my dad's shoes and he's wearing nothing but boxers. We're both brushing our teeth, me on the counter, looking up at him in the mirror with a smile on my face. *I need to find that picture.*

My favorite memories are when he would take me to the garage with him. He had a custom jumpsuit made for me that said Peterson's Auto Repair on it with my name stitched right underneath. He used to have to beg me to take it off so he could clean it. He would teach me about cars, throwing in life lessons like "A car runs on oil just like humans run on love. Cars won't drive without oil and humans can't live without love." I always understood things better when he described them to me through metaphors.

It kills me to think that he might not be proud of me. What if I've let him down? I dropped out of college, have no plans for my future, and spend most of my free time locked up in my room as of late. I honestly feel like there isn't much he could be proud of.

In another box I find a couple of hacky sacks, a letter from one of my elementary school teachers, a diploma from graduating fifth grade, more random pictures, a trophy from when I played lacrosse in middle school for one year, a yearbook from tenth grade and a hospital bracelet from the first time I went to the hospital. I fell out of a tree and sprained my ankle. Unsurprisingly, I wasn't able to find the picture of me and my dad in the bathroom brushing our teeth. Hopefully I'll find it somewhere in my things.

I start to close the box when I notice another piece of paper sticking out from under the flaps, all the way at the bottom of the box. I pull it out and flip it over. It's a piece of paper I haven't thought about for a long time. Seeing it makes me freeze up and I feel the color drain from my face. I'd recognize those colorful stars anywhere.

Sprawled across the top: "Lane & Laurel's Bucket List."

I sit back so I'm leaning against my bed, the paper shaking in my hand. I thought we'd lost this. Neither of us could remember what happened to it, and that was six years ago. We were seniors in high school the last time I remember thinking about it. I can't believe I've had it all this time.

My first instinct is to grab my phone and call Laurel, but I quickly realize that probably isn't the smartest thing to do. Telling her I found our bucket list we made when we were thirteen should not be the first thing I say to her after months of avoiding her. Especially after I hurt her.

I read the bucket list over and over and I realize how much of these we haven't done. I grin at the memory of writing this as I start to think about that day in the treehouse. She approached me that day like she had known me her whole life. She truly was meant to be my best friend. I've been hoping since that day that we would eventually become more than friends.

You see, Laurel isn't like other girls. And I know people say that a lot about the people they love, but when it comes to Laurel, it's true. She tells me what she's thinking, even if she knows I don't want to hear it. She puts others before herself, even if they're total strangers. She believes in herself when others doubt her. She used to get bullied all throughout middle school because she would sit with the lonely kid at lunch or talk to the smelly boy on the bus. But she was bullied not because of anything bad about her. She was bullied because she didn't care what others thought about her. She is just so unapologetically herself and I love that about her the most.

I sit and try to remember doing some of the things we already checked off the bucket list and I remember we added a couple as we got older: get drunk, kiss a stranger, go skinny dipping, and weirdly, name a star. There were some other things we added, too.

In ninth grade, we went on a field trip to New York. We stayed in a run-down hotel outside of the city and drove into the city everyday on the school bus that was rented for the trip. We had three whole days in the city, learning about the history, visiting important buildings, and most importantly going to see the Statue of Liberty.

Our first full day in New York was reserved for the Statue of Liberty. We were given a scavenger hunt of information we were supposed to collect throughout the tour, which would basically prove that we learned something through the trip.

We got in line to ride a boat over to the Statue of Liberty, in the wet, cold rain. The lines seemed endless, so Jey, Laurel and I played a couple games of ninja to pass the time. Eventually it was our turn to get on the boat. Once we got closer to the Statue, Laurel was so excited she started jumping up and down screaming "Oh my gosh, look! It's the Statue of Literby!"

She was so in awe and distracted by taking pictures that she didn't even notice she had said it wrong. Jey and I both noticed and we were trying so hard not to laugh. I hold it in better than Jey, but when he starts to really laugh, Laurel turns and asks, "What's so funny?" with a wide grin on her face. Enthusiasm is bursting out of her today. Jey and I look at each other and start laughing all over again.

"Come on, I want to laugh!" she practically begs.

"You said," I start explaining through breathless laughs. "You said….Lit…you said Literby instead of….instead of Liberty."

"HA!" Laurel joins. "That *is* funny!" She snaps a picture of Jey and me, then goes back to taking pictures of everything else. By everything else, I mean *everything*. She takes pictures of the bird sitting on top of our boat, and ones of other people we don't know. She stands up from her seat and takes a picture of it. I even saw her stick her hand over the side of the boat and take a picture of nothing but the water.

We got off the boat and Jey, Laurel, twelve other students and I were in a group together with our English teacher, Mr. Reech. His job was to give us a tour of the Statue of "Literby" and tell us all about its history, but he couldn't have cared less about seeing it. This trip happens every year and he's evidently lost his enthusiasm for the experience. He pulled out his phone and started fidgeting with it while quoting a driveling monologue about the importance of Lady Liberty.

We snuck off from the group and ditched our scavenger hunt assignment and went touring the Statue ourselves. We took selfies, had strangers take pictures of us, and even took pictures jumping off the steps using the timer on Laurel's phone. Laurel wanted a couple of pictures of just herself in front of it, so I took her phone and snapped some. I remember she was wearing a bucket hat she brought on the trip, probably thinking visiting the Statue would be just as adventurous as going on a safari in Kenya. The rain had weighed her hat down, so it was blocking half of her face, but you could still see her smile. She somehow finds a way to enjoy everything.

We walked around the entire thing, trying to count how many steps it took, but we lost count because Jey kept shouting random numbers to mess up our count. I think we got to five-hundred-and something. What I assumed would be a boring day full of useless information I would forget in five minutes turned into a memorable day with my best friends.

That night on the way back to the hotel, I asked if I could see her phone to send the pictures to myself. I secretly sent the ones of just her, too.

I organize all the papers, notes and toys I pulled out of the boxes and place them into new ones based on categories, feeling in a better mood than I have all week. I throw away some papers that were crumbled and smeared, decide to donate my hacky sacks, and pick out all the pictures I want to keep in my desk.

I put the bucket list in the top drawer of my desk. I want to reach out to Laurel to tell her I found it, but I don't think it would be a good idea. It's been so long since I've talked to her and since I'm leaving in three months, it just doesn't make sense for me to reach out again. The way our relationship ended will always weigh heavy on my heart, but I don't want to hurt again.

After I clean up my mess, I head into the kitchen for a snack. I'm hungry since I didn't eat much of my breakfast or my lunch. I open the pantry and grab the only thing that sounds good right now: kettle corn popcorn.

Checking the time I discover it's nearly 7 p.m. Jey is still passed out on the couch, so I set the popcorn down and go over to wake him up. I grab a pillow off the chair next to the couch and hit him hard on the back with it. He jumps and groggily screams "Shit!" when the pillow connects with his back.

"Good morning, Jey. Nice of you to finally enjoy the last few hours of this amazingly, wonderful day," I say sarcastically.

He opens one eye and finds me standing over him, threatening to hit him again. He looks like a bird with one eye open like that. He moans and flips his head to the other side.

"I'll hit you again," I say, raising the pillow.

"Alright, alright, I'm up. Happy?" He sits up like a zombie but keeps his eyes closed. He stretches and lets out a loud screech.

"How was Ms. Elsie's today?" he asks me through mid-yawn.

"It was fine," I lie, walking into the kitchen. I sit on one of the bar stools at the island and face him, popping a few pieces of popcorn in my mouth. "Was your game canceled?"

"Yeah, this stupid rain is never ending. I thought April showers bring May flowers, but it's almost the end of May and it's still fucking raining. It's so depressing."

I chuckle, thinking of the song in Bambi that goes "drip, drip, drip, little April shower." Laurel used to love Bambi.

"Yeah, it makes us depressed individuals even more depressed."

He stops rubbing his eyes and looks up at me. "I'm sorry, man, I didn't mean it like that. I just meant -"

"It's okay," I say, cutting him off. "I was joking."

I swivel around in my chair, not wanting to look at him because now I feel awkward. I actually was joking.

It stays quiet for a second.

"I'm sorry if I made you upset earlier this morning," he starts. I turn around to look at him. "Lane, I care a lot about you, and I'm worried you aren't okay." *Here we go.* "I know you've been through a lot and you need to take your time healing," he starts. "But I just need to know you're okay. I know you go to therapy, but I feel like that isn't enough. I haven't asked you to open up to me about it in a while because I know how you are, but seriously man, please tell me something."

I look out the backdoor, wishing I could escape this conversation. He's right, he hasn't asked me to open up to him recently. He hasn't in nearly two months. But I don't want to do this right now. I emotionally and mentally *can't* do this right now.

I don't answer so he starts speaking again, taking a more aggressive route this time.

"You know what, man, if you want to be like that, fine. But the day you decide to commit suicide, it won't be on me. I tried to ask you, but just like always, you don't ever respond. I'm so tired of this fucking silence." He throws his hands up in the air and starts to walk away.

Now, I'm mad. I jump out of the chair and quickly crash into him on his way to the bathroom. I push him up against the wall and yell, "You want to force me to be open with you and talk about something that I'm not ready to talk about, well, here you go. Today I saw Mrs. Malani at the shop and the second she left, I ran to the bathroom and had a panic attack. I sat on the floor and cried like a fucking pathetic baby for thirty minutes. My chest literally felt like it was going to crush in on itself from the guilt."

I let go of Jey and stare down the hallway, through the large window above the sink. I watch the trees sway in the wind as the raindrops continue to fall. My life is a storm.

My voice is so quiet when I start talking again that I don't even know if he can hear me. "I can't ever take back what I did, Jey, and I have to live with that for the rest of my life. It's all my fault Laurel isn't in my life anymore and I can't handle it. So, no, I'm not okay. I will never be okay again."

I finish and let out a deep breath through my nostrils. I can feel my whole body shaking with adrenaline. I look down at the floor, tears spilling from my eyes. Jey stands there, completely stunned like he doesn't know what to say.

He wanted me to open up and now he has nothing to say to me.

I start to walk away, but he grabs my arm and tells me to wait. I freeze, still waiting for him to say something. I wait five seconds and shove his hand off my arm then head toward the front door. I hear Jey call after me as I slam the door behind me and head to the one place Jey will never look for me.

Magic is in the Air

Chapter 8

The summer after Laurel and I met, the first thing we picked on the bucket list was to read Harry Potter and watch all of the movies. We borrowed the first book from the public library and sat in the treehouse and read the entire day. I was a faster reader than her, but I only think that's because she takes her time to understand what's really happening. Around 6 p.m., she asks, "What page are you on?" We just got back to the treehouse from eating a dinner of chicken, mac and cheese, and Mrs. Malani's famous brown sugar carrots.

"What page are *you* on?" I respond. I don't want her to know I'm ahead of her. I can tell by looking at her book that I have fewer pages left than she does.

"I just got to page one hundred and sixty-three, the chapter titled Halloween," she informs me. I just got to the chapter on Nicholas Flamel.

"Oh, me too," I say. She shoots up from slouching down in her chair and says, "Oh my gosh, that midnight duel chapter was wild! I for sure thought they were going to get eaten by that three-headed dog!"

I laugh at her enthusiasm. It's so like Laurel to actually be worried that they would get eaten by the three-headed dog. They couldn't have or there would be no plot for the rest of the books. It would be illogical to think they would actually get eaten.

We spend the rest of the day reading. I finish well before she does, but I pretend to keep reading so we can finish at the same time. It's nearly 9 p.m. when she closes her book and jumps to her feet onto the seat of the couch. She throws the book into the air and shouts, "OH MY GOSH, I LOVE HARRY POTTER!"

I knew her reaction would be nothing but dramatic.

"Lane, wasn't that just the best book you have ever read? I can't wait to start reading the second one. We HAVE to go back to the library tomorrow!" She squeals and jumps up and down then she joins me where I lay on the ground.

Laying on the treehouse floor, Laurel and I talk about Harry Potter for the next two hours, using the ceiling as the backdrop for our imaginations. We discuss our favorite characters, what house we think

we belong in, who our best friend at Hogwarts
would be, and what classes we wish we could take.

We eventually leave the treehouse and I walk
Laurel to the backdoor. We make a plan to go to the
library first thing tomorrow to get the first movie
and the next book. We decided that we would read a
book and then watch the movie and then read the
next book and so on. After Laurel goes inside, I
bike back to my house and shower before I go to
bed. That night I dream of my own magical life. A
life where Laurel is by my side forever.

The Locket

Chapter 9

As soon as I wake up, I run to Laurel's house and just as I'm about to bang on the front door, she opens it with a wide smile. She runs past me and I hear keys jingle in her hand. I follow her as she opens the front passenger door of Ms. Malani's car. Five seconds later, I hear the engine. She yells over her shoulder at me. "Let's go! We're going to the library!"

"I can't drive," I tell her, just as Ms. Malani comes out of the already open front door.

"Laurel, did you take my keys?" she asks. She nods her head and rolls her eyes when she hears the car running, then turns to close the door behind her.

"Get in the car already!" Laurel yells at me.

It's a rainy day so we grab all kinds of pillows and blankets from the house and trudge them up the stairs of the treehouse. We decided to watch in the treehouse on the portable DVD player. We close the blinds and make a fort out of almost all of the blankets and place the pillows all over the ground to lay on, making the floor a lot more comfortable. We use the rest of the blankets to pretend we have Hogwarts robes.

We spend the next two and a half hours watching the first Harry Potter. I was pretty impressed with how similar the movie was to the book. Some details were off, but I was expecting that. Laurel hated that it didn't include the midnight duel between Draco and Harry in the movie. I hated that it didn't include Peeves.

Laurel was amazed by the movie, claiming it was the best movie she's ever seen. She says every movie is the best movie she's ever seen, and she probably genuinely thinks that about every movie she's ever seen.

***

Over the next two weeks, we read the books and watch the movies. We would rotate our reading locations between the treehouse, my uncle Eli's house, the beach, and our secret closet at my uncle's garage. Our favorite place to read was the beach late at night. We would bring flashlights for after the sunset and we would snack on all kinds of candy and chips. We would read until our eyes were sore and then bike back to our neighborhood.

She cried when Sirius Black died while reading the book. She cried when Hermoine was tortured by Bellatrix Lestrange. During that scene in the movie, Laurel grabbed my arm and hid behind me. It made my stomach flutter when she leaned in so close to me. We both cried when Dobby died and she cried when Bill and Fleur got married. Basically, she cried a lot.

My stomach feeling weird when Laurel got close to me was a new experience for me. Laurel and I have never felt weird being close to each other, we're always comfortable despite being friends for only a month. But when she leaned in with her head on my shoulder, I liked it. But for new reasons. I don't know when the change occurred, but it made me feel what I can only assume what people refer to when they say they have butterflies in their stomach. I've never felt butterflies for a girl before.

Sometime at the beginning of the week, we got character wands from Walmart. They were surprise wands so we didn't know who we were going to get. Laurel ended up getting Luna's wand, which I thought fit her very well. I got Fred Weasley's.

During the last movie, during the Battle of Hogwarts, we got out our wands and pretended to jinx and hex each other. She would shout, *"Stupefy!"* I would counterattack using, *"Protego!"*

Then we would throw something against the wall so it made a loud noise, pretending that things were blowing up all around us. It was a lot of fun. We got so into the world of Harry Potter, we decided to take the official Pottermore House test. Unsurprisingly, Laurel got Gryffindor. I got Hufflepuff, which we also weren't too surprised about.

Those two weeks were nothing but magic and all things Harry Potter, so I wasn't at all surprised when Laurel decided she wanted to have a Harry Potter themed birthday party. Her birthday was two days later, June 29th to be exact. I had no doubt she would go all out.

***

Today is June 29th, also known as Laurel Penelope Owens' birthday. Today, she will officially become a teenager.

I wake up around eight, which is a lot earlier than I usually wake up, especially in the summer. I'm so excited to celebrate Laurel's birthday. It's the first birthday we get to celebrate since being friends. We went shopping all day yesterday at various party stores, trying to find the best Harry Potter decorations.

I get dressed and skip breakfast with my uncle Eli and Ivy and run over to Laurel's. When I get there, they call me into the kitchen and I find them making pancakes that look like different Harry Potter characters. Mr. Matthew holds one up in the air that looks like Dobby, or maybe it was a really bad Ron Weasley. I couldn't be sure. Laurel made one that somewhat looked like the Hungarian Horntail dragon, and Mrs. Malani made one that looks like a mandrake, save for all the colors. They invite me over to make one so I pull up a picture of the Golden Stitch on their iPad and get to work. I've always been a detail-oriented individual, so this should be fun.

It takes me fifteen minutes to do one side of the snitch, but I keep going, despite their jokes about how serious I look.

When I finish, I turn the burner on low and carefully pour some extra pancake mix on top, covering my tedious artwork. I let it cook and flip it over. I let out a gasp because I'm blown away by how good it actually came out.

Laurel comes over to look at it. "Lane! Oh em gee, that looks amazing! Can you make me one?" She looks at me with her big green eyes and so much enthusiasm covers her face, and I can't say no to her. But I didn't want to spend the next thirty minutes making it again, so I just switch pancakes with her instead. She coats it with butter and syrup and gives me two thumbs up after she takes her first bite.

We clean up breakfast with Mr. Matthew while Mrs. Malani goes to the garage to get all the decorations out. The party officially starts at two, but we have a lot to do. Hanging decorations, putting snacks out, cleaning the house. Laurel's so excited, she put the bowl with the extra pancake mix right into the dishwasher.

"Laurel, you dumped pancake mix all over the place!"

"Oh, sorry," she says. I can tell her mind is elsewhere. I think her dad knows that, too, because he tells her to wash her hands and to go help Mrs. Malani with the decorations. She rinses her hands off, without soap, and dries them on her shorts while running toward the garage.

I continue to wash the dishes off in the sink and hand them to Mr. Matthew so he can organize them in the dishwasher.

"Lane," he starts softly, sliding a fork in the utensil holder.

"Yeah?"

"I just wanted to say that I am very thankful Laurel found a friend in you. I know you haven't known her very long, but you're the closest friend she's ever had and I just wanted to say thank you. Malani and I appreciate how much you care about Laurel."

I let the water run over my soapy hands, feeling kind of thrown off. Mr. Matthew has never said anything to me like that before.

"Oh, well, thank you," I say. "Laurel's one of the closest friends I've ever had, too." I look over at him and smile with the corner of my mouth. I really wonder why someone like Laurel doesn't have a line of people at her door, waiting for a chance to be best friends with her. She's so kind and smart, and funny and unapologetically herself. Why don't more people see her the way I do?

I hand him the last of the dishes and we both wash our hands before joining Laurel and Mrs. Malani in the family room. We got enough decorations for the family room, kitchen, and for the party tent in the backyard.

When we walk into the family room, my jaw drops with how many decorations they have already put up, and at the number of decorations that still need to go up. "Wow," I say. "You guys work fast."

"Well when you're as determined as Laurel, you can just about get anything done," Mrs. Malani laughs. Her parents head outside to start putting up the tent.

Hanging in the doorway is a curtain with what looks like a hundred tassels. Being that no one has walked through the doorway and made it move, I can see that all the individual tassels make a picture. It's a picture of Hogwarts. There are balloons surrounding the entertainment center, candles hanging from random spots on the ceiling, and a large standing sign with arrows pointing in various directions, all labeled with various popular Harry Potter destinations.

I take a quick break and run to the bathroom. I literally run because Laurel's yelling at me, telling me to hurry up. When I lift the toilet seat, I lose my balance and almost trip and fall over into the bathtub. There's a picture of Moaning Myrtle taped to the lid of the toilet. I roll my eyes and let out a small laugh, finding it cute that Laurel thought to do that.

I make my way back to the living room and Laurel is standing there with a hand on her hip and her arm in the air, checking her nonexistent watch.

"Took you long enough."

"Well, I would've been quicker if I had known that Moaning Myrtle was going to jump out of nowhere."

Laurel chuckles to herself and then suddenly stops. "Wait, you put the seat back down, right?" I spin on my heels and run back to the bathroom to put the seat back down. I guess she wants everyone to be as thrown off as I was.

When I get back and am finally ready to get to work, Laurel hands me the end of a streamer and a piece of tape.

"Here," she says. "We're going to put this one across the room like this," she makes a diagonal motion, pointing towards the door and the entrance into the kitchen. This streamer has Harry's, Ron's, and Hermoine's faces on it.

I grab the stool on my way over to the entrance of the kitchen and step up on it. "Twist it, like this," Laurel demands. She starts twisting it, making me drop the streamer.

"Ugh, Lane! We don't have time for your silly mistakes today," she grunts.

"My deepest apologies, Your Highness," I say, stepping off the ladder and bowing in her direction.

She laughs so hard she snorts. She picks up a pillow and starts chasing me around the room. She tries to hit me with the pillow, and at the last second, I switch my direction, making her fall to the ground and slam her face on the bottom of the couch.

She lets out a painful screech and immediately grabs her forehead. She looks over at me and I see blood oozing between her fingers. She pulls her hand away from her head and screams "Mom!"

Mrs. Malani comes rushing into the family room from outside. "I was chasing Lane with a pillow and I ended up falling and hitting my head on the couch. Am I going to need stitches?" she asks. It's written all over her face how badly she doesn't want stitches. Not because she's scared of them, but because she doesn't want to miss her party.

"Let me see it, dear," Mrs. Malani says. Mr. Matthew brings over some paper towels and Mrs. Malani wipes the blood off her forehead. She inspects it for a minute and finally says, "No, I think you're alright. It doesn't look too deep and the bleeding has already slowed. Sometimes head injuries bleed a lot even though they aren't bad injuries."

Laurel jumps up and throws her hands in the air, hitting Mrs. Malani in the face with her fist.

"Laurel, would you be careful? You just smacked me in the face."

***

We finish setting everything up, and I have to say, it looks pretty amazing. There's a table filled with snacks from the world of Harry Potter; butterbeer, Canary creams, pumpkin pasties, cockroach clusters, treacle puffs, and so many different kinds of candy, ending with Hagrid's infamous birthday cake. Obviously, instead of Harry it says Laurel.

There are cardboard cutouts of Harry, Ron and Hermoine with holes replacing their faces, so you can take pictures pretending to be them. The first movie is playing on the TV in the living room, and there's a speaker outside playing the soundtracks from the movies. There are all differently shaped balloons, some shaped like Dobby, chocolate frogs, and wands. My favorite thing at the party though is the bounce house that's shaped like the Burrow. It's one of the coolest things I have *ever* seen.

Right before the party starts, Mr. Matthew and Mrs. Malani tell me and Laurel to join them in the family room. There are two presents sitting on the coffee table, one with Laurel's name and one with mine.

"We just wanted to say thank you to you guys for helping us with the shopping, the cooking, and all the decorating today," Mrs. Malani says handing us our presents.

We open them up and inside are Hogwarts robes from our respective houses.

Laurel sucks in a deep, sharp breath, with her jaw hanging wide open.

"This is so awesome," I say, pulling mine out the box.

I hold it out in front of me and notice my name has been stitched in yellow on the right-hand side. I look over at Laurel's and her name is stitched in red.

"Mr. and Mrs. Owens, this is too much. Seriously, thank you so much, this is so thoughtful" I say, putting my robe on.

"Don't worry about it at all! We wanted to get you guys something special to enjoy the party in!"

"YOU GUYS ARE THE BEST," Laurel shouts, running over to her parents to attack them with hugs. She hugs it around her tightly and spins around. It doesn't really fly out like dresses do, but to her it has the same effect.

About five minutes later, Laurel's family shows up and are soon followed by a bunch of kids from school. Nearly the entire class was invited, so we're expecting a lot of people to come. Jey shows up at 2:15 with the girl he's dating this week. He was dating a different girl last week. I can't keep up with him. She's a year older than us and wasn't invited to the party. I'm annoyed he brought her, but I don't say anything about it to him. I don't want to start anything on Laurel's special day. My uncle Eli and Ivy come, too.

Once almost everyone arrives, the kids go to the backyard. We have wand fights using imaginary spells and magic, but we also just use them like swords. We jump in the bounce house for hours, making up games and pretending we're flying on the back of a dragon. We take turns jinxing each other. Samuel, a boy in our history class, yells "Eat slugs" at one of Laurel's cousins, Riley. Riley spits out all the gummy candy in his mouth, pretending to throw up slugs like Ron Weasley. Laurel cackles so hard, I think she might've snapped a vocal cord for a second.

We spend the rest of the night playing pin the tail on the dragon, playing Quidditch with random balls we found in the Owens' shed, eating snacks and candy, and watching Laurel open her birthday presents. She got a couple new wands, a Harry

Potter journal set, so many gift cards, and a new bike from her parents.

By eight o'clock, everyone's gone home. It's just Laurel and me hanging out in the treehouse while her parents take all the food and decorations inside. We lay on the floor, sharing a bowl of Bertie Bott's Every Flavor Beans.

"Ew, I think that one was dog food," she says, spitting it out of her mouth. I hear it bounce on the floor.

"Laurel," I shakily say. *I can do this. It's just a birthday present.*

"Yeah?" she asks, shoving jellybeans in her mouth. She must've gotten another gross one because she spits it in her hand and throws it out the open door.

I sit up and reach for my backpack and pull out her birthday present.

"Here's your birthday present." That comes out shakier than I was expecting. My voice cracks.

She sits up and looks up at me confused.

"You got me something?" she asks. She takes it from my hand.

"Well, yeah. But I wanted to give it to you when we were alone."

She starts to untie the bow on top of the little box. She opens the box and finds a necklace. Not just any necklace, but a locket. I had it engraved on the front with the letter "L." "L" for Laurel and "L" for Lane.

She takes it out of the box and holds it up so she can see it in the light.

"Lane," she starts. She doesn't finish, yet. After a beat, "It's beautiful. How much did this cost you?"

"Don't worry about it. Happy birthday, Laurel." I'd been saving up my money for the past couple years from birthdays and Christmases just in case I wanted something special and didn't want to ask my uncle Eli for it. But this was worth spending all my money on. I'm grinning from ear to ear. *I'm so glad she likes it.*

"Open it up," I say.

She opens the locket with dainty fingers, being extra cautious like she doesn't want to break it.

Inside is a picture of us. One we took at the beach once. We're sitting on a bench, eating ice cream. Laurel has a brown smudge running down her lip, her bucket hat flopping on her head. The sun is setting in the background, giving the photo a pinky-vibe. She told me that was her favorite picture of us.

"Thank you, Lane. I love it so much. Will you put it on me?"

"Uh, yeah… Of course!" I muster, kind of flustered.

I inch closer to her as she turns around. She hands me both sides of the necklace and then moves her hair to the side. I grab the sides of the necklace and clasp them together. My hands graze her neck and I feel how warm it is.

Without thinking, I lean in and hug her from behind. She grabs my arms and leans her head on my forearm.

"This is the best present I've ever gotten," she says, clutching it tightly in her hand.

No, I'm Not Okay

Chapter 10

I arrive at the Owens' old house twenty minutes after I walked out on Jey. I park in the street and walk past the large FOR SALE sign in the front yard, punching it over and over in my mind.

Walking to the backyard and up the steps of the treehouse is muscle memory I didn't even know I still had. The path Laurel and I used to walk is now covered in tall, new grass. I walk the path, crushing the grass beneath my feet. It doesn't feel the same as it used to.

It's been a while since I've been at this house, even longer since I've been in the treehouse. I softly whistle as I make my way up the stairs, feeling a little nervous. I make it to the top of the stairs and lightly open the door, taking a peek before I step all the way in. I knew it would be cleared out, but I didn't know how empty seeing it hollowed out would make me feel. The couch is the first thing I notice is missing, since it sat directly across from the door. I step inside and glance around, overwhelmed with emotion. The wall that was covered with Laurel's Victoria Falls mural is now blank and boring. There's a smudge of blue sticky tack on the wall so I peel it off and rub it in between my fingers.

I sit against the back wall where the couch used to be, bringing my knees to my chest and resting my arms on them. I let my head fall and I drop the sticky tack. I don't stop the tears from coming. At first the tears are slow, then they come in like rapids rushing down a river.

I sob into my arms, soaking my shirt with my tears and drool. I don't even care.

I think about how much my life has changed in the past seven months. I think about how much I hate what I did to her; how I let her down. How I changed the Owens' lives. I think about screaming in Jey's face. He didn't deserve my silence and he definitely didn't deserve my screaming. I think about how I was rude to Ms. Elsie earlier today.

I think about the loss of my dad. How he died from a tumor in his brain we never knew he had. We found out when it was too late. I think about how I had to redo the sixth grade because the grief of losing him was too much. I think about how my mom left when I was little. I hardly remember anything about her. All I know is that she walked out on me and my dad, leaving a hole the size of a reliable mother in my life. I think about losing Honey, how even though we weren't exceptionally close, she loved me more than my mother did. I think about losing Laurel and how much I miss her friendship. How much I miss *her*. I think about losing Mr. Matthew and Mrs. Malani, who treated me like their own child.

I think about how I am planning to leaving those I care about in order to get away from my miserable life. At the end of the summer, I am moving across the country to forget all of this...mess.

I think about how ending it all might be the easier option than trying to pretend I'm okay every day. I wake up every morning, wishing I could go back to sleep. I don't want to face the day. I don't want to face my mistakes and my guilt and my grief. I'm overflowing with so many different emotions and I can't differentiate between them.

This is the first time I have let myself cry since the accident. The last time I cried before that was at my dad's funeral when I was ten. Sure, I've cried from an overly happy moment in a movie, or when Dobby died in Harry Potter. And I guess I cried when I saw Mrs. Malani at the pottery shop, but that was different. I was surprised by the catharsis which accompanied my crying. I've needed to let this out for almost seven months.

I cry so hard my body involuntarily shakes. My throat is sore and my head stings with a migraine. I lay down on the floor of the treehouse, my favorite place in the world. I whistle a soft song my dad used to sing. It calms me down a little. I fall asleep and dream of a different life. One where I wasn't miserable and I still had my dad. One where my mom loved me and chose to be my mother. One where I didn't lose Laurel.

***

I wake up feeling really groggy. My body is sore from laying so awkwardly on the hardwood floor. I check my watch and realize it's eleven at night. I was asleep for nearly three hours. I manage to sit up, crack my neck and stretch my arms, and begin to feel a little better. My eyes have a heaviness to them, as if all my tears somehow made them weak.

Standing up, I put my hands in my jacket pocket, ready to leave. I discover there is a pen in my pocket. I roll it in my fingers.

I walk over to the wall, meeting it with the pen. I write Lane and Laurel by the door of the bathroom, claiming it as ours. Whoever moves in here next needs to know this is our treehouse.

I walk down the steps of the treehouse and think that this will probably be the last time I ever get to come here. I take a deep breath and walk back to my car. I don't take a second look back.

I drive home with the windows open, despite the cold. I feel so emotionally numb right now, like a zombie. I need to feel something, even if it's feeling freezing cold.

I pull into the driveway.

Get out.

Shut the car door.

Walk inside.

And that's when I see Jey sitting on the couch, his leg bouncing up and down and up and down. He looks like he's been waiting for me for hours. I know Paisley was supposed to come over tonight, so he probably told her not to come so we could talk.

"Hey, Lane," he says. He's holding his hands together so tightly his knuckles turn white. I watch him relax as I close the door.

"Hey, Jey," I sigh.

"Can we please talk? I mean talk. Like we both sit down and have a conversation and you don't get to run away again."

No thank you. "Yeah, okay," I sigh, walking over to the chair next to the couch. *I can't avoid this forever.* I grab the pillow and hold it in front of me. It feels like a million pounds holding me in place. I squeeze it as I feel my body tense up.

"Okay." He pauses, takes in a deep breath, and continues.

"First, I'm sorry for saying what I said. That was so wrong of me to say and I've been beating myself up for it since you walked out the door."

"It's oka-," I try to say, but he cuts me off.

"No, Lane, it wasn't. That was such a shitty thing to say. If you ever did commit suicide, I would one hundred percent blame myself, for that comment alone."

"Well, thank you for apologizing," I say awkwardly. *Why is it so hard for me to say what I'm thinking?*

So instead, I try to not *think* about what I'm saying.

"But you know how hard it is for me to open up. Even earlier this morning I overheard you and Paisley talking in the kitchen and you told her I have a hard time opening up. Yeah, maybe it is because of my dad and that was a long time ago, but it's still hard." I fidget with the tassels on the pillow. "He died so suddenly and I didn't know how to cope so I just shut everyone out and kept everything in." Even telling him all of this is difficult and I haven't even really started sharing my feelings yet.

Besides Laurel, Dr. Therin is the only person I've ever really shared my feelings with. Jey and I used to tell each other everything, but that was before I started losing people.

"I'm sorry it's hard for me to open up and I'm sorry it frustrates you. But the difference between us is that I need to do it on my own time. You have no problem sharing your feelings, but that's harder for me to do. Forcing me to open up isn't going to make me open up, if anything it's just going to push me away."

He shakes his head up and down slightly, like he already knows all of this. Which he probably does. He's known me for a long time.

"I know, and I'm sorry for trying to push you. I just want you to feel better. I know it's going to take time, but I wish you were there right now. I just want you to be happy again."

Jey may be a cocky guy, but he has no problem crying, being vulnerable or sharing his thoughts and feelings. I appreciate that about him, but also envy how naturally it comes to him.

"I'll try harder to be more open, but I can't promise anything. I also have a harder time saying anything in front of Paisley. You know I love her, but she," I start through a forced laugh "she looks at me like I'm a sad puppy."

"Yeah, I've talked to her about that. She can't help it though, she wears all her emotions right on her face," Jey says, making a circular motion around his face.

He places his hands back in his lap and starts picking at his fingers. He does that when he's nervous.

"I'm just worried about you. You've become a little bit of a misanthrope." He says it with a pained look on his face, like he's waiting for me to disagree. But I can't disagree because it's true. I've stopped talking to just about anyone outside of my immediate life. My buddies from my semester of college, the old intern from the pottery shop, the guys at the garage, mine and Laurel's trivia night gang. I've become a hermit.

"Yeah, I know. I just need...time," I say through a breath. I run my hands through my hair and down my face.

"Can I ask you a question?" Jey asks, looking up at me.

"Yes."

"Can you just tell me that you're not okay? I need you to say it out loud to me. I need to know that you know you aren't okay."

I understand why he's requesting this of me. At this moment, it reminds me how much he cares about me.

Yes, I admit it, I am not okay.....

Now say it out loud, Lane.

"I'm not okay," I finally say, with a shaky voice.

"Thank you," Jey says, letting out a breath.

The Tipping Point

Chapter 11

I wake up the next morning with a splitting headache. Probably from all the emotion and crying yesterday. I'm not used to that. I shut my alarm off and go back to sleep. I've set another for fifteen minutes from now.

Fifteen minutes later, it sounds. I'm not ready to get out of bed. Even though I took a three-hour nap last night, I feel like I could sleep for twelve more hours. I turn off my second alarm and head to the bathroom to take a shower, hoping it'll help my headache. I shower much faster today.

Arriving at the pottery shop ten minutes before opening, I unlock the door, turn the lights on and get ready to open in, now, eight minutes. I turn the music on, count the cash in the drawer, display a couple of new pieces we worked on last week, and flip the closed sign to open.

I do not want to be here today.

The first couple hours go by slowly, with only a few customers. It's still pouring outside, keeping everyone locked inside their homes. I decide to start sketching a few new ideas for a couple weeks from now when we'll need new displays. The phone starts to ring and I grab it while continuing my sketch.

"Hi, Ms. Elsie's Pottery shop, this is Lane. How can I help you?"

I'm greeted with silence on the other end. "Hello?" I ask.

I start to hear breathing on the other end and before I can say anything else, they hang up.

That was weird. Must've had the wrong number.

I continue my sketches and do a couple of other things before Ms. Elsie arrives. Today I have my second meeting this week with Dr. Therin.

Ms. Elsie walks in with a bright yellow umbrella. She shakes it outside the door before putting it in a tall pot and hanging her coat up.

"The weather is so horrible right now. I'm glad we both made it here okay. You heard about the storm warming, right? It just keeps getting worse. Be careful when you leave, darling."

She comes behind the counter and I catch her up on everything that's happened since I opened. I told her about the random phone call, but she didn't seem all that surprised by it. Except I see a flash of...panic?... in her eyes. I notice she breaks eye contact with me when I tell her about it. Maybe it happens often.

I tell her to close and leave if the storm gets any worse before the end of the day. I don't like the thought of her driving in this weather.

I grab my stuff and run out to my car. I turn on the heat even though it's almost summer. The rainy weather makes me so cold.

I slowly drive to Dr. Therin's office, just outside the middle of town. The last time I drove in weather like this is the reason I see Dr. Therin now. It was pouring the night of the accident.

I arrive twenty minutes early because I didn't think I would have enough time to go home beforehand. I sit in the parking lot, trying not to think about how much I am dreading this meeting. He's going to ask how I've been since Monday and I'll have to tell him everything that happened yesterday.

Ten minutes later, I walk inside and find Ms. Shelia sitting behind the reception desk.

"Hello there, Lane," she says cheerily. I'm used to what happens next, so I take out my debit card and pay for this week's sessions. It isn't super expensive with my insurance, but it adds up.

She hands me back my card and tells me to take a seat and that Dr. Therin will come get me when he's ready.

I stare at the clock on the wall and watch the second hand tick by. I'm still two minutes early. I shake my right leg up and down and feel my heel connect with the floor every time I make it go down. *Tick tock, tick tock.*

I bite my lip and look around the room. I want to leave.

Dr. Therin comes in what feels like an hour later and greets me with a nice "Hello, Lane."

We walk to his office and I follow him in and sit down in my regular seat. Usually, it's a pretty comfortable chair, but right now I feel like I'm sitting on a chair made of nails and concrete.

His office is decorated with his degrees, random, obscure art, and dim, gray walls. He turns on the white noise machine sitting just outside the door and then closes the door behind him. Confidentiality. He sighs as he sits behind his desk. He opens his file with my name on it and pulls out a piece of paper. The light coming in from the window hits it and I can see scribbles.

"So, Lane. How have you been? Has anything new happened since I saw you last?"

He sets the paper on the desk and looks up at me through stylish glasses and grins through a perfectly trimmed beard. He wears a blue and white checkered button up shirt, probably ironed by his wife this morning.

"Fine." I purposefully don't answer his second question.

He nods, hopefully getting the point that I don't want to talk today.

"Have you worked on any of the things we talked about on Monday?"

On Monday, I was actually in a pretty good mood. After our meeting, I felt like trying harder. I want to feel better mentally and emotionally. But after the past couple of days I've had, I don't want to try at all.

I think of yesterday in the pottery shop bathroom. I did do the homework he gave me. All those techniques to help calm me down. I've had a lot of panic attacks since the accident and he's been trying to help me work through them instead of letting them hit me like a ton of bricks.

"Yes, I did actually." I know he's going to ask me what happened so I start to share before he gets it out. For some reason, the thought of him asking annoys me.

"I saw Mrs. Malani yesterday. It led to a panic attack so I went to the bathroom and calmed myself down using the grounding technique you told me about."

He looks at me with his hands folded, holding up his chin.

"Was it hard seeing Mrs. Malani for the first time since the accident?"

Well, it technically isn't my first time *seeing* her since the accident. But definitely my first time talking to her. Any time I've seen her I've walked away and avoided her.

"Yes, it was." I'm annoyed because this seems obvious to me.

"That makes me very happy to hear, Lane, that you used a grounding technique. I'm glad it worked. So, you said you saw Mrs. Malani and that led to a panic attack. But what do you think it was that took you over the edge of your tipping point?"

"My tipping point?" I ask, growing irritated.

"Yes, your tipping point. A tipping point is basically the point at which a series of small things or incidents becomes significant enough to cause a bigger change. You were fine until one specific moment, right when the panic attack happened. So what do you think was your tipping point yesterday? What pushed you over the edge?"

I mull over this new concept and try to think back to yesterday. What was it that made me freak out like that?

"Um….I don't really know."

"Okay. Do you think it was seeing Mrs. Malani unexpectedly?"

He's obviously trying to get me to share the details of yesterday. If I'm paying for this, I might as well give him the full story.

I tell him I got called into work early, that Mrs. Malani was there when I arrived. I told him I apologized for the accident and how she seemed so cold.

"I don't really know what I was expecting. I guess not a hug, but she used to treat me like I was her son. And yesterday she treated me like I was a complete stranger."

"Hm. So you think it was because she was treating you differently?"

I feel like that's not it. I've gone months without talking to Mr. Matthew and Mrs. Malani. I know what I did, and while I was wishing I would get a hug and understanding, I knew I wouldn't get that.

"No, I don't. But I don't know what it was that led to the panic attack." I fidget with my fingers and cross my feet.

The rest of my meeting we talk about my conversations with Ms. Elsie and Jey. It makes me feel bad, but somehow my conversations with them are less important than what happened with Mrs. Malani. Not that they meant less to me because I care for Ms. Elsie and Jey but talking to Mrs. Malani for the first time hit me with a new level of anxiety.

I leave Dr. Therin's office and head to the mechanic shop for the rest of the day. I haven't stopped thinking about what my tipping point could've been. Something had to have happened during that conversation that was too much. Something had to have pushed me over the edge. I just can't pinpoint what it was.

I park my car in the back parking lot and meet my uncle Eli in his office. We usually chat a bit before he puts me to work. I finished all my assignments two days ago, so I need something new to work on.

My uncle Eli owns a mechanic shop, Peterson's Auto Repair, in the middle of town. When I was younger, I used to run around the shop trying to find the best and most original places to hide for hide-and-seek. Before my dad died, they were business partners. People always said there wasn't a car the Peterson brothers couldn't fix. My uncle Eli struggled for a while after my dad died because he had to take over all the expenses. And take care of me.

Now I work in the shop.

"Yo," I say, entering his office.

His back is to me and he's facing his computer. He jumps when he hears me and quickly exits out of whatever website he was on.

"Hey, kiddo," he says. "How was your meeting with Dr. Therin?"

"It was good, actually. Have you ever heard of something called a tipping point?"

He looks up, like he's thinking through everything he's ever known.

"No, I haven't. What's it mean?"

"Oh, nothing. I was just wondering. Whatcha up to on that computer, huh? I saw you close that browser *pretty* quickly." I give him a smirk, knowing I caught him doing something mischievous.

"What? Oh, nothing," he says, waving his arm, dismissing my question. "Just some parts I was looking at. You scared me though," he admits. "I just jumped is all."

I sit down on the seat next to his desk, giving him a sassy "Mmhmm, right." I'm in a much better mood than I was an hour ago. He shuffles through some papers on his desk when I ask, "What do you have for me today?"

He tosses me a couple of papers that are paper clipped together. I take off the paper clip and shuffle through them. They all need minor things like a new headlight or brake fluid. Shouldn't take me too long.

I head over to the garage and bump into Al. Al's been working here for as long as I can remember. If I'm remembering correctly, he was the first employee hired when my dad and uncle Eli opened up this shop. He used to play hide-and-seek with me. He looks a lot older now.

"Hey, Lane," he says, grabbing me into a tight, quick hug. He's a very affectionate man.

"Hey, Al. How's the baby doing?" Al and his wife Natalie just had a baby last month.

"Oh, she's great! I have to show you some pictures!" He grabs his phone out of his jumper, despite the grease that covers his hands.

We flip through pictures of baby Callie for a couple minutes. He starts to get teary-eyed at one point.

"She's beautiful," I say, really meaning it. Most babies I find to be kind of ugly. But she's actually pretty cute.

"All she does is eat, sleep, poop, and cry, but I love her to death."

"That's great. I'm glad you and Natalie are so happy."

I pat him on the back and walk away, thinking of how he has the life I someday wanted with Laurel. A life that I know I could never have.

The Flapping of Eyelids

Chapter 12

The summer before ninth grade, Laurel and I managed to cross off a couple of things on our bucket list. We went to a Red Sox game, snuck into a movie, and visited the Kings Dominion theme park in Virginia.

The Red Sox game was more of Laurel's idea. She's lived in Massachusetts her whole life and had never been to a game before, which seemed crazy to me. I grew up with a dad and an uncle who religiously watched every single game, so I've been to my fair share of them. I assumed everyone from Massachusetts had.

Mr. Matthew and my uncle Eli took us. We took the train into Fenway and ended up having to buy our tickets when we got there. Usually we get our tickets ahead of time but I guess there was some confusion between my uncle Eli and Mr. Matthew about who was getting the tickets.

The game doesn't start for a couple hours and there are people everywhere.

The line for tickets was so long that by the time we actually got our tickets, the game had already started. Laurel was complaining about being hungry so my uncle Eli ran out to get us some food while we waited in line. He was able to go get us food and come back all before we had gotten our tickets. I was frustrated and annoyed because we were missing the game and this wasn't how I pictured our day going. But I noticed Laurel was as cool as a popsicle, so I tried my best to let it go. After all, there was nothing I could do about it.

The line hasn't moved for a long time so Laurel and I decide to walk around for a little while the "grown-ups," as they refer to themselves, wait in line. We're standing on the David Ortiz Bridge when a guy selling tickets on the side of the road approaches Laurel and me. He's a scalper and scalpers make me uncomfortable. My uncle Eli always tells me to never look them in the eye.

"You guys looking for tickets?" He wears a leather jacket with a Red Sox hat fit tightly on his head, making his ears fold a little. Rings line his fingers.

"Yeah!" Laurel told him. I look down the sidewalk over at the "grown-ups" and feel stuck. They aren't paying attention to us but I can't leave Laurel alone with this man. Why would he ask two kids if they need tickets? It puts a weird feeling in my stomach.

Before I can decide what to do, Laurel starts talking again. "Let me go get my dad!" She grabs my hand, pulling me toward my uncle Eli and Mr. Matthew who are still waiting in line. I turn around and the scalper is following us.

"Dad, this guy has tickets for us!" Mr. Matthew looks confused before realizing we have a scalper trailing behind us. Mr. Matthew and my uncle Eli give each other a look. I'm assuming they're considering the option, being that we have no other options right now. After a second, Mr. Matthew starts pulling out his wallet.

"How much?"

***

I spent most of the game explaining how baseball works to Laurel. The rules, what ball and strike mean, who the players were. She knew the gist of the game but didn't know or understand the rules.

She playfully slapped me on the arm when I told her what a strike was. "I already know what that one is," she told me.

In the seventh inning, we all stood up and sang *Take Me Out to the Ballgame*. Thankfully Laurel knew the song. I know Laurel well enough to know that she would've hated not knowing it. "I would've been left out of the 7th inning stretch experience," she would've whined to me.

The Red Sox ended up winning and we left the stadium to go get ice cream. We rode the train back to the station where we parked our car and drove the rest of the way home. Laurel fell asleep on my shoulder. I had my eyes closed, just resting, when I was suddenly startled by a flash of light in my face.

I slightly open one eye and see my uncle Eli showing Mr. Matthew the picture he just took of us. Laurel's mouth hangs wide open and I can see a line of drool on my shirt. I smile, not really caring.

Overall, it was a pretty good day. Laurel got to experience her first ever Red Sox game and I got to experience Laurel drooling on me.

A couple weeks after that, Laurel and I decided to go to the movies. We bought tickets to see some random movie Laurel chose and then went to the refreshment counter to buy some snacks. I got us a bucket of popcorn and a slushy and Laurel got us Sour Skittles and Rolos. We always get popcorn and a slushy and then something chocolate-y and something fruity.

We made our way into the theater and found our seats. There weren't many people in there, which was fine with me. There's always too much snack noise when the theater is filled. People rustling their snack trash, slurping on their drinks and munching too loudly on popcorn. I like the theater when it's empty.

I spent the entire movie trying to convince myself to man-up and grab her hand. I wanted to hold it, but I was scared she would pull away from me. I don't think she actually would have, but her thinking about not wanting to hold my hand is just as bad as her actually pulling away from me.

At this point, Laurel and I have been friends for a couple of months, but I've had a crush on her since I saw her that first day in home ec.

I decide against holding her hand and try to focus on the movie. I guess I didn't focus well enough because I forgot what it was about. Laurel had all my attention. She gasped at things that shouldn't surprise her, she cried at all the wrong times, and she laughed during the parts that she should be crying over. I wonder what it would be like to listen to her thoughts during movies.

As the movie ends and we head toward the front door, Laurel pulls me to the side, in between two large movie posters.

"Laurel, what are you-" she cuts me off, pulling a piece of folded paper out of her pocket. She unfolds it and I see that it's our bucket list.

"Lane, tonight is the night we sneak into a movie." She grips the paper in both of her hands and squeals excitedly. "We're already here and it's only 8 o'clock." She shoves the list in my face. She anxiously checks our surroundings, her eyes darting from side-to-side.

I wasn't expecting that. I always figured that we wouldn't actually do that one.

"Laurel, I don't know. That's stealing. What if we get caught?" I lower her hand with mine and meet her eyes.

"Well, we haven't even gone past the ticket booth yet. Nobody would ever know that we didn't buy tickets. Look," she says pointing to a theater. "That one starts in," she looks down at her watch, "5 minutes. Let's go!"

She grabs my arm and yanks me in the direction of the theater. I look around, hoping nobody heard or saw that conversation. I don't even know what movie we're about to watch.

We sneak into the theater and decide to grab seats in the front row, just in case. Nobody ever buys seats in the front row.

"Once the movie actually starts, we can switch. People do it all the time," Laurel assures me. The credits roll through and the lights start to dim. Laurel looks over the seat and whispers to me to "Come on."

I follow her and she takes us three quarters of the way to the top. She picks a row and finds two empty seats with open seats in front of us so we can put our feet up.

We sink into our chairs and she starts to giggle, hiding her face in her hands. She gets hushed by someone behind us and I want to yell at them for telling her to stop laughing. We try to focus on the movie but we're too hyped up on adrenaline to calm down. Just when we finally get ourselves under control, an usher comes into the theater and shows his flashlight.

Laurel grabs my hand and draws it up to her face, hiding behind it.

"Oh no, what if we get caught? He's going to see us and know we didn't buy tickets," she loudly whispers. She holds my hand tighter. I can feel her breath meet my hand, and I try to ignore how warm it feels.

"Well, yell-whispering about it isn't going to make him less aware of us," I whisper while my eyes follow the usher. He turns to walk up the stairs on our side of the theater. I knew we shouldn't have done this. We're gonna get busted. I don't want to go to jail. Laurel hushes me.

I watch the usher get closer and closer to us. He must realize the seats we are in aren't supposed to be occupied. Just like the last theater, this one is pretty empty. I want to whistle to help calm my nerves, but I don't want to make noise and draw attention to us or get shushed like Laurel did earlier.

He comes up to our aisle and I think he's going to turn into it. I can feel Laurel tense up next to me. I can feel her palm start to sweat in mine. Our heads move in sync as we follow him with our eyes. My heart picks up speed, pounding fiercely in my chest. I wouldn't be surprised if the usher would hear it.

But instead he walks one aisle past us and turns right, making his way to the other side of the theater. I watch him until he's no longer in my line of sight.

"Laurel, he's gone," I say, leaning in closer to her. I almost pull my hand away to get her attention, but then I stop, remembering that I want her to hold my hand. She looks up from behind my hand and slowly sits up higher in her seat.

"Okay, good. I for sure thought he was going to kick us out."

She held my hand for the rest of the movie.

***

Three weeks later, we convinced Mr. Matthew and Mrs. Malani to take us to Kings Dominion in Virginia. Laurel became obsessed with the idea several years ago when she overheard a girl talking about how her family goes there every summer. She even has the layout of the park memorized. We bought the tickets a week before we were set to leave. The plan is to drive down to Virginia, spend the weekend at a hotel nearby, and spend our entire Saturday at Kings Dominion. I'm excited, but I've never been on many roller coasters before, at least not big ones like at Kings Dominion.

We planned to leave the next morning at 5 am, so the night before, I go through my suitcase, making sure I have everything packed. A couple changes of clothes and socks, toothbrush, bathing suit, deodorant. Laurel told me three times to make sure I bring comfortable shoes for walking in. I throw a hat in my bag too. It's toward the end of the summer, so I'm expecting it to be a hot, sticky day. I decide to throw a disposable camera in my bag so we can have some pictures to remember this trip.

Once I have double checked everything three times, I decide to say goodnight to my uncle Eli and Ivy. They tell me to have a good time and to ride all the rollercoasters I possibly can. My uncle Eli gives me fifty dollars for food and souvenirs, which I thought was really thoughtful of him. I head back to my bedroom and go straight to bed.

I wake up seven hours later to my alarm clock going off. Is it 4:15 already? I punch the top of it, making it shut off. I don't want to wake my uncle Eli. I throw my covers off of me - more like lazily toss them across my bed - and I slither out and head to the bathroom. I take a quick shower, hoping the water will help wake me up. I brush my teeth and quickly tiptoe back to my room to get dressed. I throw on sweats and my most comfortable sweatshirt for the long drive, making sure to spray it with my body spray so Laurel will think I smell good.

Next, I pack up my backpack with some snacks, a book, headphones, and some small games. I unzip my Ipod case and make sure it's inside. I throw that into my backpack as I head to the kitchen to make some breakfast.

I eat a quick bowl of cereal and head back to my room to gather all my things. I carry them all to the front door and sit them outside on the porch. Mr. Matthew said they would pick me up so I didn't have to carry my suitcase down the street.

I'm sitting on the porch, waiting for the Owens family when I hear the door open. I turn around and see my uncle Eli standing in his boxers and a white t-shirt. His hair is tousled and going in many different directions. "Oh, sorry, Uncle Eli. Did I wake you up? I tried to be quiet."

"No, I set an alarm last night. I wanted to see you off," he says, yawning.

"Oh, thanks." I don't know why I didn't assume he would do that. He's always been caring like that.

He sits in the chair behind me and starts to rock it back and forth.

"You excited for the trip?" he asks.

I spin around and meet his eyes. "Yes! I can't wait. I've only ridden one rollercoaster before so I am so pumped!"

"I'm sure you'll have a great time, bug."

Just then, Mr. Matthew, Mrs. Malani, and Laurel pull into the driveway. Before the truck is even in park, Laurel throws the door open and runs over to me. She grabs my hands and pulls me off the steps. I quickly grab my pillow and run to the car, following her. I can hear my uncle Eli laughing at her enthusiasm.

My uncle Eli grabs my suitcase and backpack and puts them in the back of the car. Mr. Matthew rolls down his window, along with mine, as Uncle Eli shuts the trunk door.

"Good morning, Owens family," he sings, resting his arm on my window.

"Hi!" Laurel shouts. "Thank you so much for letting Lane come with us, this is going to be the best weekend ever!"

"No problem at all, thank you for inviting him," my uncle Eli says. He looks at me and adds, "Make sure you listen to Mr. Matthew and Mrs. Malani, wear your sunscreen, and have a great time. Take lots of pictures for me!" He places his hand on the side of my face and gives me a soft smile, then takes a step up to Mr. Matthew's window. Laurel starts talking to me, showing me all the movies she brought that we can watch on the drive.

Six minutes later, we pull out of the driveway and set off. Our first stop is coffee for the adults and breakfast for the kids. We stop at Dunkin Donuts and get a box of munchkins which we tear into before we even make it out of the drive-thru.

The Owens' luckily have one of those cool vans that have a TV in it, so Laurel asked me to bring some movies with me. I grabbed the *Back to the Future* trilogy and *The Goonies*. Mrs. Malani sets up the TV while Laurel and I decide what movie we want to watch. I pull out the two I brought and we flip through their collection of movies they keep in the car. We settle on *The Goonies* and Laurel puts a pillow across my lap and lays down. I place my hands awkwardly behind her head. It's not comfortable but I don't want to make her move. Within five minutes, she's asleep.

Instead of watching the movie, I watch Laurel. Her breathing is steady and she looks peaceful. We hit a bump in the road and a strand of her hair falls in front of her face. I grab the strand and tuck it behind her ear. I continue to play with her hair while listening to the movie. I feel myself start to drift to sleep and I let my eyes close, my hand still resting on Laurel's head.

***

I wake up several hours later and Laurel is sitting up in her seat. She's reading a book and listening to music. She looks over at me when she realizes I'm awake.

"Hey, sleepyhead," she says lightly. Mr. Matthew is asleep in the passenger seat. I didn't even realize we had stopped at some point.

"Hey," I say stretching.

"Wanna play a game?"

***

We made it to our hotel around 4:30 that afternoon. After unpacking our things and getting settled, Laurel and I decided to go swimming in the hotel pool. It felt good to move around after being in the car for eleven hours.

We swam, played games, and had splashing competitions until Mrs. Malani and Mr. Matthew brought us some pizza for dinner. Between the four of us, we ate two large pizzas. We go back up to the hotel room and take turns showering after we finish eating. Mr. Matthew and Mrs. Malani let us pick a movie to watch before we go to bed.

Laurel picks a romance movie and she takes her newfound position laying across my lap again. I smile knowing she's comfortable around me.

I bravely place my arm across her side. I look over at Mr. Matthew to see if he noticed where I put my hand. He's looking down at his book, not paying attention to us.

I feel Laurel snuggle closer and I relax. Except for the butterflies in my stomach. Those don't relax.

We watch the movie and Laurel's parents have fallen asleep on the bed. Laurel turns the TV off and sits up from laying on my lap. I've only known her for a couple of months, but I have such strong feelings for her. I would do anything for her.

Laurel starts to get up to head over to her trundle bed when I grab her arm.

"Laurel," I whisper. She turns to face me. "Yeah?"

I stare up at her and I can barely see her face in the darkness. But I've studied her face enough to know exactly what it looks like. The moss color of her eyes, the freckles speckled on her face, the scar on her forehead from when she fell at her birthday party, and the curve of her lips.

I wait a second before responding and let go of her hand. "Nothing….I just wanted to say I'm excited for tomorrow."

She laughs quietly and reaches for my head. "Me too," she says, messing with my hair. "Goodnight, Lane."

Sweet dreams, Laurel.

***

The next morning, we're up by 8:30. We eat breakfast in the hotel and gather everything we need for the day. Snacks, water, cash, medicine, extra socks, bathing suits, towels, sunglasses, sunscreen. Mrs. Malani double checks that I'm comfortable and have everything I need. We're ready to go by 9:15 and head to the car to drive the half hour it takes to get there from our hotel.

Thirty-five minutes later, we arrive, park, and get checked in. While we're standing in line, waiting for the park to open I grab a map from the ticket booth and Laurel and I begin circling all of the roller coasters we want to ride. She knows all the ones she wants to go on.

We get an invisible stamp on our hands in case we want to exit the park and come back, and Laurel pretends we've been inducted into some private mission; one that only the four of us knows about. Even though everyone entering the park is getting stamped.

The first thing we do is use the bathroom by the entrance. We want to empty everything out so we can go for as long as we can without stopping. That was Laurel's idea. We pull out the map once we've all emptied our bladders and pick the closest couple of rides to us. We ride a boat one called The Berserker that flips you upside down. I felt like I was going to hurl and Laurel was sitting next to me laughing as I began to turn various shades of green.

Our first roller coaster of the day is called The Dominator. Despite it being a weekend in the summer, it isn't as busy as we'd expected it to be. The wait was about ten minutes and the whole time, Laurel was jumping up and down and hanging on the poles that separate the lines. She was told to get down at least three times.

The four of us fit into one row; Mr. Matthew, Laurel, me, and Mrs. Malani. The floor drops below us and over the speaker we hear the ride operator giving instructions, finishing with an encouraging "Ride on!"

The moment the ride starts to move, Laurel squeals so loud I think my ears start to bleed. She immediately reaches for my hand and I gladly let her squeeze it. We make it up to the top of the incline and Laurel snaps her eyes shut. I yell at her to open them, just as we tip over the edge and zoom through a loop. Laurel is screaming at the top of her lungs and I'm laughing so hard that I can barely keep my eyes open.

The ride finishes and we rush down the steps to look at the picture the ride took of us. Mr. Matthew is pretending he's asleep, Mrs. Malani has her arms up in the air with a crazy look on her face. My eyes are closed and I look like I'm laughing the hardest I've ever laughed in my life. Laurel's face looks like a mix between excitement and complete terror. We're still holding hands.

After we all finish laughing at the pictures, Mr. Matthew pulls out the map and we figure out our next destination. We make our way toward some of the other larger roller coasters. We spend the next four hours waiting in line and riding some of the most exhilarating rides I've ever been on.

We go on one called Flight of Fear, which is alien-themed, indoors, and speeds off so fast Mr. Matthew said he heard his neck snap. We ride The Volcano, which also zooms off really fast, and spits you out the top of a volcano. We ride The Shockwave, which is a rollercoaster where you stand the entire time; we ride Avalanche, Anaconda, Apple Zapple, and The Grizzly.

We decide to take a break and get lunch at the Chick-Fil-A located in the park. It's nice to get out of the heat for a little bit. After lunch, we get some much-needed ice cream and head to the Intimidator 305: one of the fastest and tallest roller coasters on the East Coast. *Dun, dun dun.*

We stand in line and eat our ice cream while I'm pumping myself to go through with riding it. I won't back out because I don't want to look like a coward, but I'm going to be nervous until we hit the first drop. The inching to the top of the drop makes me anxious every time.

I sit with Laurel and the ride attendants get us buckled in; Mrs. Malani and Mr. Matthew are sitting directly behind us. Laurel and I look back and we all wish each other good luck.

Over the speakers, a guy starts talking and all I hear is car engines revving and someone says, "Start your engines!" and we make our way to the top.

I quite literally feel like I am laying flat on my back. That's how steep this drop is. Three hundred and five feet in the air. Gulp.

We've held hands almost every ride, but she's always the one that initiates it. This time I'm the one grabbing Laurel's hand. We reach the top and I can feel my heartbeat all throughout my body. I make the mistake of looking over the side and Laurel yells my name. I snap my head over, expecting her to be freaking out.

She looks at me with soft, calm eyes and says, "It's okay, Lane. I'm right here," as she squeezes my hand.

That's when we start to dive down straight toward the ground. I literally black out and can't see anything for a couple of seconds as we fly around a turn. I hear Laurel beside me screaming at the top of her lungs and I can feel my cheeks jiggling in the strong wind. A worker told us this ride goes so fast, that it can't have loops because it would make people pass out. *It doesn't need loops for it to make me pass out.*

After a couple more seconds I feel better now that the scariest part of it is over. I raise my hands in the air and scream as loud as I can. I feel drool slide out of my mouth and across my cheek, but I don't stop screaming. We ride really close to the ground and I lose my vision again for a couple of seconds.

The coaster comes to an end and Laurel is laughing harder than I've ever heard her laugh before. I look over at her, more like side-eye her because of the seats obstructing my movement, and she looks like she has a wild lioness' mane that has never been brushed.

She slaps her hands on the pads of her seatbelt and simultaneously squeals, "That was so amazing!" She flips her head back to look at her parents and asks if we can do it again. We grab our backpacks once we are free of the seatbelts and run straight to get in line again.

This time I'm not so scared. Laurel offers me her hand as we ascend into the sky and I take it, even though I don't feel like I'm going to vomit this time. We raise our hands in the air and we fall towards the ground. I lose control of my arms and the flail all over the place, bumping into Laurel's, who also doesn't seem to have much control.

We scream and laugh and scream again some more, only stopping when the ride does. We get off and grab our backpacks. I take a sip of water because my throat is so dry. We talk the whole way to the building where the pictures are to look at them. I didn't even realize it took our picture last time.

Laurel and I both have our hands up and are blocking Mr. Matthew and Mrs. Malani behind us. Laurel's face is bright red and one of my eyelids is pushed up from the wind.

"Oh my gosh, look at my eye!" I say pointing to my eyelid, chuckling.

Laurel bursts into laughter and we spend a good thirty seconds laughing so hard, I start gasping for breath.

"That is the craziest thing I have ever seen! Why the heck does it look like that?" Laurel asks.

"The wind must've pushed it up. It looks so funny." Mrs. Malani says.

Mr. Matthew comes over to us with a small bag in his hand. He gives it to me, and Laurel and I dig our hands inside to find two small keychains with our picture on it.

"No way! A keychain! I can't wait to show my uncle Eli and Ivy."

Laurel attaches hers to my backpack then steps in front of me so I can attach the one in my hand to hers.

***

We spend the rest of the day riding roller coasters like the Hurler and the Twisted Timbers, which was my favorite of the day. We get soft pretzels and nachos for dinner and get some more ice cream for dessert. We ride some of the children's rides after dinner and take turns steering the car on the Antique Cars ride. We ride White Water Canyon more times than can I remember. At one point, the two of us snuck away while Laurel's parents wanted to cool down in the lazy river at the water park. So we went on all of our favorite roller coasters again.

Today really was one of the best days I've ever had. Mostly because I got to come here with Laurel.

Once the sun has set and the firework show is about to start, the four of us find a spot in the grass to sit down on. We get ice cream for the third time today and happily eat it while waiting for the show.

Fifteen minutes later, the fireworks start. Pops of blue, yellow, red, green, and even purple splatter the sky, making it look like a sporadically painted picture. Laurel gasps almost every time another one is set off. I'm not completely sure if it's from the loud pop or the colors. Probably a mix of both.

I lean back on my right hand and watch Laurel taking all of the colors in. She looks like a kid seeing fireworks for the very first time: surprised, confused, and filled with awe. Laurel always finds a way to appreciate the small things.

I tap Mrs. Malani on the shoulder and ask her to take a picture of Laurel and me with the fireworks behind us. I put my arm around Laurel's shoulders and she grabs ahold of my torso with both arms, hugging me as tightly as she can. I look down at Laurel just as Mrs. Malani takes the picture and see that she's grinning from ear to ear. I promise myself from that day forward, I will do whatever it takes to make her smile like that every day.

Ghosts of Regret

Chapter 13

It's been ten days since I saw Mrs. Malani. Ten days of anxious thoughts, regret, obsessing over how I apologized, and wishing I could change the past. I've done a lot of whistling these past ten days. Even after all these years, whistling still helps calm me down. Dr. Therin says it's because our brains have sense memories. He thinks my dad's whistling is a strong sense memory for me. It makes sense. There wasn't a problem that my dad's whistling couldn't fix.

I woke up in the middle of the night last night from a nightmare. The details of the accident were all different from what my usual nightmare consists of, but the end was still the same. I slept on and off after that all night and finally got up around seven.

I decided to go for a run on the beach, hoping it would help clear my head and fill me up with endorphins. Dr. Therin says that exercise is good for you when you're depressed because it releases endorphins, which are essentially "pain decreasers." *I will take all of those that I can get.*

I run and run and run until I notice that I ran five miles without realizing it. I walk back to the house and find Jey doing a load of laundry. I see he's washing his jersey so he must have a game tonight.

I go to the fridge and take out some chocolate milk and find a glass in the dishwasher. "Do you have a game tonight, Jey?"

"Yeah, I do. It's at our normal field at five, if you want to come. You can sit with Naomi and Dallas."

"That actually sounds like fun. I think I'll go. Is Paisley not going?"

"No, she has to work late tonight at the soup kitchen," Jey explains.

"Oh, gotcha. Yeah," I say, rubbing the back of my neck, "I think I'll go. Thanks for the invite."

"Sweet. I'll let Naomi know."

***

At 4:30 I close up the pottery shop and head over to Jey's game. I'm a little nervous about who I may run into. Our area is small and almost everyone knows about the accident. It made the news and everything, so I'm expecting at least one person to say something to me about it. Which is another reason why I put on my hat when I get out of the car.

I texted Naomi and Dallas about the game tonight, hoping we could meet up like Jey said. Dallas can't make it because he has too many finals right now, which bummed me out. I'm excited to see Naomi though. *It's been a while since I've seen h-*

My thoughts are interrupted as Naomi shouts "Nicky!" her nickname for me, and crashes into me from behind. I used to make fun of her for her obsession with Nick Jonas from the Jonas Brothers. Instead, she turned the joke on to me and started calling me Nicky.

I stumble forward and barely catch myself as I spin around to greet Naomi. She's in jeans and a casual, plain hoodie with our matching hat on. We always used to wear our matching hats to Jey's games in high school so he could easily find us.

"Hey Naomi," I say, knocking her with my shoulder. "How was the drive?"

"Eh, it was fine. I hit some traffic, but I made it right on time. It's good to see you," she says, sliding her arm into mine. Naomi goes to school in New Hampshire but occasionally comes home on the weekends to watch Jey play and visit home. I get to see her every now and then, but it's always nice when I do.

"Yeah, it's good to see you too. I feel like it's been so long. When was the last time you came home?" I ask.

"Hm. I think it was two-ish months ago," she says, kicking a rock. "I'm lucky I don't have as many finals as Dallas does. I feel like freshmen get it a little easier than juniors."

"Yeah, that's probably true."

We make our way to the bleachers just as the teams are lining up to introduce the players. Jey's team, the Lake Hawks, is introduced first. Jey is called second and Naomi and I cheer for our favorite number seven.

The other team is introduced and Naomi stops paying attention and asks me questions. "So, how have you been?" I don't need to pretend with Naomi, but I also know she isn't asking me about the accident. She knows I don't want to talk about it.

"I've been good. Just working in the pottery shop and with my uncle Eli in the garage. How are classes going?" Even though Naomi is six years younger than me, she's only five grades below me.

"Aw, how's Ms. Elsie? She's the tiniest, cutest, little old woman I've ever met."

"She's good," I say laughing. Naomi has always had a soft spot for Ms. Elsie.

"Freshman year has been pretty good actually," she says, answering my question. "My classes are pretty much just general education classes right now, but next year I'll start taking classes for my major, which I'm so pumped for. There's one class a girl in my major told me about that takes you to an aquarium where you get to swim with dolphins!"

She tells me about her messy roommate and how she joined a volleyball intramural team, and even though they've lost every game they haven't given up. She tells me about the cute girl she met in the library and how they've gone on a few dates. I listen to her talk for fifteen minutes, until Jey scores the first goal of the game. Jey does his victory dance, which consists of him making a complete fool of himself. Noami gets out her Hawks flag and waves it back and forth, chanting our cheer we wrote for Jey so many years ago.

At one point, I see one of the guys from our trivia night team. Rys and I were never the best of friends, and he hasn't reached out since I stopped showing up to trivia night. He sees me, but I'm not worried he's going to come talk to me. He knows about the accident. And he knows me well enough to know I probably don't want to talk about it. He gives me a nod and I nod back at him, grateful for the space he gave me.

At half-time, the game is 3-2 and Jey has scored two of our goals. Naomi goes to the concession stand to get a snack so I decide to go to the bathroom so I'm not vulnerably sitting alone. I've made that mistake before.

I'm half-way to the bathroom when I spot an old teacher of mine walking toward me. He's looking past me and I'm hopeful he won't look directly at me. I avoid eye contact with him. We walk closer to each other and just when I think I'm in the clear, he stops me. Ugh.

"Well, if it isn't Lane Peterson," Mr. Flannery says.

"Hi, Mr. Flannery. How ya doing?" I ask him before he can ask me.

"Oh, I'm just peachy," he says, patting his large, circular stomach, plate full of funnel cake in his other hand. Mr. Flannery was my English teacher in high school. He's in his late sixties and has been teaching for over forty years. I'm pretty sure he wears a toupee.

"That's great. I'm glad to hear it," I say, backing away. He starts to open his mouth, so I tell him I have a friend waiting on me. I head to the bathroom once he's out of sight and close the stall door behind me. I lean against the door and exhale sharply. I run my hands through my hair and stretch my neck.

That was fine. No big deal, I tell myself. *Nothing even happened.*

I spend two more minutes of alone time in the stall; I only leave when I hear someone else come in. I wash my hands even though I didn't use the bathroom and head back to our seats. Naomi's munching on a bag of Cheetos when I find her. "Here," she says, throwing me a Twix. "That was the last one."

Forty-five minutes later and the game has ended. The Hawks ended up winning 5-3. Naomi and I head over the trash can to throw our snack trash away and I do a double take when I see long caramel hair in my peripheral vision.

Laurel.

I take a step closer and blink.

Laurel?

She's gone.

I look over the shorter people and below the taller people. My eyes dart around Lake Hawk fans, all wearing large hats and carrying giant foam fingers. My hands clench into fists and my heart starts to beat faster at the thought of seeing her. At the thought of speaking to her. I spin in a circle, thinking maybe she went the other way. Naomi asks me if I'm ready to go get ice cream, something we do with Jey after every game, when I finally spot her.

Our eyes meet from across the way and I don't know what to do. I'm shocked she's here and very thrown off at seeing her right now. I stand here unmoving, trying to decide if I should go say something or pretend I didn't see her. But I feel too stunned to move. *What would I even say to her?* Someone steps between us and breaks our eye contact and then she's gone. Like she was never even there. My pulse picks up again, but this time it's because the thought of not talking to her is what's scaring me.

I scan the crowd again, looking for her. I want to talk to her. I *need* to talk to her. But I can't find her anywhere.

I'm startled when Naomi hits my arm, saying, "Dude, are you alright?"

"Ow!" I say, grabbing my arm, my search for Laurel interrupted. "What was that for?"

"I asked if you were ready to go get ice cream. Are you okay? You look like you just saw a ghost."

"Uh, yeah. I'm fine." I start. "Just thought I saw someone." I scan the crowd one more time. Hoping I'll see her again, but also hoping she was never really there. I'm not sure if I'm ready to face her yet, but I also can't go another second without seeing her.

Just then, Jey comes running up to us and pulls us into a group hug.

"Great game, Jey!" Naomi congratulates. "This time you only managed to play about half the game like a toddler playing soccer for the first time." Jey mocks Naomi in a whiny voice.

"Well, at least I scored two of the goals." He turns to me. "Thanks for coming Lane!" he says as he pats me on the back. I'm suddenly brought back to what's happening in front of me and I'm smacked in the face with disappointment that I couldn't find Laurel.

"Oh, yeah, no problem," I somehow mutter.

"Fair," Naomi shrugs in response to Jey's boasting of making two of the five goals.

"Who's ready for some Ben & Jerry's?"

"I am," Naomi shouts, shooting her hand up in the air. She puts her arms around Jey and me as we walk toward the parking lot. She grabs a hold of us tightly and lifts her legs off the ground, making us carry her.

"To the chariot, my humble servicemen!"

***

"Okay, but how can you say that Sporticus couldn't be an Olympian? He's so athletic," Naomi argues with Jey. She takes a bite of her ice cream as she's speaking, which causes some of it to drip down her face. She grabs a napkin and wipes it off.

"Yeah, he might be athletic and can do flips and stuff, but good enough to be in the Olympics? Please," Jey retorts, holding up a hand. Jey religiously watches every Olympics.

"I don't know, I think I agree with Naomi on this one," I say. "He's from a place called Lazy Town but he's most definitely not lazy. You couldn't even do any of his tricks if you tried, Jey."

Naomi places a hand on my arm, saying "Thank you, Lane. See, Jey, he understands."

Jey rolls his eyes and takes another bite of his banana split. I've missed this. I've missed going to games and getting ice cream with Jey, Dallas, and Naomi. I've missed spending time with them, talking about stupid things like if Tigger or Papa Smurf would win in a fight.

One of my favorite memories of the four of us was after one of Jey's games in middle school. Noami, Dallas, and Mr. Reggy and Mrs. Elora, and I all went to the game. Jey scored all three goals so we celebrated by going laser-tagging. I had never been before, so naturally I was pretty excited. We played a bunch of the arcade games before laser-tag so we made a bet. Whichever group won in laser-tag would get all of the tickets and could pick out whatever prize they wanted. Dallas and I were partners and Jey and Naomi were partners. Dallas and I won, obviously. By a lot. But we felt bad for Naomi because she was so much younger than us and she kind of got sucked into giving her tickets away. So we decided to get her the giant stuffed Sully from *Monsters Inc.* she desperately wanted.

We finished celebrating by getting Ben & Jerry's and that was how the tradition started.

I've recently been so caught up in my own life and have been so down lately; it feels really nice to be here right now. Laughing with them, celebrating Jey, and eating ice cream just like old times, except Dallas was always with us. Laurel was with us most of the time, too.

And then I remember that I saw Laurel tonight. Not only saw her but made eye contact with her. I zone out of the next debate Jey and Naomi are having and I think about seeing her again. *Did she look happy to see me? Surprised? Angry?* I can't remember what her face looked like. All I can remember was my panic.

All I know is that I want to see her again.

The Proposal

Chapter 14

Two months after that first day on the beach with Laurel, my uncle Eli is finally ready to propose to Ivy. Laurel interviewed my uncle Eli about him, Ivy, and their relationship so that she could make the proposal meaningful for them. I wasn't surprised by how seriously she took it.

Laurel wouldn't let me inside the treehouse for two weeks because she was working on…whatever it was she was working on. All I know is that she recruited Naomi to help her. I didn't see Laurel for two whole days while she and Naomi were working. I'd go to the treehouse, knock on the door and receive a "Go away!" from either one of them. Most of the time though, if Naomi didn't respond, I wouldn't hear from either of them. Laurel gets way too in-the-zone to respond to anyone.

The proposal is happening tonight and I have no idea what's been planned. I don't think my uncle Eli even knows what's going to happen. All I know is that my job is to meet everyone at the beach in an hour. My uncle Eli and Ivy have spent the whole day doing things together. I know he took her to a make-your-own-candle shop in Boston because she loves candles. And they went to the movies to see some new action movie that they wanted to see and did some other things like that.

Right now, I'm getting dressed in my new outfit that Laurel picked out for me. Khakis with a "sage green" button-up shirt, as she called it. I guess Laurel's eyes must be close to sage green because it almost matched them perfectly. Her eyes are slightly darker.

As I'm putting on my shirt, Laurel busts through my bedroom door, scaring me, and making me fall backward on my bed. I look up at her, then down at my naked torso. I instinctively cover myself with my shirt.

"Oh, good, you're getting ready," she says, as she exits as quickly as she came in. "Hurry up!" she yells as she slams the door behind her. I see her through my window, sprinting back in the direction of her house. I finish buttoning up my shirt and head to the bathroom to check on my hair. It looks like it always does, so I flip the light off and find the new shoes Laurel picked out for me. They're called Sanuks and they might be my favorite type of shoe now. Laurel said they were made out of recycled yoga mats, which is why she picked them.

She said they were "environmentally conscious, so I should put my money towards them." And probably because they match my new shirt perfectly. But I like them because they're comfortable.

I start walking down toward the beach and when I get to the sidewalk, I can slightly see what Laurel's been planning. From across the street, all I can see are faded lights and a white sheet. The sun has set now, so it stands out against the dark blue of the ocean.

Once I make it to the sand, I can see she's used the sheet to create some sort of tent. There are white lights strung up all around the inside of the tent.

"Hey, Laurel," I say, rounding the corner of the tent.

"Whoa." I look around the tent and I'm absolutely amazed at all the work she put into creating the perfect setting. The sheet is held up by several wood boards, put together to create the shape of a small house. Christmas lights are wrapped all around the wood panels and hang down at the entrance of the tent, giving the whole atmosphere a soft glow. There's a large plant in one corner that reminds me of Ivy's house. She has so many plants. I realize I recognize the pot and now I'm wondering if she somehow stole it from Ivy's house. I wouldn't be surprised.

Pinned to the white sheet are pictures of Ivy and my uncle Eli, some of them even include me. There are pictures of us hiking, the two of them at my birthday party, some of them kissing and hugging, and some of them just doing random things, like cooking dinner or grocery shopping. They look really happy.

Along with all the pictures hanging on the sheet, are notes. I step closer to read a couple and I realize they're from family members and friends of Ivy and my uncle Eli. I read a note from Ivy's favorite coworker that says, "Congrats! Can't wait to hear all about it while we're prepping for surgery." There's pictures of flowers peppered around the pictures of us and the notes. I can't help the smile forming on my face because Laurel is so thoughtful.

In the corner of the tent is a small table with a pitcher of what I'm assuming is pink lemonade, and a large plate of various cookies. Ivy's favorite drink and my uncle Eli's favorite dessert. Hanging directly in front of the entrance are small gold balloons that read "Marry Me."

It really is amazing.

"How did you do this? This is amazing!" Laurel looks up from brushing sand off the rug placed in the middle of the tent.

"Well, my dad helped me build the structure and my mom helped me sew two pieces of white fabric together. I stalked Ivy and Eli on my mom's Facebook for the pictures and messaged their friends and family for the notes. I went to the garage and the hospital to get notes from their coworkers and Naomi made the pink lemonade and blew up the balloons and I helped my parents make the cookies. This is the rug from my treehouse. The plants are from…Lowe's. And I bought the lights from Target." There's a pause as she looks around. She eyes the table in the corner and lifts up the light pink tablecloth to show me what's underneath. "Oh, and I stole this generator from your garage. Hopefully your uncle won't care." Underneath the table is my uncle's generator, easily recognizable by the soundproof contraption he made to contain the loud cacophony of noise it produces.

I'm shocked. Ivy and my uncle are going to love this. I can't believe she pulled this off.

"This is so great!" I say, taking another look around. "When are they going to be here?"

Laurel looks down at the watch on her wrist. "They should be here in about ten. Everyone else is hiding at a restaurant across the street. Everything looks okay, right?"

"Are you kidding? I can't believe you did all of this!" I say, rushing over to her and pulling her into a hug.

"Oh, it isn't that big of a deal," she says, waving me off. But it *is* a big deal.

"Can I eat one of these?" I ask, grabbing a cookie. She lunges toward me and smacks the top of my hand. "Not yet! Anyway, you need to go and wait for them. Your Uncle knows where to park, and you're supposed to walk them down here," she says, pushing me out of the tent, being careful not to get sand on the rug.

"He'll be directly in front of us, parked right next to the blue trash can with the peacock painted on it. Go get them!"

"Okay, okay," I say, putting my hands up in surrender. I walk through the sand and I finally start to get excited. I'd love to have Ivy as an aunt. She's caring, loud, and doesn't have a selfish bone in her body. I used to worry about my uncle being lonely, but now that I know he has someone, I can stop worrying that he'll be lonely for the rest of his life.

I make it to the blue trash can with a peacock painted on it but I don't see them yet. I wait for about thirty seconds before I see my uncle's truck pull up, right in front of me. I wave, but I can't see them because of the headlights. They get out of the car and I give them both hugs and ask them how their day was together.

"It was really nice," my uncle Eli responds. "Ivy made you a candle for your room."

"Yeah, I was thinking it might get rid of that teenage boy smell," she says, gently ruffling my hair.

I force a laugh, because I didn't know I smelled like a teenage boy and lead them onto the sand. When they aren't looking, I sniff my armpit. *Smells fine to me.*

"I think there's something down there on the beach for us," I tell them.

Ivy and my uncle walk hand-in-hand behind me and I can feel the excitement radiating off of my uncle

Eli. I can't really hear what they're talking about, but Ivy laughs. Every step we take, the more excited I get.

We make it to the tent and I notice that Laurel's not here, so I'm assuming she went to get everyone hiding in the restaurant. I hear music playing. *Nice touch.* I stay at the entrance of the tent and stand like a waiter as I say, "Ivy, Eli, may all your dreams come true tonight."

Laurel gave me that line.

I step to the side so they can enter, and Ivy gasps and throws her hands in front of her mouth. "Oh my gosh, this is so beautiful!" She looks around the tent, missing the balloons. While she's distracted, my uncle Eli gets the ring from his pocket and places himself on the rug on one knee. He looks over at me and I give him a thumbs-up and a smile.

Ivy's reading a note when my uncle Eli clears his throat. Ivy turns around and gasps again when she sees my uncle Eli on his knee. He reaches out to her, taking her hand in his. "Ivy, when I first met you, I had no doubt in my mind that you would be the woman I would marry. Your caring heart, your infectious smile, and the love you show to everyone around you is what made me fall in love with you.

You are everything that I could ask for in a partner and it would be my honor to be your husband. Ivy Grace Riddenhouse, would you marry me? I can't wait to spend the rest of my life with you by my side. By *our* side," he adds, as he reaches out to me. I walk over to them, they're both crying, Eli more than Ivy. She looks at me, her eyebrows raised, asking me if I'm okay with this. I nod and she wraps me in a hug as she cries even harder. And that makes me cry.

With shaky hands, my uncle Eli puts the ring on her finger and Ivy squirms with laughter. She pulls both of us into another hug and says, "I love both of you so much." They kiss and then she kisses me on the side of my head and pulls me in closer to her.

"I guess you can start calling me Aunt Ivy," she jokes, as she gently strokes my cheek.

"I'd like that," I say. And I really would.

Just then, Mrs. Elora, Laurel, Naomi, Honey and Ms. Elsie, the guys from the shop, and Ivy's best friends from work come into the tent, surprising both my uncle and Ivy. Everyone's taking pictures and laughing and Ivy's still crying while she laughs. I find Laurel and I help her pass out cups of pink lemonade and napkins with cookies on them.

There's chatter all around me as everyone asks to see the ring.

"That's the perfect ring!"

"It's so beautiful in here! Who did all this?"

"It's the perfect night!"

"I can't believe my best friend is getting married!" That comes from Mrs. Elora. Her and Ivy have been best friends since the Bishops moved here.

We spend the next hour and a half drinking pink lemonade, taking pictures with Laurel's polaroid, and listening to stories of Ivy and my uncle Eli. I watch my uncle and Ivy and think about how happy I am for them. How I can't wait for them to get married and have a new mother figure in my life. I have Honey and Ms. Elsie, but they're more like grandmothers to me. Honey actually is my grandmother. Ivy would be my aunt and I've never had an aunt before.

Ivy must be matching my enthusiasm for this new relationship because she pulls me to the side and tells me how excited she is to have me as a nephew and that makes me smile.

We play some games, one Laurel calls pin-the-ring-on-Ivy's-hand and we play a couple rounds of telephone where all the phrases are about Ivy, my uncle Eli or marriage. Everyone raves about the Owens' cookies. Ivy tells them they should start making cookies to sell, and they really should because they're the best cookies I've ever had.

I decide to take a break from all the excitement and go sit out on the sand. When I make it out of the tent, I find Laurel so I sit down next to her. "Hey, what're you doing out here?" I ask her.

"Just getting some fresh air." She plays with the sand at her sides, picking up a handful, and letting it slip between her fingers.

"Tonight was great, Laurel. I can't thank you enough for all you did for my family tonight." She grabs my hand and holds it in hers, squeezing it once before she places our folded hands in her lap.

"I just hope that someone loves me as much as Eli loves Ivy one day."

"You don't need to worry about that," I tell her. "Someone will. And they'll be the luckiest person in the entire universe."

Reunions

Chapter 15

Another two weeks of the pottery shop, the mechanic shop, therapy, and summer goes by. I spend most of my time in the pottery shop making new sketches and creating different types of pottery. Most of our customers are older women who appreciate fine pottery, so I try to design things that cater to that specific demographic.

But this week I tried something a little different. I designed a teapot that looks like a pirate ship, and surprisingly, I had a good amount of people ask me about it. The water comes out of the bowsprit. It was a pretty clever idea if I do say so myself. It took a lot of researching, though. I had to research all the different parts of the ship and then delicately make it out of ceramic clay. It took me nearly two weeks to complete.

I spent four days this week with my uncle Eli in this shop. I did a lot of ordering and picking up new parts. A couple of paint jobs. Fixed a radiator and changed a couple tires. All the basic stuff. Then, I had therapy on Monday and Friday.

I told Dr. Therin during our Monday session about the game. How I was nervous to go but went anyway. How someone tried to ask me about the accident and I avoided the conversation as much as I could. How I saw Laurel.

He congratulated me on going to the game and encouraged me to attend more this summer. He thinks my relationship with the Bishop family is great, especially because I don't have any siblings. He says I should keep things in my life that make me happy. Recently, Jey hasn't been making me too happy, but we're working on that. Naomi and Dallas always make me happy though.

We decided that next time someone tries to talk to me about the accident, I will either work my way around talking about it, instead of straight up avoiding or leaving the conversation, or simply tell people that I would rather not talk about it. That will take me a while to work up to. If someone tried to talk to me about it today, I would bolt. Baby steps.

Then we talked about seeing Laurel.

"How did you feel when you saw her?" he asks.

"Honestly, I don't really remember. I think I may have blacked out a little. I remember seeing her and feeling frozen. I wasn't sure what to do. I haven't seen her in seven months."

"What do you think would have happened if she approached you?"

"I don't know."

Even though seeing Laurel is what I want, the thought of it scares me. *Does she blame me? What am I saying? Of course she must blame me.*

After my session with Dr. Therein, I go home and pull out the bucket list from the top drawer of my desk. This piece of paper is so familiar to me, but it feels foreign in my hands now. I rub my thumb on the grease stain from the popcorn Laurel was eating. I smile at the memory. That day was the day we became friends.

I think back to that conversation we had about bucket lists; how people write them so they know what they want to experience in life. Well, having Laurel be a part of my life forever has been on my bucket list since the day I met her. The promise I made to her one night in the treehouse flashes in my memory. I can't break that promise.

I sit in my chair and pull my phone out of my pocket. I pull up the picture of Laurel sitting on the Statue of Liberty steps, her hat so wet it sags on her head. I chuckle at the memory as I rub my thumb over the picture, wishing I could relive that day. I grab my keys and head out to my car, hoping I can talk myself into going to see her.

Thoughts rotate through my head while I'm driving, as if my mind was a never-ending cassette. *What if she doesn't want to see me? What if she hates me? What if she doesn't answer? What if she walks away from me? What if she* wants *to see me?*

Fifteen minutes later, I'm parked outside the Owens' old house. I didn't mean to come here, but I somehow ended up here. I never thought I would be back, but I guess I subconsciously needed a better ending to the chapters of my life that happened at this house.

I get out of my truck and head up to the treehouse. I sit on the floor and take the bucket list out of my pocket. I read it over and over, wishing I had the guts to reach out to Laurel. I drop the list in my lap and run my hands through my hair. *Just go see her. What's the worst that could happen? Well, she could slap you across the face. Or spit on you. Or tell you she never loved you.*

It doesn't matter what I could do to Laurel, she would never do any of those things. I spend the next thirty minutes sitting there, playing over and over in my head all the different possible scenarios of seeing Laurel. I move over to the window. I always liked looking out this window. You can see the neighbors' rich-ass pond in their backyard. I'm watching some birds play in a bird bath when I hear a creaking on the stairs of the treehouse.

I snap my head over my shoulder and I watch the door slowly open, creaking with anticipation. My heart is pounding in my chest because I shouldn't be here. *Should I jump out the window?* I could get in trouble for being here. The door is now halfway open and I see caramel colored hair swish back and forth before I can see the rest of her. I instantly know who it is. My pulse quickens.

Laurel.

She spins around to close the door so she doesn't see me at first. When she fully turns around, she screams so loud that she throws her hands over her mouth when she realizes how loud it was.

My feet are frozen to the spot I'm in, my legs feel like jelly, as though they may buckle in on me. A tingle flows through my body, as if I just consumed too much alcohol.

"Laurel? What are you doing here?" I blurt out. I'm so shocked I could even find the words to speak, that I stumble backward into the wall.

"What am *I* doing here?" she asks, stubbornly putting her hands on her hips. "I should be asking what *you're* doing here."

"Well, I-" I stutter.

"Wait, what *are* you doing here?" She asks, genuinely interested in my answer.

I look over through the window, avoiding eye contact with her. I feel my insides mix all around, threatening to dispel my lunch.

It just now hits me that Laurel is standing in front of me. My Laurel. The one I've been avoiding for the past seven months. The one I've spent every single day of life thinking about. Well, every day since I first saw her in middle school. The same Laurel I hurt.

I look over at her and her eyebrows are furrowed, a sign that Laurel is genuinely confused. The sun is streaming through the window and it makes the scar on her face very prominent. I know she got injured there in the midst of the accident, but I could hardly look at her after it happened.

You did that to her. An intrusive, yet true thought.

I feel awkward admitting it, but she knows how important this treehouse is to me. "I just wanted to see it one more time, I guess." She walks over to the doorway of the bathroom, leans against it and crosses her arms. My body stays completely still, except for my eyes, which follow her.

"Yeah, I get that. It's actually kind of cool, don't you think? We spent so much time here and now some other little kids will get to spend all their time in this treehouse." She glances up and sees where I etched our names in the doorframe. Her fingers trail to the ink and she gently skims her pointer finger across our names. "Huh," she says, "when did that get there?" She smiles, like she knew it was me, and gives me a side-eye. I feel myself start to blush and I'm suddenly filled with a desire to leave. Before she can tell me to leave. *Before she can slap me across the face and tell me how much she hates me.* She doesn't look like she wants to slap me though.

"Well, I think I should go," I say, walking toward the door.

"Wait," Laurel says. I stop in my tracks and turn towards her. She takes a couple steps closer to me, until she's standing directly in front of me, and I feel like all the air has been sucked out of the room.

She doesn't look like she wants to slap me. I can usually know what she's thinking just by looking at her face, but right now I can't tell. If anything, she looks kind of...lonely.

She hesitantly reaches her hand out and I don't dare move, even after she connects with my cheek. She rests her hand on my face while she searches my eyes. "Lane," she starts, her eyes never leaving mine. "Will you stay?"

I fall into her, relief shooting through me. It's not that I was expecting her to actually slap me because she would never do that, but rejecting me would be far worse. That would be equivalent to being punched in the face over and over and over and over. I grab her hand on my face and rub my fingers over hers. I nod and we sit on the ground with our backs against the walls. She curls up beside me, just like how she used to.

***

Saturday morning, I'm wide awake at 6 a.m. I had diarrhea this morning, probably due to the amount of anxiety I've been having about tonight. I asked my uncle Eli if I could skip the mechanic shop today; I would be too nervous to do anything. I need to just sit in my room and daydream about what's going to happen tonight. I read for a couple of hours, go on a run, shower, and spend some time outside on the deck. I watch an episode of some random cooking show and lay in my bed and stare at the ceiling, watching the fan go around and around and around.

Laurel and I made plans to meet tonight at six. I wasn't sure if this was such a good idea, but I couldn't say no to her. I need to see her. I can't keep avoiding her.

It's now 5:45 and I've been watching the second hand on my watch tick for three minutes. I stand up from the bar stool in the kitchen and pace around the living room. I do some jumping jacks and hype myself up. *You can do this. It's just Laurel. She doesn't hate you. If she did, she wouldn't have agreed to meet you.*

It's 5:49 and I decide to start walking to the beach.

I make it seventy-nine steps before I convince myself to turn around. I pivot and head back in the direction of my house.

I don't deserve her friendship again.

But I want it. I want to see her. I want to hug her and feel her warmth around me.

I audibly groan, annoyed at myself, and pivot again, spinning around and head toward the beach, making up my mind to see Laurel.

Nine minutes later, I see Laurel sitting on the wall that separates the beach and the sidewalk. Her long legs are swinging over the side. She's looking out at the ocean, her caramel, wavy hair flowing in the wind.

The closer I get to her, the calmer I feel and I know I made the right decision to meet her. I see the scar on her face and before I can convince myself to speed walk away again, I approach her.

"Hi," I say, sitting down next to her. She looks over at me and she smiles. A smile that reaches her eyes.

"Hi," she says back.

"Laurel, thank you for meeting me here. I-" I begin.

"Lane," she says, grabbing my hand, "I've missed you." She reaches up and pushes my hair back, which kind of surprises me, but also makes my stomach hurt. In a good way, but also in a way that makes me feel guilty. *Why is she the one consoling me?*

"I've missed you too, Laurel. I'm sorry I never reached out to you."

"It's okay. We've both been through a lot." She looks at me directly in the eyes, almost as if she's searching me. Reading my thoughts.

She swings her legs and claps her hands together. I speak up before she decides to leave me. "I found our bucket list," I say, pulling it out of my pocket.

"What? You're kidding! I thought I accidentally threw it away at lunch one day at school." She mumbles that last part. I hand her the folded-up piece of paper and watch as she delicately opens it up.

She's smiling from ear to ear and I can't help but smile with her. I lean in and we read through the list together. I can smell her pear shampoo. I lean in a little closer so my chest is barely touching her shoulder. We laugh at some of the things we wrote and all the memories we made together because of this list.

"I can't believe you had this. I'm so happy you found it!" She looks out at the water then turns her head toward me. "So what are we going to do first? We need to choose one to complete right now."

I'm a bit thrown off by her eagerness to do something from the list right now. I was thinking we would talk and I would apologize and we would cry and hopefully begin to move on. But, I guess that isn't what she expected. "Um, I don't know. Which one do you want to do?" She looks over the list again and says, "How about we buy a meal for someone in need?" She turns to face the road and waves her hand in front of her. "There are people all over Hull who need a good meal."

"Alright," I say, loving her heart. "Let's go."

We stand up and start walking. We walk for a couple of seconds when she reaches over and grabs my hand in hers. I can't say I'm surprised that Laurel is being her normal self. She's never anything except herself. But I'm thrown off a little at how quickly she takes my hand in hers. We've always been touchy with each other, but I wasn't expecting it to happen so quickly. It brings me an immense amount of relief though.

She swings our arms back and forth and we walk in silence, all the way to the sandwich shop Ms. Elise and I love. The feel of her hand in mine sends sparks igniting in every direction of my body. I've missed her so much.

We walk inside and order a sandwich, a large fry, and a strawberry milkshake to share. We sit down at a table and eat our food in more comfortable silence.

I take a bite and look up at Laurel and she starts laughing at me. "You have a piece of spinach hanging on your lip," she says through laugh filled breaths. I chuckle, grab the piece of spinach off my face and place it in between my thumb and middle finger. I flick it and it lands on her forehead and she laughs even harder. So hard that strawberry milkshake shoots out of her nose.

"Ow!!" she says, grabbing a napkin. "That was just cruel!" She takes the spinach off her face and wipes her nose with a napkin.

"You look like you snorted pink yogurt," I say, guffawing. I wipe a tear from my eye and hold my stomach, my abs aren't used to this much laughing.

"That probably would have been just as painful," she says. She snatches the last couple of fries out of my hand, pink milkshake still on her face, and says, "I deserve these," and dunks them into ranch.

We order a duplicate of what we just ate and head outside to find someone to give it to. We walk around town for a while, talking about what we've been up to the past couple of months. I tell her I've been going to therapy and she tells how proud of me she is for going.

We head down an alley and find a woman laying down in a corner. I look over at Laurel and she shrugs. We walk over toward the woman and Laurel bends down onto her knees.

"Excuse me, ma'am?" Laurel says. She startled the woman awake and Laurel takes an awkward step back.

"What duyou want?" the woman asks, sitting up. "Leave me alone," she practically barks, swinging her arm out in front of her. She seems irritated that we woke her up. Her hair on the side of her head she was laying down on is matted down. It doesn't look like she's had a shower in a while.

"Um, we have an extra meal if you'd like it," Laurel says placatingly. I hand her the bag and she takes it from me. "There's a sandwich, some French fries, and we got a milkshake, too."

The woman sits up straighter and her face shifts from confusion to hope. Laurel sets the things on the ground, but the woman doesn't say anything. She hasn't even looked at me.

Laurel stands up and I offer her my hand as we turn and walk away, just as the woman starts to speak.

"Wait. Why would you do this for me? You don't even know me."

We turn around and face her again. We both drop to our knees and this time I speak.

"We wanted to do something kind for someone. We just thought you might need a nice meal." She looks over at me and legitimately looks startled when she finally takes in my face. Like she's surprised.

She looks back and forth between both of my eyes and settles hers on the ground in front of me. A look of shame washes over her face and Laurel reaches out to touch the woman.

"Ma'am, what's your name?"

"I go by Milly," she says. "I can't tell you enough how much I appreciate this." Her eyes soften and she grabs the bag in front of her.

"Milly, where are you from?"

Milly takes a sip of the milkshake and gulps hard. "I'm from Hull. Born and raised here."

She refuses to look at me, but stares at the ground as she eats her food.

"So, if you don't mind me asking, how did you end up here?" Laurel asks.

"Um, I just made some bad decisions some years back. Got into drugs, met some bad people. That's all I wanna say about that," Milly tells us.

"Okay, that's fine. Well, is there anything you need? We would be happy to run to the store for you."

"No, that's really okay, you've already done enough for me. I don't want to be a bother."

"No, it isn't a bother to us at all. Lane can drive us, won't you Lane?" Laurel looks over at me with sharp eyes, telling me to agree.

"Yeah, of course. Anything you need."

Milly takes a quick look at my face and turns away just as quickly. I can see her face turn a dark shade of pink. "Well, that would be very nice." Laurel helps her stand up and she gathers her backpack and blanket and follows us back to the beach. Laurel introduces herself and talks to the woman like they've been best friends. My heart can't handle how much I love her. How much I never stopped loving her even after all these months. My stomach starts to hurt thinking about what happened seven months ago and I try to flick those thoughts away.

I run home and grab my truck and drive it over to the corner. They get in my truck and I drive the three of us to Walmart. Laurel offers Milly the front seat, but she refuses, flashing another quick glance at me.

I put the truck in reverse once we're all buckled and look in the rearview mirror. Just as I'm about to pull out, I see Laurel and immediately realize this will be the first time I've driven her since the accident. I take a quick second to compose myself and I drive the entire way to the store with my fingers clenched around the steering wheel, my heart in my stomach.

We go through Walmart and Milly starts to put some things into the cart. Some basic things like shampoo, toothpaste, and a toothbrush. Then we go to the food section and she picks out some peanut butter, bread and honey. One of my favorite sandwiches growing up. We get her a small pillow and a new blanket. Some new socks and a couple of new shirts and shorts.

We head to the checkout and I pay for Milly's new things. We drive back toward where we found Milly and in the rearview mirror, I see her holding something. Looks like a piece of paper. Or maybe a picture? She's looking at is with an intensity I've never seen someone look at a picture before with. She snaps out of her trance and wipes at her eyes, then tucks the picture into her bra.

We drop Milly off at her corner and Laurel tells her we'll be back next week. We say goodbye and Milly finally looks at me. She takes in my face and gives me a small smile, then looks away again, fidgeting with her new things.

"What made you want to do that?" I ask, heading back to the beach.

"I don't know, I just felt like we should help her. I would have wanted someone to do that for me." The way that Laurel's heart just embodies everything good and kind reminds me of why reconnecting with her was a good idea.

We drive back to the beach and Laurel steps out of the car. I was a nervous wreck all day about seeing her and now I'm worried that our time together is coming to an end tonight. I open my door and watch as she shuts hers.

"Thank you, Lane. For doing that," she says, tucking her hair behind her ear.

"Yeah, I'm glad we got to check something off of our bucket list tonight." She walks around the car and pulls me into a hug. I've never felt more at home than I have right now. I squeeze her hard and rest my cheek on the top of her head. The ache that's been in my chest slightly lifts as she nuzzles her face in my arm and squeezes me back. We stand there hugging for a little longer and then she suddenly pulls away and I'm left feeling naked and empty again. She starts to take a couple steps backwards when she says, "I missed you, Lane Andrew Peterson." Before I can even answer, she turns and sprints away from me.

I feel a smile form on my face, despite how hollow I feel now that she's gone.

My Eurydice

Chapter 16

My last memory of the bucket list was one of the best nights of my life. It was sometime during the end of the summer and Laurel and I wanted to cross "spending the night in the treehouse" off the bucket list. We also decided to try sushi for the first time. We went to a local sushi place and ordered some things we thought sounded good. We order almost two of everything on the menu and take it back to the treehouse. We taste each piece together and then rate it on a scale of one to five, one being, "disgusting, I would rather starve than eat that again," and five being, "amazing, I would eat this every day for the rest of my life." My favorite was one with mango in it. I don't remember what it was called though.

We spent over an hour trying all different types of sushi and rating them. Laurel gagged a couple of times and ended up spitting one of them out the window. We use soy sauce, teriyaki from Laurel's fridge, and the pickled ginger that came with the sushi. We weren't sure what it was at first, so Laurel made me taste it. I remembered the taste of the ginger from Ivy's juices and assumed that's what it was.

It was around 8 o'clock when Laurel went inside to tell her parents she wanted to sleep in the treehouse that night. She would sleep in the treehouse often, so they wouldn't think anything of it. There's a lock on the inside of the door, so they knew she was always safe. This was one of the things on the bucket list that I am most excited for. Not because I think anything will happen, but spending that much time with Laurel, having her fall asleep next to me, would be truly ethereal.

We were seniors in high school, so there was no way Mr. Matthew and Mrs. Malani would willingly let me stay over. She was giggling all the way up the stairs of the treehouse, tripping over the blankets and pillows that were falling out of her hands. I help her up the stairs and we dive onto the floor, hoping her parents didn't see me from the kitchen window.

We set up a fort with all the blankets like we used to do all the time, throwing pillows all over the floor to make it comfier. We put on *10 Things I Hate About You* with Julia Stiles and Heath Ledger, one of Laurel's favorite romances. We've seen this movie more times than I can count. We lay up against the couch and she curls up against me, my arm around her, pulling her close to me. She rests her hand on my chest and I play with her hair as we watch the movie.

I can't pretend like I haven't thought about making out with her the entire movie. The treehouse is dark, with only the light from the moon shining in from the window and the small amount of light coming from the T.V. The blankets and pillows everywhere give the treehouse a cozy feel and we're already snuggled up against one another.

Obviously, I never make a move. One, I'm too chicken. Two, I can't ruin what we have by trying to kiss her. It would complicate things. So, I keep it in my pants. Or I guess I keep my lips to myself.

The movie ends and we angle ourselves so that we can see the sky through the window. The window is small and a tree in the neighbors back yard blocks most of the view, but we don't complain. We lay on our backs and look up at the stars. I pick up a piece of Laurel's hair and start to twist it in my fingers when she asks me a question.

"Have you ever heard of the constellation called Lyra?"

I shake my head no, then remember that she can't see me. "No," I respond. It comes out as a whisper because my voice gets stuck in my throat.

"In Greek mythology, Lyra represents the lyre of Orpheus. Orpheus played music on his lyre so charming that even the trees and streams would sway and dance." I can see her arms straight out in front of her, like she's dancing to Orpheus' music. "He married a woman named Eurydice, who was killed by a snake bite and was sent to the Underworld. Orpheus traveled to the Underworld to save her by playing music on his lyre. His music was so calming that even Hades was enchanted. Orpheus asked Hades if he could have Eurydice back. Hades let Orpheus take Eurydice back, but only on one condition. Guess what the condition was." Her tone is playful, so I play along.

"Uh...that he could only eat slugs for the rest of his life?" I guess, somewhat jokingly.

"Ew, gross. No, that isn't it. Guess again. You have two more guesses."

"Okay, um let me think for a second." I try to think of something more like what Hades might do. "Oh, Orpheus would have to be his slave? Like he would have to take her place."

"Nope. I'll just tell you," she says, but I cut her off. She's impatient.

"Hey, I thought I had one more guess."

"Yeah, you do, but you're not good at guessing."

"Well, there's a billion things that his condition could be. Do you really think I'm going to be able to guess it?"

"I guess that's true. Okay, fine, what's your last guess?"

"Hm." I think a little longer than last time. "That Orpheus would have to bring Eurydice back to the underworld every now and then. Sort of like a fifty-fifty type deal. Hades gets her half the time and Orpheus gets her half the time."

"That's actually not a bad guess. But that's not it. The condition was that Orpheus couldn't look back until they reached the outside world again. Unsurprisingly, at the last second, Orpheus looked back, and Eurydice was gone forever. Lost amongst the stars. He aimlessly traveled, playing his lyre for her, hoping one day she would return to him," Laurel explains. "I think it's beautiful that he never stopped looking for her."

She sits up and scoots closer to me so she can lean across my chest. I cup her face, slowly moving a piece of hair behind her ear. She rests her chin on her hand and says to me, "Lane, if you ever lose me, promise me you'll always keep looking for me, like Orpheus did for Eurydice."

I smile and move my arm behind her and rest it on her lower back, bringing her closer to me. I look back and forth between her dark sea glass eyes, saying, "I'll never lose you, Laurel."

"But if you did, I want you to promise me you'll never stop trying to get me back." She draws circles on my chest, making the skin she's touching tingle.

"I promise," I say, taking her hand on my chest in mine. I rub my thumb across her fingers and she slowly leans in towards my face. A smile spreads across her lips. For a second I think she's going to kiss me. Then she leans in further and now I know she's going to kiss me. Oh, god.

I want to question why she's kissing me, but my only thoughts are of her lips.

Her lips connect with mine slowly yet confidently. I've wanted to kiss her since the first day I laid eyes on her. My stomach fills with butterflies, each one for the number of times I've thought about kissing her. The butterflies travel down my torso and my legs and they shiver with pleasure. I need more of her.

I respond to her kiss by moving my lips against hers and tightening my grip on her lower back. I kiss her as if this is the only chance I will ever have to kiss her. It isn't sloppy or forced. It isn't uncomfortable or weird. It's gentle and it's perfect.

She lets go of my hand and holds the side of my face, deepening the kiss. Her lips are soft and taste like the vanilla chapstick she always uses. I grab a hold of her thigh and pull her leg across mine, inch by inch getting closer and closer to touching her someplace I know I shouldn't. I keep my hand where it is, despite how badly I want to move it. She kisses me for another couple seconds before slowly pulling away from me. My eyes flutter open, wondering where her lips went. She looks me in the eyes then plants a single, soft kiss on the side of my mouth. I can feel her warm breath across my face and as she pulls away to lay on my chest again, my face flushes with intense desire for this girl.

"Laurel, I have a question for you."

"Hm?" she quietly grunts.

"Why did you ask me to come over that day? The first day we met." She doesn't answer right away, but when she does, I'm surprised by her answer.

"Well, I knew about you because of home ec. I knew you and Jey were friends, but I was curious about you. We were the only two kids that got off at our bus stop and we would practically walk home together, but we would go our own separate ways every day. I guess it just made me... sad." Her voice goes up on that last word, like thinking about it now is making her sad. "That we had the opportunity to be friends, but neither of us were doing anything about it. So, that day I did something about it."

"Huh. Well, I'm glad you did."

We don't talk the rest of the night, but she lays on my chest, hums a song, and eventually falls asleep. I switch back and forth between twirling her hair in my fingers and drawing on her back. I fall asleep to the sound of her gentle breathing, feeling like the luckiest guy in the world.

Food Trucks & Naked Swimming

Chapter 17

A week goes by of Laurel and I hanging out, and we cross off one more thing on our bucket list: try pottery. Even though I've worked in a pottery shop the last four years, Laurel and I have never actually made anything together. Laurel visited me at the store and we snuck into the back and I showed her how to use the wheel. I sat behind her, guiding her hands up and down as she made a curvy, non-symmetrical vase. At one point, she pressed on the pedal too hard and wet clay hit us both in the face.

While I obviously enjoy having Laurel back in my life and spending time with her, I've been worried this week that Laurel and I are spending too much time together. I don't think I'm good for her anymore. I'm a nervous wreck all the time, and not to mention the accident. It probably also isn't good for me; good for *us*. I mean, I'm moving across the country at the end of the summer. Selfishly, I want to spend as much time with her as I can before I move. But what will that lead to? A broken heart? Losing each other again?

A few days later, we decided to go check on Milly. We surprise Milly this time with some pizza. We found her in the spot she was in last time, and Laurel woke her up again from a nap. She responded grouchily at first, then I think she could smell the pizza, and eventually realized it was us. We took the pizza over to the beach and ate every single piece. Milly told us stories about her childhood and what it was like growing up in Hull all those years ago: what she and her friends did for fun, the boys she would show up in surfing competitions, and all the sneaking out she did in high school.

Laurel brought a deck of cards, so we played a few rounds of a game called Golf while the sun set behind us. Milly still wasn't really looking at me and I don't really know what that's about yet. We talk until the sun fully set and we walk Milly back to her spot in the corner.

Laurel and I are walking back to my house when Laurel says, "Milly's pretty cool. It makes me feel bad that she sleeps in the corner every night. If we still lived in our old house, I would let her stay in the treehouse."

"Yeah, it makes me feel bad, too. Maybe we should tell her about the soup kitchen Paisley works at."

"That's a good idea, Lane." Laurel grabs my hand and we walk the rest of the way to my house in silence. We get to the door and I turn to face Laurel behind me. I've been preparing a speech for the past two days about how I'm no good for her and I'll just end up hurting her again.

"Thanks for seeing Milly with me again tonight," she says. "What should we do tomorrow?"

I stare at her green eyes and search for any hint of regret. I know she keeps hanging out with me, but I'm nervous she's going to realize that I'm not good for her anymore and she'll leave me. I'd rather be the one to tell her that than for her to realize that. I need to say something.

"Laurel," I start, "I feel like we shouldn't be spending so much time together." My heart breaks as I say it. I watch her face for any movement, but she stares at me like I didn't even just speak, so I continue. "I'm no good for you, Laurel." I look away from her, feeling like I need to cry. "It just…" I stutter, thinking of a way to get my point across, but not wanting to say it. "I think we've been spending too much time together. I'm worried things won't end well, and -"

She takes a step closer to me and punches me in the shoulder. "Ow! What was that for?"

"For saying something so stupid," she laughs. She pauses. "Lane," she says more seriously, "I've been a complete mess for seven months. The best thing for me was running into you in the treehouse. Don't push me away."

I sigh. "Laurel, I hurt you. I'm the reason you've been a complete mess for seven months. Just think about-"

"Stop," she says, firmly. She places her hands on my chest and looks up at me. "Don't do that." Her hand touches my face and she gently runs her hand through my hair. I'm suddenly calmer. "Meet me at the bookshop tomorrow at 5. I have a fun night planned for us." She spins around and sprints away from me. "Don't be late! And bring our bucket list!" she adds over her shoulder.

I head inside, so grateful that Laurel didn't let me push her away, but still feeling like a trash human being.

***

I meet Laurel outside the bookshop just like she told me. The Owens family owns this bookshop, which has through the years, turned into a bookshop/bakery/coffee joint. Laurel and I used to spend a lot of time here; doing homework, helping organize books and dusting shelves, and sneaking baked goods when nobody was looking. I actually worked here many summers ago. All the books are used, donated books. Laurel used to love looking through newly donated books and checking to see if any of them had sweet, little messages inside. She found a grocery list, a happy birthday note, a drawing of a seahorse, and a note from a teacher to one of their students.

I don't go in because I know I'll see Mr. Matthew or Mrs. Malani, so I sit in one of the patio chairs and wait for her to meet me outside. A few minutes later, Laurel comes out with a chocolate chip gingersnap muffin in one hand and a white macadamia cranberry one in the other. She hands me the white macadamia cranberry one while she shoves the other one in her mouth.

"Let's get this show on the road!" she says, hoping into my car. "Where are we going?" I ask. I have a few ideas, being that she wanted me to bring the bucket list, but I'm not really sure what she has planned. "I'll tell you where to go." For the next ten minutes she gives me poor directions, which I assume is on purpose to throw me off. I know exactly where we are.

We park the truck and walk over to the boardwalk where there are more food trucks than I have ever seen in one location. Mexican food, Vietnamese food, vegan food trucks, ice cream trucks, sushi trucks, burger trucks, southern food, and even Mediterranean food.

"Tonight, we are going to try something from every food truck!" she exclaims, pulling my arm.

"What, there's probably like fifty food trucks here. And we just ate muffins like fifteen minutes ago." I say.

"We don't have to get whole meals," she says, rolling her eyes. "Come on, it'll be fun! Where should we go first?"

We start with the truck closest to us which is selling breakfast food. We split a kid's omelet, which I have to admit was one of the best omelets I have ever had. We walk around a little and try to come up with a plan. Laurel takes out her phone and starts making a list, putting the ones we want to try at the top and the ones we don't really care about trying at the bottom. That way if we get too full, we know we at least ate all the good stuff.

All around us, kids are eating ice cream, jumping in bounce houses, and dancing with their friends to the different music coming from each truck. There are people walking their dogs, a clown making animals out of balloons, and families taking selfies with their various dinners.

We decide to hit up the Mack's Mac & Cheez food truck second. We order a kids mac and cheese with bacon bits and sausage, crusted with Ritz crackers on top. It takes about a whole thirty seconds to devour. We make our way to the Mediterranean truck and order some falafel and a piece of pita with a side of honey. We get a slice of pizza topped with pineapple, barbecue sauce and chicken. We get a tray of sushi, a spicy cauliflower and avocado taco, and some Pad Thai. To finish off the night, we hit up the Cookie Monster food truck that serves cookies the size of a small dinner plate with ice cream inside. We get two "Everything Including the Kitchen Sink" cookies with a scoop of mint chocolate chip, cookie dough and toffee heath with three cherries and a mountain of whipped cream. I take out my phone to take a picture of us with our monstrous dessert. Laurel smiles her biggest smile while I lick some whipped cream off the top.

"I am so stuffed," Laurel says, rubbing her stomach in a circular motion fifteen minutes later. We ate all that we could of the cookie ice cream sandwich and there's still over half of it left. We found a place to sit on some rocks and have been waiting for the food to digest before we go do the next thing Laurel has planned.

"I know, I never want to eat again," I say, picking up a cherry and plopping it in my mouth.

She playfully pushes my shoulder and I pretend to fall off the rocks, making her laugh. Before she's done laughing, a giant burp escapes from her throat and her hands fly to cover her mouth in utter shock, her eyes wide.

"Oh my god, Laurel. What is happening in your stomach? Are you okay?" I ask through fits of laughter.

"I have no idea where that came from! I didn't even know I needed to burp," she cackles. She burps again, but this one is much smaller. Still impressive, though. "Wow, I feel a lot better after that," she says, as she pats her stomach.

Walking around with her tonight was a lot of fun. It felt like us again. Lane and Laurel against the world. We laughed, we fed each other food, and we even got matching airbrush tattoos of a lightning bolt. We both agreed it was the most badass design.

"Alright, let's get going to our next destination."

"Don't make me move. I'll fall over and I may never be able to get back up," I warn.

"Hop on," she says, crouching down in front of me.

"You want me to get on your back? You're going to carry me to the truck?"

"Yeah," she says, motioning for me to jump on. "Let's go. We don't have all day."

"I don't think you can carry me, Laurel." She stands up and spins around, placing her hands on her hips.

"Why? Cause I'm a girl? How very sexist of you, Lane. I thought I taught you better than that."

"I'm five inches taller than you. My feet are going to drag on the ground." She crouches back down in front of me without saying anything.

"Ughhh," I sigh. "Fine. But if we fall over it's all your fault."

"Ye of little faith." I put my right leg up against her back and she latches onto the back of my knee. "Ready?" I ask.

"Just do it already!" Just as I'm about to jump on her back, she drops my right leg and spins to face me. "Hey, what are you -"

"If I can carry you on my back the entire way to the truck, you owe me a foot rub," she says, poking me in the chest.

"Okay, you're on. If you can't, then you owe me a foot rub." I poke her back on the shoulder. She shakes her head when we shake hands, sealing our deal. "I'm stronger than you think, so make sure to rest your hands because you *will* be giving me a foot rub."

We decide it'll be easier to start on the concrete, so we leave the sand. Knowing her, she'd twist an ankle and then blame everything on me.

"Alright, get on." she says, once we've made it to more stable ground.

Like I thought, my feet touch the ground, so I hold them up so she won't trip on them. We bob and weave around people with various foods and drinks and I'm more than shocked when we make it to my truck in one piece.

"Looks like you owe me a foot rub," she says, getting into the truck. We drive for twenty minutes, windows down, music blasting through the speakers. Laurel tells me to take a left turn and when we make it onto the next road, I can finally see where we are. It's Paragon Park.

"Next, we cross visit an abandoned theme park off our list!"

"Whoa, I didn't know Paragon Park was still here...Or I guess what's left of it." It closed in the late 80's but growing up in Hull, I've heard about it before.

"Well that makes sense since only the cool people know about it."

I roll my eyes at that comment, hiding my laugh, and lock my truck behind me. We walk under the entrance sign, which has been graffitied all over and is barely hanging onto the wooden post behind it. It looks like a faint gust of wind could make it fall off.

"Pick a number one to infinity," Laurel says, skipping ahead of me.

"Um...873,759,721," I say, exaggerating the number one.

"Interesting. That's exactly what I was going to say."

She leads me through a bush-infested path, kicking aside a branch that had fallen, probably from the bad storm we had a couple of weeks ago. We meet a fork in the path, one way going left, one way going right. She continues to the right without hesitation making me think she's been here before. Branches are smacking me left and right when she lets them go. I look down and see I have scratches on my arms and legs.

After what feels like a trek through Narnia, we make it to what I'm expecting used to be a carousel. Half the horses are missing legs, the benches have been carved out and stolen, and there are penises spray painted nearly everywhere.

"This is what you wanted to show me?" I ask.

"Isn't it so cool?" I follow her to the horses and climb on the one next to the one she straddles.

"It's sad that these rides don't ever get used anymore." I look past her and notice some other rides in the distance, or what used to be at least.

"Yeah, but I guess it had it's time. Think about all the kids' butts that have sat on these horses, right where we're sitting now."

"How poetic," she says, chuckling. I take my phone out and snap another picture. I figured we may as well capture evidence of us completing the items on our bucket list.

She jumps off her horse and when she lands her foot breaks through the rotted wood.

"Oh shit," I say, jumping down to help her. "You okay?" I grab her shoulder and while I should be concentrating on her leg, all I feel is her warm skin under my hand. My fingertips skim across her neck as I help her stand up. A soft tingle runs through my body.

These past couple weeks Laurel and I have been hanging out have been nice. Better than nice. Laurel and I have always been touchy with each other. Holding hands, hugging, and cuddling. We haven't really had an opportunity to do anything more than hold hands so touching her neck and being so close to her mouth sent shivers through my body, making me crave more of her.

"Yeah, I'm fine. Look, no scratches. It's just rotted wood," she says, lifting up her leg. "Let's go run around!"

We run through the maze of horses with missing eyeballs and added tattoos, jumping over holes in the wood. If this thing worked, I definitely would be throwing up by now. I'd be so dizzy. Even though the mirrors around the base are covered in gunk and hard to see, it's still a little trippy.

"I bet you can't catch me," she plays, swinging herself around a horse that has an arrow pointing to its butthole.

"What happens when I do catch you?"

"When you don't catch me or if I catch you," she pauses, looking over my shoulder, "you have to get in the pond. Naked." She points toward the pond over by a large piece of a fated, bright green metal, which I'm assuming was the base of a rollercoaster. It looks like it has merpeople living in the bottom of it.

"Oh ho ho. No no no. I won't be the one getting in the pond naked. If I catch you, same rules apply," I tease, crossing my arms.

"I guess we'll just have to see." And with that, she sprints away from me, running in between and through a giant labyrinth of metal. Twisting left and turning right, I almost catch her two times. But she's faster than I remember. She runs between two buildings and when I finally catch up to her, she's disappeared. I stand there, listening for any sudden movement or for the slow, deep breaths she respires.

"Oh, Laurel," I sing.

Out of nowhere, she comes running at me from behind and jumps on my back. I stumble forward and my foot lands in a small hole in the grass, causing me to twist my ankle. I fall on the ground and bring Laurel down with me.

"Lane!" she screams, as we go down. Instinctively, she throws her arms around my face, trying to catch herself from falling. My neck shoots back and I can hear, and feel it crack. We land on the ground in a tangle of arms and legs, her still clinging onto my back. "What just happened?" she asks through chuckles. "You're crushing my entire body," she cry-laughs.

"Oh, god," I say, rubbing my neck and feeling a pang in my ankle. "I wasn't expecting you to jump on my back and nearly break my neck. I lost my footing and twisted my ankle."

"Sounds about right. You blaming your loss on *twisting an ankle,*" she says, using air quotes "Looks like you're getting naked," she smirks, crossing her arms.

"Fine, don't believe me. But I did twist my ankle."

We make our way over to the pond and while it doesn't smell too great, the sun setting behind it actually makes for a nice sight. "Alright, strip, Bernie Barker." I glare over at her while I take my shirt off, making sure to flex just the right amount. I watch her eyes take a quick look at my body. I don't have an eight pack or anything, but I workout every now and then. I smirk because Laurel Owens just checked me out.

I slide off my shoes and pull off my socks and start to step out of my shorts when I notice Laurel taking off her shirt. Every muscle in my body freezes, except my jaw, which falls to the floor.

Oh fuck.

"What are you doing? You won; you don't have to get in." I don't know why I'm trying to convince her not to come in with me. *Shut the hell up, Lane.*

"I know. But what's the fun in that?" she says, lifting her shirt over her head.

Laurel Owens is standing in front of me shirtless. And holy fucking hell she is stunning.

Don't get me wrong, I've seen Laurel in a bathing suit more times than I can count. But this is different. It's so much more intimate. I realize I'm staring so I slide my shorts off the rest of the way and clear my throat. "Uh, turn around."

"What, you don't want me to see anything?" she asks with her hands on her hips.

"Nope," I state. I might be trying to hide something else, too.

She rolls her eyes and turns around. I whip my boxers off and toss them over my shoulder and book it to the pond. I know she turned around at some point because she's laughing at me. Probably laughing at the way I dove into the pond, my bare ass-cheeks mooning the sunset.

I flit around in the water while Laurel slides off her shorts and I swear I've never seen anything so hot. "You gonna join me?" I ask. I am internally begging her to. I place my arms parallel with the water and skim them back and forth, making calm ripples all around me.

"No, I'm taking my clothes off to go ride the carousel again," she mocks. "Wait, that came out wrong." She covers her face with her hand. I throw my head back in laughter at what she just said. "Come on in, I won't look." I say, covering up my eyes with my hand. I'd be lying if I said I wasn't tempted to peek.

I only remove my hand when I can feel her presence next to me. "Ugh, did you pee?" she asks me, disgust written all over her face.

"That's for me to know and for you to never find out." I didn't, it was warm when I got in. But I like seeing her squirm.

"Ew, Lane," she says, splashing me with water.

"I don't pee and tell," I say, laying my head in the water. I'm trying very hard to concentrate on anything except Laurel's naked body next to me.

I close my eyes and take a breath, feeling peaceful, just floating in the water. Laurel is with me and it's just like old times, of course, except right now we are naked. Something I cannot forget. I hear water moving and then I feel Laurel's hands touch my hair. I look up and see her standing above me, her fingers tangled in my hair. I smile up at her and she smiles back at me. She scratches my head and neck and twirls my hair in her fingers. She traces small circles around my temples, her fingertips gliding on my skin. They travel under my eyes and across my nose, following the trail of my freckles. Her touch literally makes me feel intoxicated.

"I like your freckles," she whispers.

We're quiet for a few minutes while she plays with my hair. I lift my hand and touch her cheek with my thumb, which makes her grip my hair just a little tighter. Water trickles down my arm and gently

217

plops back into the pond. She blushes and before I know what I'm doing, I'm speaking out loud.

"You're beautiful," I say.

She blushes again and her cheeks match the setting sun behind her. "Stop it," she says, covering my mouth with her hands, pulling me closer to her chest. I grab her hands and remove them from my mouth and twist around to meet her face-to-face. She turns away from me and I tilt her chin so she's looking at me. We are inches apart. I stand up a bit so she's looking up at me. I like how short she is compared to me. I look down at her and I can see the curves of her breasts just above the water. Her face is sprinkled with new freckles from spending days in the sun. Her wavy caramel hair is pulled into a bun on the top of her head with pieces sticking out in all the right places. Despite all the greasy food we just ate, she smells like vanilla and clementine. I meet her green eyes.

"You're beautiful," I say again.

"You're only saying that because we're naked right now." She puts her hand on my cheek and pushes my face, causing me to look away from her. I grab her hand and hold it tightly.

"No, Laurel. I can promise you I'm not." The sun is almost fully set and it's getting darker with every minute. I see her smile to herself right as she submerges herself under water.

Spooning with Danny

Chapter 18

It's been four days since I've seen Laurel. Four days since we were naked in that pond, literally inches apart from each other. I haven't stopped thinking about her. I never stop thinking about her, but this new memory is one I will never ever forget.

We swam around the pond for a while before it got too cold. I drove back to my house and we sat in my truck for a couple seconds before Laurel spoke up. "Well, we can cross skinny dipping off our list," she says. Then she leaned over and kissed my cheek and got out of the truck and I haven't seen her since. I haven't tried contacting her because I'm worried she regrets skinny dipping with me. I want to give her the space she might need.

So I've just been going to work at the pottery shop and my uncle Eli's garage, waiting for her to reach out to me again. But today is the fourth day of no contact, so I figured maybe she's waiting for me to contact her.

I decide to go to the Owens' store after I get off from the pottery shop. I switch out one of the displays for tomorrow morning. I turn off the lights, flip the open sign to closed, and lock the door. It takes twenty minutes to get there with all the beach traffic. I'm not ready to see Mrs. Malani or Mr. Matthew, but it was going to happen sometime soon.

The bookshop door is open so I walk in and look towards the checkout counter for Laurel. She's there, wearing a matcha colored sundress with daisies all over it. I can tell her eyes are popping from over here. I get in line and when I make it to the front, she has her back to me. It looks like she's wiping the counters down.

"Hi," I say, just as she turns around.

"Lane, oh my god!" I guess I surprised her, which sends her arms flying in the air, and the dirty rag shoots out of her hand and lands on the floor with a thud.

"Lane, oh my god, you scared me." She runs a hand through her hair and places the other one over her heart.

"Sorry, I wasn't trying to," I say through laughs. It's then that I notice how beautiful Laurel looks today. She's wearing a pretty green colored dress. It looks like the color of Paisley's matcha lattes. It's peppered in little white daisies and it hugs her body in all the right places.

She picks up the rag she threw and rinses it out in the sink before throwing it under the counter and into the bucket where dirty rags go then washes her hands. She opens the glass window to where all the freshly made goodies are and hands me a gingersnap snickerdoodle cookie. I eat it in three bites. Those cookies are to die for.

"You wanna go do something? I'm off innnn…" she checks the nonexistent watch on her arm and says "…*now* actually!" She rips off her little apron that says Half & Half Cafe and throws it in the back room.

We exit the shop and decide to walk three blocks to see if we can find Milly.

We find Milly a few streets away from her usual spot surrounded by a couple of other people. They're all sitting spread out, making a circle around the pavement, some of them smoking and drinking. "Milly!" Laurel shouts. Milly looks our way and mumbles something to one of her friends and walks towards us.

"Hi guys," Milly says. She looks embarrassed.

"Lane and I were wondering if you wanted to do something with us tonight. We were thinking of going down to Tipsy Tuna."

Milly looks over her shoulder at the group of people then turns back to us. "Yeah, sure, that sounds good." She fidgets with her hands. She's wearing the new clothes we bought her. I know she found a spot at a homeless shelter so she's been staying there. She looks newer, cleaner, healthier.

We walk down to Tipsy Tuna, which is a restaurant and bar with karaoke. The three of us get a table and decide to split the seafood nachos. While we eat, Laurel and I enjoy our drinks, and Milly drinks her water. She's seemed a little uncomfortable this whole time. I'm about to ask her if she's okay when she speaks up.

"Um, back there," she points over her shoulder, "I just want you guys to know that…" She looks down at her hands while she fiddles with the napkin in her lap. "I don't want you guys to think something is wrong about me."

Laurel senses Milly needs comforting and reaches for her hand. Milly looks up and gives her a quick, small smile. "I'm sober. I've been sober for seven months. I know it isn't smart of me to be hanging out around that group, but they've got my back.

Even if I asked for a drink, they wouldn't give it to me. She chuckles then continues. "They're proud of me and don't want me to backtrack on my progress."

"Thank you for sharing that, Milly. I'm proud of you for being sober for seven months. That's an amazing accomplishment," Laurel says.

"Truly, Milly, you should be so proud," I add.

"Thank you guys. I just didn't want you to think wrongly of me or be worried about me or anything. I guess I was nervous you guys were going to judge me, is all. I actually found a recovery center called The Anchor. I've been going there multiple times a week for services and meetings. Everyone there is so great. I've been wanting to ask you guys about coming to a meeting with me one time. I would sure mean a lot to have your support."

"Milly, we don't judge you. We know you have a past, and that's okay. We're just proud of how far you've come. And absolutely, we'll be there!"

"Thank you, Laurel." Milly starts to get teary eyed.

I take another bite of the seafood nachos while I think. I hadn't known that she was sober. I didn't even think that she could possibly be using since we met her. She told us when we first met her that she used to be involved with drugs, but that thought never even crossed my mind. But I am glad to know that she's come so far. From what I know about her, she's such a strong woman and I look up to her for that.

Milly wipes a tear from her face. "Well enough of this," Milly says. "Let's go dance!"

She finds an older man dancing alone and goes to join him. Laurel grabs my hand and I follow her to the dance floor. It's mainly all old people. The Tipsy Tuna is usually packed with old people, especially this early on a Friday night. The music playing is a mix of oldies and some modern pop, but mostly oldies. Sam Cooke. Air Supply. Chicago. Right now, "Make You Feel My Love" by Adele is softly playing in the background. Laurel and I are slowly dancing in the corner. Her arms wrapped around my shoulder and mine wrapped around her waist. We sway to the music as Laurel cuddles into my neck and plays with the tag on my shirt. Her dainty fingers connect with my skin and it gives me goosebumps.

"You smell nice," she says to me.

"What do I smell like?"

"Like a mix of coconut and mint. With maybe a hint of honey." I nuzzle my face closer into her hair and exaggerate a giant breath in. "Your hair smells like pears." I already knew that though. I kiss the side of her head and pull away from her, searching her face. "Laurel, I," but I get cut off.

Milly comes over laughing with the guy she's been dancing with for the past ten minutes. "Just wanted you to know I'm heading out." The guy behind her tugs on her arm, pulling her away from us. Milly laughs and waves at us over her shoulder. "Bye guys!" Her smile makes her look radiant.

Laurel and I dance through a couple more songs when a guy, probably in his seventies, comes over to us and tells me that I look a lot like his grandson.

"He must be a good-looking man," I brag.

"What's your name, sir?"

"I'm Danny. Hey, you wanna come play a game with me and my buddies?"

"Yes, that would be so fun!" Laurel cheers. "Come with me," he says, waving us toward him. He slowly hobbles away, his age showing. We follow Danny over to the table he's sitting at with his friends. A younger guy sitting next to Danny has a deck of cards in his hands and there's a pile of spoons laid out in the middle of the table.

"Gents," Danny gestures to the table, "this is….."

"I'm Lane and this is Laurel," I say as our introduction.

"Ah, yes, Laurel and Lane. They're gonna join us." Danny goes around the table and introduces us to Arthur, Otto, Willy, and Lloyd. They all greet us kindly as Arthur passes out the cards after shuffling the deck. "You guys know how to play Spoons right?" he asks.

"Yes, we know how," Laurel answers, smirking over at me. Jey, Naomi, Dallas, Laurel, and I used to play spoons in Laurel's basement. We used to place the spoons around the room and the second someone went running, you had better remember where the other spoons were located. One time when we played, Dallas and I went for the same spoon and he tripped over the carpet as I slipped on my sock and we smashed heads so hard, I had a purple bump on my forehead for the next week.

"Cool, let's get to playing now, youngin's"

For the next hour we played three games. Three. They moved so slow, I was sure one of them would die before they picked up their next card. After the second round, I looked over at Laurel and rolled my eyes back and stuck my tongue out, pretending to die. She giggled for a whole thirty seconds and didn't miss anything in the game. The crazy part was neither Laurel nor I won.

After our third round, they call it a night. We chat for a couple minutes before walking them to their cars. We wanted to make sure they got there safely. Suddenly, Laurel and I were alone in the parking lot with no plans for the rest of the night. The sun is starting to set and the roads are empty, despite it being a Friday night in the summer of a beach town.

I follow Laurel across the street, back toward where we found Milly earlier this evening. I can hear "You Send Me" by Sam Cooke from the restaurant. It's one of my favorite songs. Without thinking, I grab Laurel's hand in the middle of the street and spin her towards me.

"Let's finish our dance," I mumble into her hair.

She smiles at me and lets me pull her in. She rests one hand on my chest and holds my hand in her other one. I find her waist and lightly squeeze it. The silk of her dress feels soft in my hand, making me feel dizzy. She grabs ahold of my shirt and rests her head on my shoulder. We stand under the streetlight, swaying back and forth. I'm drunk by her.

I can feel endorphins shooting around my body.

Her hair blows in the wind and it tickles my arm. Her hand is light and delicate in mine. Her thighs graze mine as we sway. Her breaths are even, imponderous. She follows my rhythm, a slow undulation of waves. I drop my face to the crook of her shoulder and breathe her in. I can feel her heart beating. It matches the beat of mine. If I had to pick a moment to experience forever, it would be this moment.

A car drives by us but we stay where we are. Two songs go by when we finally look at each other. Without saying anything, we grab each other's hands and walk back to my truck.

"I have an idea," I say.

"What is it?"

"You'll see."

I drive us to one of our favorite spots overlooking the water. It's up on a hill, so you can see the water and the sun setting behind it. I pull in backwards and Laurel gets out of the truck while I grab some blankets in the backseat.

"Wow. This sunset is beautiful. Look at all the colors."

I look over my shoulder and see Laurel studying the water. Her face is illuminated by the setting sun and it makes her hair look like copper and her eyes look like pools of sea salt. God, I've never seen anything as beautiful as her. I snap a picture of her silhouette in the sunset.

I jump in the back of the truck and motion for Laurel to follow me. I put one blanket down and sit against the back of the truck, propping myself up. She sits right in between my legs and covers us with the other blanket. She rests against my chest and I wrap my arms around her waist, pulling her in closer to me.

"This is the most beautiful sunset I have ever seen," she says, "and I've seen a lot of them." A pause. "Look at how the colors are bouncing off the clouds. It's like I'm looking at it through a kaleidoscope." She puts her hands around her eyes, pretending she's using one. "That would be pretty dope to look at through one."

"Yeah, it would," I agree. There are a couple beats of silence.

"Weren't Danny and his friends just the cutest things? Otto has my heart forever. And Arthur? What. A. Doll. I could pinch his cheeks every day for the rest of time and I would never get bored of it."

Laurel has always had this weird thing for old people. Most people are annoyed by their turtle-like pace and their inability to comprehend modern ways, but Laurel isn't bothered by that. I think if she had to choose between people her own age or old people, she would choose old people.

She spins around, making my arms fall from her waist. She scoots back and moves the blanket higher up her body to expose her feet. "I think you owe me a foot massage now." She stretches her legs so her feet are now resting on my chest. I grab them with my hands and move them down to my lap.

"I already got naked, though. How about another time?" I playfully squeeze up and down her shins. It's really just an excuse to be able to touch her in the future.

"Hmphf," she says, crossing her arms. "That's what happens when you lose a lot. You have to keep up your end of the deal."

"C'mon," I say, pulling her body back to mine. "Let's just watch the sunset for now." I just want to enjoy this moment with her.

"Fine." She snuggles back up against me and covers us with the blanket. "But I will not forget that you owe me one. Don't think you're out of giving me a foot rub, Lane Andrew." Oh, no. The middle name. I know she's serious when she uses my middle name.

"I wouldn't dream of it."

We sit in silence for a couple minutes. I've been thinking about our day today and how happy it's made me. I was so scared to welcome her back into my life, for reasons I don't even necessarily know or understand. But now that I'm here with her, it isn't as scary as I thought it was going to be. But there's something I need to do. I need to apologize to her. I need her to know how sorry I am. I've been thinking for a while now that I need to talk to her about the accident. Apologize for everything. I spent countless nights wishing I could apologize to her and take back what happened. Countless hours crying so hard, my ribs hurt the next morning. Right now feels like the right moment.

"Laurel."

"Hm?" she hums. She lightly plays with my fingers.

"Laurel, I need to apologize to you."

She sits forward and turns to face me, concern written all over her face. "For what?" she asks. I tuck a strand of hair behind her ear.

"The accident, Laurel."

"Lane," She puts her hand on my chest to reject me, but I grab it. "No, please let me finish."

She slightly nods and waits for me to continue. I hold her hands in mine and stroke them while I get the courage to speak. I open my mouth to speak but tears stream down my face instead. She catches one with her thumb and searches my eyes, waiting for me to talk. I breathe out a sharp, quick breath and spill out everything.

"Laurel, I am so sorry." My chin quivers but I keep going. "That night, I think about it all the time. Every single day, I carry with me what I did to you. I will never forgive myself for it. This scar on your face…" I gently run my finger along the mark on her cheek.

"I blame myself. I blame myself for that." I take a deep breath. "I wish I never invited you to come home with me that night. I wish you never got in the car with me. I wish I listened to you about the rain. I wish I could go back to that night and keep it from happening. I am so sorry. I am so sorry for what happened. I have spent countless nights lying awake in my bed, thinking through what I could have done to prevent it from happening. If I had seen the truck sooner. If I was going slower or faster, we wouldn't have been hit. My dreams consist of nightmares where the accident happens over and over again, in a never-ending loop. I hear you scream in my dreams. The scream that left you when we got hit….." *I never knew a scream could leave a scar.*

I can't even finish my sentence because I start sobbing. I hid my face in my hands and curl against Laurel. She puts her hands around me as I cry. I cry and cry and cry until I feel like I have no more tears. Until I feel like I have let out every possible tear my body could produce. I sit up and meet Laurel's eyes, searching for understanding and grace.

Instead, I see that she's been crying, too. Laurel is usually a really hard crier, which is something that I admire about her. When she needs to cry, she just lets it out. Seeing tears spill over her cheeks reminds of the night her bunny died. He was a black and white rabbit with chocolate brown eyes. His name was Spencer. She really wasn't good at naming her pets. That night, my uncle Eli told me I needed to head over to the Owen's house for something. He told me that Laurel had been crying. I got there and she told me what happened and we sat in the treehouse together, talking about all the things she loved most about Spencer. She sobbed. Like almost hyperventilating sobbed. Once she calmed down, tears continued to quietly trail down her cheeks.

The look in her eyes right now reminds me of that night. Tears quietly falling down her face. Every time I see her cry, it breaks my heart. I hate thinking she's hurting enough to produce tears.

I'm brought back to reality when she moves around and straddles my body. Not in a sexual way, but so she can see me face-to-face. She can probably tell I'm overthinking. She holds my face in her hands and speaks. "Lane, please do not blame yourself. Please do not do that. I chose to get in the car with you. Neither of us knew what was going to happen. You cannot do this to yourself." She looks back and forth between my eyes, the concern and worry on her face growing with every word she speaks. I look away from her and she pulls my chin, forcing me to look at her again.

"I am to blame just as much as you are. We both made a choice that night to get into the car. It's not your fault, or mine." She pushes my hair out of my face and rubs her thumbs across my temples, keeping my tears from falling.

She puts her forehead against mine. "Lane, please listen to what I am saying. It was not your fault." I nod, knowing it will take me a long time to accept that. But hearing her say that breaks me into a million pieces. Most pieces contain relief, some still contain guilt.

"It's going to take me a long time to get to that point but thank you. I needed you to know how I felt. I needed you to know how sorry I was, how sorry I am. I ignored you for seven months because of how guilty I felt. I couldn't face what I did to you, so instead I ran. I'm sorry for that. You didn't deserve to be abandoned. I regret not reaching out to you every day, but I just didn't have the strength to face you."

"I don't blame you, Lane. I never did and I never will." It's quiet for a second. Then Laurel slowly pulls up her dress, exposing her upper thigh. There's a massive scar that runs diagonally across it. She takes my hand and runs it along the length of the scar. I can feel the ridges on her skin, the ins and outs of what all those stitches did to it. I feel her soft skin that surrounds the scar. It's perfection contradicts the imperfection of the jagged scar.

"I was once in pain. But I'm okay now."

As if I couldn't be broken anymore, what's left of my heart shatters. She's so strong.

She leans against my chest again, this time with her chest flush against mine. She wraps her arms so tightly around me I feel like I may pop. I squeeze her back and cry a little more into her chest. I haven't told her I'm planning on moving at the end of the summer and I know I need to because once I do tell her she's going to be blindsided. But I think we've talked about too much tonight to bring it up.

We stay like that for so long, we fall asleep. I suddenly jolt awake, my eyes staring up at the black expanse above me. And I realize the alluring sunset has been replaced by the moon and stars. Laurel starts to shift from my sudden movement but eventually finds a comfortable position against me.

I had another nightmare. This time, it wasn't about the accident. Laurel and I had spent a great day together. We went strawberry picking, kayaking, and then got dinner and ate in the park. We climbed in the back of my truck like how we're sitting right now, drinking wine and watching the stars above us. After over fifteen years of being in love with her, I finally tell her how I feel. I tell her how much I love her, that I've loved her since the day I first saw her in home economics. How I watched her get off the bus every day, wishing I could join her in that treehouse. I tell her how I want to chase sunsets with her, visit Victoria Falls with her, and spend the rest of my life trying to make her happy. When I finished, she laughed in my face. She said "How could you think I would love you back? Don't you see what you did to me?" She points to the scar on her face and then lifts her dress to show me the one on her thigh. She starts bleeding from the gash on the side of her head and blood trickles down the gaping hole on her thigh. "What makes you think you deserve my love, Lane? You ruined my life." Blood starts oozing from every orifice of her body as she crumples to the ground. I run over to her but by the time I reach her, she's disappeared, her clothes lying in a bloody pile in the bed of my truck.

I shake the dream from my mind, reminding myself that even if Laurel didn't love me back, she would never say those things to me, even though I deserve it. I wrap my arms around her and squeeze her tight, nuzzling my nose into her neck. I breathe her in and try to replace the memories of my nightmare with the smell of her skin, with the memories of this night.

I fall asleep after a while, dreaming of nothing.

The Accident

Chapter 19

It was October third. The weather was cool and crisp and the leaves were changing colors. Fall has always been my favorite season. There's just something about the crispness in the air and the autumnal hues that blanket the earth that seem so cozy and inviting to me.

Laurel and I are at Half & Half, stacking some books when I get a call from Jey. I take my phone out of my pocket and answer it.

"Hey, Jey. What's up?"

"Heyo. I got a game tonight and I was wondering if you and Laurel wanted to come along. You in? Dallas and Naomi will be there."

I lower the phone and ask Laurel if she wants to go. She nods her head, confirming she wants to.

"Yeah, we'll come. Tell Dallas and Naomi we'll find them there."

"Cool, cool. See ya later," Jey says, and hangs up. Jey doesn't like unnecessary phone chatting.

I lock my phone and put it back in my pocket and continue helping Laurel with the books.

"The forecast says it's supposed to storm," she says looking at the weather app on her phone. "I wonder if his game will end up getting canceled."

"I guess it's possible. But games are always so much more entertaining when it's raining. There's more slide tackling and the ball just flies across the turf. What?" I ask. Laurel's shaking her head at me, holding back a laugh.

"You're such a dude."

***

A couple of hours later, we arrive at the game and find our seats with Dallas and Naomi. We scoot between excited guests and rowdy college students decked out in their respective college gear.

"Hey, guys," Laurel and I say at the same time when we finally make it to Dallas and Naomi.

"Waddup?" Naomi says, smacking a hand clapper together. The teams are making their way to the center of the field to begin announcements.

"Nicky, where's your hat?" Naomi asks me, using her nickname for me.

"Right here," I say, grabbing it out of Laurel's arms. I put it on and take my seat next to Dallas. Wearing our matching hats is a tradition at Jey's games.

He fist bumps me and asks what we've been up to today.

"Well, we worked at Half & Half some and then went to the park and Lane pushed me on a swing. He pushed me so hard I fell off and scraped up my elbow," she says, pulling her sleeve up to show Naomi and Dallas her battle scars.

"Damn, dude. You don't know how to treat a girl," Dallas jokes.

"Eh, it was my fault. I told him to push me higher." I made up for it by placing a gentle apology kiss on her wound right after rushing to her side to see if she was okay.

Laurel straightens out the blanket we brought and places it over our laps. It's a chilly night, especially with the rain coming in and all.

The players are announced and we all stand up and shout when they call Jey's name.

"Where's Paisley?" Laurel asks.

"She couldn't make it. She has a major project due on Monday so she didn't have time," Naomi responds in between cheering for the team.

"Oh, that's too bad. I wanted to talk to her about something," Laurel says.

"What do you need to talk to her about?"

"None of your business," she nudges.

"Girl stuff?" Dallas asks. "It's usually girl stuff."

"It's not 'girl stuff,'" Laurel says, using quotations. "I just want her opinion on something."

"Soooo girl stuff," I joke. I get another nudge to the stomach.

The first half of the game flies by and the score is 2-1. Jey scored one of our goals and a player I don't know the name of scored the other. I take a break and head over to the concession stand to get us some apple cider and hot chocolate. The clouds are getting darker every minute and I know it's going to rain soon. It's only a matter of minutes.

I take the drinks back to our seats and see Naomi and Laurel chatting. Dallas is talking to some girl a few rows in front of us. Naomi notices me coming and motions for Laurel to stop talking. *Odd.*

"What are you ladies chatting about?"

"Like I said, none of your business," Laurel reiterates playfully. "Did you bring me a banana Laffy Taffy?" she asks when I hand her a cup of apple cider. She loves banana Laffy Taffy and I get her one every game, as long as they have it of course. I place it in her hand and she immediately shimmies off the wrapper and takes a bite.

Dallas comes back to his seat with a smile on his face while putting his phone back in his pocket. "What are you smiling about?" Naomi asks. "Did you finally use the bathroom without mommy and daddy there to wipe your ass?" she asks in a baby voice.

Laurel chuckles beside me as Dallas answers. "Ha ha, you're so funny. I got that girl's number, actually, if you must know. I've seen her at a couple of the games and we've made eye contact like at every single one of them. So I finally asked for her number."

"Good for you, brother. Now shut up, cause the game's starting again."

The game ends and Jey's team wins 3-1. It started raining about ten minutes ago and it's pouring now. When the game ended, Laurel and I booked it to my car after finalizing our plans to meet at Ben & Jerry's for ice cream.

We drive to the ice cream shop and the roads are nearly flooded. Laurel kept telling me to drive slower but I was already going fifteen under the speed limit. We hydroplaned once, but we made it safely. We get inside and meet everyone at our usual table in the back while we wait for Jey to show up. Once he gets here, we order our ice cream and make our way back to the table.

Everyone praises Jey on his goal tonight and we start bowing down to him and he curtsies before he takes his seat. "Number 13, that guy Derek Williams, man I wanna bash his face in. Did you see him slide tackle me? He should've gotten a yellow for that. He blamed it on the 'slick grass.' Such a pussy."

We spend the next thirty minutes talking and eating our ice cream. Laurel and I always switch ours when we've finished half of it. That way we get two flavors for the price of one. Well, I guess it's still technically for the price of two. But we each pay for one, so it's basically like the price for one. We finish up and say our goodbyes and I pull Naomi to the side when Laurel heads out to my car.

"Hey, what was Laurel saying to you? Is she okay?"

"I don't know, she never got to start because you came back so fast. I'm sure she's fine, Lane. Don't worry about it. She'll talk to Paisley and Paisley will tell Jey and then Jey will probably tell you. You'll find out soon enough."

I meet Laurel out in the car. I spend about eleven seconds in the rain and I'm completely soaked.

"Damn, it's really coming down out there," I say, cranking up the heat.

"Yeah, I'm soaked," she says, squeezing out her hair. Drops of rainwater drip from the ends of her hair onto the floor of my car.

"Wanna come over and watch a movie? I can drop you off at home once the rain slows down."

"Sure, that sounds great." She pulls the hood of her jacket over her head and sinks back into the seat, her knees facing the door.

I drive back to my house with the windshield wipers on at their fastest speed. I'm surprised they haven't flown off yet, they're moving so fast. I can't help but notice how off Laurel seems. She didn't say anything the whole way to my house.

I pull into the driveway, and we run inside with wet shoes and leaves stuck to the bottoms of them.

I give Laurel a pair of my shorts and a sweatshirt to change into while I throw her clothes in the dryer. She makes her way to my room and selects a movie on Netflix. She has it pulled up on the TV and is sitting on my bed waiting for me when I get back to my room. I shut the door and turn off the lights and climb onto the bed, sitting down next to her.

She starts the movie but I'm sad and distracted because she's sitting so far away from me. We cuddle every single time we watch a movie, so I'm wondering why she's being so distant right now. The movie plays for a couple of minutes when I grab her arm and whisper for her to "Come here." She scooches over with a faint smile on her face and finds her spots in between my legs. She lays against my chest and I wrap my arms around her, pulling her closer to me. I slide my hands through the pocket on her sweatshirt and kiss the side of her head. She snuggles into me and I finally feel relaxed.

I nod off every now and then and I'm suddenly startled awake. Laurel's smashing my cheeks together with her hands.

"Wake up," she whispers.

"I'm awake," I say, my voice cracking. "What time is it?"

"It's nearly 4 a.m."

"Yikes," I say, sitting up. "I should probably get you home. Your parents are probably worried. We don't usually stay out this late."

I stretch and grab her wrist and pull her to me. "Or you could just spend the night?" I want her to spend the night. That was the best sleep I've ever gotten. I always sleep better when I'm with her. I hug her tight and she hugs me back. I feel so content right now. She brushes her hand through my thick hair, sending chills down my spine. "I tried calling my parents when I woke up, but my phone died and I'm assuming they're asleep." She squiggles out from underneath me. I let her go and she leaves my bed. I shiver in her absence.

I get up and grab her clothes from the dryer and bring them back to my dark room. She comes back from the bathroom and I hand her her clothes and tell her to get changed. I can hear her strip but I can't see anything because it's so dark.

Dammit.

"I'll grab my keys," I tell her. I shine my phone flashlight around my room, looking for my keys. "Lane, I'm not sure you should drive tonight. It's still pouring outside. It'd probably be better if I just spent the night here," she says peering through my bedroom window.

"Maybe, but after the stern talking to your dad gave me when we were in high school about making sure you get home at a decent hour, I think it's best if I drive you home tonight," I say, finally finding my keys. I had never been so scared of Mr. Matthew than during that conversation. I have always dropped her off at an appropriate hour simply because of that one conversation.

I so badly want her to spend the night with me. But I'm terrified of Mr. Matthew's protective side and I don't want to disappoint her parents. Or make them mad at me. Or assume things about Laurel and me that aren't true, no matter how much I wish they were.

She follows me out the front door. We stand on the porch and find that it's still pouring. "Are you sure you wanna drive me back? It's raining really hard. And it's 4 a.m." She crosses her arms across her chest, making her look cold and small.

"Yeah, I'll just drive slow. I don't want your parents upset with either of us tomorrow and I'm not even tired anymore."

"Lane, I'm twenty-two years old. I don't think they can punish me anymore for coming home too late. Plus, they would understand. It's raining real bad." We walk toward the front door; Laurel still has her arms wrapped around her torso.

"It doesn't matter how old you are. I don't want to disappoint or disrespect them. Or make them worry for no reason," I add. I run to the car and I slide in, checking to see if she followed me. Laurel looks back and forth between my car and the front door. She ultimately decides to follow me.

I pull out of the driveway and make my way to the main road. It's *pouring* and the roads are flooded.

"Just be careful," Laurel reminds me. She sounds upset. I turn onto the next road.

"Laurel, I'm sorry if I said something that upset you. I wasn't trying to, I just -"

"It's okay, Lane. I'm not upset," she says, sighing. I side-eye glare at her, giving her a look that says I don't believe her. "Really. I've just got something on my mind," she persists.

"What is it? Was it what you wanted to talk to Paisley about?"

"Yeah, it is. I'm okay, no need to worry about anything," she assures me. It's quiet as I drive down the road. She stares out the window, tapping her fingers on her knee.

She looks like she's about to burst from keeping whatever it is she's hiding from me a secret. She's antsy and fidgety and isn't acting like herself.

It's obvious she's deep in thought. For a split second, I see a small smile on her face. When I look back over at her, it's gone.

"Lane?" Her voice is so heavy. It sounds full of confusion and contemplation and worry.

"Yeah?" I ask, trying to mask my concern. I think she's sniffling now. *God, what did I do? Is she crying?*

We're coming up to a red light. I slow down and stop. I look at her again, trying to see the expression on her face, waiting for her to say something. My eyes don't leave her until I see the light change to green in my peripheral. I quickly look forward so I can proceed through the light.

I look back over at Laurel when I step harder on the gas. "Laurel?" I ask. She looks up at me and screams my name, gripping her seat belt. There's terror in her eyes so I snap my head in a one-eighty so I'm looking out my window. I'm blinded by two headlights, and I don't have enough time to react.

We're gonna be hit.

I shout Laurel's name and find her hand in the split second before we're hit. Laurel shrieks so loud, I wouldn't be surprised if it was her voice that shattered the windows. It's the kind of shriek that gives me goosebumps and my heart drops to my stomach.

The back left side gets the most impact, but we're spun until Laurel's side of the car smashes into the semi-truck that hit us. We bounce off the truck and hydroplane on the water until we skid off the road, smashing into something else.

It happens so fast; I don't even have time to stop it from happening. Everything around us stills once the car finishes bouncing from the third impact. Glass falls. Everything is quiet for a second.

My head is laying against the headrest, feeling so heavy. It pounds as I try to lift it up. It's too heavy. I can't lift it. I try again, grunting from exertion and it comes off the seat. I begin looking around, trying to understand what just happened but I can't really make anything out. It's too dark and there's too much rain and my head feels too foggy.

I touch my forehead because it hurts and I feel thick, warm liquid. I see we hit a tree. There's a sharp pain in my side and I look down to find a large piece of glass sticking out from my abdomen. I throw my head back against the back of my seat, my entire body throbbing with pain.

I remember Laurel's with me. It's so dark, it takes several seconds for my eyes to adjust.

"Laurel," I cry. "Laurel." It comes out quieter. "Laurel," I scream for the third time, looking over at her seat. It takes everything in me to shift my head to the side. She's slumped forward, laying on top of the dashboard. Her seat belt is ripped in half. I let out a loud sob and reach for her with my right hand. The glass in my side moves and it sends a bolt of pain through my body.

"Oh, god," I cry, my head throbbing.

"Laurel," I say, desperately trying to get her attention. I lean forward and scream through the pain in my side. I get frustrated and grip the piece of glass with my left hand and yank it out of my abdomen. There's blood everywhere. I scream out in pain, my head still throbbing, my side gushing blood. I let out a breathy scream through clenched teeth.

I drop the piece of glass and unbuckle my seat belt and reach over the center console to get to her. I pull on her shoulder and let out a muffled sob when I see the piece of glass sticking out of her face. It looks like a horror movie- one that I'm somehow in. With trembling hands, I take the piece of glass out and throw it out the busted window in front of me. Blood seeps down her cheek as I scrape a couple of smaller pieces of glass from the wound.

"God! This cannot be happening!" I scream. I frantically wipe blood from her face, hoping whatever I'm doing will make it somehow stop the flow. I wipe Laurel's blood on my pants, giving up, the blood continues to trickle down her face.

"Laurel," I say, shaking her. She falls back in my arms and it's then when I see the bloody slash across her left thigh. Blood has soaked through her shredded jeans and I wail when I see her bone. My hands are shaking and I feel bile rising in my throat. I place Laurel against the seat and lean behind her to empty out my stomach. I gag and choke on throw up and bile for what feels like hours. I look over the seat at Laurel and she still hasn't moved. *Her pulse.* I don't know why I didn't check before, but I grab her hand and put my fingers on her wrist, *praying* I feel a pulse.

I do.

I immediately get a rush of adrenaline. I gently drop her arm on the seat and turn to my door and start kicking it open. All I can smell is blood. There's rain coming into the car, soaking my clothes and hair. I push my hair out of my face and kick the door open with everything I have in me. It opens awkwardly and I immediately squeeze out of the small gap and head toward Laurel's door. The front of the car is smashed into a tree, so I make my way toward the back of the car.

The pain in my side is excruciating. I stumble and drop to the ground from the throbbing in my abdomen and the sting coming from my right leg. I look down and see a cut on the back of my ankle, blood soaking my sock and shoe. My sweatpants have tears in them and I'm missing my left shoe.

I hop around to the other side of the car, taking shallow breaths every couple feet. My ribs ache every time I take a breath. I must have broken a rib. Pieces of broken glass stab through my sopping wet sock as I walk. I make it to Laurel's side after what feels like a lot longer than it should've taken me and I finally get the door open after seven tries. I fall to the ground on my knees when it finally creaks open, barely hanging on its hinges.

The rain continues to pour down around me, making it harder to see in the dark. My fingers

tremble as I think about my next move, not only
from the adrenaline pumping through my body, but
because it's cold. The rain mixed with the chilly
October night and the reality of the situation I'm in
sends goosebumps up and down my arms.

I look in the grass next to me and make sure there's
no glass scattered around. I grab Laurel's arms and
as gently as I can, I pull her out of the car and sit
her up against the side of the car. She looks awful.
Blood is still oozing out of her leg. There's a trail
running down her cheek from where I pulled the
piece of glass out that flows down her chest,
staining her white sweater. Her face is bruised and
scratched all over. Her left eye already bruised and
swollen shut.

Her sweater sleeve is pushed up and from the light
in the car, I can see the scratches on her arm from
earlier when she fell off the swing. I wish I could go
back in time to when that was the only mark upon
her perfect skin.

I rake my hands through my bloodied hair,
screaming at the top of my lungs. A thought
interrupts my screaming. *Phone.* I look around me,
searching for a phone. I can't see, it's so dark
outside and the rain continues to pour. I hobble back
to the driver's side of the car and search the
floorboards for my cell phone. No luck. I pick up

the hat I was wearing and throw it on the asphalt as hard as I can, screaming out in frustration. My ribs ache.

I remember there was another vehicle and a surge of hope, desperation, and fear run through me. I run, more like hobble, back to the road and find the semi-truck that hit us. I move over to it as fast as I can and open the driver's door. I must've asked the driver a question because he's mumbling. He's slumped over the steering wheel, so I sit him up-right and begin looking for any injuries. It's then that I notice the bottle of beer in his hand. All I feel is *rage*. I take the bottle from his hand and throw it against the asphalt and scream out every curse word I can think of.

I take the guy out of the truck, who's mumbling and trying to push me off of him. I sit him up against the large wheel and question him. I want to beat him until he looks worse than Laurel does but I don't have the energy.

"Do you have a phone? Where's your phone? I need to call an ambulance," I question him desperately. His eyes roll to the back of his head.

I kick the tire next to him several times, causing the cut on my ankle to gush blood and my ribs to burn.

I scream at him. "*You fucking piece of shit*! Where's your phone?"

It's obvious he won't be answering me so I climb into the truck cab and find a cell phone sitting in the passenger seat. I grab it and run back to my car to check on Laurel, grabbing my chest, trying to ease the intense pain there. I dial 911 as I make it back to her. Her face is so pale and she's lost a lot of blood. She suddenly coughs and blood spews out of her mouth. I drop the phone and grab her. "Oh, god, Laurel. Stop it!" I grab her and force her forward so she doesn't choke. She's still coughing and blood continues to drip down her chin and come out her nose. "Stop it, Laurel!" I cover my ears with my hands and squeeze my eyes shut, wishing I wasn't in this nightmare right now. I have no idea how to help her.

If only I had listened to her when she said she didn't want to leave.

I remember I was calling the police. I pick the phone back up and hit the green button, finally calling. It rings twice before someone picks up.

"Hello, this is the Hull Police Department. How can I help you?"

I yell, "There's been an accident on Wylee street! There's a girl....she's lost a lot of blood!"

"Have you checked her for a pulse?" the operator asks me.

"Yes, she has one, but she's unconscious. But she's lost a lot of blood. I can see her bone," I say, trying to explain the severity of what just happened. I look back at her leg and almost throw up again. I take a deep breath, despite the searing pain in my chest, and swallow. I start crying and the operator tries to calm me down. She asks me what happened and I relay the events of the past - I don't even know how many minutes - telling her the guy that hit us had a bottle of beer in his hand.

She tells me there are ambulances on the way and not to hang up. I sit next to Laurel, pleading with everything inside of me that she hasn't lost too much blood. She's still unconscious, despite me shouting her name over and over again. I straddle her on my knees, careful not to touch her leg. I cup her cheeks in my hands, telling her how sorry I am, begging her to open her eyes. I pull her face to my chest and sob. I can feel blood matted in her hair so I check her head for a wound. There's a small cut at the back of her head. I feel so helpless. *What can I do?*

I take my soaking wet sweatshirt off slowly and peel my undershirt off. It's glued to my skin with blood, rain and sweat. Only then do I realize how bruised my ribs are, the bloodied gash from the glass, and the burn mark across my body from my seat belt. I put my sweatshirt back on and take my shirt in my hands. I lightly wrap it around Laurel's leg, hoping to keep any dirt or glass or grass out of it. I sit next to her and I realize then that I'm whistling. But it's a heavy whistle, not the light kind my father used to sing. It goes in and out and shakes with my scattered breathing.

I need to watch her to make sure she's okay, but it's so difficult to look at her. This isn't my Laurel. I'm concerned she doesn't seem at all aware of what's going on.

I lay on the ground and rest my head against her good thigh, taking her hand in mind. I lace our fingers together and sob. She isn't holding my hand back. Her fingers are slack in mine and it scares the hell out of me. I lay there, praying with everything inside of me that the ambulances will be here soon.

Just then, I hear the distant sounds of sirens, and then out of nowhere three ambulances park in front of us. They move quickly but methodically when they grab Laurel's limp body and place her on a gurney. Her body looks lifeless. The EMTs say things I don't understand and are asking me questions I don't have the voice to answer. I scream and cry when they put her in the ambulance and drive away from me. Another EMT tries to get me to calm down, telling me they're taking her to a hospital, ensuring that she's in good hands, all the while trying to drag me to the ambulance meant for me.

The adrenaline is leaving my system and I can feel myself starting to lose consciousness. I drop to the ground, my knees making contact with the asphalt first. The EMT is in my face, saying things to me I can't comprehend right now. My eyes are heavy and my head throbs and my side hurts and my throat is sore and I'm soaking wet and my ankle stings and my heart has never been more broken. I let my eyes close and the last thing I remember is hearing Laurel scream.

One Day, Two Mistakes

Chapter 20

Laurel wakes up a couple minutes after I do. I sat there for a while just listening to her breathing and watching the waves roll in and out, thinking about our conversation from earlier and the nightmare I had. I deserve to be slapped across the face, forgotten about. But Laurel would never do that to me. In some ways, I feel as though I've slapped *her* across the face. Those seven months of avoiding her are evidence of that.

Laurel's asleep next to me on the blanket, her face pressed up against my thigh.

She moves around, trying to get comfortable again. "Laurel," I whisper.

"Hm?" she moans, groggily.

"We should probably go," I tell her, even though I wish we could stay like this forever. I nudge her until she finally sits up. She sits up and to my surprise, climbs into my lap.

"Do I have drool on my face?" she asks, rubbing her eyes.

"Actually, yes you do," I say, laughing. "I think there's some on my shirt, too," I say, looking down at it.

"Oh, gosh, that's embarrassing," she says, rubbing at the dried spot of drool.

"Not as embarrassing as the farts I heard…"

Laurel takes the blanket we were using and wraps it around my head. "Hey, you jerk! I do not fart in my sleep." I take the blanket off my head and shoot her a look that says, "Come on, be honest." "Okay, fine. Maybe I fart in my sleep." I chuckle and grab the blanket and fold it up.

"What time is it anyway?" I check my watch. "It's three am. We've been asleep for nearly five hours."

"Yikes, good thing nobody needs me tomorrow."

"I need you tomorrow."

I can see her blush in the moonlight.

***

I drive us back to my place and we both crash again. Laurel fell asleep in the car so I carried her in and put her in my bed while I took the couch. It was all I could do not to crawl into the bed with her. She probably wouldn't have minded, but come on, she's asleep.

I wake up around ten o'clock and decide to start cooking breakfast. I pull out my phone and play some Frank Ocean while gathering some fruit and the necessary ingredients to make breakfast sandwiches.

I'm reminded of my nightmare last night from a smudge of ketchup left in the sink. The blood oozing from Laurel's thigh, soaking her silk dress, staining it crimson. Laurel gave me something I haven't been able to give myself: relief from my guilt. She told me everything I thought I needed to hear but it still wasn't enough.

My thoughts are interrupted when Laurel joins me in the kitchen as I begin to fry some eggs and toast some bread.

"Good morning," she sings through a stretch. She joins me over the stove and rubs her hands together when she sees what I'm making.

"Yummmm. I'm so hungry."

"Could you grab the avocado from the fridge?"

"You have avocado? Since when did you get so bougie?"

"I think Paisley bought it but I'll replace it." Laurel spreads avocado on the toast and peppers it with different spices. I slide the eggs on top and sprinkle cheese on top, letting it melt down the side of the toast. She cuts up some strawberries and places them on the plate, making it look like a flower.

"You know the second I sit down those are going straight into my mouth, right?"

"Yes," she swats the hand towel at me. "I just thought it was pretty," she says, perfecting the flower.

We shove our faces like we've never eaten before and finish our toast in what feels like a world-record time. We clean up our dishes and decide to go for a walk before I have to go to the mechanic shop this afternoon.

We head over to the beach and walk up and down the shoreline. The whole walk to the beach, I was thinking about last night. I want so much with Laurel. I want a life with her. I want to be happy with her. I want to dance with her in the rain all night and buy sandwiches for hungry people on the street together. I want to have kids and grow old with her. I want late nights with her where we fall asleep together, holding one another. I want endless adventures and happy and sad moments. I want everything with her. And I'm terrified of what her response would be if I ever told her. She would probably tell me she doesn't feel the same way and I would be heartbroken; my world completely and utterly shattered. I can't imagine being with anyone else. And being told that won't happen...I can't bear it. It seems easier to never have her than to be rejected by her.

Flashes from my nightmare from last night blind me. Even if she did feel the same way, I wouldn't deserve her.

I'm brought back to reality by the heat. It's a hot day, so fifteen minutes into our walk, we run into the waves fully clothed. I shake off my thoughts, trying to enjoy the moment I have with her right now. We spend the next thirty minutes floating in the water, splashing each other, and having hand-stand competitions. Laurel's a lot better at hand standing than I am.

We walk uncomfortably back to my house, my socks sloshing in my shoes with every step. It's awfully humid outside and my skin feels sticky and moist. My shirt is suctioned to my body and when I move my arms when I walk, I can feel a rash starting to form. I feel so uncomfortable, my mood is turning sour.

"Don't you think that's important, Lane?" Laurel asks me. I was so consumed with my thoughts that I don't even know what she's talking about.

"Uh, yeah, it is." She stops in her tracks and swats at my arm, which makes me annoyed. "I knew you weren't listening to me," she says, slightly rolling her eyes. I just look at her. She lets out a quick breath of air. "Lane, I just asked you if you thought collecting pebbles off the side of the road was important." She walks past me and continues walking, saying "What's wrong with you? You seem off." I know she doesn't say it to make me angrier, but it does. She probably doesn't even know I'm angry.

"Nothing's wrong with me, I'm fine," I retort, flouncing away.

"Yeah, that's not true." She catches up to me and grabs my arm, turning me toward her. "Hey, what's wrong? Talk to me." I'm getting angrier the longer we spend in this heat. I need to go shower off and clear my head.

"I said I was fine, Laurel. Let me go." I snatch my arm from her grip.

"Lane…"

"I said I'm fine!" I snap at her. She draws away from me, looking equally hurt and confused.

"Can you just drop it?" I ask, walking away, leaving her behind me. I don't hear her footsteps and I know she isn't following me. I keep walking, my stubbornness getting the best of me.

***

After a shower I go to work at the garage, hoping to pop in my headphones and fly through my assignments. I walk into my uncle Eli's office, ready to get this shift over with. I open his door and he has music playing so loud he doesn't hear me come in. Ivy is leaning against the wall, looking at a magazine, coffee mug in hand.

"Hey, Lane! Good to see ya," Ivy nods at me.

"Hey, Aunt Ivy. How's it going?" She sips her coffee and I take that as her answer. I guess it's been a long morning.

As I walk closer to his desk, I can see my name across the screen and the name of the hospital I was taken to after the accident. I can see he has my medical bills pulled up on his computer and a credit card in hand. *Is he paying my medical bills?*

As soon as I realize what he's doing, I feel betrayed. And enraged. I urgently walk over to his desk and slam my hand down beside him. "What are you doing?" I yell. "Are you paying my medical bills?"

He jumps so high his glasses fall sideways on his face. He fixes them and says, "Lane, please don't be mad at me. Let me explain."

"No," I cut him off. "You promised me months ago that you would let me pay for them by myself. You told me you stopped helping me."

"Please calm down," he says, shifting in his chair.

"I told you *I* wanted to pay for them from now on. I told you that like three months ago! You've been lying to me for three months!" I know I'm irrationally angry right now, but I really couldn't give a shit.

Ivy's been watching us, waiting for a good time to butt in. "Lane, please calm down. Let's sit and discuss this," she adds. I wave her off, focusing on my uncle Eli.

"Lane, I'm trying to help you. I didn't tell you I was still paying them because I was worried you would be upset. I'm just trying to help you, son. That's hundreds of thousands of dollars that you owe - "

"Don't." I cut him off. "Don't call me son." I watch his face fall as I say it. I know I've hurt him. "I didn't ask you to help me. I don't want your help." I spit. "The accident was my fault, so I have to pay for it. Don't you dare finish that payment."

"Lane Andrew Peterson!" Ivy yells at me.

Shaking, I turn around and slam the door shut behind me, feeling so much worse than I did this morning.

Shit to Clean Up

Chapter 21

A week and a half has gone by. Ms. Elsie's, my uncle Eli's, therapy, avoiding Laurel at all costs.

In my most recent visit to Dr. Therin's office, I relayed everything that happened between me and Laurel and me and my uncle Eli. I told him about apologizing to her, leaving out all the intimate details of the night. Those were too personal to share. I told him about losing my shit on both of them. I felt so ashamed. I *feel* so ashamed. So we spent the past couple sessions this week discussing my shame and where my stubbornness and sudden anger might've come from. It reminded me of our conversation about my unexpected run-in with Mrs. Malani, when he asked me what I thought my tipping point was. I still haven't figured that out.

Giving Dr. Therin a replay of what happened this past week was hard to do. It was hard to talk about. It's embarrassing explaining two outbursts as a twenty-three-year-old. After talking with Dr. Therin, I understood I was feeling out of control from my dream about Laurel. I'm terrified of losing her for a second time. Then, I pushed her away again to regain that control and on top of that, I took it out on my uncle. I said some horrible things to him, which I still haven't apologized for.

I've been hyping myself up the past couple of days, preparing to apologize to my uncle Eli today. I've never been good at conflict or apologies. I get to the garage a little before opening so we can talk in private. Being one of the most hard-working men I know, he's at the garage long before it opens and long after it closes. It's just who he is.

I find him in the kitchen, waiting for the coffee to finish brewing. One of the guys recently bought him a Keurig and he's been trying to figure it out for a while now. He looks determined and concentrated, his brow furrowing with impatience. You'd think since he's a mechanic he would be able to figure out how to operate a Keurig, but I've shown him how to use it multiple times and he still has trouble with it. I open the door fully and walk in. *Breathe in, breathe out.*

"Hey, bug. You're here early."

"Yeah, I was um, actually hoping we could talk." He pours the finished coffee in his mug. "Sure thing. Let's go somewhere quieter." We walk to the back of the garage, which has a little lounging area for breaks. Most of the time, the guys hang out in here after work and play poker. He takes a seat and I sit down across from him, my leg bouncing up and down.

"Okay, um." I start. "Look, what I said to you last week…" I pause. *Breathe in, breathe out.* "Uncle Eli. I can't even begin to tell you how sorry I am for what I said to you. First, I yelled at you for doing something so kind. Only a terrible person with horrible anger issues does that." I chuckle awkwardly, trying to make this easier. He doesn't laugh. I shake my head to collect my thoughts.

"Look, I should have never said those things to you. I was mad about something else and I took it all out on you and that was so wrong of me. I said horrible things to you that I knew were going to hurt you. I apologize for that. You've been nothing but a father to me since I lost mine and I can never thank you enough for that. I'm sorry for losing my shit on you." I look down at my hands and play with the tablecloth in my lap. "You've spent so much time and money on me these past thirteen years and you don't deserve to have to pay for my medical bills. I'm an adult now and I meant it when I said I didn't want you to pay for them. You've helped me more than you know. Please, I can pay for them myself." He's quiet, thinking. There's a silence that lingers in the air, making goosebumps appear on my arms. He rubs his beard and places his hand on his cheek. His eyes look old and tired and my heart breaks for how I hurt him.

"First, thank you for apologizing. Those words did hurt me." He pauses and I can see his eyes growing tears. "I've thought of you as a son for the past thirteen years and hearing you say that broke my heart. Losing my brother was hard, and I know losing a father was so hard on you, especially at such a young age. Add growing up without a mother on top of that. But I have *never* tried to replace your father, Lane."

"I know. And I've never thought that. I don't even know why I said it. I think I was just hurting and I wanted someone to feel the pain I was in. So I said something completely false and so terrible. Please forgive me."

"I do forgive you, Lane. I will always forgive you. But there's something you should know about the medical bills." He shifts in his seat, his eyebrows furrowing. Whatever he's about to tell me must be important, making me equally nervous and curious. "When your father died, he left me a large sum of money. Money he wanted me to use to care for you. It was meant for medical emergencies or for school, if and when you decided you wanted to go to college. I'd been saving it all those years so you could go to the school of your dreams, get away from Hull for a while. But you decided college wasn't for you, so I had all this money left over. When the accident happened, I immediately started paying the bills with the money your father left for you." He stopped for a second, letting me soak in all this new information.

"Thank you for being concerned about me spending my money, but it wasn't mine, Lane. It was your fathers. I'm sorry I kept that from you, but he never wanted you to know about it."

I'm stunned. I never knew my father had left me any money. I didn't even know that he had any money to leave me. "Uncle Eli, I'm so sorry." I place my head in my hands, ashamed of my actions as of late.

"You can stop apologizing, Lane. I already told you that I forgive you. I think you should go find the person you really need to apologize to." He winked at me and starts to leave with his coffee in his hand.

"Um, could you also apologize to Ivy for me? I know she'll understand that this next apology is a little more pressing."

A soft smile warms his face. "Sure thing, bug."

Of course, the second I see Ivy next, I'm going to apologize to her myself. But Ivy's understanding.

I immediately head over to Half & Half, knowing exactly who I need to apologize to. I speed walk inside, my hands shaking in my pockets. I hear Mrs. Malani's laugh before I see them, so I follow it. I round the corner and see them sitting on the floor behind a shelf, organizing a new box of donated books.

She leans around the shelf to welcome in the customer and is obviously surprised to see me instead.

"Oh, Lane. What are you doing here?" She stands up as Mr. Matthew looks over his shoulder at me. He follows suit and rises.

"Um, I was wondering if I could talk to you guys." My whole body is sweating.

"Yeah, sure, Lane. Everything okay?" Mr. Matthew asks. He wipes his hands on his pants after placing the book he was holding on the shelf.

"Yeah. Can we go to the back?" I follow them to the back room where their office is. I sit down on the funky couch and hold a pillow to my chest. Laurel and I picked out this couch. Laurel's parents took us to Goodwill and told us we could pick out a couch. She fell in love with a loveseat that looked like it was made with thirty different types of fabric.

It kind of hurt my eyes to look at, but I told her she could pick.

I shake my leg up and down as Mrs. Malani shuts the door and sits on the desk in front of Mr. Matthew, who sits on the rolly chair behind her. *Are my toes sweating? I didn't know toes could sweat.*

Here we go. I squeeze my thighs.

"I owe you a major apology. Both of you. For hurting Laurel in the first place and then for ignoring her and you for seven months. Your family has done so much for me and I sincerely apologize to both of you for how I've treated you. I was messed up for a long time after the accident, I still am, but I'm working on it. I blamed myself for the accident and I still haven't completely worked through that. But, since reconnecting with Laurel, I've been getting closer to accepting that. I hope we can work through the hurt I caused your family. I miss you guys and I want nothing more than to rekindle our relationship."

They stare at me, as if they weren't expecting me to say any of that. I finally meet Mrs. Malani's eyes and I can see the tears forming. One falls, leaving a small wet trail all the way down her cheek.

"Thank you, Lane." She walks over to me and kneels down to look me in the eyes. She cups my face with her hands, making me feel comforted and understood. "What happened was difficult, Lane. And I can't lie and say we weren't hurt. We still feel it every day. We love you like our own son and losing you was difficult, especially after watching Laurel struggle for so long. We don't blame you at all for the accident, please know that." She wipes a tear away with her thumb, making my skin prickle under her comforting touch. The touch of a mother.

"We do love you, Lane. We never would have blamed you. Like Malani said, we really struggled for a while, but we've been doing better and we're glad to see you've been doing better, too."

"And we're so happy you reconnected with Laurel! That's all I've been hoping for. And I understand you had to do it on your own time. I also need to apologize for that day in the pottery shop. I gave you the cold shoulder and that was wrong and immature of me and -"

"Mrs. Malani, you don't need to apologize. I completely understand." She pulled me into a tight hug and then Mr. Matthew joined in. We all sniffled and then started laughing as we sat in our hug.

"Thank you, guys, really. I'm so lucky to have you."

"Nonsense! We're lucky to have you."

***

I drive to the spot Laurel and I watched the sun set nearly two weeks ago. I sit in the back of my truck and hang my legs off, swinging them back and forth, matching the motion of the waves beneath me. The conversation I had with my uncle Eli rotates around my mind.

One thing I've learned about myself through therapy is that it takes me a long time to process things. Learning this new information was a shock to my system and I had no thoughts. Just absorbing it, taking it all in. Hours later, I now realize how many questions I have. *Where did my dad get the money from? Was it just his savings? Why didn't he want me to know about it? How much money was it? Why did he save it for me?* Maybe I'll never know the answers to these questions.

Squeezing their way in between the questions about my dad's mystery money are thoughts about the Owens's. Now that I've calmed down and have apologized to Mr. Matthew and Mrs. Malani, I need to apologize to Laurel again. I don't know why I keep trying to push her away. I'm the worst version of myself without her. These past two-ish weeks have left me feeling empty and craving her.

I sit in the sun for a little while longer and feel the breeze flow through my shirt. It ruffles my hair, making it look wilder and more tangled than it usually looks. I get in the front seat of my truck and drive, determined to find Laurel and make sure that I never lose her again.

The only thing is, I'm moving in a month.

Betty Rose

Chapter 22

I drive to the Owens' old house, hoping to God that I find Laurel in the treehouse. I park my truck and bolt it up the stairs, cracking the door open. Before I see her, I hear a sniffle, confirming she's here.

I step inside and she whips her head in my direction, startled. "Lane, oh my god! What the hell are you doing?" Her tone turns sharp. "What do you want, Lane?" She clutches her chest and takes a few deep breaths.

"Sorry, I didn't mean to scare you. I was hoping I would find you here."

"Why, so you can leave me again?" I can tell she's been crying. *Ouch*. But I deserved that.

I breathe a deep, hurt sigh. Not because she hurt me, but because once again, I've hurt her. Once again, I've let her down.

I walk over to her on the ground and sit beside her, taking her hand in mine. She tries to pull away, but I keep my grip and she immediately stops pulling away from me.

"Laurel, I could never do enough to show you how truly sorry I am. For everything. For the accident. For ignoring you for seven months. For being indecisive. For treating you as anything less than my best friend. I hurt every day, Laurel and it's easier to blame someone else and lash out than it is to face what I've done."

She looks at me, then looks away, not quite convinced I'm here for good.

"I apologized to your parents today." I say quietly. She snaps her head in my direction and meets my eyes, concern and wonder overflowing from her face.

"What do you mean you apologized to them?"

"Well, I had a conversation with my uncle Eli two weeks ago and I kind of lost it on him. I apologized to him this morning and then he said I needed to go make things right with some other people. And that's where your parents come in. I told them I was sorry for the accident. Sorry for leaving you and ignoring you. Sorry for letting them down. Sorry for everything. We cried and thankfully they forgave me. I don't know what I would've done if they didn't."

Her face has softened and I can tell she isn't as mad anymore.

"Once again, I owe you an apology. And an explanation." She looks at me, urging me to continue.

I've never been good at being vulnerable and open. I usually hold it in tight, lock it up inside. It's easier to let people think I'm okay. But I've learned that doesn't get me anything except more hurt and heartbreak. I give Laurel all the details, holding nothing back.

"That night we went to watch the sunset, I had a horrible dream. It was about the accident. You were gushing blood from all the places you were injured and you told me you blamed me. I just couldn't shake those words, that image of you bleeding. I'm sorry, Laurel. I've been working on accepting your affirmations and acceptance from that night. But it's hard. I have good days, but I also have bad days. I get really in my head, and it's hard to keep from spiraling. I'm not asking you to forgive me right now, but I'm just asking you to be patient with me."

She nods, taking my confession in. "I think I can do that. However, I want you to be honest with me. Please stop pushing me away, Lane." Her voice gets shaky as she looks me in the eyes. They swell with tears and spill over. I hold her face and wipe a tear away. "I'm here, Laurel. I'm not leaving anymore. I've got to learn to face it and not back down. And that starts with you."

***

I went to work at the pottery shop feeling much better than I have the past two weeks. I patched things up with my uncle Eli, finally got the guts to apologize to the Owens's, made things right with Laurel, and even learned that my dad has been looking out for me since he died.

I busy myself with some new plate and bowl designs. I was inspired by the couch in the office at Half & Half and decided to make a matching set, each item a completely different pattern than the next. I even made some matching cups.

It was a pretty slow day customer wise. Most of our customers consist of older women, all who love to hear about my life. Most of the things I tell them are untrue: how happy I am, what I'm looking forward to in life. This one customer's name is Betty Rose. She used to be good friends with Honey and Ms. Elsie. She came over sometimes to watch soaps with them. Well, she comes into the shop pretty often and usually buys items for birthdays or anniversary gifts.

She always asks me the same questions. How I'm doing, my plans for the future, and if I have a girlfriend yet. Her thick, Caribbean accent and sassy attitude makes the questioning a little more tolerable.

I haven't had a girlfriend, if you could even call it that, since the ninth grade. She was some girl I really couldn't have cared less about. But Jey told me that she liked me and there was no way I was going to tell Laurel how I felt, so I figured, why not? We "dated" for like two months before I finally stopped sitting with her at lunch. It was all the talk at school that week.

Betty Rose likes to hear all the gossip. So, today when she asks me whether or not I have a girlfriend, I respond, "Nope, I still don't Betty Rose. The girl I love...I don't deserve her. Never will."

"Now that's just wrong, Lane. You deserve any girl out there. Whole wide world, seven point something billion people innit. Ain't nobody out there you don't deserve. Who she be, child?"

"Someone I have history with, for starters, which probably isn't great. She means too much to me to possibly ruin what we have by professing my love to her."

"Any girl would be lucky to have a kind, handsome man like you. Wouldn't she?" she turns to a customer to ask. The customer ignores us. "I can tell you right now, you wrong about that one, son." Betty Rose laughs and gently slaps my cheek, making me laugh with her. Her rings feel cold against my skin, sending a small shiver down my spine. Her chuckling stops abruptly and she gets serious. The shiver intensifies.

"Let me tell you right now, Lane. I don't know who this mystery girl is," she says, flicking her hands in the air like a fortune teller, "but I bet if ya told her how ya heart felt, ya might just sweep her off her damn feet."

"Yeah, well, I guess we'll never know."

She gives me a face like she's going to beat me with her purse. Sometimes she genuinely scares me. "Let me know when you finally tell her how ya feel. " With that, Betty Rose sashay's out of the store, leaving me to contemplate telling Laurel how I really feel.

I shouldn't, right?

The Camping Trip

Chapter 23

This weekend is our annual camping trip. The Bishop family and I used to go camping every single summer on the Cape. We would sleep in tents, roast marshmallows, go kayaking, cook breakfast over the fire. All that classic camping stuff. Mr. Reggy and Mrs. Elora stopped coming once Naomi was in eleventh grade. Somehow Jey convinced them that it was weird that they went camping with their "adult" children. I think it was more about Jey wanting to have fun without his parents there than him thinking it was weird that we all went camping together. I never thought it was weird though. I thought it was nice.

I haven't really been looking forward to this weekend. Things between Jey and I were a little tense earlier this summer and I've been trying my best to avoid spending too much time with Paisley. I am looking forward to spending some time with Dallas and Naomi though. I haven't gotten to see them much so far this summer.

We leave in an hour and I've just finished packing when Jey walks into my bedroom, shirtless and sweaty from soccer practice. "Hey, you gonna be ready to go soon? Dallas, Naomi, Paisley and Sonali should be here in ten."

"Sonali? As in Paisley's friend from school? I didn't know she was coming."

"Yeah, Paisley asked if she could come. Sorry, I guess I forgot to tell you."

"Are you serious? You know how I feel about Sonali. She's always flirting with me and being so touchy. I hate it."

"She does not. And I'm pretty sure she has a boyfriend now. She'll probably leave you alone." I hate this. I already wasn't really looking forward to this weekend and now Sonali's coming? She's always touching my hair and "accidentally" bumping into me. This weekend just got worse. I decide it's better to ignore that comment and move on.

"Are you gonna be ready?" I say, motioning toward his disgustingly dirty body.

"Yeah, I just gotta hop in the shower and pack some clothes. Paisley and I gathered everything else up last night. It's already in Paisley's van." Paisley drives one of those old Volkswagen buses and it's perfect for hauling loads of camping gear.

"Cool."

"Mind letting them in when they get here?" he shouts, heading into the bathroom and turning the shower on.

"Yeah, I can do that." Just then, Naomi swings open the front door.

"They're here!" Laurel shouts from her spot on the couch. I've been trying to keep her out of my room so she doesn't see that it's practically empty. So when she runs over to let me know, I bolt out of my room and shut the door behind me.

"Guess you don't need to let them in," Jey says as he steps into the shower.

Naomi slumps down on the couch and takes out her phone, probably fidgeting on Instagram or Snapchat. Laurel runs back over to the couch and lays on Naomi's shoulder. Dallas comes in last behind Paisley and grabs a glass from the cabinet and fills it with the last bit of chocolate milk from the fridge.

"Really?" I ask.

"What?" he looks at the carton and then back at me.

"You should've just drank it from the carton. Why dirty a glass?"

"I was trying to be polite. This isn't my house."

"Well, thanks. But next time, don't dirty a glass. Now, you have to wash it." I grab the sponge and put a dab of soap on it. "With soap and water." I know I'm acting unreasonably upset about a dirty cup, but I can't shake the annoyance I feel about Sonali coming.

"Fair," is all he says. Sonali finally comes in and I roll my eyes. She's dressed in white jeans and a sequin tank top with matching sequin flip flops. *Who wears pants in the summer?* I hide my annoyance and greet her. She answers me with an exaggerated smile and gives me a hug, which I reluctantly give back by patting her once on the shoulder. She makes herself comfortable on the couch and starts chatting with Naomi.

Jey's just finished his shower and he walks through the living room in his towel. His bedroom is on the other side of the house, which means he usually walks around half-naked a lot. Most of the time, he's fully naked.

Laurel covers her eyes as she passes by her and says, "Ew, Jey. Put some clothes on."

"That's literally what I'm going to do. Besides, it's not like you've never seen me shirtless before." He flexes and Naomi rolls her eyes.

"Yeah, but you're…." she doesn't finish her sentence.

"What? I'm what?" Jey asks, his arms out at his sides.

"You know...naked." Laurel whispers.

"You mean like *this*?" Jey asks as he yanks his towel from around his waist.

"Jey!" Paisley and Laurel shout as Laurel covers her eyes again.

Paisley loudly exhales when she realizes Jey's wearing boxers. "Why would you do that? I almost had a heart attack!" Laurel says with her hand over her heart.

"Yeah," Naomi chimes in. "I almost just threw up and passed out at the same time."

Naomi throws a pillow at Jey and he catches it with his quick reflexes. "Calm down, geez. I wouldn't have done that if I was actually naked."

"Yes, you would've," Paisley and I say at the same time. "Go get dressed, would you?" she adds.

***

Two hours later, we've finally made it to the campsite. Jey, Paisley and Sonali rode in Paisley's van and the rest of us are piled into my truck. I was glad Sonali didn't try too hard to ride with me. Laurel and Naomi took the back so Dallas could have the front since he's so much taller than them. He's built like a football player. He could be a human sized Hulk. Everyone always says it's a shame he went into wrestling instead of football.

After we've unloaded Paisley's van and set up the three tents, Laurel and I head to the store for some food and ice for the coolers. We find a little grocery mart a few miles down the road and decide to stop there. We get stuff for hamburgers and s'mores and grab bagels and cream cheese for breakfast. Laurel adds some fruit snacks and Clif bars to the cart while I grab the ice.

When we make it back to the campsite, Paisley already has the fire going. When she started the fire two years ago with only a stick and a match, Jey deemed Paisley the official fire starter. Dallas is setting up the foldable chairs around the fire pit while Jey hangs a hammock on some nearby trees.

"Wow, you guys turned it into a home in the thirty minutes that we were gone," Laurel says, grabbing some bags out of the back seat of my truck.

"Yeah, we work fast. We've been doing this for as long as I can remember. Did you grab those sticks for roasting marshmallows, Lane?"

"I checked but they didn't have any. We can just use sticks from the ground." I tell Jey.

"Fine with me," he says, jumping into the hammock. It stays up for a couple seconds before slipping an inch or two down the tree.

"Oh shit." The rope stays and we all watch it for a couple more seconds until we're certain it won't fall. Just as I look back down at the cooler, I hear the rope slide down the tree and I watch as Jey's ass meets the ground below him. He groans and rolls onto his stomach, holding his lower back.

"God damn, that hurt. I think I landed on a rock right on my tailbone," he groans. I feel bad, but I can't help but laugh.

"That's why Dad always used to tell us to double check the security of the ropes," Dallas says.

"Is no one going to check on me?" he asks.

It's silent.

"Oh, sure, leave me here on the ground in pain." He whimpers like a baby and Paisley goes over to check on him. I dump the rest of the ice into the cooler and start putting the food items that need to stay refrigerated on top of the ice.

Then I hear Sonali's voice. Don't get me wrong, she's a beautiful girl. Long, black hair, dark brown skin that shimmers in the sunlight. She's sweet, too. But what bothers me so much about her is her obvious obsession with me. When I move, she moves. When I say something, she always laughs, regardless of whether it was funny or not. I've never told her I don't want her attention because that requires uncomfortable confrontation, but I hate dealing with it.

"So," Sonali says. "What have you been up to these days?" She leans on the back of my truck and twirls her hair in her fingers. She changed her clothes, which I didn't notice before. Now she's wearing a t-shirt and shorts. Much more appropriate clothing for camping.

"Not much. Same old same old. You?" I grab the chocolate and put it in the cooler. I think it's obvious in my tone that I don't want to talk.

"Oh my gosh, Lane, you're so mysterious" she says, laughing. When I don't laugh back, she clears her throat awkwardly and answers my question. "I've just been taking the summer off. I start a fellowship at the Boston Aquarium in the fall, so I'm taking time off for the summer. Been going to the beach, hitting up some parties. You know. Just summer things."

"Sounds nice." I roll my eyes again. Good thing she can't see me. I put the cream cheese in the cooler.

"So," she says awkwardly, clearly thinking of something else to talk about. "How have you been since the accident?"

Nope, not happening.

"I'm gonna run to the bathroom."

"Okay," she says, standing up straighter. "Catch up with you later." But I've already walked away.

***

It's now ten at night and we've eaten our burgers and our marshmallows are being toasted. Just as I finish my first s'more, Sonali comes over with a box in her hands. "Alright, who's ready to get wasted?"

"Oh, hell yeah!" Jey says. We usually drink during this annual trip, but I don't really feel in the mood tonight. Sonali passes out some beers and Seagrams and we settle back around the fire. Sonali, Paisley, and Naomi are chatting about a music festival they're going to in a couple weeks and Dallas is showing Jey a new wrestling move he learned recently.

Sonali hasn't actually bothered me that much, besides asking me about the accident. Maybe Jey's right. Maybe she will leave me alone. She isn't staying tomorrow night, so I just have to make it a couple more house until we all go to bed.

Suddenly, Sonali announces that we're going to play truth or dare. I don't think I've played truth or dare since Jey and I were teenagers. But everyone seems excited, so I decide to play along, despite the growing anxiety in my stomach, telling me this isn't going to end well.

"Truth or dare, Dallas?" Sonali asks.

"Um, dare."

"I dare you to make a s'more."

"Okay, that was the lamest dare ever," he scoffs, grabbing a marshmallow.

295

"I wasn't done," she says.

Dallas pauses, waiting for Sonali to continue.

"Make a s'more with a worm in it."

Dallas looks up at her, trying to figure out if she's being serious. Dallas is a wimp when it comes to food. He's not a very adventurous eater. In his defense though, I wouldn't want to eat a worm-s'more either. He swallows and awkwardly laughs.

"Go find me a worm then," he says with fake confidence as he unconsciously straightens his posture. Sonali gets up and turns on her flashlight and begins to dig around in the dirt for a worm. "Someone else go," she says over her shoulder.

Paisley turns to Naomi. "Truth or dare?"

"Truth," Naomi says.

"What is the most disgusting thing you've ever done to or with another human?"

"Ew, Pais, I do not want to know that about my little sister."

"I didn't mean something sexual."

"Oh, I got it! One time my friend and I were at a party and I was dared to do a body shot off of

Smelly Mike. In case you couldn't tell by his nickname, Smelly Mike is a very smelly dude. It was disgusting."

"Oh, gross," Dallas says.

"Found one!" Sonali says. She comes over with a decent sized worm and places it on Dallas's s'more. He adds more chocolate to it after realizing the worm is bigger than he was anticipating. "Can we cut it in half?" he asks.

"Ugh, fine." Sonali takes the worm out of the s'more and rips it in half with her bare hands.

"God, what the hell was that?" Dallas asks, obviously horrified.

"What?" she asks.

"You just split the worm in half with your bare hands." Dallas shivers. "It was kinda hot though," he murmurs. Sonali takes the now mutilated worm and puts the smaller piece on his s'more. "You may now feast," she says. Naomi's face shows pure disgust.

Dallas shoves the whole s'more into his mouth and chews so fast. I've never seen someone chew that fast before. His eyes are shut tight and his fists are in balls on top of his knees. He gags for a second and then swallows. He shows us his empty mouth and then immediately chugs a can of beer.

Sonali claps and finds her seat next to Paisley. "Good job, Dallas. I commend you," she says. Dallas lets out a loud burp and it makes Paisley jump beside him.

"God, that was massive. Sounded like a truck horn!"

"Alright, who's next?" She looks around the circle and her eyes land on me. *Oh great.*

"Truth or dare, Lane?" I'm not sure how to answer. I don't want her to dare me to do something stupid, but what if I pick truth and she asks me about the accident? Dare seems safer.

"Dare."

She smiles at me for a second before giving me a dare. "I dare you to kiss me." *Are you kidding me? Maybe truth would've been safer.*

"Not gonna happen."

"Well, you have to. I just dared you to. If you don't complete your dare, then you have to do two dares in its place."

"No, that's what happens to a hydra when you cut one of its heads off. Two grow back in its place," Laurel says. Everyone looks at her. "What? I like Percy Jackson."

"Well, you have to do it," Sonali says, as she rolls her eyes at Laurel's comment.

There are many reasons I don't want to kiss Sonali. One, I just don't want to. I have no desire to kiss her. Two, Laurel is sitting right next to me. Obviously we aren't officially together, but like everyone knows that we're *together*. Three, I *knew* she hadn't changed.

"Don't you have a boyfriend?" Dallas asks.

"No, we broke up last night." *Great, so I'm a rebound?*

How can I get out of this? If I don't kiss her, then her two other dares are going to be just as stupid. I guess I could just leave. "I think I'm gonna go to bed now," I say getting up from my chair.

"C'mon, Lane. It's just a game. Unless there's someone else here that you want to kiss?" She looks at Laurel and I see Laurel curl into her chair in my peripheral. Now I know she's screwing with me.

"Like I said, not gonna happen. I'm going to bed now." I grab my backpack from my truck and head into my tent. I'm sharing with Dallas tonight, but I'm hoping he ends up falling asleep in the hammock.

I change into some sweatpants and wrap myself in my sleeping bag. I grab the strings on my hoodie and pull tightly, making the hood cinch around my face, wrapping me up like a cocoon. I lay there, feeling angry and annoyed. *Why did she have to do that?* I probably reacted a little immaturely, but something about Sonali brings it out of me.

I hear the tent unzip and someone come in. "I'm fine, Jey. I just didn't want to kiss her."

"Yeah, I could tell," Laurel says. I sit up and look over at her. She has her sleeping bag and her pillow in her arms. "Mind if I crash with you? I already asked Dallas if he'd switch with me."

"Yeah, I don't mind." I lay back down and tighten my cocoon. I instantly feel better with her beside me. She lays her sleeping bag next to mine, gets inside and lays down on her pillow.

"You okay?" she asks me. I know I was being immature. I didn't have to walk away like that. But it made me angry. Sonali was acting like Laurel wasn't even sitting there.

"Yeah. She just knows how to get under my skin. Why did she dare me to kiss her?"

"Well I guess she must have wanted to kiss you." I think about that.

"I guess you could be right." Maybe it wasn't about Laurel after all. "Sorry about that. That was immature of me."

"Eh, it's fine. I wouldn't have liked it if someone dared me to kiss them like that either."

"Yeah," is all I say. We lay in silence for a while and I think. Tonight would have gone pretty differently if Sonali hadn't come. She always ruins everything. Okay, obviously not *everything*, but she always seems to put me in a bad mood. I'm just glad Laurel's here with me right now. I loosen the strings on my hoodie and look over at her.

"Hm?" she asks.

"If there was one person I would've kissed tonight, it would've been you."

Prom?

Chapter 24

We were juniors in high school getting ready for our first prom. I was going with Laurel and Jey was going with his girlfriend at the time, Bailey. I wanted to come up with a creative way to ask Laurel to prom, but I knew she would hate it if I did one of those prom-posal things. That isn't really my style anyway. I'd rather be buried alive than draw attention like that to myself.

I did want to do something somewhat special for her though.

One night when I was doing homework for my astrology class, I got the best idea I think I've ever had. One of the things we added to our bucket list was to name a star. So I decided I was going to name a star "Prom?" and that would be my way of asking her. When the paperwork and certificate arrived, I took her to the treehouse and told her there was a new star I wanted to show her. I got really into astronomy since taking my class and I made a habit of showing her new stars we were learning about.

"Look right through there," I say, as I direct her to the telescope.

"What am I looking for?" I take out all the papers for the star and tell her the coordinates of it, and that it's directly next to the rightest star in Orien's belt. It's smaller than the tip of a pencil, but she "finds" it and looks back at me. "What's it called?"

I hand her the certificate with our newly named star. She takes it from me and looks at it, confusion clouding her face.

"I don't understand. Did you name a star?"

I nod.

"You named a star and you named it 'Prom?'?" she asks. Her voice goes up at the end, showing her confusion. I don't answer her because I want her to figure it out herself.

After a minute passes she gasps. "Wait! Is this your way of asking me to prom?"

I laugh and confirm her question with a nod. "Are you serious?" she asks me, giddy.

"Yes, I'm serious. Will you go to prom with me Laurel?"

"Yes, I will," she says, dropping the paper and throwing her arms around my neck. "I was wondering if you were going to ask me. I was also wondering how you would ask me. I was fully prepared to say no if it was stupid." She leans back, her arms still around my neck, and looks me in the eyes.

"Well it must not have been stupid," I say.

"No, Lane. It wasn't."

***

Jey and I got ready together at his house, which took about ten minutes, then we drove to Bailey's house to pick her up. Bailey's mom wanted pictures, so Jey and Bailey spent nearly forty-five minutes getting pictures, doing all sorts of cliche prom poses. I felt bad because we were going to be late picking up Laurel, but I didn't have the guts to speak up.

We're finally in the car. Me in the backseat, Jey and Bailey in the front. Bailey's wearing a pale pink dress with rhinestones and gems covering nearly every single inch of it. Her hair is pulled back in a loose braid. She looks pretty. Jey's suit matches her dress perfectly.

We finally make it to Laurel's house and when we pull in, I see her sprawled out on the driveway. I get out of the car and make my way over to her while Jey and Bailey sit on the bench by the front door, waiting for me to get Laurel.

I love that she doesn't care about ruining her dress, but I'm a little concerned as to why she's laying in the driveway.

"You're late," she says, checking the invisible watch on her wrist.

"I know, I'm sorry. They took forever taking pictures at Bailey's." I walk closer to her and begin to sit down next to her when she lifts her hand in the air so I pause mid-squat and grab her hand. Once she stands up, she runs her hands down her dress and I nearly fall over when I look at her.

"Oh my god, Laurel," I whisper. I feel my cheeks flush when I realized I said that out loud.

"What? Is something wrong?" she asks, looking down at her dress.

"No. No, not at all." I walk over to her smiling and take her hand in mine and lead her to the front door where Mr. Matthew, Mrs. Malani, Jey, and Bailey are waiting for us.

Her dress is a silk material and is a deep, Slytherin green. It's tighter fitting than Bailey's dress and far simpler. It hugs her in all the right places. The straps are skinny and dainty and lightly lay on her shoulders, like how a butterfly sits on a flower. There's a dip in the chest area and the fabric ripples, accentuating her chest. Her hair is half-up half-down and the curls flow naturally around her shoulders, making her face look light and round. She has never looked so breathtaking. I catch myself looking somewhere I shouldn't as we make our way over to everyone and I have to quickly situate myself.

We take some pictures with Jey and Bailey and Laurel's parents. We get some with just the two of us and even though Laurel whines, Mrs. Malani snaps some of only her. I have never seen anyone so beautiful. *I* need *those pictures.*

We head to dinner, a local Italian restaurant Jey picked out. "What, I like breadsticks," he responded when I asked him why he chose Italian. We get in on our side of the booth first and Laurel plops down next to me. We order our drinks and get some appetizers and chat while we wait for them to arrive.

Bailey plays on the girls soccer team so Jey and Bailey talk about their upcoming games and how their seasons are going. I use this opportunity to talk to Laurel.

"Are you excited for tonight?" I ask. It's her first ever high school dance. I was too embarrassed to ask her last year. Instead, we just hung out in the treehouse and ate snacks all night.

"Yeah, I actually am," she says, taking a sip of water. I want to tell her how beautiful she looks.

I lean over to her and grab her by the waist so I can pull her closer to me. She glides across the booth and stops when she hits my right leg. I nuzzle closer to her face, forgetting that Jey and Bailey are across the table from us. "You look beautiful," I whisper in her ear. She tries to hide her smile.

"Do you like my dress?" she asks me, turning towards me. My arm is still around her back and I slightly drop it to her waist. I can't help but bite my lip. I nod so slightly; I'm surprised she noticed it.

She can't hide her smile any longer. She twists her body so she's facing me now and she reaches to mess with a button on my shirt.

"Well, I like your suit." We get interrupted when the waiter comes with our food. Laurel ordered spaghetti, which probably wasn't the smartest thing for her to get. I take a napkin and fold it into a triangle and put it across the front of her dress, then take my fully open napkin and place it in her lap. "Just in case," I tell her.

Not even five bites later, a noodle covered in red sauce drops from her fork.

"I'm always thinking ahead," I wink at her.

***

We've been at the dance for about an hour now and it's loud and dark and there's too many sweaty bodies. We found a table when we first got here and Laurel immediately took off her shoes. "These are killing me. Why do women have to wear heels? I wish I had my pig slippers with me."

We dance to a couple songs but stay away from the giant circle in the middle of the dance floor. I've had enough of this dance and I can tell Laurel's done too.

"Wanna ditch?" I practically yell in her ear. She grabs her shoes and goes over to the snack table and comes back with a handful of different snacks. "Let's get out of here."

Jey drove and we're only a couple miles from the beach so we decide to walk to the boardwalk. Laurel's feet start hurting from walking barefoot so

I carry her on my back for a while. She eats some of her snacks and I can feel crumbs bounce off my neck, some falling inside my shirt.

We make it to the boardwalk and I set her down on the concrete. "Thanks," she says, slapping my back.

I take my shoes and socks off and set them next to Laurel's heels before I roll up my pant legs. I follow Laurel to the sand, while I shake the crumbs off my neck, where she plops down and lays back. I sit down next to her and play with the sand in between my legs, letting it fall in between my fingers.

"What's something you would change about me?" she randomly asks. She's looking up at the black sky above us, only when my vision fully focuses do I realize her eyes are closed.

Nothing, obviously. "What do you mean?"

"I mean, if you could change something about me, what would you change about me?"

I give her my answer because it's the most honest one. "Nothing. I wouldn't change anything about you." She darts an unconvinced look at me.

She clicks her tongue and rolls her eyes as she sits up and faces me. "There has to be something you would change about me. My hair? My personality?

The shape of my fingernails?" she says, raising her hands in front of her face. She spreads her fingers out wide, making them look alien-like.

She sits up, slightly facing me as I confess. "First, I love your hair. I wouldn't change that. Second, you're the best person I know so I wouldn't change anything about your personality. And third, what's wrong with your fingernails? That seems like a shallow thing to change about somebody."

"I don't know, I guess they could be a little more girly," she shrugs.

I choke back a laugh. "What makes fingernails girly or not girly?"

"I don't know. I guess I was looking at Bailey's hands and hers look daintier and cutesier than mine. You really wouldn't change the shape of my fingernails?" she asks me, with a pout sitting on her lips.

"No, I really wouldn't. But I'm not like other guys," I smirk, laying back on my arm. She scoffs and lays back down next to me.

"Why are you asking me what I would change about you?" She's quiet for so long, I don't think she's going to answer me. But then she does.

"I guess, I was just wondering why I don't have a boyfriend, is all," she finally admits. "Ugh, now I'm embarrassed." One, we don't usually talk about relationships, because neither of us have ever really been in one, but two because I can't stand the thought of being with someone else or her being with someone else. I hate that she thinks she needs to change for someone to like her. I like her more than if you combined how much everyone likes her from the entire school. It makes me sad that she thinks no one likes her like that.

"Hey," I say, turning to her, moving her hands from her face and lightly grabbing her chin. "Don't ever let a boy tell you that you have ugly fingernails. If someone does, send them my way," I joke. She pushes my hand from her face and lets out a mixture of a groan and a laugh. "I'm being serious, Lane. Why isn't anyone interested in me?"

"Why do you think I asked you to prom?" I ask her.

"Because you're my best friend. And because no one is interested in you either," she jokes, playing with a button on my shirt.

"Fair," I shrug.

I want to tell her that I love her. That I'm *in love* with her. But I don't think I'm ready to do that yet. I

311

would love nothing more than to kiss her under the stars right now, with the waves crashing in front of us. I would pick her up and put her on my lap and make out with her all night. But something is stopping me.

Rejection.

Instead, we sit in silence and listen to the waves. I start to whistle "Somebody to Love" by Queen. I thought it was a fitting song choice. She continues to play with the button on my shirt until her hand finally stops. I lift my head and see that she's fallen asleep on my chest. I lay there with her asleep on me for nearly two hours. I scratch her back and play with her hair and think about what it would be like to share a life with her.

Yeah, I wanna marry her someday.

I wake her up at 11:30 and carry her back to our shoes. We walk back to our neighborhood in a comfortable silence with her wrapped in my arm.

Strawberry Pie

Chapter 25

The rest of the camping trip was actually pretty good. We rented some bikes and went riding on some trails around the campsite. Bikes probably weren't the best idea since Jey's tailbone was still hurting. But he just tied a shirt over the seat to make it more comfortable. Sonali didn't stay for the second night, so that was much better. I'm still annoyed about last night.

We all sat around the fire reminiscing on previous camping trips. Naomi told everyone the story about how Dallas used to have really bad nightmares when we would camp because he didn't feel safe enough in a tent. It was one of the first years we went camping and he had such bad nightmares, he threw up in his sleep. It's funny now, but I didn't think it was funny back then. When it happened, I felt really bad for him. Every year after that we put luggage locks on the insides of the tents.

The second night made me forget all about Sonali's stupid games. Even though Jey and I haven't had the best relationship lately, I couldn't imagine not having him in my life. I couldn't imagine any of these not being in my life anymore. I wasn't really looking forward to the trip, but I think it was just what I needed. Well, except for the Sonali shit.

This past week, Laurel has been by my side every day. She comes with me to the pottery shop and talks with me until my shift is over. She helps me paint, though I give her bigger things to paint since she doesn't have very steady hands. She comes with me to the garage and helps me run errands for my uncle Eli. She comes over every night and we watch movies while we eat the dinner we made together. We spend time at Half & Half, helping Mrs. Malani and Mr. Matthew with organizing books and making pastries.

This morning, Mrs. Malani asked us to bake some pastries for the shop. We're in the kitchen making maple pecan and apple cinnamon muffins when Laurel suddenly yells, "Ah, shit!"

"What, what happened?" I say rushing over to her from the oven.

"I nicked my finger on the knife," she says, squeezing her finger in a paper towel. I check the apple slices for any sign of blood.

"Let me see it, do you think you need stitches?" I lean in and grab her hand to look at the cut, my eyebrows pinching together. When she pulls the paper towel away from her finger, her hand crashes into my face and I feel a thick, sticky mud-like substance run down my face.

"You did not just do that." I threaten. I look at her in between the chunks of hair covering my eyes, smothered in muffin batter. She's holding back a laugh as she grabs another hand full. She throws her arm backward and releases another clump of muffin mix, aiming right at my face. I duck just in time and it connects with the oven behind me.

"Oooooh, your mom is gonna be so pissed," I tease. She throws her head back and guffaws so loud, she starts snorting. I take the opportunity to grab a handful of the batter and chuck it at her. It connects with her chest and slowly *plops* onto her shoes.

"Oh, you're going to pay for that one, Lane Andrew." I sprint away from Laurel as she grabs the mixing bowl and follows me around the kitchen. I grab a cookie sheet and use it as a shield. It takes most of the hits, but Laurel gets a good throw in, right on my ear. I grab a muffin from the cooling rack and throw it in her direction. It hits her right in the eye and she flies backward, shocked from the impact. "Ow, meanie! That one actually hurt!"

"Hey, don't step into the kitchen if you can't handle the heat," I joke. She laughs and throws her hands up in surrender. "If I knew we were playing with objects, I would've thrown that blender at you," she says, pointing to a Vitamix.

"That definitely would've hurt way more than a soft, delicious muffin." I take her hand and help her up. There's a crumb in her hair so I pick it out and eat it. "Mmm. Apple cinnamon."

"You're disgusting," she laughs. "And an idiot." I take a picture of our faces covered in a variety of muffin mix. Laurel licks the side of my face right as I hit the button and I laugh so hard, the picture comes out blurry. I love it though.

"Yeah, and I have a clump of muffin batter in my ear," I say, putting my phone back in my pocket. I turn my head toward her and grab as much of the mix as I can with my fingers. I lean against the counter as she grabs a paper towel and starts wiping the excess batter off my skin. She pushes my hair out of the way and it sends shivers down my back and legs. Her touch is delicate as she wipes the crusted batter off the side of my face.

We've spent nearly every hour of every day together during this past week and we've hardly touched. I think she's scared I'm going to leave again and I don't blame her for that. But I can tell she's holding back. We've always been touchy with each other.

We sit in silence as she finishes and throws the paper towel on the counter. I meet her eyes and take her hands in mine, pulling her to me. She walks closer to me and I can feel the hesitation in her steps. I pull her until she's flush against my body. I play with her fingers, feeling each one intertwine with mine. I smell apple cinnamon and maple on her skin. Her shirt cuts low and I can see dried batter smeared across her chest.

I take the paper towel off the counter and gently scrub at the crust on her chest. Her breath hitches and she looks surprised. I can feel her eyes searching my face. I hold back a smile as I continue to lightly wipe at her exposed chest. My fingers gaze her honey hued skin and I see goosebumps crawl up her arms, mirroring the quickening of my heart rate. I finish and I drop the paper towel on the ground, looking her directly in the eyes.

I push her wavy, caramel hair behind her ear, and take her face in my hand. She leans against it as she closes her eyes and smiles. She lets out a breath, one I think she's been holding since I last told her I wasn't going to leave her again. I can see her hesitation fading with every touch.

She takes my hands in hers and slowly puts them on her waist. My hands connect with the section of skin exposed between her shorts and shirt. She's so warm. She lets go of my hands and lets me move them around her torso, exploring places I've never really purposefully touched before. I settle on her back and pull her closer to me. She stands on her toes and wraps her arms around my neck, pulling me into a tight hug. I can feel that her breath is quivering as it bounces off my neck.

God, I love you.

I feel her lips skim across the side of my neck, making my eyes roll back. I bite my lip in anticipation. She grips my hair and lightly tugs on it, giving my goosebumps. I'm lost in her and I want where this is going so much, but I don't want it like this. I think back to my conversation with Betty Rose. *It's now or never.*

I take her hands from my hair and bring them between us. I put my forehead on hers and breathe her in as I get the courage to tell her how I feel.

"Laurel," I whisper. "Since the day that I first met you -" She jerks away from me as I hear the kitchen door swing open. Mrs. Malani walks in with her back to us and a giant box in her hands. She spins around and the second she sees the mess, I know we're in big trouble.

"What the hell happened in here?" she shouts, setting the box on the ground. I can see all sorts of baking supplies inside. Sugar, flour, chocolate chips, butter.

She doesn't seem mad, just caught off guard. "Um...would you believe me if I said the oven exploded?" I ask.

"No, I wouldn't. Would you help me real quick?" Still, her tone isn't one of anger. I walk over to her, careful not to step on the clumps of muffin mix on the ground. I grab the box from her hand and set it on the counter. She points to the wet rag on the counter and then motions to the rest of the kitchen. "Now," is all she says as she leaves the room.

"I hope you know this is all your fault," Laurel teases.

"Is not."

***

After we finally finished cleaning up the kitchen and making new batter, we decided to head over to my house to wash up. We each took showers and I gave Laurel a clean shirt of mine to wear. I like seeing her wear my clothes. I've always liked when she wears my clothes. She put her hair up in a bun, one of my favorite ways she wears her hair.

Once I shower, we make a quick lunch of sandwiches and some veggies before we go down to the beach for a walk. We bumped into Milly, who invited us to a service being held in a few days at The Anchor, the addiction and recovery resource center she's been going to for support. Of course we told her we would go. I've really grown to appreciate Milly. She's been through a lot from what I know about her and I can see the strength within her.

We catch up with Milly for the next thirty minutes, until she says she's meeting up with the guy she left Tipsy Tuna with.

"He's a really great guy and I've actually been staying with him a couple nights a week. He sees my past and he doesn't judge me for it. He tells me I'm something special and that I have a bright future and all that shit. I act like his words don't mean anything, but he knows how they make me feel."

"Well, he's right Milly, you are something special. I'm glad you found him!"

"I think he found me," she says, smiling, twirling her black hair in between her fingers. Milly and Laurel continue to gossip about boys -or *boy* - while I notice how different Milly seems. Not only has Milly's spirit risen since we met her, but she's looking more and more healthy every single day. She's not as skinny or frail. She looks clean, more relaxed and less stressed. Her face looks fuller and her eyes look happier and more full of life.

We leave the beach after enjoying the crash of the waves on our feet for a while.

"How've Jey and Paisley been?" she asks me. "I feel like we haven't seen them in so long."

It's true, we haven't seen them in a while. I've been so busy working and spending time with Laurel that I haven't spent much time at home. I've even skipped his past couple games. That resulted in a few angry texts from Naomi containing quite colorful language. Luckily, she sent a heart emoji afterward, letting me know she didn't actually mean it. Okay, maybe she did a little.

"I don't really know, but I guess they're doing fi-" but I get cut off.

"Oh my gosh! We should have a dinner party with them, Lane! It would be so much fun! We can all cook together and dress fancy and spend the night drinking wine and eating cheesecake!" She twirls on her feet, her shoes scratching against the sidewalk. We reach my truck and get in, ready to head to today's adventure: strawberry picking.

"You know, that actually isn't a bad idea. I bet Jey and Paisley would be into that."

"I'll talk to Jey about it!"

***

Surprisingly, I picked today's activity. We added it to our bucket list sometime during high school. For Jey's birthday one year, Mrs. Elora made a strawberry pie with freshly picked strawberries and the second the sweet dessert touched my tongue, I knew I was in trouble. It's been my favorite dessert ever since. Top it with some whipped cream. Chef's kiss.

We drive to Wards Berry Farm, which is about a forty-five-minute drive from my house. The whole way there we play a game where Laurel asks me hypothetical or random questions.

"No way you would pick eating nothing but olives for the rest of your life over wearing the same pair of socks every day for the rest of your life. You can clean your socks, Lane."

"Okay, maybe I didn't think that one through well enough. I didn't think about doing laundry. Next one."

"Okay...hm. If you had three wishes, what would you wish for? And no, you can't ask for unlimited wishes." She flashes me a look that says she knows that would have been one of my wishes. She was right.

My first thought is *you*. But I'm still not ready to tell her that yet. Not the place or time. So I answer with my next three wishes.

"Number one, definitely to be able to experience Queen at the Live Aid concert. That one should be obvious." Laurel shakes her head like she knew that was coming. "My third one would be -"

"You mean your second one," she corrects.

"Yes, thank you. My second one would probably be to travel anywhere I wanted, all expenses paid. There are 195 countries in the world and I've only been to three, including the United States."

My first time outside the country was for a trip with my dad and my uncle Eli. We went to Chile to visit some family when I was younger. I hardly remember it. My most recent trip out of the country was to the Philippines. Jey's family went on vacation to visit some family one year in high school and I met them halfway through the trip. The Philippines was amazing. Culture I had never experienced before, food I had never tasted. It made me want to experience more of the world. There's just so much out there to see.

"My third one, well you're not going to like it, but it's the truth." She looks at me hesitantly before I speak. "I would go back to the night of the accident. I would take that night back in a heartbeat."

She looks at me with a sad look on her face. I can tell she wants to tell me to pick a different wish, but instead she strokes the right side of my face and tucks my hair behind my ear.

"What about you? What are your three wishes? Same rule applies." I look over at her as she pulls her hand from my face. She looks at her window, contemplating.

"I would want to star in a super popular, action-packed movie as the badass heroine that girls all over the world look up to. One hit wonder kind of deal. My second wish would be to have a farm. Not the animal kind, but like a massive garden farm. I would grow all my own fruits and vegetables and have goats so I could make my own cheese. I would have all different kinds of flowers. I'd live off my garden farm." Laurel talks with animated hands, imitating the sprouting of plants and the milking of goats. She gets quiet thinking about her third wish. She turns to look out the window again. "My third wish would be to eliminate poverty. To fix the world. It breaks my heart knowing that there are children dying in undeveloped countries. No food, no water, no one to care for them. I would create hospitals and schools and put in freshwater systems and donate to every cause imaginable. I want to leave the world a better place than what it was when I got here. That would be my third wish."

Only when she stopped talking did I realize that a tear had fallen down my cheek. I know how strongly she cares for complete strangers across the globe. Laurel literally has a heart full of gold and hearing her talk so passionately about what she cares for is suddenly making me feel emotional.

"I like that one," is all I say back.

***

We arrive at the farm and find a place to park under some shade, then head to the front stand to get some buckets. We've been picking for all over thirty seconds when a strawberry hits my cheek. I look to my right and see Laurel folded in half doing her best to contain her laughter. I chuckle and pick up a half smushed one and throw it at her. It bounces off her head, leaving a trail of red juice across her forehead. We both laugh harder as I make my way over to her. I wipe the juice off her forehead with my thumb and lick it off my finger.

After I did it, I realized how seductive that probably looked and I'm suddenly filled with an urge to kiss her. I always have the urge to kiss her, but it's stronger in this moment. I try to push it away but the desire loiters and travels through my body, causing me to feel…feelings.

We continue picking and before long, I fill my buckets. I make my way over to Laurel and when I see what strawberries she picked, I consider dumping them on the floor.

"Laurel, what is that?"

"What?" she asks. "Do I have something on me?" She inspects her clothes and her hair. "No. I mean what is in your bucket?"

"What do you mean? They're my strawberries."

I bend down and pick up her half-filled bucket. "Laurel, this one is almost completely white and this one literally has a worm in it." I drop it on the ground in between us. "Hey," she starts. "I felt bad because I knew no one else was going to pick the white strawberries and I picked the one with the worm in it because I figured it must be a good strawberry if the worm was eating it."

I laugh because her logic is so stupid but so incredibly cute. "Laurel, we can't make strawberry pie with under-ripe strawberries and strawberries with creatures in them."

"Okay, yeah I guess you're right." She takes the bucket from my hands and chucks the berries out of it. At the last second, she accidentally lets go of the bucket and it goes flying with the discarded strawberries.

"Oops!" She jumps over the rows of berries and fumbles trying to catch the bucket. To my surprise she catches it right before it hits the ground. Except she fell to the ground instead. "Ha! Did you see that, Lane? No more making fun of me," she warns, wagging her finger at me. She stands up and wipes her hands on her sides, getting the dirt off. She walks away, determination settling in her stride. Little does she know she has a smushed strawberry on her ass. I snap a picture as she struts away.

***

We drive back to my house and when we get into the kitchen, it's only then that I realize Laurel's eaten half of the strawberries. Luckily, there's still enough to make pie with.

I check my phone when I feel it vibrate in my pocket. It's Mrs. Elora with the strawberry pie recipe. I text back a quick "Thanks!" and instruct Laurel to start rinsing off the berries, cut the tops off of them and then to lay them down on a towel so they can dry.

I put the three ingredients in a pot and put it over the stove to boil. It's a pretty easy recipe. Once it's boiled, I add the strawberry Jell-O and stir it for a couple minutes. Laurel takes the pie crust and loads it up with strawberries. Then I pour the Jell-O mix over the strawberries and stick it in the fridge so the Jell-O can harden.

While that sits in the fridge, we decide to hang up the hammock I bought last weekend in the backyard. Laurel follows me into my room and I realize she hasn't really been in it since before the accident. I know she slept in my bed a couple weeks ago but she was hardly conscious. Most of my random things are packed so my room looks a little emptier than usual, but I hope she doesn't notice that. I still haven't decided when I'm going to tell her I'm moving.

I grab the hammock from the closet and I notice her looking around. She finds her way to my desk and picks up the picture of me and my dad from my birthday on the boat. She stares at it and I can see a smile form on her lips. She looks over at me but she doesn't know I was watching her.

"I like this picture," she says, putting it back down. "You look so happy."

"Yeah, I was. That was the first fish I caught that day."

"Do you miss him?"

"Yeah, I do, Laurel. Everyday."

"Well, let's go set this thing up," she says, taking the hammock from my hands. I follow her out of my room, but not until I steal a look at my dad's smile.

I'm reminded of what my uncle Eli told me about the money my dad was saving for me. He must've had a separate savings account for me. We were never tight on money growing up, but we also didn't have money to throw around. For some reason the gesture makes me feel more confident. Confident in my dad and our relationship. Confident that he loved me. I was never given any reason to doubt his love for me, but I had one parent who loved getting high more than she loved me. It doesn't matter if you had the most loving parent in the world; having one choose drugs over you plants some serious doubt. Doubt in yourself. Doubt in your other parent. Doubt in the people you're supposed to know you can trust.

And now I'm thinking of my mom. I sometimes wonder where she is or what she's doing. What her life looks like now. She could be in Europe for all I know or slumming it somewhere in the Caribbean living off of the land. I try not to think about her because questioning things when I don't have the answers usually leaves me feeling helpless.

I meet Laurel outside and she's studying the instructions, untangling a rope. I grab the other end and start tying it around a tree.

"Remember when I told you that I apologized to your parents?" Laurel shakes her head. "Well, that same day, I apologized to my uncle Eli. I got mad at him, too." She slowly shakes her again, letting me know she's listening. "Well, I was angry at him because I saw him paying my medical bills from the accident. I told him they were my responsibility, but he continued to pay for them behind my back. Except, he told me it was my dad's money. That he had given my uncle Eli bank account information for a private account for me. For college, or for emergencies or whatever."

"Wow, that's a lot to process. You didn't know about it before?" She gets her side tied around the tree and sits in the middle, waiting for me to join her.

"No, I never knew about it." I take a seat next to her and place my arm around her. She snuggles in close to me and throws her arm around my stomach.

"Well, I bet that meant a lot to you to find out. I guess your dad's always been looking out for you."

I smile. "Yeah, I guess so. But, I can't help but feel like I've let him down. I dropped out of college, I have no plans for the foreseeable future. I've made a lot of mistakes. Just...I worry that he wouldn't be proud of me. What if he isn't proud of me, Laurel?"

"Hey, if there's one thing I know for sure, it's how much your dad loved you." She sits up so she's looking at me. She twirls my hair in her fingers while she talks. "I know I didn't know you when he was alive, but I've heard how your Uucle talks about your dad. He loved you, Lane. Of course he would be proud of you. You dropped out of college because it wasn't for you. He'd be proud that you did what was right for you. Don't question that."

"Yeah, I guess you're right." She twists her body so she's leaning on my torso.

"Now, I believe you owe me a way overdue foot rub."

The Dinner Party

Chapter 26

Another week of summer has come and gone.
Laurel and I tried paddleboarding, went laser
tagging, went to a couple of Jey's games, and even
picked a date for our dinner party with Jey and
Paisley. I missed going to Jey's games with Naomi,
Dallas and Paisley. All four of us were there to
support our favorite Lake Hawk player and it
reminded me of old times. Dallas shouting at the
other team, Naomi fighting with opposing fans,
Paisley calling out the refs, cheering loudly for Jey.
It's one of those things that feels nostalgic even
though you do it all the time.

I even got some packing done when Laurel wasn't
with me. I was hoping I would find that missing
picture of me and my dad in the bathroom, but I still
haven't found it. Instead, I swipe through all the
pictures Laurel and I have taken from our bucket
list adventures. I can't stop smiling at them.

Paisley was over the moon about this dinner party. I
could tell she's missed her friendship with Laurel.
Looking back at those seven months, it makes me
realize avoiding Laurel was hurting more than only

me. Just another reminder of how selfish I was being.

Unsurprisingly, I was better at paddle boarding than Laurel was. That girl has no coordination. We stopped counting the number of times she fell in after we got to ten. Laser tagging was fun. We decided to go on our way home from the movies. They were doing their last group of the night, which happened to be a pre-teen boy's birthday party. After much hesitation and defiance from the birthday boy, we were allowed to join. Laurel and I only tried to shoot each other because we didn't want to ruin his birthday completely. But neither of us did very well because the group of kids ganged up on us.

The dinner party is set for tonight and Milly's service at the Anchor is tomorrow night. Laurel keeps reminding me. She thinks it's important that we go to support Milly.

After work, Laurel and I plan to go grocery shopping for all the supplies we need for our dinner. On the menu is pecan crusted chicken and scalloped potatoes with a kale and apple salad for the appetizer and lemon blackberry cheesecake for dessert, courtesy of Half & Half.

If anything, the food will be amazing.

It's three o'clock and it's been a really slow day at the pottery shop. I told Ms. Elsie about our dinner party this morning and she's been asking me about it on and off all day. I can tell she's glad I'm actually spending time with people now. "Oh, I'm just so happy you'll be having a nice night," or "What a lovely night you have planned with friends" or she tells me stories about her favorite nights spent with friends as a twenty-something year old.

She told me a funny story about one night when she was hanging out with her girlfriends. Her best friend had been crushing on the cutest boy in school so they decided to ding-dong-ditch his house. They all ran after pounding on the door, but Ms. Elsie tripped and twisted her ankle. The cute boy came outside and found Ms. Elsie sitting on the sidewalk, clutching her swollen and already bruising ankle. He asked if she was okay and he carried her inside and gave her a bag of peas to put on it while he got his keys so he could drive her home. "I told him I twisted my ankle while on a walk and he was the closest house to me, so I banged on his door. I still don't know to this day whether or not he knew I was lying. But all the girls had to walk home while I got a ride from the cutest boy in school." I was laughing so hard my cheeks hurt.

I'm in the middle of switching out a display when Ms. Elsie interrupts my thoughts. "Well, Lane, it's three and you only have two more hours til' you're off. So why don't you just head out now and get that shopping done for your lovely dinner tonight."

"Are you sure? I don't mind going after work. I don't want to make you close by yourself."

"Who do you think closes when you aren't here, darling? I have it under control. You go on now." She shoos me out the door, telling me to have a wonderful night.

I pick Laurel up and we go shopping to get all the necessary ingredients. We drive back to my house and unload the car as Jey and Paisley pull into the driveway. They help us carry everything in and Jey showers while we start preparing dinner. At first, Laurel was annoyed that Jey was getting out of cooking, but he smells like a sweaty sock so Laurel finally obliged.

There's a moment when I find myself alone with Paisley in the kitchen. There's this weird tension between us ever since I heard them talking about me on the back patio that day at the beginning of the summer. I told Jey to talk to her about looking at me like I'm a fragile little flower, so I'm wondering if he actually did. Her voice interrupts my thoughts.

"Lane? I just wanted to apologize to you. I feel like I sometimes don't know what to say to you or what I can do to help you, but I think it may come across as pity. I don't mean for that; I just wanted to fix your broken heart and I-"

"Paisley," I say, cutting her off. "It's okay. There's no need to apologize."

"Are you sure because -"

"Yes, I'm sure." She reads my face and I see her shoulders visibly loosen up. She goes back to cutting up some chicken.

"So, we're good then?"

"Yeah, we're good," I tell her, and I actually mean it.

***

Forty minutes later and dinner is ready, the table is set and everyone is dressed in their Sunday best. We decided to eat on the back patio since it's so nice out so we quickly move everything to the patio table.

We load up our plates and just as I'm about to take my first bite, Laurel clears her throat and raises her wine glass in the air, tapping it with a knife.

"Ahem. I just wanted to say a few words before we start dinner." She takes an awkward bow. No clue why she just bowed. She's so awkward but it's so fucking cute.

"First, I'd like to thank those who helped with this meal." She clears her throat and nods to me and Paisley and raises her eyebrow at Jey and looks him up and down. His shoulders slump and he frowns as she continues. "Second, I would like to say that I'm happy to be doing this with you guys tonight. It's been a long time since the four of us have been together like this and it makes me really happy." Paisley reaches for her hand and squeezes it. "Third, I'd like to say, Jey, you're in charge of the dishes. Cheers everyone!" We grab our glasses of wine and cheers in the middle of the table. Laurel laughs as she sits down because she nearly misses her seat. She must've snuck some wine while we were all cooking.

We dig in and when I take my first bite of chicken, I literally drool. Laurel and Paisley have perfected this recipe on their first try. We eat and make small talk. Paisley asks about how Laurel's parents are doing and Jey asks me how our bucket list has been coming along.

"Wow, this chicken is so good." Jey says, taking the last bite of his chicken. "I think I might have a food-gasm." Jey says exactly what I'm thinking.

"Ew, keep the sex talk away from the table, Jey," Paisley threatens.

"Why? So we can save sex talk for after dessert?" he asks.

Paisley rolls her eyes as Jey breaks out into a dance and sings "*Bow chicka bow wow.*"

"Speaking of, how have you guys been? You've been dating for what, like a hundred years already!"

I can see a moment pass between Laurel and Jey and I suddenly realize I'm missing something. I notice Jey's hands visibly start shaking and he starts licking his lips and fidgeting with his fingers. I can tell he's nervous, but I have no idea why.

"We've been good. Really good actually." He pauses and looks over at Paisley who is munching away on some scalloped potatoes.

"Actually, Paisley, can you come here for a second?" Jey stands up and walks Paisley over to the fire I started before we started cooking dinner. I figured we would end up sitting around it while we ate dessert.

He grabs Paisley's hands and looks her up and down, her mouth still full of potatoes. "Paisley, from the moment I met you, I knew you were someone special. And I knew you and I were going to be unstoppable together. You make me feel as if I can face anything in this life, the good, the bad, and the ugly."

This is the perfect opportunity to take another picture, so I wave Laurel over and take a selfie with Jey and Paisley in the background. Jey's on his knee and Laurel's giving two thumbs up.

"And you are the one I want to share all those moments with." He slowly gets down on one knee and pulls a small box from his pocket. He opens the box up and Paisley immediately starts crying. "Paisley Raye Aberforth, will you marry me?"

She squeals and jumps into Jey's arms, which makes both of them fall over. They kiss on the ground as Laurel is jumping up and down, cheering at the top of her lungs. For a second I think she's going down, but then she regains her balance. The wine's making her clumsier and more unstable than she usually is. I laugh at what's happening around me. I laugh because this is a happy moment!

My best friend is getting married!

They stand up and get themselves situated and Jey starts to put the ring on her finger. "Wait, do you want to marry me?" he questions. "You never answered."

"Of course I want to marry you, dummy!" Jey slides the ring on Paisley's finger and the girls break out into squeals again while Laurel celebratorily taps a knife on her glass of wine.

I walk over to Laurel while the happy couple is still showering each other in kisses. "Did you know about this?" I ask. I can see the mischievous grin on her face.

"Yeah, Jey might've asked me to help him," she says, slyly. "It was my idea to do it tonight."

"Well you couldn't have picked a better night." I grab a bottle of unopened champagne and shake it up before opening it. I spray it all over Jey and Paisley, showering them in sticky, sweet smelling rain.

***

An hour and a half later, we've finished eating, dinner is cleaned up and we've just finished eating our lemon blackberry cheesecake. We all had another glass, or more, of celebratory wine and have been chatting and laughing around the fire.

Paisley sits on Jey's lap as they FaceTime friends and family, telling them of the exciting news. Laurel sits beside me on a chair, sipping her wine and watching the two of them. I reach for her hand and hold it in mine, stroking her soft skin with my thumb.

I need to tell her about my plans to move in three weeks. I can't keep putting it off. I'm going to feel so guilty if I wait any longer. I already feel guilty for waiting this long.

"You wanna go on a walk?"

"Sure," she smiles. I grab her a sweatshirt before we walk down to the beach. She's a lot smaller than me so my hoodie engulfs her, making her look even smaller. She's had a couple glasses of wine and I can see how tipsy she is in how she walks. She's staggering every few feet and holds onto me for support.

We find a completely empty spot in the sand and sit down, her in between my legs. This is one of my favorite ways to hold her. She fits right against my chest and I get to wrap my arms around her torso and nuzzle into her neck. Right now though, I'm leaning back on my arms.

"What an exciting night! I can't believe they're finally getting married! They really do belong together."

I don't answer because I didn't bring her down here to talk about Jey and Paisley.

"It's nice to see two people in love like that," she adds. She picks up a shell and throws it in front of us. Sand platters as it lands with a soft thud. It's quiet for a second, then she turns and looks at me. "Lane," she starts, but hesitates. "Do you think anyone could ever love me like that?"

I literally almost start laughing because *Oh my god*, how could she possibly wonder that. But I don't laugh. I gently drag her body toward mine and pull her flush to my chest. I look her in the eyes and say "Yes. You know why?" She shakes her head. "Because I love you like that." I look her in the eyes and I can see every memory of us play through her mind. The day we met, the night we first kissed, the first time she beat me in Mario Kart, that time I held her hair back when she threw up from eating nothing but ice cream all day. The accident. I can see her think through what our relationship has meant to me. It happens in all of two seconds, because that's when I decide to kiss her.

The kiss burns with all the passion I've been holding since the first time we kissed in the treehouse. She doesn't kiss back right away, but when she does, fire ignites through every inch of my body.

My hands trail down her hips, back up to her face and through her wavy hair. Her hands find my neck and she pulls me closer to her, deepening the kiss. I slide my tongue through her parted lips and it makes her sigh. She straddles my waist as she continues to kiss me and shivers travel through me, begging for the kiss to never end. I place my right hand on her thigh and slowly inch my way to the bottom of my sweatshirt she's wearing. I push it up and my fingers connect with her soft skin under her dress.

God, this is everything I've ever wanted.

My brain goes foggy and all I can think of is releasing the tension that has built up in every inch of my body. I've thought about kissing her like this probably every single day since I've known her.

I kiss her harder and a few seconds later, I pull away from her mouth to kiss her neck. Her sun-kissed skin tastes like honey. I move her hair to the side and kiss the small, square shaped birthmark I've always adored. She runs her hands through my hair and that just reassures me to continue. I meet her lips again and she starts to move on my waist.

I need more of her and I can tell she needs more of me. I kiss her and kiss her and kiss her.

She's drunk.

Somehow, I break from Laurel's spell and I remember that she isn't in a clear state of mind. And this isn't what I brought her to the beach to do, even though I'd rather make-out with her. I came to tell her I'm moving across the country in three weeks.

"Laurel," I say through panted breaths.

"Hm?" But she continues to kiss my neck. I grab her shoulders and pull her away from me. "Laurel, we can't do this right now."

"Why not?" she asks, trying to push my arms off her shoulders to lean into me again.

"Well, for one, you're drunk. And two, we're in public."

"I'm not that drunk," she states matter-of-factly. "And there's nobody here, we're all alone." She motions toward the empty beach surrounding us. We're all alone.

"Yeah, you are. And I don't want to do something we'll regret or push you or -." I stop because I don't know what else to say. I can't tell her I'm moving across the country after we just made out and she was basically dry humping me on the fucking beach.

She moves off of my waist and sits beside me in the sand. She crosses her arms with a big sigh.

Oh man, I messed up bad.

"Laurel, I didn't mean -"

"It's okay, Lane. Let's just forget it happened, okay? I don't want to ruin what we have right now. Maybe I'm a little more drunk than I thought." She laughs it off but I can tell it was forced.

Why can't I ever do anything right? I always screw everything up when it comes to her. I've waited so long for this moment. I've wanted this so bad for so long. And I tell her to stop after I'm the one that decided to kiss her. What is wrong with me?

"Okay," is all I can say.

With that, we stand up and start walking back to the house and I still haven't told her I'm moving yet.

Tickets to Zimbabwe

Chapter 27

I wake up this morning so confused and feeling like total shit in more ways than one. *I made out with Laurel last night.*

Not only did I make out with her, but then I basically told her to stop. I did tell her to stop. Looking back, I never should have kissed her. I shouldn't have kissed her when I plan on moving in three weeks. How could I have been so careless and stupid? I let temptation get the better of me and I feel awful about it. How could I do that to us? How could I do that to her?

I spend the morning packing and thinking about last night. Wondering if she regrets kissing me. Wondering if she liked it. If she wanted it to happen. If she wants to do it again. And most importantly, how and when I'm going to tell her that I'm leaving. How will she react?

My thoughts are interrupted when Jey and Paisley enter the kitchen, where I'm packing up some of my dishes we don't typically use. Jey's hanging all over Paisley.

"Aw, would you look at that? How'd the happy couple sleep last night?"

"All I'm gonna say is that we definitely saved the sex talk for after dessert," Jey replies.

Paisley and I choose to ignore his comment.

"Where'd you and Laurel run off to last night?" Paisley asks while pouring a cup of coffee.

"We went to the beach. I know what you're going to say, so lay off. But I still haven't told her I'm moving." I wince, waiting for Jey to drill me.

"Dude, are you serious? What the hell man? She's gonna be blindsided and so pissed at you."

"I said lay off. And I know that. I tried to tell her last night, which is why I asked her to walk to the beach. But that didn't exactly happen."

"What do you mean?" Jey shouts.

"Well, basically that I didn't tell her."

"Why didn't you?" Paisley asks.

"Don't you think she deserves to know?" Jey adds, making me feel like even more of a terrible friend.

"Obviously she deserves to know. But last night just wasn't the right time. And now I think she's upset with me."

"Why would she be upset with you?" I don't really want to tell them about the intimate moments Laurel and I had last night. They probably wouldn't be very happy with me. I can see it now. Jey would call me a dick and Paisley would look at me with disappointment clouding her eyes. Not that I don't deserve that...but still.

"I did something I probably shouldn't have but I don't really want to talk about it further, Jey."

Neither of them says anything. They're usually all up in my business and now they decided to shut up. I need advice. But I'm not willing to give details, so getting advice is becoming rather difficult.

"How do I fix this? She's going to ignore me or things are going to be so awkward. What do I do?"

Paisley contemplates. She's always been good at giving advice.

"Hm. Well you guys have been doing things on your bucket list all summer, right? Is there anything on it that she really wants to do that you haven't done yet? You could surprise her or somethi-"

"Pais you are a genius!" I kiss her on the forehead as I run to my room and search for the cheapest flights to Zimbabwe on my laptop. We're going to Victoria Falls.

***

Tonight is Milly's service at The Anchor and Laurel and I said we would go. I meet Laurel at Half & Half and we drive to The Anchor. It's a little uncomfortable, but it wasn't as bad as I thought it was going to be. She's pretty much acting like it never happened. I, however, cannot stop thinking about it. One, because I kind of regret it. Well, I regret the timing. I don't regret kissing her. Two, because I can't stop thinking about her lips and her body. What it felt like, how it made me feel.

But I can't think about that right now because tonight is about Milly.

We pull into The Anchor and there are people all around. Adults, teenagers, kids. They're having what seems to be an end-of-the-summer barbeque (that's what the sign says) and it looks like the whole neighborhood has been invited. Milly introduces us to some of the people she's gotten close with over the past couple of weeks. I recognize one of them to be the guy she left with that night we went to the Tipsy Tuna. She tells us his name is Sash, and Sash goes on to introduce us to some of his friends. One of them is Arthur, one of the men we met at the Tipsy Tuna. We greet Arthur but he doesn't seem to remember us. I look around for Milly, but I can't seem to find her anywhere. She must be in the bathroom or something.

We spend the next thirty minutes chatting with strangers, laughing with kids and eating way too many hotdogs. I don't know any of these people, but I can tell this is a good place for Milly. It's radiating positivity and is oozing support. I'm so glad she found it.

People gather in chairs all around the room, so I assume the service must be starting. The "room" is more of an outside room. There are walls but there isn't a door or a ceiling. Just an archway for people to enter through. The sun has started to set, which paints a nice background in front of us. The kids have all disappeared so I assume they're playing at the park right around the corner.

Laurel and I sit near the back and we save a seat for Milly, but we realize that she's disappeared. A guy named Blair introduces himself as one of the leaders of The Anchor and tells us that a special guest will be sharing their story tonight. "It will be personal and I'm just giving a drugs and alcohol trigger warning for anyone who might need it. Please feel free to exit at any time. Now, without further ado, Amelia everyone!"

Amelia?

Milly stands up from what looks like the front row and makes her way to the little podium at the front of the room. I can tell she's nervous just by her body language and I get nervous for her. Speaking in front of people is hard, especially when you're about to share something so personal.

She sets her papers down on the little table and takes the microphone from Blair.

"Hi, everyone! First, I just wanted to say thank you for coming tonight. My name is Milly and tonight I will be sharing my story with you all. There's someone in this room that I need to apologize to. You'll understand what I'm about to say soon. And I'm truly sorry." The room goes quiet and all I can hear are some birds chirping and kids laughing in the distance. Laurel leans over to me and says, "Uh oh, I wonder what happened."

"Maybe something to do with Sash?" I question. Laurel shrugs her shoulders and looks at Milly, smiling and encouraging her from afar. Milly looks our way and Laurel gives her a positive two thumbs up.

"Now, I'll start at the beginning. I met this boy in high school. He was everything I could've ever dreamed of. Handsome, popular, an athlete, dimples, and the best smile I had ever seen. We started hanging out one day and he invited me to a party he was going to that night. I decided to tag along, hoping I would get a kiss from him or he would ask me to be his girlfriend. You know, I was 'in love.'" Milly uses air-quotes to show her sarcasm. A few people laugh as she continues on.

"That night, I had no idea what I was getting myself into. He picked me up, treated me like a queen, and never left my side the entire party. It was a great party. Lots of music and dancing. Food and friends. And he did end up kissing me, for all those hopeless romantics out there. After the party is when things got bad. He took me to an after party and the second we pulled up to the house, I had this nervous energy, like I should leave. But I was with the guy who I had the biggest crush on, so there was no way I was going to blow it.

"The first thing we do when we get to the after party is get more drinks. By this time, my crush, I'll call him Doug, had had too many drinks. After about twenty minutes of being there, Doug takes me upstairs and says he has something exciting for me to try. At first I was nervous because I wasn't sure what was about to happen. Maybe make out? Maybe more? I wasn't sure. But I definitely wasn't expecting drugs.

"Cocaine to be exact. Sparing you of all the details, that was the first time I had used drugs. And it was to impress a boy I liked. I ended up in the hospital, I got in a shit ton --sorry, just a ton-- I got into a ton of trouble with my parents and was grounded for three months. I was kicked off the basketball team at school. I didn't use drugs or drink after that experience for a long time. I was ashamed of myself. All for a boy. A couple years later in college, I had been hanging out with a group of friends that I knew probably weren't the best influence on me. I had learned at that point that I was easily persuaded, so looking back, it was stupid of me to have spent so much time with them. I was really lonely, though.

"I hung out with them a lot. We smoked weed a lot, went to parties. I wanted them to like me, so I did whatever they did, even when I knew I was making bad decisions. We had gotten some ecstasy, we did some inhalants, and basically used whatever we could get ahold of to get high. Once I graduated college, I had become addicted to a couple different kinds of drugs. I was an alcoholic. But I hid it well from everyone I knew.

"Eventually, I started dating this guy. We had a chemistry lad together and we got partnered up. Anyway, I started dating him and we decided to make thing official after we graduated college. A couple months after graduation, we got married and two years later, we had a son together."

Chemistry lab? What does that sound so familiar?

"He never knew about my drug addiction in college. Like I said, I hid it well. He started to notice it more after we got married. Obviously, we were spending so much time together, I was expecting he would find out sooner or later. I was hoping for later. He questioned me about it and I told him that it wasn't a big deal. I just liked to get high with my work friends sometimes. He let it go and after that I stopped using for a while.

"After my son was born is when things started to get bad. I was suffering from severe postpartum, was struggling with having a child and feeling so unprepared and unfit to be a mother. Work was too much too soon. Eventually it all became too much and I started drinking again. It didn't take long for me to spiral. I never got rid of my dealer's number, so I reached out to him. I was using for two months before I finally had the guts to tell my husband about it.

"One day, he gave me an ultimatum. He told me it was either drugs and alcohol or him and our son. I was so pissed at him for doing that to me. Drugs and alcohol had been a crutch for me for so long and here he was making me choose between my husband and my son and my only other comfort. So, I left. I couldn't stand the thought of losing either option. So I just left. It was the only thing I could think to do.

"My son was three years old. I regret leaving him every single day of my life." Milly makes eye contact with me as a small sob escapes from her throat, which echoes throughout the silent room. I see Laurel turn and look at me in my peripheral vision. There are tears in her eyes and she grabs my hand. A small sigh escapes from her lips. "Oh, Lane."

Bile rises from my stomach and into my throat. Holy fucking shit. *Milly's my mother.*

I immediately leave. I speed walk to my car and fumble with my keys, dropping them on the ground. I can hear Laurel calling my name, running after me. My hands are shaking and I can't get the fucking key into the fucking lock. Laurel's beside me now and she's pulling on my arm.

"Lane, would you talk to me, please?" I can hear the desperate pleading in her voice.

"SHIT!" I scream. I drop my keys and run my hands through my hair. I pace back and forth, trying to clear my head. Trying to make sense of what I just found out. Maybe I'm acting irrationally, but it takes too much strength to be still. I don't have that strength right now.

Milly's my fucking mother. What a fucking lying piece of shit.

I drop to the ground in a puddle of questions. I feel so violated, used, and betrayed.

Before I can control it, I'm sobbing in Laurel's arms. "She's my mom, Laurel. She's been lying to me all these months about who she is," I say with a cracked voice.

I cry as she rocks me in her arms and plays with my hair and tries her best to reassure me. "Maybe she was waiting for the right time to tell you," and "You don't know the whole story." But I ignore her.

We sit on the ground by my truck, my head in her lap, eyes staring straight ahead, brain switched off. I don't think I've had a single thought in the past hour. People start making their way over to the parking lot so I sit up and I see Milly making her way towards us.

Oh, *hell* no.

I grab my keys from the ground and unlock the car and get inside. Laurel stands in the way so I can't shut my door. "Lane, please talk to her. Hear her out," she pleads.

"I don't owe her anything, Laurel. Please move," I ask, coldly.

"No, you need to talk to her. She's your mom, Lane." Her face is so soft and her eyes hold so much emotion, pleading with me to listen to her. Some people don't show emotion, some people wear their hearts on their sleeve. All of Laurel's emotion is in her eyes and it breaks my heart to see her pleading at me like that. For a second, I almost give in, simply because Laurel wants me to.

Milly's right behind my truck now.

But I can't give in. I don't want to.

"Fuck her," is all I say, loud enough for Milly to hear.

"Lane, please let me explain. Let me explain everything to you. Please."

"Why the hell should I listen to anything you say?"

She hesitates. "Because you're my son, Lane. I know I've been a terrible mother. Hell, I haven't even been a mother. But I need you to know. I can't pretend and lie to you anymore. You need to know the truth." She doesn't even bother wiping her tears away anymore.

"I think I just heard the truth."

"There's more to it. Please. Just let me explain."

I think back on these past couple months. Part of me is curious and wants to know why she left me and my dad. Why she chose drugs and alcohol. I think back to all our encounters these last several months. The first day Laurel and I found her in the corner, I remember how she wouldn't look at me. *Couldn't* look at me. She knew who I was. She knew I was her son.

"You've known all this time? All these months. You knew exactly who I was."

Her shoulders fall and I can see shame blanket her face.

"Yes, I did. But I was going to tell you who I was, Lane. I just didn't know the right time or how to. How do you tell someone that found you in a corner, a complete mess, that you're the mother that abandoned them?"

"Well how you just did it probably wasn't the best way," I spit back.

"I'm sorry. I understand if you never want to talk to me or see me ever again." She turns to leave, finally recognizing that I don't want to hear her out.

But as she starts to walk away, I feel a pang of guilt. But I can't tell if it's from turning her away or being so mean to her. I've always been good at putting myself in other's shoes and while I don't completely understand why she abandoned me or lied to me for so long, I deserve the chance to understand. And I don't know why, but before I can talk myself out of it, I'm telling her to wait.

Her head shoots in my direction and I'm surprised she didn't just break her neck.

"Fine. I'll listen."

Ignorance Isn't Always Bliss

Chapter 28

The next day, I meet Milly at a quiet diner in the middle of town so we can chat. Laurel asked if I wanted her to come with me, but I felt like this was something I needed to do by myself.

I'm sitting down in our booth and the waiter has just dropped off my iced tea when Milly enters the restaurant. She looks nervous as hell. She takes her seat across from me and I feel so many different emotions. Anger, frustration, betrayal. Sympathy.

"So, when did you decide to start going by Milly?" Her real name is Amelia. To my knowledge, she had always gone by that or Amy.

"A little while after I left. I needed a new name. Needed to forget about my past, my mistakes, and move on."

"Move on from abandoning your family, you mean?" She sighs a frustrated sigh. If anything, I should be the one sighing frustratedly.

"Lane, in order for you to understand what happened, you're going to have to stop being such a dick."

I start laughing. But not because it's funny, but because she's kind of right. That comment reminds me of Honey. That forceful bluntness is something that was inside Honey and I recognize it in her daughter. I notice Milly has the same high, tight cheekbones Honey had, too.

"Alright, tell me what I need to know then." My arms instinctively cross at my chest.

"First, I want you to know that your father tried to help me. He tried so hard to encourage me to quit and get some help. But I didn't want to quit and I didn't want help. Addicts can't be helped unless they choose to be helped. He did everything he could to help me but I didn't want his help. I just need you to know that he tried."

"Okay."

"Well, you know the story of how everything started. But I left out some details about what actually happened. You see, I was so stuck between wanting to be a perfect mother to my amazing new son, one I thought I didn't deserve, and I was also craving getting high and being drunk.Two major parts of me were clashing and I didn't know how to deal with it. I was majorly depressed. I was thrown into being a mother, going back to work, and trying to be a good wife. It was all too much. The drugs and alcohol were a crutch for me. I know it doesn't make any sense, but they made me feel better. Then when your dad gave me that ultimatum, I cracked. I couldn't take it anymore."

She pauses and I wait for her to continue. She starts to fidget and I can tell she's getting increasingly nervous.

"This part I needed to tell you in person. I changed the story a little at The Anchor because I needed to tell this part to you face-to-face." She looks into my eyes, searching for something. But I don't know what.

"It was a couple days after the ultimatum that your father and I had another fight. He was pressuring me to choose and was so beyond angry that I didn't immediately choose the two of you, which was completely understandable. He said some awful things and threatened to take you away. I just couldn't handle it anymore. So, I tried to kill myself."

My chest falls in on itself and I am desperate for some fresh air. I can feel my heartbeat in every inch of my body.

Milly's crying.

"Your dad was packing a suitcase for the two of you and I was so scared of him leaving me. I wanted him and you and I also wanted drugs. But it was clear I couldn't have both. He was choosing for me. And I couldn't stand the thought of losing either of you or losing drugs. While he was distracted, I took multiple of every pill I could find in the house. I locked myself in the bathroom and when he came to tell me he was leaving with you, he found me unconscious on the floor."

The waiter comes back with Milly's lemon water and takes our order. Neither of us orders any food. She takes a second to wipe her tears with a napkin.

"He took me to the hospital and a week later, he told me we were done. That I wasn't welcome back home until I could get myself under control. Until I got help. I thought I couldn't feel any lower, feel any more numb or worthless. So, once I got out of the hospital, I contacted my dealer and have basically been doing drugs ever since."

I'm uncontrollably shaking at this information. *My dad was the one that left?*

"Well, up until ten months ago. Ten months and six days sober to be exact. But, Lane, I need you to know that your dad isn't to blame. I am. I forced him to make the decision to kick me out. But I also asked him to tell you that I was the one that left. I *wanted* him to tell you that I was the one that left. That I chose drugs over you. I didn't want you blaming him or resenting him. Since I was already out of the picture, it made sense to just put the blame on me. I deserved it anyway."

"I did blame you. For twenty years."

"Good. I didn't want you growing up hating the only parent you had."

"But I lost my dad when I was ten. Why didn't you come back when he died? I was all alone, Milly."

"I couldn't have Lane. You wouldn't have understood. You would've been too confused and you were grieving the loss of your father. Not to mention, I was using at the time. It would have been wrong to do that. But I did go to the funeral. I did check up on you. For the past four years, I've called the pottery shop once a week to check up on you. Ms. Elsie fills me in on your life. Every week, the exact same time. You usually don't work that shift, but I guess you did one time when I called. You answered and I was completely shocked and didn't know what to say, so I just hung up."

I remember that phone call. When I confronted Ms. Elsie about it, she brushed it off, saying it wasn't a big deal. But she knew who was calling.

All this new information is bouncing around in my mind like a pinball machine. *Milly is my mother. My dad is the one that left. My mom's been checking up on me since she left, which I guess that means while she did abandon me, she was still looking out for me.*

I'm so consumed with confusion. I don't know what to think, but I do know I need to get away and try to figure out my feelings.

"I can't believe all of this." My hands are barely holding up my head anymore.

"I know, it's a lot to process, so I understand if you need time." She takes out her wallet and pulls out some cash, enough to pay for both of our drinks, and puts her hand on mine.

"I never wanted to lose you, Lane." I drop my head to my arms, feeling so many emotions. I look back up when I hear the door close. And that's when I see something sitting on the table. I reach over and grab it and flip it right-side-up.

I realize then that it's the picture of my and my dad in the bathroom brushing our teeth. The one I couldn't find.

And that's when I start crying.

Eleven Days

Chapter 29

Two days later I tell Laurel, Jey, and Paisley
everything Mil- my mom - told me. Jey is in utter
shock, muttering a few choice words, and Laurel
has been listening the entire time, holding my hand.

"So, yeah. That's what happened. While she
couldn't decide between me and drugs, she still
didn't *choose* to leave me. Well kind of. It was all
my dad. I don't know - I'm very confused still."

"What the fuck, man. That is some fucked up shit. I
can't believe -" but he cuts himself off. Laurel's
darting her eyes at him. "I mean, I'm sorry, Lane.
That's a lot. How do you feel about it?" I roll my
eyes at him but answer honestly.

"I don't really know. I feel like I should be mad at
my dad, but I'm not. At all. If anything, I'm kind of
glad he had the balls to do what Milly couldn't."

"I guess that's a good way of looking at it. Are you
thinking you want to have a relationship with Milly
now that you know she's your mom?" Paisley asks.

"I don't know. Part of me wants to. But another part of me doesn't trust her after she lied to me for so long. I don't know what to do. I think I just need more time to figure everything out."

***

After everything that's happened over the past couple days, I never got the chance to tell Laurel that I bought us tickets to see Victoria Falls. We leave in eleven days, which is still plenty of time.

Going to Victoria Falls has been one of Laurel's biggest dreams so I need to deliver the news in a creative way. But everything I think of, I don't really like. At this point, I might just put the tickets in an envelope and give it to her.

I spend the rest of the evening making a list of things we'll need for our trip and packing for my move. I organize all my stuff into boxes and clean my bedroom. I had to Google how to clean floorboards.

We'll be in Zimbabwe for five days and I leave three days after we get back. I plan on telling Laurel that I'm moving once we make it to Victoria Falls, I just haven't decided how I'm going to tell her. Do I just come out and say it? It seems like a stab in the back to do it that way. We've been best friends for as long as I can remember and I'm moving away in just nine days. How do I break the news to her? What if it ruins the rest of the trip once I tell her? What if she decides to leave the trip early?

Thinking about that conversation nearly brings bile to my throat. *For now, I'll just focus on the trip and spending the last week or so I have with her in good spirits.*

Drive-Ins and Take Out

Chapter 30

We leave for our trip in five days, but I wanted to surprise Laurel with two more things from our list: a drive-in movie and riding on a motorcycle. We've been to drive-in movies before with some friends from high school, but we never counted those. Someone else was always with us. This time, it'll just be the two of us.

I rented a motorcycle for a couple hours today. I'm gonna pick Laurel up from Half & Half and then take us to the Blue Hills, which has always been one of my favorite areas to spend time. One of *our* favorite places to go. When we were younger, but too old to trick-or-treat, we would dress up in creepy costumes and go to the Blue Hills on Halloween. We would basically play a massive game of hide-and-seek. Sometimes as many as twenty of us would play. Jey would recruit some soccer players and Laurel and I would ask some of our friends from school. Naomi was a little too young, which she was always pissed about. One year, we had an incident where one of the girls got lost. She accidentally went past our border and couldn't find her way back. We learned then to always carry a phone and flashlight with us. We would all act brave, but it was creepy as fuck. Looking back, I wonder how none of us were murdered by some psycho in the woods or ended up seriously injured.

The Blue Hills is massive and covers several cities in Massachusetts, but we usually go to the Braintree area. That's where we're going today. It's close to Barnes & Noble so Laurel and I like to stop there afterwards. We always split a blueberry scone and a hot chocolate while browsing.

I have about five minutes before I need to leave to head over to the place where I'm renting the motorcycle from. I know nothing about motorcycles, so I'm assuming or at least hoping, whoever's giving it to me will give a rundown how to operate it. It can't be that difficult right?

I'm brushing my teeth when there's a knock on the door. Jey pushes the door open before he even finishes knocking and heads over to the toilet. "Mind if I pee?" he asks while he pulls his pants down.

"Be my guest," I say while spitting.

He yawns. "Are you gonna be around today? Paisley's having a crisis over at the soup kitchen. A couple of her volunteers got sick and she's low today. I was gonna help out for a couple hours before soccer, but I was wondering if you could cover the rest for me?" This isn't the first time I've covered for volunteers at the kitchen. Most of the volunteers are older so they have to call out pretty often: doctor appointments, someone comes down with the flu and then it spreads around like wildfire, etc. I'm annoyed that my plans for today are going to need to be shifted, but I can make it work. I know how busy it gets and I don't want to leave Paisley hanging.

"Yeah, I can help out. What time?"

"Around two to four-ish. Is that okay?"

"Yeah, that's good," I say, putting my toothbrush back in its cup.

"Thanks," Jey says, grabbing my head and kissing my cheek. I push his hands off me. "Ew, you didn't wash your hands yet. Your pee is now on my face."

"Probably isn't the first time. I hardly ever wash my hands after I pee," he says while leaving the bathroom.

"You're disgusting," I shout after him.

"Yet, you still love me!" he yells back. He's right, I do.

Forty-five minutes later, I've made it to the motorcycle rental place and have been given a rundown on how to operate the bike. The guy, Wes, was not what I was expecting. I was expecting a motorcycle enthusiast decked out in leather, but Wes is a cowboy. He wore a pair of the tightest jeans I've ever seen and a belt with the biggest belt buckle I've ever seen. He wore a plaid button up shirt with a bolo tie and a tight jean jacket, with a cowboy hat to complete the outfit. He didn't say much, just answered my questions.

I was slightly nervous about operating a motorcycle. We drove around the empty parking lot a few times at my request. I don't want to take any chances. It actually isn't as hard as I thought it was going to be. It's kind of like driving a dirt bike, which I've done once before for one of Dallas's birthdays. I give Wes the keys to my truck and he hands me some protective gear and I head over to Half & Half to get Laurel.

I gotta admit that I was nervous at first to ride it on the main roads. But the feel of the wind and the rush of cruising down the beach is amazing. It's euphoric. It's different from riding in an enclosed vehicle for multiple reasons. For one, I feel like I have a more intimate relationship with these roads I drive every day. I see them differently. Riding in a car is boring compared to this, I've decided. While it's a much cooler form of transportation, it's one hundred percent a lot scarier. One wrong move and I'm thrown off the bike. That's terrifying.

I make it to Half & Half in one piece and I walk inside to find Mr. Matthew talking to Mr. and Mrs. Bloom. They're an old couple that's been buying books from Half & Half since the Owens' first opened. They come once a week, buy one book and take turns reading it. When they finish, they get a new book. I can hear them talking about the weather outside. Mr. Bloom is saying it's a beautiful day to tend to his garden. I walk past them and find Laurel sitting on the spiral staircase in the back reading a book.

"Hey, you. You ready to go?"

"Go where?" She doesn't look up from her book.

"I have a surprise for you, actually. So I need you to put the book down and come with me." Now I have her attention. Laurel lives for surprises.

"Say less," she says, throwing her book over her shoulder. It tumbles between two stairs and falls to the floor with a loud smack.

"Okay, I'm glad you're excited, but I have a request first. Paisley's really tight at the soup kitchen and Jey has soccer so he doesn't have enough time to cover the entire shift. Wanna come with me this afternoon?"

"Yeah, of course. I actually haven't volunteered there in a while. Sounds fun."

"Okay, ready for the surprise?"

She covers her eyes with her hands and motions for me to lead her. I take her elbow in my hand and lead her down the steps and out the door. I walk her to the parking spot with the motorcycle and tell her she can open her eyes.

She removes her hands and her face is full of excitement. She looks around for a second and looks confused. "I don't get it. What's the surprise?"

"What do you mean? It's right in front of you." I point to the bike.

"You mean the motorcycle? That's *yours*?" Shock replaces confusion.

"Yep," I say, crossing my arms across my chest, feeling pleased.

"There's no way you drove that here. Am I being Punk'd?" I roll my eyes.

"No, you're not being Punk'd. Would you stop looking around for hidden cameras? Ashton Kutcher isn't here. Well he might be, but not because you're being Punk'd."

"Okay, so you're telling me you rode this here? Like you sat on the seat and did whatever you have to do to make it move and it got you here?" She points to the ground in front of her.

"Yes."

"Okay, I'm officially impressed." She walks over to the bike and straddles it, placing her hands on the handlebars.

"Did you forget it was an item on our bucket list?"

"No, I didn't forget. I just thought we would never do that one."

"Well, I never thought we would movie hop since that is literally stealing. But, we did that one. So, now, we're going to ride this motorcycle."

***

I had a whole speech planned in case she refused to let me drive. Laurel would want to drive, despite not knowing how to operate one. There are three reasons she isn't driving today. One, she doesn't know how to operate one. Two, I rented it, so it's under my name. I'd rather have control of it in case something were to happen. Three, *I* don't trust *her* to drive. But to my surprise, she didn't put up a fight.

We made it to the Blue Hills after driving aimlessly around for an hour or so. It's a beautiful day, just as Mr. Bloom said earlier. We park the motorcycle and decide to hike for a little bit before we go to Barnes & Noble. We hike up to one of my favorite spots. You can see part of Boston from there and I think this specific spot deserves to be on a postcard. After we've found a rock to sit on, I take out some of the snacks I packed while we chat. Once we've finished our snacks, we hike down to the motorcycle and head over to Barnes & Noble. We spend about fifteen minutes looking around the store when I find an interesting book. It's called Silent Patient by Alex Michaelides. I've heard about it before and I love psychological books, so I decide to get it.

As we head back to Hull, we drive up and down the beach, stopping to take a picture of the two of us on the motorcycle with the ocean in the background. It's getting close to one thirty, so we take the bike back to the shop so we can head over to the soup kitchen to help out Paisley.

We thank Wes for the ride and he gives me back the keys to my truck. We head to the soup kitchen and when we get there, Jey's pulling out of the parking lot. He gives me a quick nod and Laurel and I walk into the building, ready to do whatever it is Paisley might need us to do.

We've both been here before, so we let ourselves in and search for Paisley in the kitchen. She's instructing a very old looking man on how to use a potato peeler saying, "Do it away from you, so you don't cut your fingers." She hands the potato peeler back to the man, whose name tag reads Grant, and wipes her hands on the rag attached to her hip.

"Hey, Paisley," I say.

"Hey, I can't thank you enough for coming in today. Three of our volunteers called out sick and one of them has an eye appointment. I'm down four people, so seriously, thank you so much."

"Yeah, no worries. What can we do?"

Paisley gets us started on kneading the bread that's being paired with the beef stew being served tonight. This soup kitchen, The Chef's Table, is more than just a soup kitchen. It's connected to a homeless shelter, which also provides groceries and clothes and other necessities. It's actually a pretty cool place. Jey and I used to volunteer here for service-learning hours in middle and high school.

We spend the next two hours kneading dough, cutting an absurd number of carrots, onions, and potatoes and making small talk with some of the other volunteers. When we finish, Paisley gives us thirteen boxes of brownie mix and tells us to make all the boxes. I crack so many eggs, flour gets all over Laurel's shirt and both of our hands and arms are tired of cutting and mixing by the time we finally get the brownies in the oven.

We end up staying until five because Paisley's running around like a chicken with her head cut off. We help dish out the soup and cut up the brownies once they've cooled down. "I've never seen such a large amount of food in one place before," Laurel says.

"Yeah, honestly, we had to make a smaller batch today. There was a mess up with some of the deliveries, and we only got about two-thirds of the ingredients we were supposed to get. I hope we don't have to turn away hungry people tonight."

"Is that a possibility?" Laurel asks.

"Yeah, it's a possibility every night. We have numbers figured out for the most part, but sometimes more people come than expected." Well, that makes my heart break.

"Turning people away at a soup kitchen must be hard," I say. "Kinda defeats the purpose of there being soup kitchens."

"Yeah, it's not an easy thing to tell someone who's starving. But at the same time, we can't serve everyone. There has to be a cut off somewhere." She looks really sad when she says that. "Luckily, it hasn't happened in a while, but I'm worried it'll happen tonight since we didn't get our full delivery. Sometimes if it's just one or two people, I'll order a pizza. I feel too bad sending hungry people away."

"And that's why you're the most caring woman in the world, my Paisley," Jey says, as he dramatically bursts through the kitchen door.

"Thank you, babe," Paisley says, meeting Jey in a hug.

"How'd practice go?" she asks.

"It was good. Glad it's over though. Coach was being so annoying today. I ran home to shower so I don't smell when serving food," he says, smearing his finger on the side of the nearly empty brownie batter bowl. Paisley swats his hand away and turns on the faucet to fill the dirty bowl with water. She ducks below the sink and grabs a large bottle of dish soap and squirts some of it into the bowl.

"Well, thanks for helping, and staying late. Seriously, I appreciate it so much. Jey and I got it from here. I don't want to keep you from your evening plans."

"Yeah, of course," I say as Laurel asks "What evening plans?"

I grab her hand and walk toward the kitchen door, telling Jey and Paisley we'll see them later at home. "Thanks again!" Paisley shouts.

"Wait, so what are our evening plans, Mr. Peterson?" Laurel asks as we weave our way through the hallways, back to the front door.

"You might be able to guess. We don't have many things on our bucket list left." I grab the list from the glove box of my truck and hand it to Laurel. She opens it up and studies the list, thinking.

"Hm...are we waxing your entire body?" she asks with a little too much excitement. That statement and excitement don't belong together.

"What? That's not even on the list."

"I know, I was just hoping you would go along with it."

"Well, no. I would never go along with that. I have too much hair. That would hurt."

"Yeah, you do have a lot of hair," she says, running her fingers across my hair as if petting me. She tousles the hair on my head for a second before giving her attention back to the bucket list.

"Oo, do that again," I say, closing my eyes and leaning my head against the headrest.

"No, you have to drive me to our mysterious evening plans."

"Fine. But later?"

"Promise."

I pull out of the parking lot and head to the restaurant we're eating at tonight. It's a really popular taco place called Loco Por Los Tacos. They have every kind of taco you can imagine. Breakfast tacos, regular tacos, shrimp tacos, fish tacos, vegan tacos, pulled pork tacos, mac and cheese tacos. It's pretty new, so neither of us have been before. I'm very excited.

We order three different types of tacos and head across the street to eat them on the beach. We sit in the sand facing each other and lay our array of tacos out in front of us.

"I'm going to try the cauliflower taco first," she tells me, grabbing one from the to-go container. "Which one are you going to try first?"

"The pulled pork one," I answer, licking my lips. I love pulled pork. I take a bite of my pulled pork taco and I accidentally moan out loud. "I think I just had a food-gasm," I say, covering my mouth with my hand. I can feel a train of sauce drip down my chin.

Laurel laughs and grabs a napkin to whip my chin with. She takes her first bite and her eyes go wide as a soft moan escapes her mouth. "See? I told you." We swap tacos and then we both try the shrimp tacos at the same time. "Oh my god, I thought it couldn't get better than the pulled pork," I say, licking the sauce off my fingers. "These are the best tacos I've ever had."

I scootch over to Laurel and lay my head in her lap. Her hands instinctively move to my hair and I realize how greasy her fingers must be. "Wait, stop! Your hands are all greasy." She stops and inspects her hands. "Actually, I don't care. Keep playing with my hair." She chuckles and we lay in the sand, with my head in her lap while her fingers dance in my hair. I think I drift off for a little while because when I wake up, the sun has started to descend. Laurel's still playing with my hair.

"Laurel, what time is it?" I ask, snuggling into the crease of her crossed legs.

"Um," she says, checking the invisible watch on her wrist. "I'm not sure. Do you have your phone?"

I stretch then take my phone out of my pocket to check the time and see I have a text from Paisley, thanking me for all our help today. I shoot her a heart back, letting her know she's welcome. "It's seven thirty, which means we need to go." I stand up and grab Laurel's hands, helping her up to her feet.

"Where are we going next?"

"I'm not telling you."

She defiantly crosses her arms over her chest as I pick up our taco trash. There isn't a crumb left.

"What about if I guess it?" she asks when we reach the closest trash can.

"You can try to guess, but I'm not gonna tell you if you get it right or not." I reach out for her hand as I press the walk button next to the cross walk.

"Hm. Are we going to a museum? Wait, no! The aquarium. We haven't been to the aquarium yet." I don't answer her.

"Why can't I tell if I'm right or not? You usually suck at keeping a poker face."

***

We arrive at the drive-in movie location. This specific organization runs all summer long but what makes them cool is that they change locations every week. Tonight, it's at a playground that just so happens to be right across the street from a cemetery. The cemetery my dad is buried in, to be exact. I realize it's been a while since I've visited him, but I've just been really busy lately.

I pull into a spot and we can finally see the giant screen being set up in front of us. We're early, so I get out of the truck and meet Laurel at her door.

"Oh, a drive-in movie!" she says as I open the door for her. "I could be wrong, but don't we have to stay in the car to watch it?"

"Yes," I say, chuckling. "But we're early. So let's go on a walk." We follow the walking trail around the park and end up at the part of the path where it splits. One trail leads back to where our cars are parked and the other leads to the other side of the street where the cemetery is.

Laurel's talking to me, but I'm not really listening. I'm distracted. I'm thinking about my dad. Everything my uncle Eli told me about him and his secret stash of money. About what Milly told me about him and the truth about how their relationship ended. I look through beyond the iron gate and I feel something pull at me. I need to go visit him.

"Hey," I cut Laurel off. It comes out a little harsh.

"What?" she asks, her voice pinches at the end and it makes her sound nervous.

"Sorry, I didn't mean to come off harsh. I was just thinking. Do you mind if we take a detour real quick?'

"No, not at all. Are you okay?" She looks around and I can tell that she finally notices where we are.

"Oh, Lane. I'm sorry, how could I have been so stupid. I didn't realize where we were. Do you want some space?"

"No, I want you to come with me."

"Are you sure?" she asks as I reach for her hand for the millionth time tonight.

"Yeah. I want you to come." She nods and follows my lead across the street and into the cemetery. We walk along the trail that snakes its way around the burial ground. We get to the section with my dad's headstone and we turn into the row. Laurel only lets go of my hand when I sit on the ground in front of his tombstone. There are flowers here. And they look fresh. I pick them up and look for a card or something attached to them, but I don't see anything.

"Did you bring these here?" I ask her.

"No, I didn't do that. I wonder who it was."

"Yeah, I'm not sure. Probably just my uncle Eli."

Neither of us speak for a couple minutes and that's when I hear Laurel walking away. I turn and watch her find a bench at the end of the row. She smiles at me. I'm tired of sitting so I lay down, right on top of where his casket probably is. I put my arm behind my head and stare up at the sky watching the clouds drift.

"Hey dad," I say through a sigh. I don't usually say things out loud when I visit him, but I guess I feel bolder today.

"I've been thinking a lot about you lately. I know it's been over ten years since you've been gone, but I miss you every day." I take a break and watch the clouds above me make new shapes as they overlap and float around the sky.

"Would you be proud of me, dad? About where I am in life right now. I hope you would be, but I feel like I've done enough things recently that would make you exactly the opposite of proud. I lost you when I was so young. We never talked about my future plans. College. Girls. I was too young to be into girls yet. It's hard. I feel like you don't know anything about me, and I feel like I've let you down." A couple tears escape and trail down my temples.

I lay there with my arm under my head and my legs crossed at my ankles, wishing my dad were here to tell me he was proud of me. And that's when I hear it.

A whistle.

***

The movie playing tonight is *The Sandlot.* I've seen this movie more times than I can count. This was also Naomi's go-to movie when we were younger. I used to be able to quote at least, like, seventy percent of the movie.

Laurel and I are sitting in my car, listening to the movie through the radio. I can't stop thinking about kissing Laurel...among other things. I try to concentrate on the movie, but it's proving to be difficult. I look over at Laurel and the flashing colors from the screen illuminate her side profile. My eyes look to her hairline and follow the shaded curves of her silhouette, all the way down to her chin. She has a dimple in her chin and it prominently shows, even in the dark. My eyes work their way down her throat and I imagine what kissing her neck would feel like. Warm probably. My eyes drift lower and just as I'm about to reach her breasts, she sighs.

My eyes shoot up to hers and she turns and looks at me. "Would you rather sneeze uncontrollably for the rest of your life or have pickles as boogers for the rest of your life?"

Her random and unusual question would probably throw most people off, but I don't hesitate when I answer. "Probably sneeze uncontrollably for the rest of my life. There's something so.... releasing about sneezing."

"I figured you were going to say that."

"Do one for me."

"Would you rather sit in this truck and pretend to watch this movie or would you rather go get ice cream and milk and make some milkshakes?"

She smirks at me and I know her answer.

The Envelope

Chapter 31

We leave in two days for Zimbabwe and Laurel still has no idea. I decided to wait this long because I feel like the anticipation of leaving in forty-eight hours will make it so much more exciting for her. She's all for spontaneous adventure.

I invite her over for dinner, which consists of some instant noodles and juice boxes on the hammock. I have the envelope in my back pocket, ready to give to her. We finish our noodles and when Laurel comes back out from taking our dishes inside, I'm gonna give it to her. Ah, I'm so excited. *What is taking her so long?*

Just when I'm about to go check on her, she comes out the back door, looking more beautiful than I've ever seen her. We spent the day at the beach and her face is slightly burnt and her skin is more tan than it's been all summer. Her hair is pulled up in a messy bun and she's wearing my ACDC shirt again.

I'm smiling so hard that when she greets me, she asks me if I'm okay. Despite my confused feelings about finding out Milly is my mother, I'm actually mentally ready for this trip. Or, at least I think I am.

"You're acting weird, are you okay?"

"Yeah." I try to mellow my mood. I don't want it to be too obvious that something great is about to happen.

"Here, I got this for you." I hand her the envelope and she hesitantly takes it from my hand.

"What is it?" she asks, holding it up to the sun, trying to see through the thin paper.

"Open it up." She opens the envelope and takes out the tickets.

"What is it?" I don't answer, instead I let her figure it out. She gasps and grabs onto my arm.

"Lane. Are you serious? Are these tickets to Zimbabwe? As in the Zimbabwe in Africa?"

"The one and only." I'm smiling so damn hard.

"We're going to Africa?" she screams.

"Yes, we're going in two days, actually." She's jumping up and down and hollering and singing "I'm going to Africa!" Then suddenly stops.

"Wait, we're leaving in two days?"

"Yep. Less than forty-eight hours." I cross my arms, feeling so smug. She squeals and hugs me and showers my face with kisses.

"Are you actually serious?"

"Yes, Laurel, I'm serious!"

"Oh my god! I feel like I'm gonna pass out!" She plops down on to the ground and starts fanning herself with the tickets. "Oh my god, I can't believe I'm actually going to Zimbabwe!"

"There's one more thing." She's teeming with jitters.

"What? What could possibly be better than Zimbabwe?" she asks, excitement crippling her.

"Well, we're staying at a hotel right next to Victoria Falls."

"OH MY GOD!" she screams and I laugh at her and how dramatic she is. She wraps me in a hug and I spin her around as she sings "We're going to Zimbabwe, we're going to Zimbabwe."

She stops singing and looks me in the eyes, still hugging me around my neck.

"Lane, why are you so good to me?"

If only that were true.

Airplane Bathrooms Have the Worst Lighting

Chapter 32

Laurel and I are sitting in our gate at Logan International Airport, getting ready to board the plane to Zimbabwe. Well, not directly to Zimbabwe, but that's our final destination. We have three flights. Our first flight leaves from Logan and goes to Dubai, where we have a long layover. The next morning, we leave Dubai and get on our flight to South Africa. Our last flight goes from South Africa to the Victoria Falls airport. I'm not looking forward to forty hours of traveling, but there isn't anyone else I would choose to do it with.

Laurel's asleep next to me. It's currently 9:45 p.m. and she stayed up all night last night packing. We ran to the store and got some new hiking shoes, comfortable travel clothes, travel sized toothpaste and soap, and a bunch of snacks for our journey. She was so excited, she was putting everything she touched into the cart. When she wasn't looking, I put most of it back.

We board in ten minutes, so I wake her up.

She looks really groggy and out of it at first. But once she remembers where we are, her mood instantly shifts and she becomes the happy and overly excited Laurel I love. She runs to the bathroom right before we board the plane. She hates using the bathroom on airplanes, but being that our flights are so long, she'll have to do it eventually.

I take a couple selfies of us after we get on the plane and find our seats. I want to remember everything about this trip. One with us pretending to be asleep, one with us looking out the window, and one of us smiling at each other. That one was kind of an accident but she looks gorgeous in it.

Because the flight is so long, we've been given a pillow, a blanket, compression socks, ear plugs, headphones, an eye mask, and a food menu. This flight is around thirteen hours, so I'm glad for the little goody bag of things I didn't think to bring. Like a travel sized toothbrush and the tiniest little tube of toothpaste I've ever seen. I'll be grateful for that after these first thirteen hours.

Beside me, Laurel is fidgeting with her TV, pushing all kinds of buttons and flipping through the complimentary movies. "Lane, this is so cool! I've never been on an international flight before. There are so many goodies."

"I'm going to watch the new movie Horizon Line," she tells me.

"Isn't that the one about the plane crash?"

"Mmhmm," she responds distractedly. She fiddles with her headphones, trying to get them connected.

"Why the hell would you watch that?" I ask concerned.

"So just in case we go down, I know what to do. I'm not watching it for enjoyment, I'm watching it for educational purposes."

"Okay, well I will not be watching that with you."

"That's okay, you can watch American Pie or whatever you're into these days."

"Ow, Laurel," I say dramatically, clutching my chest. "I thought you knew me better than that. I've never even seen an American Pie movie."

"I thought you were kidding about that." she shrugs.

Thirty minutes later, we're in the air, headed straight for the Dubai International Airport. I pick a random movie and put my headphones in. I get comfy with my pillow and blanket and plan on falling asleep. I look over at Laurel and her head is all the way against the back of the seat, completely knocked out, mouth wide open. I chuckle while I pause her movie, take her headphones out and get her situated with her pillow and blanket. I watch about fifteen minutes of my movie before I crash.

***

It's hour eight of this ever-lasting flight. We were woken up sometime after we fell asleep to a warm meal, which was very nice. Laurel and I chatted for a while, eating our chicken alfredo and steamed vegetables. I did some reading while Laurel took another nap, obviously still wiped from not sleeping last night. We play some games, use the bathroom, stretch, and eat some snacks we brought. We decide on a movie and press play at the same time on our respective TVs so we can watch it at the same time. Laurel fell asleep halfway through the movie.

It's daylight now, wherever we are. I've been staring out the window, looking around at all the clouds. It's amazing how high up we are; how fast we're going. It doesn't even really feel like we're moving.

Even though I don't want to, I start to think about Milly. How she's my mom. I gotta admit, I feel like I should have seen that coming. All her awkwardness around me, the shame that flashed across her face nearly every time we saw each other. I mean Milly is a nickname for Amelia.

I still can't believe it, though. Here, I thought my mom was living it up in Germany or cruising around the Amazon River in Brazil. Honestly, for all I know, she could've been dead. But nope. She's been in Hull the entire time, spending the last several months lying to my face about who she is. I feel a little shameful about the way that I reacted when I found out. I basically told her to go fuck herself. While I feel bad about it, I know it wasn't necessarily a surprising reaction.

I don't know exactly what to think about *all* of it. How my dad was the one that tried to leave, how my mom couldn't decide if she wanted me or drugs more, how she tried to commit suicide, how I've thought the wrong things about my mother for all these years. I grew up believing that she chose drugs over me, which isn't technically the entire truth. I grew up believing that I only had one parent who cared about me and all this time, I had two parents who cared about me. My dad showed his care by trying to keep me away from Milly so she could get help she so desperately needed. And my mom showed her care by staying in contact with Ms. Elsie all these years, by taking the blame for everything that went down between her and my dad, and by finally getting the help she needs. She's been sober for ten months - *Wait.*

I think back to my conversation with Milly at the diner. How long had she said she's been sober? I think it was ten months and six days. I open the calendar app on my phone and do some calculating. Milly and I talked at the diner on August 9th, that would mean ten months and six days from August 9th is October 3rd.

The day of the accident.

My mind begins to swarm with thoughts. *Did Milly know about the accident the night it happened? Did she decide to become sober because she thought I was going to die? Was it a coincidence?*

I get up to go to the bathroom. I splash some water on my face and rub my eyes. Thoughts and questions flood through my mind, all desperately wanting to be the thought I focus on. But there are too many of them.

I look myself in the mirror, realizing that Milly and I have the same nose. I hadn't noticed that before. The bags under my eyes look ten times bigger from the awful lighting in this bathroom. Or maybe they are just that big. My eyes look red and irritated and

I can assume that's from the amount of stress I've been under this entire summer.

I take a couple breaths and remind myself that once I get home, I can talk to Milly and try to figure out what she knows about the accident. If I had to guess, I don't think the day she decided to become sober just so happens to be the day I was in a terrible car accident. I wonder if Ms. Elsie told her about it. For now, I can't do anything about it. No need to stress about it now.

Dr. Therin would be so proud.

I make my way back to my seat and find Laurel awake. She looks cozy under her blanket. Once I sit down, I lean against her and she wraps her blanket around me, pulling me to her chest.

"You okay?" she asks.

"Never better." I respond, smiling up at her. She plays with my hair until I fall asleep.

Elephant Crossing

Chapter 33

After nearly forty hours of traveling, we finally make it to the Victoria Falls airport. I've never been so happy to touch the ground before. We collect our bags from luggage claim and pass an indoor waterfall on our way outside. The second we step outside, both of us are instantly in better moods, despite how tired, hungry, sore, and smelly we are.

Laurel takes in a huge, dramatic breath next to me, her arms spread out at her sides. "I just took my first breath of Zimbabwe air."

We get a taxi and tell the man the name of our hotel. Our driver's name is Bright, and when Laurel asks how he was given such a unique name, the story he tells doesn't disappoint.

"While my mother was giving birth to me, she said the sun was in her eyes, peeping in through the window. It was the brightest sunrise she had ever seen. So, she named me Bright," he tells us with a crooked smile. His accent surprises me. It's not an accent I've ever heard before, obviously.

"Ooh, interesting," Laurel coos. "I think I was named after a dead baby on Oprah. My mom was watching Oprah and it was talking about how a baby died and her name was Laurel."

"Huh, I never knew that." I say, looking over at her.

"Where are you guys from?" he asks us, somewhat oblivious to the conversation about how Laurel was named after a dead baby on television.

"We're from the United States. We live in Massachusetts. Have you ever heard of Boston before?" I ask.

"Ah, yes, I have heard of Boston. One of the popular cities in the United States, yes?"

"Yeah, well, that's where we're from."

"Wow! It is so nice to have come all the way to my country from Boston, Massachusetts! What an honor." Laurel giggles beside me and tells Bright it's an honor for *us* to be *here*.

We ask Bright questions about what it's like living in Zimbabwe. Laurel asks how to say hello and Bright responds with "Salibonani." Laurel leans out of the car and yells it to every person we pass.

Suddenly, the car slows down. I look from my window toward the windshield, looking to see what the issue is, but I don't see anything except a bunch of cars. "If you look up ahead, there are some elephants blocking the road. Sorry to slow you down, but we will be stuck here until they leave the road. They are slow creatures."

Laurel shouts next to me. "THERE'S WHAT IN FRONT OF US?" her head starts darting all around as she searches for the elephants.

"Elephants, Miss Laurel. It is common to have them walk across the roads. You don't see that in the United States I guess," he says laughing at Laurel's enthusiasm.

"No, we sure don't! Can I get out and look?" she asks, her hand on the door handle.

"Actually, that is dangerous, miss. I think it would be best if you stayed in the car." It's obvious Laurel is upset by his answer and it makes me sad knowing that she was told no. I want her to have anything she's ever wanted. But I cross the line at being trampled by elephants.

"But you can look out my sun roof," he says, opening the window above us.

"Yes yes yes, I want to!" Laurel grabs my hand and we stand up, our bodies squished in the small window. "Oh my god! Look at them, Lane. They're so beautiful!" She's jumping up and down and is literally shaking the van. There are four cars in front of us, and it looks like there are two kids popping their heads out of the sunroof like me and Laurel.

"Laurel, calm down, you might start an earthquake and scare them away," I laugh. She smacks me on the chest and gasps when an elephant continues to make its way across the road. It's eating a tree branch. "Lane, get your phone. We need to take a selfie!"

I grab my phone out of my pocket and we shift to face the opposite direction, so the elephants are now behind us. I stretch my phone out in front of us, making sure you can see the elephants in the background. I snap a couple pictures as Bright tells us we need to sit back down. I guess the roads are cleared enough to keep driving.

We say "Siabona," which means thank you, to Bright a hundred times when he drops us off at our hotel and he says "Siabona," us a hundred times when we tip him. Thankfully, I was smart enough to get some ZWD, or Zimbabwean dollars, at the airport.

406

Once we get our room keys and get the tour of the small hotel, we head to our room to start unpacking our things. Our room leads right out to the back patio where the pool is, which is pretty sweet. The room is decorated in subtle yellows and reds, the colors of Zimbabwe. There's a bathroom with a walk-in shower and a bathtub, both of which look heavenly, especially after traveling for forty hours. Above the toilet is a black and white picture of an old man wearing what I assume to be a tribal costume. His mouth is wide open, like he's chanting or screaming. *Remember not to use the bathroom in the middle of the night.*

The main room has a little kitchenette area with a coffee pot, a mini fridge, and a microwave, with a little basket of snacks and water bottles inside. The bed takes up most of the room, which is topped with various throw pillows and blankets. Next to the bed are two nightstands that perfectly fit the vibe of the room.

Obviously, I notice that there's only one bed. It wouldn't be a new thing to sleep next to Laurel. I mean, we did sleep in the treehouse together multiple times, even though some of those were by accident. But we've never slept in the same bed the entire night before, though. The thought of sleeping next to Laurel and waking up with her next to me, most likely cuddling with me, gives me goosebumps and makes me wish it was bedtime.

"Are you cold?" she asks me.

"What?" I notice I'm rubbing my arms. "Oh, no."

Laurel pulls the curtains open so we can see the pool. There are a couple of kids in the pool and some teenagers playing a card game at one of the tables. "This is amazing!" she sings, as she throws herself on the bed, cozying up with a pillow.

"Yeah, I don't think I would ever get used to this," I reply joining her. She turns towards me and takes my face in her left hand. "Thank you for this, Lane. This is one of, no, actually *the* nicest thing anyone has ever done for me." I smile at her when I meet her eyes and remember I brought our bucket list.

"Wait right here." I rummage through my suitcase until I find the list and a pen and meet her back on the bed. "Would you like to do the honors?"

She laughs when I hand her the piece of paper. "We can't cross it off, yet. It specifically says visit Victoria Falls. We haven't been to Victoria Falls yet."

"Oh, I guess that's true," I say, peeking over her shoulder at the list. "Well, you can cross off traveling for forty hours."

"That's not on our list," she says, flipping it over to examine it.

"I know, but honestly, after all of that, it should be."

She scribbles "travel for forty hours to Zimbabwe" on the list and then crosses it off.

The Phallic Fountain

Chapter 34

We spent the rest of our first day out by the pool. The hotel gave us brochures and pamphlets of fun, touristy things we could do around the area. There's alligator hunting, ziplining across part of Victoria Falls, so many restaurants, river boat cruises on the Zambezi River, outside markets, elephant sanctuaries, helicopter rides over the Falls, so many different safaris, and obviously, visit the one and only Victoria Falls.

There are so many options, we had a hard time picking and agreeing on what we wanted to do. We sat in the shallow end of the pool, flipping through all the brochures, drinking celebratory, freshly made orange juice, generously provided by the hotel. We decide to save Victoria Falls for our last day. Laurel points out a restaurant overlooking the Falls next to a place that does ziplining across the Falls. I'm not sure I want to zipline across a massive waterfall. I mean, what if the cables broke? I would die.

"Come on, you won't die, Lane. You know how many people probably ride that thing every day?"

"Yeah, that's exactly why I'm nervous. It's probably old. The chances of me dying are probably really low, but I've always thought of myself as a one in a million kind of guy, so…"

That makes Laurel laugh. Then her expression changes into a pout as she grabs my hands. "Please, Laneeee," she sings. "'I'll be right there with you."

"Okay, fine," I say, happy to make her happy. I'll do anything to make Laurel happy.

***

We eat dinner, which is also provided by the hotel. It's buffet style and everyone that stays at the hotel has the option of eating every meal here. We load up our plates with chicken, French fries, veggies, and some sort of macaroni salad and choose a table off to the side of the pool. The view here is amazing. The hotel is entirely gated to ensure the safety of guests, at least that's what it said online, so I bet if there weren't gates surrounding the entire hotel, it would be a much better view.

And now I'm wondering what guests need to be protected from. I'm assuming from all the trees behind us, it's probably wild animals, which is a terrifying thought.

On this side of the hotel, for as far out as I can see, there are trees and trees and trees. With the sun setting behind it, I feel like I'm in *The Lion King*. I've never seen a sunset so red before. Right now, it's bouncing off the back of Laurel's head and it makes it look like she has a tint of red in her caramel hair.

At the front of the hotel, it's more of a touristy vibe. Lots of shops and restaurants right down the road from us, which we plan on browsing through. Maybe after I zipline to my death. I might need something calm to do and browsing through shops sounds like the perfect, relaxing activity.

I'm back up at the buffet, filling my plate with more French fries. French fries have always been a weakness of mine. I grab another Sprite bottle and head back over to the table. I pass some kids sipping on grape soda in the pool. There's a younger group of kids swimming in the shallower end, playing Marco-polo.

"So, what should we do tonight?" I ask Laurel as she dips a fry in some ketchup.

"I was thinking we could go on a walk and find somewhere to get some ice cream. And then maybe take a late-night swim. Well, assuming we don't collapse from exhaustion first."

I am extremely exhausted. We're seven hours ahead here in Zimbabwe, but with all the traveling, our bodies are confused and depleted of energy. But a walk to get ice cream sounds nice.

We finish eating dinner and walk toward the lively part of the town. Laurel is in a flowy skirt with a matching top and she looks stunning in it. The dark forest green fabric compliments the color of her skin and makes her green eyes pop. The sunlight streams in through the trees and bounces off her perfect caramel hair, making it look smooth and shiny. I swear, she gets more and more beautiful every day.

We walk hand-in-hand in a comfortable silence until we hear some live music. All around us are shops, markets, restaurants, and people. Laurel gasps at everything we pass, telling me to "Look at that!" and "Lane, come here!"

We choose the first ice cream shop we see and head inside. The music instantly quiets as the doors shut behind us and my senses are blasted with sweet smelling cream.

I order a mint chocolate chip in a cup and Laurel orders blueberry cheesecake on a cone. We take our ice cream outside and sit on the edge of a very large fountain. I take my phone out and snap a picture of us eating each other's ice cream, with the fountain in the background. I show the picture to Laurel and when she starts to laugh, it scares me and I nearly drop my ice cream.

"What are you laughing at?" I ask, startled and a little irritated.

"Look at the picture! The fountain makes it look like you have a penis coming out of your head," she says through gasps.

I look at the picture and start laughing along with her. "Ha! You're totally right!" Laurel's laughing so hard her shoulders are bouncing up and down. She tries to lick her ice cream but she's laughing so hard, she doesn't have control of her arm, or her tongue, and the ice cream cone slowly falls out of her hand and onto the ground, right next to my shoe. That makes her stop laughing.

"Oh no, my ice cream," she pouts, her shoulders slouching. Now I'm laughing.

"Well, if you weren't losing your mind laughing at the penis on my head and had a better grip on your cone, it wouldn't have slipped through your hand," I say through a chuckle.

She starts laughing again when I say the word "penis." She eyes me for a second and then quickly snatches the spoon out of my hand and takes a massive spoonful of my ice cream, shoving it into her mouth.

I roll my eyes and hand her the cup.

***

We spend the next two hours walking around, entering shops, talking to the locals, and listening to the live music playing from various shops and restaurants. We buy two bananas from a produce market and decide to eat those for breakfast tomorrow. Laurel finds a crossbody bag with different Zimbabwean fabrics on it. The woman selling it told her she made it by hand with the fabrics she got from Botswana. I can tell Laurel internally squeals as she holds the bag in her hands. She gently rubs her thumbs across the fabric.

"I'll take it!"

I hand her some money and she buys it with a smile on her face and we put the bananas inside as we head back to our hotel.

On our way back, we pass a couple more shops, the owners grabbing our hands and pulling us in, shoving items in our faces, and asking for our personal belongings in exchange for theirs. I tell them no, but Laurel doesn't want to disappoint so she buys some warm peanuts, a bracelet, and a pair of red flowy pants with elephants on them. It was honestly a little overwhelming. Everyone's shouting at you and trying to get your attention. Then they bring you their items from across the street because you *aren't* paying attention to them. I've never really experienced anything like that before.

After Laurel's satisfied, we finally make our way back to the hotel.

I change into my bathing suit and while Laurel's changing into hers, I check the pool to make sure there aren't teenagers still swimming around. All clear.

We make our way out to the pool and for some reason, we're both whispering and walking on our tiptoes. It isn't that late, but we both feel like we're breaking the rules. Maybe it makes it more exciting.

I prefer to wade in the water, letting each body part get more comfortable the longer I spend in the water. The water is usually always cold in Massachusetts. It doesn't matter if it's in the dead of summer, it's always cold. Laurel likes to jump in and get it over with. However, tonight, she joins me, slowly wading into the water. This water isn't cold, though. It's actually warm.

"What are you thinking about?" I ask her.

"You," she says, smiling. Her fingers glide along the top of the water, sending ripples all around us. The water is currently at my waist, but it goes higher than that on Laurel's shorter body.

"What about me?" I ask, instantly curious.

"Just thinking about how amazing you are." Her eyes meet mine and they sparkle with the moon's reflection in them. We take five more steps into the water. We inch closer together this time.

"Hm," I mumble.

"What are you thinking about?" She takes a couple more steps forward and I follow her lead. The water's now up to my chest and it's just below Laurel's neck.

"You," I repeat back to her.

"What about me?" she asks in a mocking tone, her arms swirling the water around.

I take a couple more steps toward the deep end, knowing Laurel won't be able to stand here. I grab her hand and pull her close to me. She wraps her legs around my waist and her arms simultaneously find their place comfortably around my neck.

"Just how beautiful you are," I say, switching up my answer on her.

"Hey, that's not what I said! You're supposed to say, 'Just thinking about how amazing you are.'"

"Fine. Just thinking about how beautiful you are," I tease.

Her face drops but her eyes remain locked with mine. I smile at her and I can tell she's trying hard not to smile back at me. The right side of her lip raises and I can see that she forces it back down.

"You are. Beautiful." My voice sounds much deeper than it normally does. It does that when I'm nervous. It's as if I lose my voice.

She rolls her eyes at me and starts to splash me with water. I splash her back and she's barely hanging on to me as we continue to throw water in each other's faces. She puts her hands on top of my head and pushes down, forcing me to go under the water. I grab onto her waist and pull her under the water with me. We resurface and we laugh as I spin us in a lazy circle. She wraps her legs tighter around my torso as she leans back. She's laying on top of the water with her arms spread out as I spin us around and around.

Water rushes over her chest, causing the light from the moon to glisten off her body. God, her body is amazing. The bathing suit she's wearing accentuates her curves and just barely pushes her breasts together. Her tight, toned stomach is tan from hours spent at the beach. I notice new freckles that cascade down her arms and feather her chest.

I slow down the speed in which I'm spinning until I'm slowly rocking her back and forth, left and right. Her hair sways in the water when I change directions. Lazy ripples bounce around us.

Her laughing eventually slows and she sits up and wraps her arms back around my neck. She stares intensely into my eyes for a few seconds before slightly opening her mouth. We're both breathing heavy from all the splashing and playful drowning.

Her fingers intertwine in my now wet hair. Her nails scratch my skin and it sends goddamn shivers all over my body, leaving my paralyzed by her touch. My hands instinctively begin to roam her waist, touching every inch of her slippery skin. I'm careful not to miss any part of her. I can feel her tense against my body. Her back curves under my touch and she wraps her feet together behind me, drawing herself closer to me. I let out a slow, deep breath and it literally makes Laurel shiver.

"So are you going to kiss me or not?" she asks.

Ben and Alice

Chapter 35

The last four days have gone by fast. We've done lots of sightseeing, market shopping, late night swims, and doing whatever we can find to make the most of our time here. We went to an elephant sanctuary and got to see and feed elephants. Laurel was over the moon that day. I have more pictures of elephants than I'll ever need.

Yesterday, we went to Outlook Cafe, which is the restaurant overlooking part of Victoria Falls. It's also where the zip lining is. We ordered our lunch, ate our French fries and drank our milkshakes. Laurel hasn't brought up the zip lining yet, but I know she's going to before we leave.

I pay for our meals and I redirect her toward the gift shop at the entrance of the restaurant, praying she'll get distracted and forget about the zip lining.

I realize I'm torn. Because if she wants to do it, then I want her to be able to do it. But *I* don't want to do it and there's no way she'll do it without me.

We continue to look around the gift shop, and for some reason, probably because I love her, I bring up the ziplining.

"So, are you wanting to zipline?" Dread fills my stomach.

Her eyes light up, like she's surprised I asked. Honestly, she should be surprised. "Are you serious?" she asks, quietly.

"Yes, I'm serious." She grabs my hand and plants a big kiss on the top of it before snuggling it against her cheek.

"Are you sure? Because I won't be able to handle it if you chicken out." It's true. If we go over there, get all suited up and are ready to go, and I chicken out...she'll be devastated. I take in a deep breath.

"Yes, I'm sure. Let's go zip lining across freaking Victoria Falls."

We head over to the zip lining area, get all suited up, helmets on. My nerves are through the roof. Laurel's been holding my hand the entire time, her thumb lightly rubbing mine while the instructor tells us what to do.

I think I black out for a second because I'm not comprehending what he's saying. He tells us again.

He points across the falls, which I've been avoiding looking at, and reminds us that there's another instructor on the other side who will catch us and help us dismount.

Laurel gets hooked up first. She's just about ready to go, her knees bent, getting ready to fling herself off the side of a cliff, right above deadly water. "Wait!" I scream.

She jolts, backward, fear splattered on her face.

"Oh my god, Lane!"

"Are you okay?" The instructor asks me.

"Uh, yeah. I'm fine. I'm just nervous." My palms are so sweaty. I rub them on my shorts, but it doesn't really help.

Laurel waves me over, so I hesitantly take several steps until I can reach her hand. "We don't have to do this." I love her for that. But we have to. I can't bring her all the way to Zimbabwe and not let her experience everything it has to offer.

"Yes, we do. It's okay, I'm fine." I kiss her knuckles and back away.

The instructor double checks Laurel's still connected and counts down. "One, two, three…"

And Laurel's off. I shut my eyes, but I hear her scream echo through the rocks that surround us. Only when she laughs do I open my eyes. By that time, she's made it to the other side. The instructor unconnects her and she's jumping up and down, yelling "Woo-hoo!" at the top of her lungs. The instructor turns around and Laurel stops jumping, so he must have told her to be careful.

I'm up next.

I concentrate so much on keeping myself calm that I don't even notice I'm ready to go. I grab the bar with both hands and hold on to it for dear life. The instructor counts down. One…two…I hear Laurel scream, "You can do it!"…three.

I push off the ledge without thinking and scream so loud, my throat instantly hurts. I squeeze my eyes shut and I hear Laurel yell at me to keep my eyes open. I quickly open my eyes and look down. The raging water looks like death, so I keep my eyes focused on Laurel. She's clapping and I finally feel a little calmer.

I can't deny that the view is amazing.

I land safely on the opposite ledge and the instructor disconnects me from the line.

"Was it fun?" he asks.

"And extremely terrifying." I add. Laurel laughs at that.

We thank the instructor and make our way back to the car, my legs feeling a little wobbly.

"Thank you."

I look over at her and she answers before I can ask.

"For following through."

***

We're currently on a riverboat cruise on the Zambezi River. We've been chatting with the couple across from us at the table.

Each round table is set with four to six chairs. Ours only has four. The tables are topped with an off-white tablecloth and a small bouquet of flowers in the middle. Each table has different flowers, though. We chose to sit with this couple because they seemed the most approachable.

"So where are you guys from?" Laurel asks after we finish discussing how amazing the food is. It's a dinner cruise so we've been served a full course meal along with an endless number of drinks.

"Oh, we're from South Africa, actually," Alice, Ben's wife, answers.

"We moved there about fifteen years ago after we left Germany," Ben adds. I was wondering what their accents were a mix of.

"Why'd you leave Germany?" I ask, intrigued.

"Well," Alice starts, rolling her eyes in Ben's direction, "Ben here decided he wanted to up and move to a new continent after we had a bad experience trying to find a new home. We're both originally from Germany and we wanted to move after our son had moved out. We didn't move until years later, though"

Ben interjects, "And I suggested we move to South Africa. We'd never been and I thought it would be a fun adventure."

"It sounds like a great adventure to me," Laurel says.

"'Adventure' isn't the term I would use to describe that move," Alice says, popping some warm peanuts in her mouth.

"Then what would you use to describe it?" Ben asks, obviously curious.

"Unnecessary," Alice says, winking at Laurel while Ben rolls his eyes. I hear Laurel's giggle next to me.

"Oh stop it, you know you love it in South Africa." He leans over and rubs her cheek.

Alice playfully rolls her eyes and glances at Ben with a smile on her face. I don't even know Alice and I can tell she loves it there.

"And now we've been living there for fifteen years," Alice says, never breaking eye contact with Ben. I don't know how old they are, but I would assume they are in their sixties. I look away from the happy couple and glance at Laurel. She's watching them with a smile on her face. One that doesn't reach her eyes. Her eyes look sad, like she's longing for something.

I think back to the conversation we had at the beach the night of our dinner party. Why can't she see how much I love her? We haven't talked about the kiss that night at the beach or what I said about loving her. Or about what happened the other night in the pool.

I don't want to ruin the night with my never-ending overthinking so I ask them a question.

"So, what are you doing in Zimbabwe?" I ask, taking a sip of my water bottle.

"Just going on another adventure," Ben responds. "I retired last year and we've been trying to travel as much as possible."

"What about your son?" Laurel asks. "Do you ever see him? Does he have any kids?"

Alice's face slightly drops. "Our Ronan passed away when he was in college. We try to visit home every once in a while, to visit his grave. He wasn't married when he passed."

"Oh, I'm so sorry to hear that. Was he sick or -" Ben cuts Laurel off.

"He was in a car accident. It was raining and he just lost control of the car. Hit a telephone poll and died on impact."

I feel Laurel move under the table. Her hand finds my knee and gives it a reassuring squeeze. If she's thinking that I'm thinking about our accident, then she's right.

"I'm sorry to hear that," I say, grabbing onto Laurel's hand on my thigh.

"It's been a long time, and the grief never goes away, you just get better at living with it. " Alice says.

Laurel removes her hand off my thigh and grabs her bottle of soda. She raises it in the air and says, "To Ronan." I hear Alice release a quick, quiet sob. I grab my glass and join the cheer. "To Ronan," Ben, Alice, and I say in unison.

Laurel's hand finds its way back to mine. My mood has changed a little since finding out their son was killed in a car accident. My heartbeat quickened. Laurel's hand still hasn't left mine and I'm thankful because that is what's grounding me right now. I slid my thumb up and down her hand, making swirly patterns and drawing circles. I already feel better.

Our conversation is changed when dessert is delivered to the table. Ben is telling us a story about the time he almost got arrested at a carnival when he was a teenager. Apparently, it was one of those "wrong place at the wrong time" moments and he was nearly arrested for it.

"It was actually our first date, and boy did my father hate you after that!" Alice says through a chuckle. I laugh, thinking about how awful of a first date that must've been. Your date gets dragged away by the police and you have to go home to your parents and tell them what happened. Sounds horrible.

"Yeah, but he eventually came around," Ben confidently reminds Alice.

We continue to slowly float down the Zambezi River as the sun is finally starting to make its way to the other side of the globe. As we eat our dessert, we talk about all of the traveling Alice and Ben have been doing since Ben retired from civil engineering.

"My favorite place we've been so far is India," Alice explains." The food and culture was so amazing. I would definitely go back for a longer stay next time. They have the most beautiful buildings." She grabs Ben's phone and starts scrolling through some of the pictures they took in India. She scrolls one too far and we're suddenly staring at a naughty picture of her bent over, picking up something off the ground. It's very zoomed in on one particular area of her body.

"Ben!" she snaps. His head shoots up at us in alarm. "When did you take this picture? I just showed my ass to our lovely new friends!" Ben smirks and then shrugs and continues to pop peanuts in his mouth.

We find out that Alice used to be an artist. Well, still is, she just doesn't sell her work anymore. Her work is even in some museums in Germany. "Her work is unique," Ben gloats for her. "She paints and sculpts and creates using trash she's picked up. Everything she uses is recycled." *I think I've just been inspired.*

"Wow, no way! Our friend Paisley would love you," Laurel says.

After dessert the tables are cleared and we're taken to the other end of the boat. Our tour guide begins telling us all about the history of the area and about some of the animals we can expect to see. Just as he's telling us that we might see alligators, a little boy shouts and points over the edge of the boat saying, "Look, look! There's a hippo!"

"Ah, yes!" the tour guide exclaims. "There are many hippos in the Zambezi River. Mom, you might want to grab your son's hand before it gets chomped on by one of them!" The tour guide anxiously laughs into the microphone when the mother shoots a dirty look at the tour guide and grabs her son from the edge. "Hippos can be ruthless and quite unpredictable, just like any other wildlife. You can never be too cautious," she continues in a less fun tone.

We spend the next two hours floating down the river, looking at wildlife, and sipping on some sodas. We take pictures of the river with the sun setting. I snap some of the hippos and some of

Laurel leaning over the edge, trying to get a better view of them. I snap the picture then quickly grab her arm and pull her back over the edge.

We chat with Alice and Ben more and even get some pictures taken with them. They take some of Laurel and me with the sun setting behind us. She's curled up against my chest with her arm slung around my back, pulling me to her. I rest one hand on her back and hold her other hand against my chest. I smile bigger than I've ever smiled for a picture.

Fifteen minutes later, we've docked and have traded contact information with Ben and Alice. They were actually really fun tonight. Alice is so sassy and reminds me of Laurel a little and Ben had so many stories to share. He definitely seems like someone who makes decisions on a whim. Like moving to South Africa.

We make it back to the hotel and after the packed day we've had, we decide to call it a night and watch a movie. I hop in the shower and take a long, hot, soak. I can't help but notice that Laurel has been a little off these past couple days. I've been wondering if it's from jet lag or not getting enough sleep, but I'm starting to worry that it's something else. She hasn't mentioned anything, but I know if something was bothering her she wouldn't tell me about it until after the trip was over. She wouldn't want to ruin it. But I noticed the way she was watching Ben and Alice and I'm wondering if I've done something wrong. We've been sharing a bed every night and our first night in the pool was new for us, but I'm nervous I've done something to make her upset. To make her question me.

Laurel chooses *10 Things I Hate About You*, which doesn't surprise me. It's always been her go-to comfort movie. She has it pulled up and ready to go after I've showered and changed. I join her on the bed, plopping down next to her. She's wearing my ACDC shirt, which I'm guessing is now hers. I like that she wears it, though, so I don't really care. Her hair is pulled up on top of head, just the way I like it. She's scrolling through the pictures we took on my phone today, looking at each one.

"I like this one a lot," she says, showing me the picture of us hugging. I really did smile as big as I could. *Goddamn, she looks beautiful.* The sun is reflecting off her hair, giving it a red tint again. She has more freckles bridged across her nose from spending so much time in the sun. The enthusiasm in her smile matches mine and I've never seen two people look so genuinely happy in a picture before.

I take the phone from her hand and start messing with it. "Hey, what are you doing?" she asks. "I wasn't done looking through them." I lock the phone and hand it back to her. When she clicks the button, she sees that I set the picture as my phone background. She looks up at me and smiles, handing the phone back to me. I reach for it. "I thought you weren't finished?"

"Yeah, but I already saw the best one." I put my phone on the table and hop back on to the bed next to her. I throw my arm around her and she snuggles up close to me. I can smell her pear shampoo. I dig my face into her hair and kiss the top of her head. She picks up the remote and hits *play.*

Sometime during the movie, we both fall asleep. Her in my arms, exactly where she belongs.

Vic Falls At Last

Chapter 36

Today is the day. Victoria Falls.

This morning, I woke up with Laurel wrapped in my arms. Her back was pressed against my chest, my arms thrown around her. Lazily opening my eyes, I realized how close she was to me. I tighten my grip on her and pull her flush against my chest and dig my face in her neck.

"Good morning," I say, groggily through a smile.

"Morning," she barely mumbles.

"You know what today is?" I ask into her neck.

"Ummm, the day I was planning on sleeping in," she says, pulling the sheet over her head.

"Nope. We actually have to leave in…" I sit up on my arm and look at the clock on her nightstand. "…about an hour, actually." It's 8:15 right now.

"Why, what are we doing?"

"You don't remember? It's our last day, so -" She suddenly bolts up and her movements shut my voice off.

She intakes a short breath. "We're going to Victoria Falls today!" she shouts. She stands up on the bed and jumps up and down, making me bounce below her.

"Get the hell up, Lane! We have to get going!"

"Wasn't I the one telling you that *you* were the one that needed to get up?" I laugh.

"Well, I'm the one up now, so get the hell up!" she yells, hitting me with a pillow. I grab the pillow from her hand and throw it across the room. I jump up and grab her legs and back and throw her down on the bed. I land on top of her, my arms resting on either side of her head, pinning her to the mattress. She's looking up at me with a surprised look on her face.

"Now, I'm the one up."

***

We're finally on our way. Our driver wasn't nearly as friendly as Bright was. He drops us off at a little booth, which is where we get our tickets. We make our way across the street and enter a little hut looking building. Our tour guide today, his name is Enzo, greets us and gives us time to use the bathroom before we start the tour.

Once I get back from the bathroom, Enzo asks us if we're ready to go.

"I've never been more ready for anything in my entire life," Laurel responds. Enzo takes us through what feels like a small maze around the building. Well, it's not really a building. There's no roof, but there are walls. All along the walls are pictures and stories about Victoria Falls. Who founded it, what birds can be seen while walking, different types of plants and other animals we may run into. It's honestly quite fascinating.

I know I'm on picture duty today. Laurel will forget to take a single picture, she'll be so wrapped up in finally seeing the Falls. I snap some pictures of the signs, of Laurel reading the signs, and of Laurel and Enzo talking. Once we've finished going over the history, we walk a little ways before we come across an elephant skull. Laurel obviously wants a picture with it, so we take some selfies with it, including some with Enzo.

We continue our walk through the woods for about ten more minutes when we make it to a little clearing. I can hear the crashing of the water before

I see it. I meet Laurel at the railing and she's just staring out at the falls. I for sure thought she was going to scream and jump and down because we had finally made it.

But when I look out at the falls, my breath hitches in my throat. I understand her silence now. It's like nothing I've ever seen before. Mist is everywhere, lightly dusting our skin and clothes, giving me goosebumps despite the heat from the sun. The trees and other plants that surround us are the greenest flora I have ever seen. The sun reflecting off the water produces the most vibrant rainbow I've ever laid eyes on. Water continues to crash down the falls, right across from us. It's louder than I expected. I lean over the railing just a tad to see the bottom, but there's too much commotion at the bottom of the water. Bubbles, waves, foam. It's weird, but I can only describe the smell as…water. Water doesn't have a smell per say, but it just smells like water. Like Earth and nature.

I look over at Laurel and she has the most content barely-there smile on her face. I take a picture of her, looking out at the Falls. She has a hand on the railing and I cover it with mine, drawing her attention to me. "Are you happy?" She answers with a light bounce of her head. It looks like she's been holding back tears.

"This is the first section of the Falls that we'll see today," Enzo says. He sees Laurel holding back her emotion, which is something that she doesn't typically do. "It's beautiful, isn't it, Miss Laurel?"

She doesn't answer right away. "It's the most beautiful thing I've ever seen."

"Just you wait," Enzo says, smiling to himself.

We continue the walk through the Falls, taking hundreds of pictures. The further we walk, the more Laurel shows her emotions. She's getting more and more excited with each step, each section of the Falls we see, and with each picture we take. Forty-five minutes pass when we make it to a more open area.

"This is going to be the most beautiful part of the tour, so get your camera ready," Enzo instructs me.

There's a path leading to an open area with big rocks. I'm looking down at my feet, my big clunky boots making it hard to walk on such uneven ground. The second I look up I understand what Enzo means about it being the most beautiful part. We're surrounded by multiple sections of waterfall.

I walk over to Laurel who literally hasn't moved and grab her by the hand. I take us down the lengthy path, closer to the edge so we can see better. Mist is flying everywhere. I don't think a single area of my clothes are dry. I glance back at Laurel who is following behind me, a stunned look on her face. It makes me smile knowing how affected by this she is. This has been one of her life's biggest dreams. And I get to be here with her to witness it.

I take us to the tip of the cliff, where the two sides of the waterfall meet. On the left and right of us is waterfall. I stop a good couple feet before the edge of the cliff, not too comfortable with being any closer to the edge.

I lean forward over the edge and I experience something that I will probably never be able to describe. "Whoa."

"Laurel, come here." I motion her toward me and she follows my command. "Look over the edge," I instruct. I hold onto her hand and show her how to stand just in case she slips. We peer over the edge and coming *up at* us are little drops of water. It seems impossible and must defy all laws of gravity, but there are literally drops of water floating upward.

I reach my hand out and a few droplets splash against my palm. Laurel copies my movement and places her palm out in front of her. "Can you believe this?" I ask. "This is the craziest thing I have ever seen."

Laurel still hasn't said anything. She drops her hand and spins in a circle, first to the left and then again to the right. It's like she doesn't know where to look because there's too much to see. "Lane," she says.

"Yeah?"

"It's better than my Victoria Falls mural," is all she says to me, still looking all around her. I can't tell if she's crying or if her face is just wet from all the mist, but I would guess that she's probably crying. I shift towards her and bring her into a tight hug.

It's crazy to think that one day she invited me over when we were hardly teenagers, and now here we are, standing together at one of the seven wonders of the world.

I take a thousand pictures of the falls. There are rainbows everywhere you look. Some of them are even double rainbows. I take pictures of Laurel and I take pictures of the trees and I take pictures of the both of us with Laurel's selfie stick. I take some pictures of the birds in the trees and water droplets resting on the leaves. I take a picture of a "Do not enter" sign with an inconspicuous trail behind it and

I'm *praying* Laurel doesn't see that, because she *will* enter.

I walk down the path back to Enzo, leaving Laurel to bask in the ambiance of the Falls. "Does it ever get old? Seeing this, I mean." I gesture to the falls. He told us earlier on the tour that he gives around four to six tours of Victoria Falls a day.

"Never. It's like when you see a buffalo in the wild, every single time you see it, it's still beautiful and fascinating." I thought something along those lines would be his answer. How could you ever get used to this?

Over where Laurel is, there's a rock that stands higher than the others. I watch as she stands up on it and throws her arms out at her sides, lifting her chin to the sky. I want to be over there with her but I know how important this moment is to her, so I want to make sure she gets to experience it how she wants to. My heart is bursting with affection for her.

After a couple minutes, I walk over to the rock and climb up next to her.

"Lane, this is the most amazing thing I have *ever* experienced." Her arms are still out and her eyes are closed. I'm surprised she even heard me come over here, the water is so loud.

I wrap my arms around her torso and snuggle my face into her neck. "I'm glad you finally got to experience it," I say, smiling.

She grabs my head with her hands and shifts her body so she's facing me. Her eyes are still closed. She runs her thumbs back and forth across my cheekbones, then places them around my waist.

I grab her face in my hands and touch her eyelashes with my thumbs, trying to wipe the mist off of them. I trail my fingers across her eyebrows and down the sides of her face, ending at her chin. My thumbs outline the edges of her lips, stopping after I've circled them. I cup her cheeks in my hands and lean forward. I slowly put my lips on hers, stopping the second they connect. I leave them there and gently give her the smallest of kisses.

I press my forehead against hers and wrap my arms around her waist, pulling her closer to me. Our wet shirts stick to each other as mist continues to sprinkle on and around us. I've never had stronger feelings for Laurel than what I feel for her right now.

I think back to the beginning of this summer and all that has happened since I ran into her at the treehouse. The amount of grief and guilt I carry with me today doesn't at all compare to the guilt and grief I carried with me that day in the treehouse. And that is because of her.

Because of her, I have accepted that the accident wasn't my fault, that there was nothing I could have done to prevent it from happening. Because of her, I know who my mother is again. Because of her, Jey and I have a better relationship than we've had since the accident happened. Because of her, I've opened myself up again; to feeling emotions and letting people in. Because of her, I see a future, one that I get to be excited for. She's made me see that life is exciting and worth living. Because of her, I've found myself again. Because of her, I'm standing where I am right now, hugging in her a cloud of mist in Zimbabwe. I am everything I am today because of her.

"Laurel."

"Hm?"

"There's something I need to tell you."

Goodbyes, Goodbyes & Goodbyes

Chapter 37

Today is the day I move to Seattle. It's 7 a.m. and Jey and I just finished loading up the last of my things into my truck.

"Well, that's the last of it," Paisley says, bringing out a bag full of snacks and placing it in the front seat. She shuts the door and walks over to Jey, who puts his arm around her and kisses the side of her head.

"I've never had to say goodbye to you before, Lane, so I'm not sure if I should hug you or what. Actually, I should probably punch you for leaving me," he jokes.

"Well, you'll see me soon. I'll be back for your wedding, after all." They're getting married in nine months, so I'll be back before they know it.

"You won't just be 'coming back' for my wedding, dude," he says, using air quotes. "You're gonna be the best man in my wedding."

Well, this is news to me. I figured he was gonna ask me, but it doesn't surprise me that he's telling me

I'm doing it instead of giving me the option to. "Not Dallas?"

"I thought about it, but you're the one I want standing next to me." He smiles softly and looks at the ground. He raises his hand to his face to cover up the inevitable tears I was expecting today. He sniffles and Paisley pats him on the chest, encouraging him to let it all out.

"Oh, don't cry. I'll be back before ya know it," I mock.

"Yeah, that's why I'm crying." He looks up at me and drops his hand. "I don't want you to come back."

"Yeah, yeah, yeah," I say, chuckling. I check my watch. "Well, I should probably get on the road."

I got in touch with Milly yesterday and we met up. She apologized a million times, asking if there was any way that I could find it in my heart to forgive her. I told her I already forgave her. I asked her about her sobriety, too, specifically when it started.

"Well, you know how I said that I called Elsie once a week to get updates on your life? Well, the night of your accident, she called me. Right then and there, I decided I was going to be sober for you. I had no idea you would walk right back into my life, but I made that choice anyway." My mom really is special. My mom. It's still weird to refer to her that way, but it feels right.

We both cried and we were hugging and wiping away each other's tears. I told her to come visit me once I've got a place and get settled in. She said she would love that. You know, even after she kept the fact that she was my mother from me and basically lied to me all summer, I can't *not* want a relationship with her.

"Can I ask why? I mean, I'm not trying to push you away, but how can you forgive me for what I've done?"

"I guess it just made me sad...that we have the opportunity to have a relationship and the only thing keeping that from happening is me." She hugged me for five minutes before she let me go.

My next stop was Ms. Elsie. I'm pretty sad about leaving Ms. Elsie. She was the closest thing I've had to a grandmother for the last several years. For old times' sake, I went to our favorite sandwich shop one last time to get us our favorite meals. I told her I would call her every now and then so we could catch up and she could let me know how the shop's doing. I also told her she didn't need to check in with my mom anymore, that I could do that on my own now.

"I never wanted to hide it from you, but she didn't want you to know," she said, stroking my hair. I didn't cry in front of her when we said goodbye, but I cried in my car after I drove away. Ms. Elsie will always be like a grandmother to me.

Next, I drove to Half & Half to say goodbye to Laurel's parents. They hugged me and wished me well, saying they were always a phone call away. It was hard saying goodbye to them, but they encouraged me more than I thought they would. They told me they loved me like a son and that was when I started crying.

I said goodbye to the Bishops right before I went over to Ivy's. Dallas said he was sad to see me go but understands why I need to leave. Noami punched me in the face and said I was a jerk for leaving her forever. She sucker-punched me right in the lip, busted it right open. She finally hugged me after she wiped the blood off my face with a paper towel. I said goodbye to Jey's parents and thanked them for everything they've done for me all these years. They really were like parents to me.

I said goodbye to my dad one last time. Once I got to his lot, I noticed there were flowers there again.

Who was leaving them? I hummed one of his favorite songs as some birds whistled and chirped along. It wasn't until I was pulling out of the parking lot that I realized who was leaving the flowers there. It was Milly.

Ivy surprised me with dinner. It was really nice getting to spend some alone time with the two of them. We haven't done it in a while. They asked me about my plans once I move out there, but I didn't really make any plans, so I didn't have anything to tell them. They both cried, which didn't surprise me, but I surprised myself when I let my tears fall. I've cried so much this summer, what's a couple more?

And now, here I am, saying goodbye to my two best friends. As much as I don't want to admit it, I'm gonna miss Jey a lot. The summer started out a little bumpy for us, but I couldn't imagine my life without him. I give hugs to each of them, then Paisley insists on a group hug. I hop in my car and pull out of the driveway, feeling so hopeful for the first time in a long time.

This isn't Goodbye Forever

Chapter 38

I stop at Walmart and head to the back of the store to print out all the pictures from this past summer. The ones of us eating ice cream, the ones of me falling off the paddle board, the one of the phallic fountain, and my favorite picture from our Zambezi River boat cruise. I print out every single picture from this summer. From our summer.

I head back to my car and drive to say goodbye to the person I am dreading saying goodbye to the most.

***

I pull into the parking lot and put the truck in park. I grab the envelope of pictures and stick them in my back pocket along with the letter I wrote for her. I get out of my truck and shut the door. My heart starts to pound in my chest and I feel woozy so I put my hands on the hood of my truck for balance.

I suck in a deep breath and let it out slowly and start walking. *I can do this.*

I turn the corner next to the giant oak tree like I always do, finding the familiar slab of dark gray stone sticking out of the ground that reads:

Laurel Penelope Owens

June 29th 1997 - October 8th 2021

Beloved daughter & friend

I find my usual seat next to her headstone and pull out the envelope of pictures.

"I've said goodbye to twelve people in the last twenty-four hours and none of them hurts like this one does."

I lay back in the soft, green grass and look up at the sky above me. I lay there for either thirty minutes or three hours. I can't really tell.

I sit up and start taking the pictures out, showing them all to Laurel, telling stories from each picture. I laugh at some of the pictures, thinking back to the moments they were taken. I tell her about the food trucks and about breaking into the amusement park. I tell her about meeting Milly and finding out she's my mother. I tell her about the forty hours of traveling it took to get to Zimbabwe. I tell her about Victoria Falls and how much I know she would've loved it. I tell her about renting a motorcycle for the day, driving up and down the beach and all-around town. I tell her about every single thing I did on our bucket list this summer.

I place the pictures back in the envelope and rest it up against her headstone. I take the letter out of my back pocket and place it behind the pictures so it doesn't fly away.

"This letter says everything you need to know, Laurel." I trace the letters of her name on the headstone. I tell myself once I get to the "s" in Owens, it's time for me to go. I take my time, following each curve and line of the letters, dragging it out so I don't have to leave yet.

I get to the "s." It happens too soon.

I drop my hand in my lap and a tear falls down my cheek onto the dirt above her casket buried in the ground beneath me.

"I will love you forever, Laurel Penelope. I just wish I got to tell you that while you were still here."

With that, I stand up and walk back to my car. I trip over branches and rocks because my eyes are filled to the brim with tears. I can't tell if they're all sad tears or if some of them are tears of relief.

There was a period of time when I thought I wasn't ready to leave yet. When I thought I wasn't ready to be so far from Laurel. But I know this is what I need to do.

After all, this isn't goodbye forever.

The Letter

Laurel,

When I first saw you that day in home ec, I knew I was in trouble. I wanted to be your partner so bad but you had already paired up with a girl named Julia so I had missed my chance. Stupid Julia. I hoped that I would have more classes with you that year, but that was the only one.

Towards the end of the school year, one day you invited me over to your house. We had just gotten off the bus and you turned around so quickly and looked me dead in the eyes and invited me over. It kind of scared me. I didn't know anything about you. You didn't know anything about me. I didn't even know that you knew who I was. But I was so curious about you and that treehouse that I couldn't pass up the offer.

I didn't know it yet but accepting that invitation would change my entire life.

We spent the next several years by each other's side almost every single day. I was there for you when your bunny died and you were there for me when Honey died. You came with me to Jey's soccer games, even when it was freezing cold and raining. You came to my art shows, and I went to your races, supporting you from the sidelines. Our prom night was the night I realized I was in love with you. God, you looked breathtaking that night. That dark green dress did wonders to your body. I wanted to tell you that night on the beach just how much I loved you. I wanted to scoop you up in my arms and kiss you all night and tell you over and over again just how much you meant to me. But I was a coward. I've regretted not telling you that night so many times.

We were there for each other during the best and worst moments of our lives. Up until October 8th, 2021. The day I found out I had lost you.

Losing you in that accident was the absolute worst thing that has ever happened to me. Not only because I lost you, but because I was the reason that I lost you. I know, you're probably slapping me on the wrist right now or preparing to haunt me from your grave, trying to tell me again *that it wasn't my fault. I know that now. But it doesn't make losing you hurt any less.*

At the beginning of this summer, I decided that I was going to move to the farthest point in the United States from Hull. I wanted - needed - to get away. Away from the memories, away from the nightmares, away from the pain. There were days that I didn't want to try anymore. There were days when it seemed easier to end my misery than to wake up tomorrow and be reminded of the worst pain I could ever feel. But you always got me through it. It was always you, Laurel.

While I was going through the stuff in my closet getting ready for my move, I stumbled upon our bucket list. Remember that? We wrote that together the second time we hung out, up in that treehouse of yours. I felt like the luckiest guy in the world that day. You picked me to be your friend.

The day I found our old bucket list, I decided that I was going to cross off everything I could before I moved at the end of the summer. I ended up completing it. I kissed a random stranger. I rode in a hot air balloon, which was one of the coolest things I have ever done, by the way. I was scared out of my mind, but it was so cool. I got that tattoo we always talked about getting. The letter "L" on the inside of our ring fingers. You always said that was the only letter that ever mattered and that tattoo was going to be our way of never letting each other go, so I finally got it. I did the entire thing. For us. For you. Before the day I found it, I was so lost, Laurel. So lost. I was not only grieving you but felt an immense amount of guilt. I felt like I was walking around with seven backpacks filled with bricks everywhere I went, always weighing me down. Finding our list gave me hope.

I wish more than anything that we got to experience crossing off everything on our bucket list together. But I was imagining you there with me the entire time. I knew everything you would've said to me, all the emotions you would've felt during each task on our list. Not to brag, but I know you pretty well. I would give up everything *for you to have been there with me.*

I decided to go to the treehouse one night. I was having a really hard day. I saw your mom for the first time since the accident and I assume you can understand what that felt like. I was the reason her daughter was dead. So yeah, it was a pretty terrible day. I went to the treehouse after getting in a fight with Jey, hoping to feel some relief. I cried for so long that night. Several weeks later, I decided I was going to visit your grave. I hadn't yet, since I was in the hospital the day of your funeral. I went to the treehouse for the second time, hoping for...well I don't really know what. What I wasn't expecting was you. *Maybe I just felt your presence so much that night or needed you so badly that I was just imagining you there. Maybe it was you in angel form. Honestly, who knows? But you saved me that night.*

God, I miss you, Laurel. I miss your smile and your laugh. Your horrible, obnoxious, too loud laugh. I miss the way your hair always smelled like pears and the way that your eyebrow raised when you knew I was lying to you. I miss our inside jokes and I miss watching sunsets with you. I miss going to the beach with you and watching you find the prettiest shells you could find. I miss the way you would cuddle against me when we watched a movie and the way we just so perfectly understood each other. I miss having you in my arms.

In case you don't know already, I've been in love with you basically since the moment I met you. I think about that kiss in the treehouse almost every single day, wishing for the life of me that I got to kiss you again. That I got to feel your lips on mine again. That I got to hold you that close to me again. I love you so much, Laurel. I always have and I always will. You're tattooed on my heart. Forever and permanently stuck there.

I never told anyone that you were about to tell me something when we got hit the night of the accident. I've wondered for so long what you were going to tell me. I finally decided that you were going to tell me that you loved me. You were acting weird and distant that night, saying you had something you needed to talk to Paisley about. I think you wanted to tell me that you loved me. I have to believe that because that's the only thing that makes losing you the least bit more bearable. That you loved me, too. I think you were just as worried about losing me as I was about losing you and that made both of us cowards. I imagine all the time about what our life could have looked like if I just told you how I felt.

I wish I could hug you one more time. Kiss you one more time. Hear your laugh one more time. Hold your hand one more time. I wish I got the chance to tell you that I love you. Well, I had many chances, but I was too scared you would tell me you didn't feel the same way I did. I wish I told you that I loved you. You deserved to know that someone loved you as deeply and strongly as I did. As I do. But I was too afraid of your rejection because I couldn't imagine losing you. I wish I would have told you despite my fear because I regret not telling you more than I've ever regretted anything.

There's an envelope laying on your gravesite filled with pictures from our adventures this summer. I thought you would want to look through them and find the best ones. One of my favorites is from Victoria Falls. The waterfall is crushing down, spewing mist all over the place. The sun is reflecting off the water, casting the most vibrant rainbow in the sky. I made sure to take lots of pictures of the falls so you could add them to your Victoria Falls mural. I wish you got to see that in person. It was one of the most beautiful things I have ever seen. Aside from you, that is.

There's a couple, Ben and Alice, in some of the pictures from the night of the dinner cruise. I sat with them at their table and they told me that they had lost their son in a car accident. I ended up telling them about you, which is something I would normally never do. But I felt like they needed to know. I told them the truth: that I was driving and it was raining and we were hit by a drunk driver. As weird as is to admit, we bonded over losing a loved one in a car accident. I really liked Ben and Alice and I think you would've, too. Alice said something to me that I think about all the time. She said, "It's been a long time, and the grief never goes away, you just get better at living with it." And it's true. Everyday sucks because you aren't here with me but facing today is a hell of a lot easier than it was the day I found out I lost you.

I'm sorry I'm leaving you to live my life. I'm sorry that I get to live my life. Leaving you is the hardest thing I have ever had to do, next to losing you. I decided to move to Seattle and I leave tomorrow morning. It will be hard being that far away from you. I visited you every single day this summer. In the rain. On the super humid, hot days. I came to see you every single day. I just wanted you to know you won't see me for a while. I need to do some more growing and I can't do that here anymore.

I've finally realized that you are my tipping point, Laurel. Dr. Therin asked me about what my tipping point was the day I saw your mom for the first time since the accident. I may have freaked out and had an anxiety attack. He asked me what it was that tipped me over the edge. What made me lose it like that? And the answer is you. Being with you makes me happy. It makes me so happy. I feel untouchable, like nothing could ruin my day or put me in a bad mood. Not being with you makes me sad. Thinking about how I'll never see you again in this life makes me feel like I'm drowning. It makes my palms sweat and my throat fill with bile and my heart beats so fast in my chest I feel like it's going to explode. You are what makes life worth living.

If I could've chosen, I would've saved you that night. I would have traded spots with you in a heartbeat so that you could live the adventurous life you were destined to live. You could've ended up in Morocco or Tanzania for all I know. I guess that just means that I get to live the rest of my life for the both of us. What should we put on our next bucket list? Skydiving? Walking the Camino de Santiago? Living in the woods with no electricity? You name it, I'll do it.

461

You're the bestest friend I ever had and the greatest love I never got the privilege to fully experience. Because of this summer - because of you, Laurel - I have accepted that the accident wasn't my fault, that there was nothing I could have done to prevent it from happening. Because of you, I know who my mother is again. Because of you, Jey and I have a better relationship than we had since the accident happened. Because of you, I've opened myself up again; to feeling actual emotions and letting people in. Because of you, I see a future, one that I get to be excited for. I enjoy life again. You've made me see that life is exciting and worth living. Because of you, I've found myself again. Because of you, I'm sitting in my room right now, writing this letter, with tears streaming down my face, getting ready to live my life again. I am everything I am today because of you.

For that, I owe you my life.

We were always meant to be, Laurel. We just weren't made to last.

With love,

Your Lane.

Epilogue

It's been five years since I sat down on this beach.
It's been five years but it feels like I was here just
yesterday. On a run. Building a sandcastle with
Dallas and Naomi. Going to Jey's soccer games.
Hiding out in Laurel's treehouse. Working in the
garage with my uncle Eli. It's good to be back.

I'm back for my uncle Eli and Ivy's wedding. Yeah,
they finally decided to get married. They were
engaged for over ten years, and most people think
that's weird, but it just worked for them. They were
comfortable with how their lives were, living in two
separate houses, and didn't feel the need to make
anything official. They loved each other and that
was enough for them. Honestly, them getting
married isn't really going to change much of
anything, besides the fact that they'll be living in
the same house.

I was told over FaceTime that this is how it
happened:

"Hey, you wanna get married?" Ivy asked my uncle
Eli while he was reading the morning newspaper.
She was on her way out the door to head to the

hospital for her shift when she turned around and asked him.

"Do *you* want to get married?" my uncle Eli asked.

"Yeah, I do."

And that was that. Six months later, here we are. A day I honestly thought never would've happened.

I walk back to my truck and head to my uncle Eli's house to pick him up and take everyone to the church to start getting ready. I drive by Laurel's old house. There's a man in the front yard, bent over the bushes, pulling weeds. A woman is blowing bubbles and playing with a little girl on the right side of the house. My attention is brought to the treehouse when a much older girl peers her head out the door and shouts something to her mom.

I can't stop smiling as I pull into my uncle Eli's driveway, so happy that someone gets to experience that treehouse like I did. *I wonder if they painted over my writing on the doorframe above the bathroom.*

I'm greeted by my uncle Eli, Jey, and my not-so-little-anymore "nephew," Grant.

"Uncle Lane!" Grant shouts as he runs into my arms.

"Hey kiddo!" I enthusiastically shout when I pick him up. It's been a little over a year since Jey, Paisley, and Grant visited me in Seattle. He's grown a lot since then.

"How are you, lil bug? You excited to be the ring bearer today?"

"Yeah! My dad told me I have to be super careful with the rings, though. We practiced all night last night. Where's Laurel? I wanna see Laurel," he says.

"I'm glad to hear you're so prepared, little monkey. Laurel's at the church already," I say, rubbing his little head of hair.

I put Grant down and give Jey a hug. "It's good to see you, man," he says, patting me on the back. Paisley walks out the front door and she looks much more pregnant than she did on FaceTime a month ago.

"Wow, you're really showing now, huh?" I ask, walking up the stairs and hugging her around her big belly.

"Yeah," she says, hugging me back. "I really popped these past two weeks. I even had to buy a new dress for today. Where's Ava?"

"Well, I'm sure you'll still look lovely in it. Ava's -
" I get cut off before I can respond when my uncle
Eli emerges from the house. He nearly starts crying
when he sees me. "Oh, Lane, it's so good to have
you here. Thanks for coming, bug."

"Wouldn't miss it for the world."

We drive to the church and spend the next two
hours getting ready and finalizing all the details
with the wedding. I sneak off to find Ivy so I can
see her before the ceremony. I find her in a room
with her sister and her best friend. They're doing
last minute touches on her makeup and hair.

"Hey, Aunt Ivy," I say, peeking my head through
the door. "Mind if I come in?"

"Lane!" she shouts, pushing her sister's hands away
from her face. She stands up and rushes over to me
and wraps me in a hug. Ivy has always given the
best hugs. "Thank you so much for coming. I know
it means so much to your uncle to have you here,
but it also means a lot to me."

"I wouldn't miss it." I say. I pull back from her and
look down at her dress.

"You look amazing, Aunt Ivy. Prettiest bride I ever
saw."

"Oh, stop it," she says, flickering her hair back. Her sister calls her over to finish getting ready so I give her one last hug, tell her she looks beautiful and find my way back to my uncle Eli's room.

***

The ceremony goes by quickly. They've been together for so long that they decided a big wedding wasn't something they wanted. There's about thirty people here, all of their closest friends and family. I sit in the front. My wife, Ava, and our nearly three-year-old daughter sit next to me. Milly's on my right, next to two empty seats, saved for my dad and Laurel.

They exchange their vows and kiss. Everyone hoots and hollers and I notice Grant covers his eyes.

The reception is just as small as the ceremony, but some of the guys from the garage and some of Ivy's work friends come to join the celebration. Grant finds Laurel and they run off together to the dance floor.

Ava and I find a seat with Jey and Paisley and we all catch up about the happenings of our lives from the past couple months. Grant's starting kindergarten in two weeks, which Paisley is sad about. "But when the baby comes in a couple more weeks, it'll be nice to have him out of the house," Jey reminds her.

"That's very true. I love him to death, but he's quite a handful," Paisley admits. "How have you guys been?"

"We've been good," I say, looking over at my wife. Her long, dark brown hair is in a half-up half-down bun and it outlines her face perfectly, accentuating her cheekbones and almond eyes.

"We've actually been thinking about moving back home," Ava says, grabbing onto my hand.

Ava and I met four years ago, after I moved to Seattle. She lived across from me in our apartment building. I wasn't looking to meet anyone, but she quite literally fell in my lap. We met because she was coming down the stairs with a big box and didn't see me. She bumped into me, causing me to fall, which made her fall, and she landed right in my lap.

"NO way! Are you serious? When are you thinking of moving back?" Paisley asks.

"Well, we actually drove a moving van from Seattle. So, like tomorrow, I guess," I say, shrugging at Ava. She laughs. "Yeah, we're back for good now."

"I mean, I'm glad you're back, but why are you back? Did something happen?" Jey asks.

"When Ms. Elsie died a couple months ago, the bank called me and told me she left the building to me. So, we're gonna fix it up and do something new with it," I explain.

"Aw, I always knew I loved Ms. Elsie. What are you gonna do with it?" Paisley asks.

"We talked about turning it into an art therapy place for kids. Lane can do the art and I can focus on the therapy," Ava answers.

"You remember Ben and Alice from Zimbabwe? Well, I asked Alice to come help me with some planning. She's a really talented eco-friendly artist and that's kind of what we want our vibe to be."

"Ooo, I want to meet her!" Paisley says.

"Yeah, with Lane's artistry and my background in childhood trauma, we figured we could make a pretty unique place for struggling kids," Ava adds.

After spending some time with Ava in Seattle, we found out that we were both from Hull. Not only is she also from Hull but she went to the same middle school as me. I didn't believe her so she pulled out a yearbook and proved it. What freaked me out the most was that she was Laurel's partner in our home economics class. She moved after that year, so I never really got to know her.

"I thought her partner's name was Julia?" I said.

"Nope, Ava. I was her partner. I remember her," she told me.

Being that she knew Laurel, I felt comfortable telling her about what happened. We spent many nights talking about the accident and my feelings for Laurel. Surprisingly, I never crawled into a ball and sobbed like I would've before our bucket list summer. I made a lot of progress that summer.

It took a while to open my heart again to loving someone. I never thought I would be able to love someone the way that I loved Laurel. But then came Ava.

We had a very small wedding. Just her parents, my uncle Eli and Ivy, Milly, Ava's two best friends, and Jey and Paisley. Now, we've been married for nearly three years and have a two-year-old daughter, Laurel.

I'm shaken from my thoughts when Ava grabs my hand and pulls me to the dance floor. I scoop up my daughter in one arm and hold my wife in the other and swing with them to the music.

***

After the ceremony, I take Ava and Laurel to Laurel's grave. Laurel hasn't met the amazing woman she was named after yet, so that is the first thing I wanted to do: introduce them to each other.

We round the corner next to the familiar, giant oak tree and I see her grave. It's been a while since I've been here, yet it feels like just yesterday. Since Jey and Paisley's wedding nearly five years ago. I've changed a lot since then. I'm happy. I have a wife and a wonderful daughter I absolutely adore. I enjoy life.

I sit on the ground in front of her grave and place Laurel on my lap. "Laurel, this is my friend, Laurel. She's the girl you're named after," I explain.

I play with her curly hair, which is the exact same color as Laurel's; caramel brown that gets hints of red in it when the sun strikes it. Laurel picks up her hand and waves to the headstone. "She was my best friend. Did you know that?"

She shakes her head up and down then scoots off my lap and moves closer to the headstone. She flattens both of her palms on the dark gray stone and sits there for a second. Then she looks over her shoulder at me. "She says 'hi,'" Laurel says.

Ava joins me on the grass and I scoot over to make some room for her. I put my arm across her shoulder and pull her close to me and kiss her on the side of the head. "She says 'hi?'" Ava asks.

"Yeah, she told me to tell you she says hi. And she's glad you're back." I watch Laurel for a second, before she speaks again. "She says she's waiting for your next adventure."

I let out a small chuckle and say, "Yeah. I bet she is."

The end.

Acknowledgements

There are several people that I want to thank for helping me make this book a reality. First, a family friend, Jeff Scott for reading the entire book and taking his time to thoroughly make edits and suggestions. Without his knowledge in writing and editing and his insistence I publish, this book wouldn't be where it is today.

Secondly, I'd like to thank my sister Kamden for being the first person to read the entirety of my book. She believed in me and encouraged me since the very beginning and for that I am so thankful.

Other family members I'd like to thank for their support and encouragement include my siblings Kenna, Karson, Kaden and Karter. They listened to me talk about my book for an entire year, sent it to friends to read, offered advice, and encouraged me to get it published. I'd also like to thank my parents for always being my biggest fans. Thank you to my cousins Brooklyn and Gracyn and my aunt Meghan for providing edits and feedback and for talking to me about my book for two hours after they finished reading it. And to my favorite coworker Jimmy for being "literally obsessed" with my work (his words, not mine). Key Bryant and Briana Taylor, you were there the day I found out I was offered a publishing contract and when I look back on that moment, I will always think of the two of you. To Richie for being the first person to "purchase" my book. Even though you paid me through Venmo and I forwarded you the book on Google Docs. To my best friends Caroline Kalen and Becka Martell who have encouraged me from the beginning and who have always supported me.

A big thank you to the designer of my book cover, my insanely talented artist of a cousin, Karin. I sent her an email with my envision and she helped me bring it to life. And to her sister Kailey for offering much needed advice and suggestions.

Thank you all for believing in me.

The Anchor

The Anchor of Hull, located in Hull, Massachusetts is a real Christian-based recovery center for those struggling with addiction. It is a resource center for those in recovery and those supporting individuals in recovery. The Anchor offers sober activities and events, recovery coaching, access to resources and assistance to those in all stages of recovery. If you or a loved one is struggling with addiction and recovery and are living near Hull, Massachusetts do not hesitate to contact The Anchor of Hull. Contact information provided below.

Phone number: 781-534-9327
Email: theanchor@northst.org
Mail: The Anchor of Hull, 7 Hadasah Way, Hull, MA 02045

Suicide Hotline

If you are struggling with thoughts of self-harm, suicide or suicidal ideation, call 9-8-8, the National Suicide Prevention hotline for help. You are not alone.